A Likely Story appears to be an autobiography but it is much more than that.
This is a gripping, page-turning story of the American experience. For those who have also lived through Glenn's experiences there is an immediate and powerful connection. For those who haven't, Glenn's story foreshadows the pain, hope, joy and eventually triumph that life can bring.
– Chad Lewis,
Everett, WA

A Likely Story covers the extraordinary events in the author's life from the age of eight into his seventh decade. This is a fascinating narrative and written with candor, whether relating to the adventures of childhood, the sometimes arduous process of growing into adulthood, or the tragedies that life has a way of inflicting upon us. The thing I love most about this book is the wonderful sense of humor. I found myself laughing out loud while reading numerous accounts. This is a truly remarkable story.
Audrey Ling –
Los Angeles, CA

A Likely Story is an astonishing work – so very personal and revealing, like a Neil Diamond song! Don Angell -
Duxbury, MA

I started reading A Likely Story last night after I went to bed and found myself laughing out loud so many times. Dr. Adams has so many tales to tell, and he tells them delightfully. I can hardly wait to finish the book so I can pass it on to the rest of my family. Evelyn Bedenbaugh – North Augusta,
SC

I read A Likely Story as soon as it arrived. I couldn't put it down. Its humor is wonderful, the madcap adventures, the follies and reverses of youth, and the writing is all of one piece. What emerges at the end is a love story, which is very deep yet understated. I was moved to tears at the description of Glenn's wife leaving the hospital's snowy parking lot as he watched from his hospital window. It is an excellent social history of life in the United States during the turbulent '50s and '60s. This is the story of a significant life and a unique human being. Jean Musser – College Place, WA

4304-ADAM

A Likely Story

A Likely Story

THE UNLIKELY ADVENTURES OF A BOY AND A MAN

Glenn Arthur Adams

Copyright © 2001 by Glenn Arthur Adams.

Library of Congress Number:		00-193058
ISBN #:	Hardcover	0-7388-5281-3
	Softcover	0-7388-5282-1

All rights reserved. No part of this book may be reproduced or transmitted in any form or by any means, electronic or mechanical, including photocopying, recording, or by any information storage and retrieval system, without permission in writing from the copyright owner.

This book was printed in the United States of America.

To order additional copies of this book, contact:
Xlibris Corporation
1-888-7-XLIBRIS
www.Xlibris.com
Orders@Xlibris.com

Contents

Prologue 13
Reflections 15
Acknowledgements 17

PART ONE

Chapter 1 Thunder and Lightening 21
Chapter 2 Neighbors 23
Chapter 3 Delivery Men 27
Chapter 4 What's a Tampon? 31
Chapter 5 Loosen Up, Irene 34
Chapter 6 The Cops 35
Chapter 7 A Most Unpleasant Time 37
Chapter 8 The Budding Businessman 40
Chapter 9 Tastes Just Like Chicken! 42
Chapter 10 V-2 44
Chapter 11 Burning Rivers and Dying Lakes 47
Chapter 12 My War Effort 48
Chapter 13 The Flute Man 50
Chapter 14 My Sister's Girdle 51

PART TWO

Chapter 15 The Reunion 57
Chapter 16 The Farm 61
Chapter 17 Fossil Consolidated School 66
Chapter 18 Fall/Winter, '46 - '47 70
Chapter 19 Go Back to Detroit, Mister 78

Chapter 20 Never Ride The Lead Toboggan 84
Chapter 21 The Stone Boat Saga 86
Chapter 22 The Haunting 88
Chapter 23 White Bull Calf 92
Chapter 24 Stupid Old Cow aka
  Stupid Young Boy 94
Chapter 25 Shifting Gears at 50 Below Zero 96
Chapter 26 Never Store Fish In
  Your Uncle's Flooded Basement 98
Chapter 27 Fall/Winter, '47—'48 101
Chapter 28 Fossil Notables 107
Chapter 29 Gray Milk 114
Chapter 30 Chickens 117
Chapter 31 Rabbits 121
Chapter 32 Uncle George's Bull Calf 124

PART THREE

Chapter 33 Back to Detroit 129
Chapter 34 The Paper Boy 137
Chapter 35 Southwestern High School 152
Chapter 36 The Television Star 163
Chapter 37 Block-Busting 165
Chapter 38 Ford Boulevard 169
Chapter 39 Lincoln Park High School 174
Chapter 40 The Jumper 179
Chapter 41 Bwana Devil 187
Chapter 42 Death Rides the Non-Skeds 191
Chapter 43 A Sanitation System
  (And Beat It If You Can) 199
Chapter 44 Lake of the Woods 207
Chapter 45 Mizpaw 212
Chapter 46 Battle Creek 221
Chapter 47 Junk Jobs—1953/1954 227
Chapter 48 Uncle Sam Eve 236

PART FOUR

Chapter 49 Hi, There, Uncle Sam 241
Chapter 50 Over the Hill 244
Chapter 51 It's Almost Over 250
Chapter 52 Fort Lee, Virginia 254
Chapter 53 Japan Ordnance Command 261
Chapter 54 Al 269
Chapter 55 Retraining Sgt. Wyrens 275
Chapter 56 The Black Market 278
Chapter 57 Soldier of the Month? 282
Chapter 58 Command Inspection 284
Chapter 59 Say What? 287
Chapter 60 The Other Japan 290
Chapter 61 Heavy-duty Crowds 294
Chapter 62 The USNS E. D. Patrick 299

PART FIVE

Chapter 63 Wayne State University 307
Chapter 64 The Carpenter 311
Chapter 65 Back to School 314
Chapter 66 A Way Out 323
Chapter 67 The Repo Man 327
Chapter 68 The University of Oregon 332
Chapter 69 Arlene 337
Chapter 70 Cross Country—One More Time 343
Chapter 71 Snow?——What Snow? 349
Chapter 72 Time to Get Serious 354
Chapter 73 Don't Stick Your Finger in my Eye . 357
Chapter 74 The Big Horn Mountains 359
Chapter 75 The Little House 365
Chapter 76 The Last Lap 368
Chapter 77 Medford 374
Chapter 78 Disillusionment 378

Chapter 79 A Fresh Start 382
Chapter 80 High Anxiety 386
Chapter 81 Everett Junior College 388
Chapter 82 Youth Opportunity Centers............. 390
Chapter 83 Pluses and Minuses 394

PART SIX

Chapter 84 Preparing to Die 401
Chapter 85 Surprise! 411

EPILOGUE 419

Prologue

For Everything There is a Season

FOR everything there is a season, and a time for every matter under heaven:
a time to be born, and a time to die;
a time to plant, and a time to pluck up what is planted;
a time to kill, and a time to heal;
a time to break down, and a time to build up;
a time to weep, and a time to laugh;
a time to mourn, and a time to dance;
a time to cast away stones, and a time to gather stones together;
a time to embrace, and a time to refrain from embracing;
a time to seek, and a time to lose;
a time to keep, and a time to cast away;
a time to rend, and a time to sew;
a time to keep silence, and a time to speak;
a time to love, and a time to hate;
a time for war, and a time for peace.
Ecclesiastes 3:1-9

I would rather be ashes than dust!
I would rather that my spark should burn out in a brilliant blaze than it should be stifled by dry rot.
I would rather be a superb meteor, every atom of me in magnificent glow, than a sleepy and permanent planet.

> The proper function of man is to live, not to exist.
> I shall not waste my days in trying to prolong them.
> I shall use my time.
>
> Jack London, November, 1916

This note originally appeared in the *San Francisco Bulletin* on December 2, 1916, ten days following Mr. London's death.

Reflections

PERHAPS the most valuable result of all education is the ability to make yourself do the things you have to do, when they ought to be done.

Thomas Henry Huxley

Peak experiences in life, even the tragedies and crises, are things that we should treasure. These are the times in life when deep learning takes place.

Abraham Maslow

Fatherhood is a time of special awareness. It is a time for fathers to reexperience the child in ourselves. As fathers, we become both man and child. We grow in both directions.

Harold Lyon, Jr.

Sound friendships consist of many nameless acts. What matters is the intent—the intent to keep alive something worthy and mutual. This happens when people remember each other, cultivate each other, meet each other a little more than halfway. When you keep a friend, you add something to the richness and the worth of life.

Frank V. Morley

Acknowledgements

IT is just about impossible to recall and recognize the scores of people and events that have influenced my life. I'll do my best, but please forgive an oversight here and there.

The people who were the most critical forces in my life, of course, were my parents, Lester and Daisy Adams (nee Abbott), without whose dalliances my existence simply never would have been. They taught me well the rules of honesty and honor, and to accept the responsibility for doing the job at hand, whether pleasant or not, to the very best of my ability.

The next most influential and powerful force in my life has been my wife, Arlene. She has always managed to keep me reasonably on track as I careened through one adventure after another.

Next come our children, Kim, Beth, Kevin and Dawn, each of whom has brought an entirely new dimension into my world and has made me incredibly aware of the preciousness of life.

My brother Harland, his wife Lorraine, and children—and my sister Dorothy and her children have all been very influential in my growth as a youth and as a man. My extended family, uncles, aunts, and cousins, especially on the Abbott side, taught me a lot about how to live life.

Members of the Adams family seemed destined to live out their lives trapped in a poverty mentality. As far as I know none of them, with my dad as the only quasi exception, did much of anything to improve their lot in life. About the only impact they had on my life was to show me how not to live it.

Then there were the non-family people who precipitated

changes in my self-concept and ultimately the direction my life took:

People like Dick Hayne, my paper station manager when I was sixteen. Dick motivated me to sell hundreds of new subscriptions to the Detroit Times, which won me several trips around the United States when I was a sophomore and junior in high school;

And Wilson, another paper-station manager who demonstrated for me the downside of an obsessive/compulsive personality;

And the dozens of Fossilites, without whom my Minnesota years would have been cold, dark, and gloomy indeed;

Lt. Tighe, my commander in the Army at the Japan Ordnance Command, who urged me to do something constructive with my life and offered to recommend me to West Point. His counsel became a critical turning point in my life.

As life pulsated along, Arlene and I found ourselves at Everett Junior College in 1962. It was there that we made many lasting friendships with people like Jean Musser, who has been a long time, consistent friend and supporter with her constructive help along the way—and with couples like the Carbones, the Robinsons, the Mansfields, the Lerviks, the Lewises, the Palmers and the Whites. They all remain dear friends.

I think that a person is fortunate to have one or two good friends in life. I have been blessed with many.

Of special note are John-Bob and Rita-Bob Hamner. John-Bob and I were drafted into the service of our country on the same day, May 4, 1954, and have remained comrades in and out of arms ever since.

And now, for one of the damnedest stories you've ever read.

Part One
THE EARLY YEARS

Chapter 1

THUNDER AND LIGHTENING

IT was raining heavily that sultry night in 1944. It was just after midnight and a typical Midwest thunderstorm was rolling through Detroit. Lightening flashes were nearly constant. The booming, crackling crashes of thunder were first heard in the distance, but they were growing steadily closer, sharper, and louder. The war was raging in both the European and Far Eastern theaters and I thought to myself, "This must be what a battlefield sounds like." My brother, Harland, who was twenty-two and twelve years older than me, was a ball turret gunner in the Air Force and would soon be headed for bombing missions in Europe.

The blasting in the catacombs of the International Salt Mine under our house in southwest Detroit was ever-present, but it was most noticeable at night, when competing sounds were minimal. The worst race riot in Detroit history had occurred the previous summer, in 1943. Thirty-four people were kill ed and hundreds were wounded in knife and gun battles. Hundreds more were savagely beaten by those of the "other" race. Our entire family slept in one upstairs bedroom with the door locked and a loaded twelve-gauge shotgun by the bed. It had been a very bad year. A brooding, uneasy peace hung heavily over the city. I was ten, and had just moved back into my own bedroom.

At three in the morning, I was shaken from my fitful sleep by a deafeningly loud explosion. Thunderstorms in the Midwest are normally fairly frightening, but this violent explosion was near cataclysmic. The house trembled, and dishes fell from the cupboard and crashed to the floor. An unusual orange-yellow light flickered crazily over the walls. Mom, Dad, my twenty year-old sister Dorothy and I raced down the stairs and outside into the pouring rain—to a sight from Hell. "Stay back, Glenn," my Dad said to me as he enveloped me in his strong, protective arms and held me close. Scores of close neighbors joined us, buzzing excitedly about this near catastrophe.

Lightening had struck a telephone pole less than forty feet from our house. The pole was shattered and the power lines were down, spewing sparks and dancing maniacally across the ground and parked cars like possessed serpents. What was left of the shattered telephone pole was smoldering, and an acrid smoke from the burning wires filled the night air.

Within just a few minutes we could hear the wail of firetruck sirens. Soon, the fire department and a crew from the power company arrived. They worked for more than three hours, and when they left, a new power pole and power lines had replaced the downed and damaged ones, and everything was functioning properly. No one had been physically hurt this time, and property damage had been held to a minimum. This potentially disastrous episode ended reasonably well, but it was mearly a mild harbinger. I would not be nearly as fortunate with future threats to my young life.

Chapter 2

NEIGHBORS

A family of first generation German immigrants lived in the only house between our home and the lightening strike. Two brothers, Karl and Kurt, had married two sisters Gertrude and Helga. They had migrated to the United States in the late 1920's. All spoke broken but understandable English. Helga was wheelchair bound but I'm not sure why. She may have been a paraplegic, or a diabetic with minimal leg function, or simply too heavy to walk anymore, or all three. Gertrude, the much slimmer sister, ran the household and had given birth to three daughters all of whom were considerably older than I was.

The adults frequently played pinochle, and they played it with a vengeance. There was never any humor or laughter—only screaming recriminations when one or another perceived what to him or her was a stupid move. About ten feet separated our houses so our family was accustomed to the verbal carnage that exploded during the nightly card games. We simply learned to tune out the insanely audible battles.

But then, late one summer evening in 1945, the disagreement escalated into a physical battle between Karl and Kurt. They each armed themselves with a butcher knife from the kitchen and began slashing at each other with murderous intent. The fight spilled out of the house and into their front yard. We watched in horror through our front room windows as they fought, stabbing and slashing each other. Blood was everywhere. Gertrude was in the yard screaming for them to stop. One of them finally fell onto the lawn, exhausted and streaming blood from dozens of wounds. The other stood over him for a minute, and then retreated into the house to tend to his own wounds. Miraculously, no major arteries had been severed and both eventually recovered physically, but the tensions remained until their deaths, very close to one another, sometime in 1947. It was my first encounter with senseless violence in Detroit. It wasn't the last.

Across the street, in a tiny little house, lived the Holt family. They had a kid named Sonny who was my age and we were comrades. Sonny had a canvas tent in his back yard where he and I played out one adventure after another, slipping into various roles such as Superman, The Lone Ranger and Tonto, Captain Marvel, and a myriad other heroes and villains. The tent was relatively small, perhaps eight by eight, smelled of musty canvas, and had windows with frayed strands of canvas hanging from their edges. One day Sonny and I happened upon a book of matches and decided to entertain ourselves with a dangerous game. We would light the frayed canvas, and then blow out the flames. We were delighted with our little amusement—until the time inevitably came when we couldn't blow out the flames. The capacity of our tiny lungs was just not up to the job. The flames quickly spread up the dry canvas and soon engulfed the wall of the tent. Sonny and I ran inside to get some water in one of his little, but colorful, beach pails. But Sonny's mother was busy bathing his little sister and just put us off until she was done. When she finally finished her chore, she turned to us and asked what it was we wanted.

"We need a pail of water," Sonny said.

"What for?"

"My tent is on fire" Sonny sobbed.

"What?" she shrieked. Blood drained from her face as she ran out the door and into the back yard with the naked infant in her arms. The tent was by then not much more than a smoldering, stinking mass of incinerated canvas.

She got her garden hose and extinguished the remains of what had been our glorious retreat. We were devastated. Sonny was also thoroughly thrashed by his mother. We could hear his screams quite clearly, even across the street.

It was also the only time I got a licking from my father. He put me over his knee and really let me have it. Unaccustomed as I was to such treatment, I promptly urinated all over him and myself. When he was finished with his nasty little behavior modification technique he sent me upstairs to my room which I shared with my mother's brother, Howard, to await further instructions. As I plodded forlornly up the steep stairway I turned and looked back. There was Howard, laughing at me. The memory of that added insult stayed with me for the rest of my life. However, Dad's rude punishment did extinguish my tent-igniting behavior forever.

Then there was Chuck. He lived next door to Sonny in what seemed like a huge house. It had two stories and a full basement. Chuck had the most fantastic collection of comic books I'd ever seen stashed in that basement, and we spent a lot of time there reading Captain Marvel, Superman, Batman & Robin, Spiderman, Plastic Man, and a host of others, including the whole Disney spectrum. It was great until one summer evening when we were so engrossed in our literary adventures that dinner time came and went and the sun had set just west of the always odiferous Darling Rendering Plant.

I was startled back to reality when Chuck's mom came downstairs and informed me that my dad was there. Apparently, I was a couple of hours overdue, and Mom and sent him out looking for me. Clearly, this was not a good situation. He took me by the hand and walked me back across the street to our own lair where Mom was anxiously awaiting word. When I explained to her where I had been and what I had been doing, she summarily rejected my pleas for mercy and assigned Dad the job of whipping me this time because it hadn't been very long since she had beaten me up for some other transgression.

Dad reluctantly took me upstairs to his bedroom and I was preparing myself for another thorough whipping. When we got there we sat down on the edge of the bed and he said, "Glenn, I don't think you need a spanking. I'm sure you'll remember to let us know where you are from now on won't you?"

"I sure will" I responded with a great sigh of relief.

"However," Dad said, "we do have to satisfy your Mom's need for you to have a licking, so when I slap my hands together, you scream. O.K.?"

I readily agreed to the proposed charade and Dad started to slap his hands together. I screamed as though I was being slowly stretched on a rack.

Mom was happy that I was being punished. Dad was pleased that he had saved me from being punished. And I was relieved beyond measure with the outcome. I loved my Dad a lot that night.

Chapter 3

DELIVERY MEN

LARGE grocery stores, or supermarkets, began to appear during the forties, but it took many years for them to become the dominant force in food retailing. Most grocery purchases were made in small, neighborhood stores run by families. The clerk in charge was generally the male head of the household. He would greet customers from behind his counter and ask, "What would you like today, Mrs. (or Sir, or young fellow or lady)?" Then he would scurry around the store gathering the items you had mentioned. Chickens were usually sold live from their pens outside the rear door. When everything was gathered on the counter, he would lick the tip of his number two pencil and write the price of each item on a grocery sack and add it up without the aid of adding machines or computers. If Mom had too much for her to carry home, the grocer would arrange to have one of his employees, usually a son, deliver them to our home. But home delivery was the usual mode of buying several items. For example:

Ice. The iceman made his rounds through our neighborhood about every three days. He had what seemed to us kids a very huge truck filled with twenty-five and fifty-pound blocks of ice. He always made sure that there were plenty of ice chips on the floor of the truck, easily accessible to the kids in the neighborhood. Every customer had a sign that they would hang in their living room window indicating that they needed ice that day, and how many pounds they wanted. The little sign was square, and on each side was printed a number: 25, 50, 75 or 100. Whatever number was on the top of the sign was the quantity being ordered.

The ice man would chip free and select the appropriate amount, grab it with a huge pair of steel tongs and hoist it onto his shoulder, which was covered with a thick leather cape. The cape prevented his shoulder and body from becoming wet and eventually evolving into ice themselves. As he disappeared into the house, we would hoist ourselves into the truck and make away with as many ice chips as we could carry. Our pockets were full and wet, but it was a great treat in Detroit's sweltering, suffocating heat.

Milk. Most milk was purchased from the milkman, rather than the grocery store. No milkman I ever knew in Detroit had a truck. They all delivered from a single horse-drawn rubber-tired milk wagon. The horse on our route knew which houses were milk customers and would stop automatically in front of each one. The milkman would leave each customer's standing order on the porch, and pick up the clean empty bottles. Plastic cartons were unheard of, so all milk was sold in very thick glass bottles by the quart. Each had a little cardboard lid with a pull tab to remove it, pressed into an indentation in the top of the bottle.

Homogenization was still an unheard of concept in the forties, so the cream, with its rich butterfat content, would rise to the top four or five inches of the bottle, with the heavier, skimmed milk supporting it. In the wintertime, when the temperatures were freezing, the cream would freeze and expand, pushing the lid free. We would frequently find our milk bottles with a three or four inch column of frozen cream sticking straight up from the bottle with a cardboard lid on it, like a little cap.

Bread. We could, of course, buy bread in the stores, but our preference was to get our bread from the Hungarian Bread Man. He drove a small, orange and brown panel truck through the neighborhoods, ringing a little bell. Housewives would flag him down and go out to the street to buy his wonderful, fresh, aromatic loaves of bread, just recently out of his employer's ovens. He was a wizened up little man of about sixty, with a mammoth black leather purse slung over his shoulder. We would point out the loaf we wanted from the vast array of delectables, and he would spear it with a long handled implement, just like Captain Ahab might have. It was quite a show. He was always happy and laughing. Why not? He had a truck full of fresh bread and a purse full of money. That was something damn few folks had.

Melon Man. The melon man drove a huge stake truck filled with watermelons and cantaloupes (the latter we called muskmelons). He had rigged up a strange, cacophonous, but effective loudspeaker, through which he announced his pending arrival by sing-songing, "Sweet watermeleeeee, sweet matermeloooooow!" We bought lots of melons from him, and we never got a bad one. He would pick one out for us and then "plug" it. That means cutting a small wedge, or plug, out of it to let you taste it before you bought it. They were always so perfect, so sweet and juicy, that we finally just took his word for it and bought whatever one he suggested. We were never disappointed.

Good Humor Man. The Good Humor Man was the father of one of my schoolmates. We could hear him coming, jingling his little bells gently, when he was a block away. We always had ample time to beg, or somehow scrape up enough money to buy something in his truck that was cool and sweet, even if was just a nickel popsicle. On good days I could convince Mom that somehow she could afford to give me a dime so I could get a real ice cream bar.

The Good Humor Man's nickels and dimes added up. His son told me that his Dad averaged $110 a week in profits. Wow! That was unheard of. My dad earned right around $50 a week, slaving away in that awful foundry of Henry Ford's Rouge Plant. I was only about ten then, but I started making plans to become a very rich career Good Humor Man.

Chapter 4

WHAT'S A TAMPON?

MY next recollection of a significant event is one that made an impression that I have carried with me throughout my life and one that I've related many times. I was in the sixth grade at Francis G. Boynton Elementary School in southwest Detroit and a homlier kid didn't exist. It was a sizable school, two stories high and a city block long. Its teaching staff consisted of one male and thirty-five females. This was not an atypical ratio in those days.

I was in the physical process of evolving from a really cute child to a really ugly adolescent and I do mean ugly. I hadn't yet considered it necessary to comb my wild hair, my lips and teeth were far too large for my goofy looking face which was almost a solid freckle. I was *ugly*. In fact, I had reached the pinnacle of grotesqueness—at least in my mind. I can remember walking to school and passing several storefront windows, each of which repeatedly proved my perception to me. God, that was an awful time.

It was rest time for several classes, and we were sitting cross-legged or lying on mats in the gymnasium. Suddenly, a new tampon came skittering across the floor. There were a few giggles and muted screams, but some of us, including me, had no idea what this unusual thing was. The silly looking little cotton cylinder scooted along until it paused momentarily near one of the boy students who sent it on its way again. More giggling. The next time it stopped on its merry way around the room, it was coming to rest right by me, just as the teacher entered the gym and spotted it. I was in deep, deep trouble, and I didn't even know why. I was sent directly to the Manual Training teacher, Mr. Goodell for appropriate punishment.

Mr. Goodell was waiting for me. He was a man about fifty years old, and the fingers he still had were thick and scarred. He always had a mouthful of a horrible breath freshener, Sen-Sen, one of the first available commercially. Its sickeningly sweet licorice smell permeated the little wood shop and lent a whole new dimension to the concept of halitosis. One of his duties was to physically discipline young students who had violated some rule in some not always clear way.

Mr. Goodell didn't like me. I couldn't make beautiful laminated wood sailboats like his favorites could. I couldn't even make simple birdhouses or kites, the most elementary of wood projects. When I arrived in his office for punishment, he knew of my serious transgression against the whole of the female population, not only of Boynton Elementary School, but of women everywhere. He gave me a couple of whacks on the butt with his wooden paddle. The whacks didn't really hurt, but his words were devastating. He said,

"Glenn, do you know what you're going to be when you grow up?"

"No, Sir," I replied, suspecting that he might just be about to tell me.

"You know those horrible looking, bum-like guys that walk around parks with a gunnysack and a long stick with a sharp nail on the end of it, cleaning up scraps of paper from parks and playgrounds?"

"Yes, Sir."

"Well, that's what you're going to be. You're too stupid to do anything else."

I never forgot that recrimination and I never forgave him. I never will. What a devastating thing to say to any child - no matter how homely he or she might be.

Chapter 5

LOOSEN UP, IRENE

ANOTHER unsavory episode at Boynton occurred in the fifth grade. Every day, a half-pint of always warm surplus milk was provided to each student and was consumed during a fifteen-minute mid-morning break from our studies. The kids would generally mill around the room, talking and gossiping and drinking their nauseating milk. I was walking up to the front of the room for some reason or other, when I came across Irene, a cute little blond who was kneeling on her desk seat, talking with her neighbor. Unknowingly, she presented her little bottom just as I approached the area. What was I to do? Without thinking, and acting purely from instinct, I gently goosed her. I thought it was great fun. She didn't. She ran screaming to the teacher and through her tears, told her of my horrible crime against her body and mind. I spent the rest of the afternoon sitting alone in the hallway. I wonder sometimes if Irene ever mused about that event or ever thought that she might have overreacted somewhat. Relax, Irene.

Chapter 6

THE COPS

THE first of my many distasteful encounters with the Detroit police occurred the next summer. I don't remember where I got them, but I found myself in possession of a great quantity of illegal firecrackers.

One day, with a pocket full of contraband, I was walking in a relatively unfamiliar neighborhood about six blocks from my home. I was merrily lighting one firecracker after another as I headed home. Suddenly, I looked up and spotted a police cruiser at the end of the block. The cop had seen me. More seriously, he had heard me, and turned his car in my direction. I started running through yards and alleys and across streets, one after the other, thinking I could escape. But then I ran into a yard with a very high fence that I couldn't scale. I backtracked and ran into the open garage and hid under a bench at the far end. I was crouched there, panting, my heart pounding, sweat beading up on my freckled brow, thinking I would wait a little while for the cop to move on—

and then I'd be free! I was wrong. I looked up to see the cop standing in the doorway of the garage.

He said, "Come on out, you little shit. I can see you."

I crawled out from my ridiculous, unshielded "hiding place," to confront my tormentor, ready to go to prison for life. In a voice that damn near intimidated me forever, he said, "Don't you know that you should never run from the police? We can only think that you must have done something really bad if you run, and you could be shot."

He scared the Hell out of me, took my firecrackers and sent me on my way. Even though I've never been terribly cynical, I suspected then (and still do) that he probably had a great time that evening with his own kids and my firecrackers.

Chapter 7

A MOST UNPLEASANT TIME

I was in the sixth grade when a most unfortunate event occurred. It was nearing Halloween and I was eleven years old. I purchased a small paper mache' pumpkin with a few of my hard earned pennies, and put it on top of my folk's new console radio. The radio was a beautiful piece of dark walnut furniture, and held a commanding spot in our living room. Every afternoon I would rush home from school, prop myself up in front of the radio, and listen intently to the latest episode of "Superman," one of my favorite radio shows.

One beautiful fall afternoon I came bounding merrily into the house after school, full of good cheer and youthful enthusiasm about most everything. I walked into the kitchen where Mom was washing dishes at the sink.

I said, "Hi, Mom."

Without turning around to face me, she replied in a soft, but firm voice,

"You're going to get a licking, Mister."

"What for?" I asked, not having a clue about why I should deserve a licking. Later, much later, I learned that the horrendous, searing feeling gnawing at my gut was that terrible emotion—*anxiety*.

"Come here," she said, leading me into the living room. She pulled a cover off of her beautiful, new radio. It had a deep, black, scar that covered nearly half of its top. The acrid odor of scorched varnish filled my lungs. Oh, oh. Oh, shit. I had lit a candle in my little paper pumpkin when I was home for lunch, and had forgotten to blow it out before going back to school. The candle burned down, and eventually ignited the entire pumpkin. The pumpkin, in turn, ignited the varnish on the radio top and burst into a roaring flame, melting and spewing sputtering gobs of flaming varnish all over the living room. The rug had caught fire in several places, and the couch had more than a few burn spots. I was in deep, deep trouble.

"You're going to get a serious licking when your father gets home!" she shrieked and returned to the kitchen, tears streaming down her face.

I retreated to my room and pondered my fate—but not for long. There was Mom at the door.

"Come on, Glenn. We're not waiting for your father."

I slunk out into the living room where she was waiting with my Dad's razor strop, a thick, three inch wide, band of leather that Dad used to put a fine edge on his straight razor.

"Take your pants off," she hissed. I complied and lay down on the couch, face down, as directed.

My body exploded in pain as she rained blow after blow on my back, buttocks and legs. I didn't think she'd ever stop. I was screaming in agony.

"Think you've had enough?" she asked.

"Yes, yes," I wailed.

"Well *I* don't think so," she screamed, and the beating continued for another five or six sickening lashes.

Finally, it was over. I will never forget that beating. Not ever.

Chapter 8

THE BUDDING BUSINESSMAN

As an emerging entrepreneur, I was always trying to think of ways to earn a penny or two. One of my first endeavors in the business world began when I was eight years old. I answered an advertisement in the back of a comic book. The company was looking for kids to sell Cloverine Salve. If I ordered a gross, I could get them for a nickel each. I figured I could double my money if I could sell all of them for ten cents each, and I did. I just went door to door, asking people if they wanted to buy some great salve. I don't think I called on a house that didn't buy at least one of my little tins—and it *was* great salve.

My next adventure in business was selling Collier's Magazine. Every week I would get a bundle of twenty-five magazines delivered to my door. I paid ten cents a copy and they retailed for fifteen. My profit margin wasn't as great as with the salve, but I always sold my quota, and always had spending change in my pocket. My best sales sites were the neighborhood taverns. I could usually sell three or four at each joint before the bartender asked me to leave. I quickly learned that half-looped guys are big tippers, too. Many of them gave me fifty cents for a magazine that had cost me ten. What a life!

I even made a deal with my mother. I was to kill all the flies in the house, and for each one, I would receive a penny bounty. It didn't take long, however, before the supply of flies was exhausted. What to do? The answer came to me in a brilliant flash of insight. Since I needed more flies, I went into the basement and opened the windows. Viola! I had an unending supply of flies to harvest. It only took a couple of days for Mom to discover my larcenous little scheme though, and promptly put an end to it.

Chapter 9

TASTES JUST LIKE CHICKEN!

ANOTHER of my great money making schemes had to do with supplying meat to meat-hungry neighbors. Since all meat was in short supply during the war, and none of our neighbors was a vegetarian, it occurred to me that here was a market ripe for exploiting—and I was right. Mom had fed us flour dipped pan-fried rabbit one night for supper, and it was wonderful. It really did taste just like chicken, as she had promised it would. An idea quickly formed, and after a brief discussion with my parents about its merits, we all went shopping for a female rabbit.

We found the perfect candidate for my introduction into the meat raising and marketing business I was creating—a white, very large, pregnant mother lode of a rabbit. I paid three bucks for her and we left for home with my money-making machine.

I kept the rabbit in a cage in our garage while Dad quickly built some hutches. He cut a hole in the garage wall, and hung a set of hutches on both the interior and exterior walls. The rabbit could then have access to the inside or outside, depending on the weather, temperature, and her own not-to-well thought through desires. Rabbits are dumb.

One day soon after we got her set up in her new home, the pregnant mother to be gave birth to fourteen bunnies. They had no hair and looked exactly like baby rats. Their skin was a variety of colors, white, black, brown, and mixtures of those colors. We soon found that as they began to grow fur, the hairs were the same color as the skin from which they erupted. They were healthy and all of them survived to adulthood.

When the bunny brood was adult enough to butcher and sell, we saved the females for an ongoing breeding program. However, we didn't get to the males soon enough. One or more of them had mated with their mother and here she was, pregnant again. This batch of bunnies wasn't terribly deformed, but when I let it happen the second time, and more neglectfully between brothers and sisters, all Hell broke loose in our hutch's gene pool. We had many newborns with no feet. Sometimes no ears, or ears shooting off in crazy directions. It was a mess. And, at that point, we had thirty-five very original looking creatures.

I was getting tired of this project anyway. I was tired of buying rabbit food pellets. I was tired of picking clover for them. I was tired of cleaning their dirty little cages. So, we decided to butcher and then, with the help of some of our neighbors, eat the whole deformed population. They tasted great—no matter how outlandish their little bunny bodies looked.

Chapter 10

V-2

THE street we lived on in Detroit was just one long block. Almost all of the parents had migrated from one or another European country. Many were German, but there were also Hungarians, Poles, Irish, and Canadians. My father was a Canadian, and a naturalized U.S. citizen. As far as I could tell, the men who didn't work in the auto factories were cops. We had three policemen on our block alone, so we generally felt relatively safe.

The street was our playground. It was about thirty feet wide and paved with asphalt. Every fifty feet or so a two inch wide tar expansion strip ran across the street. We used these expansion strips as boundary lines for various games like touch football and baseball. Storm drains were designated as the first and third bases.

The storm drains were located next to the curb and covered with heavy steel grates. The purpose of the grates was to prevent rainwater from carrying pets and small children into the sewers during major downpours. During heavy rainstorms, we would block the drains with newspapers so the street would fill up with water—perhaps five inches deep or so. Then we'd lie down in the water and pretend to swim. We also rode our bicycles through it at the highest speeds possible, spraying water in every direction. Sometimes the water would come from the fire department's routine flushing of the hydrants. We didn't care where the water came from, as long as it came.

One of my favorite games, though, was the rubber-gun battle. We manufactured wooden pistols and rifles of various lengths. We were very creative in design. Some of our rifles could be loaded with up to ten rubbers and when fired would release a shotgun like blast of rubber missiles toward the "enemy." If one hit you, you were "killed" and out of the game. The "rubbers" were made of strips of automobile tire inner tubes, cut in strips about three quarters of an inch wide. The resulting loop was then tied in the middle with at least one tight knot. The knot provided stability in the trajectory and greatly enhanced the "kill" ratio. In a typical battle, one side would rush up to the asphalt line that divided the battlefield into "us" and "them" and everyone would fire their weapons at the other team members, who had retreated to the back boundary line. The survivors would then rush up to the dividing line and release their salvo. One day we were engaged in such a battle, and a little eleven-year-old on the enemy team named Ramie rushed up to the line and gave us everything he had.

But we were ready. We charged, firing wildly in his general direction. Ramie began a rapid retreat. He turned around to see where he was going just as he smashed face first into the rear end of a parked car.

Poor Ramie. He chipped both incisors. Split them damn near in half in fact. When he stopped crying and we got to inspect the damage, we found that he had created a very nice inverted "V" in his smile. From that time on Ramie was known as V-2, after the infamous German rocket then bombarding England. Ramie grew up to be a Detroit Policeman. I kept my distance from him.

Chapter 11

BURNING RIVERS AND DYING LAKES

EVERY so often, perhaps once a month or so, I would hear a major explosion, and it was always at night. Dad told me that the Ford Rouge Plant, where he worked, made everything needed for the manufacture of cars, including steel from iron ore and glass from the huge mountains of sand we could see from the road. One of the byproducts of the steel-making process was an extremely hot material called slag. Ford workers would move the slag on a barge from the plant to the middle of the Rouge River, which ran by the plant on its way to empty into the Detroit River, which in turn disgorged its terrible contents into Lake Erie. Then they would dump the slag into the water—as if they could do that forever. Sometimes, perhaps once a month or so, the intensely white hot slag would interact with other oils and pollutants in the river and explode, rattling (and sometimes cracking) windows within a several mile radius. It frequently set the river on fire.

Chapter 12

MY WAR EFFORT

DURING World War II, everyone was called upon to fulfill their patriotic responsibilities. One of the children's obligations was to save their pennies, nickels and dimes rather than spend them foolishly on such things as ice cream cones or comic books so we could buy savings stamps and bonds to help the war effort. Actually, ice cream was in very short supply, and we were reduced to eating sherbet—a nasty confection that was supposed to be an ice cream substitute. I hate sherbet to this day.

Every Thursday, we would bring our week's meager savings to school, and purchase as many War Savings Stamps as we could. The stamps came in denominations of ten, twenty-five, fifty cents and a dollar. We would paste them into a little booklet that each of us had. When the booklet contained enough stamps to total $18.75, we could then turn it in for a $25.00 Savings Bond. Of course, some kids were able to bring fifty cents or a dollar each week, but I was happy to bring my quarter. I managed to accumulate over two hundred dollars in bonds between 1942 and 1945, and I was very proud of that.

Everyone in elementary school also learned how to knit. At home we would knit little squares about five inches on each side. Each Thursday, at Savings Stamp buying time, we would turn in our little squares. We were told that they would be sewn together by the ladies of the Red Cross, creating woolen blankets of various sizes and patterns which were then shipped to Europe to help keep the children there warm in the winter. I'm sure those kids didn't care how wild and odd the blankets looked, as long as they worked.

Another nearly forgotten war effort was the saving of cooking oils and grease rendered from the cooking of meat. We were told that these oils were refined and then used both as lubricants for jeeps, tanks, and trucks, and as a critical ingredient in the manufacture of gun powder. We would save all such renderings in a coffee can and when it was full, turn it in at a collection point. Two blocks from our home, the local Smith Store, one of a relatively small chain of neighborhood groceries, served as such a site. Mr. Woolery, the owner of this franchise, thought he was just about as clever as a man could possibly be when he put a big strip of butcher paper in his window with the words boldly announcing in big blue letters: "***Ladies, bring your fat cans to me!***"

Chapter 13

THE FLUTE MAN

THE Flute Man traveled the alleys of Detroit. There were, of course, several flute men—probably scores of them—but the only one I knew was the one who announced his weekly visits to our alley with a squeaky horn he blew. The horn only had two high pitched, screechy notes. I figured that he was either crazy or deaf or both to be able to tolerate that interminable assault on his ears. He was a scavenger and a junk man, and probably, a very wealthy one. He would stop a fairly long, horse-drawn staked wagon at everyone's trash pile and carefully sort through it for any items he thought might be salvageable or resalable. He was scanning especially for anything made of metal which could be recycled for the war effort. He would also buy bundles of newspapers from people who were patient enough to collect, bundle, tie, and wait for him in the alley. I waited for him every week. I almost always had something I hoped he thought would be of value, and I was usually right. I almost always came away from my alley encounters with the flute man richer by a quarter or two.

Chapter 14

MY SISTER'S GIRDLE

DURING World War II it was next to impossible to find anything made of rubber. It was all being consumed by the men and machines of war. If our civilian population got anything at all made of rubber, it was generally either an outrageously priced black market item, or purchased in Canada. Shortages of everything, silk stockings, meat, and tires were never really problematical in Canada—certainly nowhere near the degree to which they were in the States. But in the States it was a different story. Everything was in short supply. Gasoline was rationed. Every car owner had a ration book issued to them according to the job they held, how critical it was judged to be to the war effort, and the distance it was from home to work. Very little latitude was allowed for "frivolous" travel, like going to a beach or a park, or to church for that matter. In addition to the ration book, car owners were issued a windshield sticker that designated the type and amount of gasoline that could be legally purchased, "A," "B," "C" or "T." As I recall, an "A" book was the best and allowed the most gas to be purchased. "B" and "C" books could buy less, and "T" was for trucks, which of course, had a much more generous allowance.

Just about everything was rationed and could only be purchased either with coupons from ration books, or special permission from the ration board. New cars were impossible to buy. Other items, such as bicycles, fuel oil, kerosene, shoes, stoves, tires, typewriters, meat, and sugar were extremely scarce and all were rationed. Of course, if a person had unlimited financial resources and didn't care what he paid for an item, just about anything could be had.

One day, in my pre-adolescent ramblings around our house, I discovered my sister Dorothy's only rubber girdle. I didn't have any idea what purpose in served or how valuable it was, and decided that strips of it would make a great slingshot. And I was right. I cut two nice strips out of her girdle, each one about a foot long and an inch wide. With those strips, a bit of leather, and a great "Y" from a tree branch, I made myself a slingshot that was "the Mother of all slingshots." I could fire marbles at speeds that I'm sure challenged Mach 2. They traveled so fast they couldn't be seen, only heard (or felt) as they pierced their target with deadly accuracy. From my upstairs bedroom window, I could send my little glass missiles through the rear windows of the apartment building on the next street. They never knew what hit them or from where.

I always had plenty of marble ammunition. I was an excellent shot in the neighborhood games and very nearly always finished the game winners. I always played for "keeps," never for "funsies." I can only recall buying marbles one time. They were in a little mesh sack with about thirty of those beautiful little glass spheres. The sack also contained a few "puries," which were miniature marbles of a single, pure color—hence, the name—puries, and a single "boulder," an oversize marble worth perhaps ten ordinary marbles on the then current marble market. I was a very good shot, and I don't think I ever bought another sack of marbles. But I won hundreds of them and kept them stored in a gallon pickle jar that I had rescued from our garbage bin.

One night, as I was on the hunt with my slingshot in a vacant lot across the street from us, I spied a guy on the next street. He was sitting in his living room with his back to me, reading the evening paper. I took careful aim. *Swoosh*!! The missile was launched. It whizzed right through the shattering window, by the fellow's ear, and tore neatly through his paper. He didn't like that. He came roaring out of the house, swearing and yelling seriously foul language at his invisible tormentor. When I saw him racing toward the door, I dropped down in the tall weeds on the lot, and remained very, very still. He only ranted ten or fifteen seconds I suppose, but it seemed like an eternity to me that evening. I figured that it might just be about time for me to leave town.

Part Two
MINNESOTA

Chapter 15

THE REUNION

IT was summer, 1946. I was twelve, skinny, and covered with freckles and excitement. My Mom, Dad, and I were traveling from Detroit to my uncle George's farm in Red Lake Falls, Minnesota. It was to be the first family reunion of the Abbott clan. As would become the custom, the reunion was held the first weekend in August. Coming from Detroit, we were accustomed to the oppressive heat and humidity. It was, however, to be the first time I had ever seen mosquitoes big enough to strut as they prowled their hunting grounds and aggressive enough to cast a romantic eye toward the farmyard turkeys. Some of the buck mosquitoes were brash enough to mount those turkeys standing flat-footed. It was a fearsome sight.

My mother, Daisy, was an Abbott—the second of fourteen children, born and raised on the wind-swept prairies of northwestern Minnesota. She was happy. My dad, Lester Adams, was one of thirteen children in a neighboring farm family, but Dad's family members were never as close to each other as the Abbotts were.

This was the first time all of Mom's siblings and their families had gotten together since the oldest ones had begun drifting away from home in their mid-teens. Most of the boys would later insist that they left home at age three to go to work on the railroad, just to escape the regular savage beatings from their father, which were doled out in a more or less random fashion. Whenever his wife or one of his children would deny that they were responsible for some imagined transgression, he would scream, "A likely story!" and proceed with the savage beating he "needed" to deliver. The animals didn't need to deny anything—they simply accepted their beatings as an unpleasant part of their lives.

It was 1946—the war was over, and all nine of Mom's brothers had survived. None had been wounded, but many had seen combat. The German Army had captured my oldest cousin, Earle, a paratrooper, within days of his first jump into enemy territory. He had spent three years in a Nazi prison camp. This was a very special reunion.

We pulled our rig, a 1936 Studebaker, into the farmyard and piled out. Dad had bought a brand new, 1941 Ford just before the war broke out. But in 1944, Dad began a series of disastrous decisions that eventually ruined us financially. He sold that beautiful, maroon car to a stranger from Kentucky who knocked on our door one summer evening. He was buying all the cars he could and taking them back home to be resold at huge profits. He offered Dad $1,000 cash, right then. Since Dad had only paid $900 for it and had driven it for over three years, he thought it was an outstanding offer, and without giving it a second thought, sold our car. The guy peeled off ten $100 bills, took the paperwork and the car and drove off. It took Dad several weeks before he could find *any* kind of replacement, but he finally did and wound up with a *very* used '36 Studebaker. It was an absolute wreck that he paid for repeatedly in repair bills.

It seemed like there were hundreds of other folks there, uncles and aunts and cousins—many whom I'd never seen before—some I'd never see again. The women were cooking and telling each other how wonderful their children were, the men were telling each other lies and drinking beer, whisky, and whatever else looked like it might contain a buzz. The kids, all first cousins, played, and ran and tumbled and got to know each other.

My Dad, Lester, had worked for awhile in his youth as a farmhand and lumberjack in Northern Minnesota after leaving school in the seventh grade. Soon World War I broke out and in 1917 he joined the Army. Sixty days after his enlistment he was under artillery fire in France. He survived the war years without being physically wounded but he would never talk about his time in combat. After the war he returned to Minnesota and struck up a romance with my mother—who had recently been divorced from an alcoholic and physically abusive floorlayer. They were married in 1932 and moved to Detroit to try to find work. Dad was a gentle man—filled with quiet dignity.

The depression was in full bloom and the only work he could find was a part-time job clearing the Detroit sewers of debris. He and the other workers all wore gas masks because the air in the sewers was so foul and full of noxious gases. One day Dad heard that Henry Ford was hiring for his Rouge Plant. The plant was just about seven miles from our home. At that time he had no car, so he walked the seven miles to get in a very long line of applicants at 6:00 am. After waiting all day, he finally got to the reception desk. The receptionist asked him if he was a citizen.

"Yes," he replied, "A naturalized one."

"Where are your citizenship papers?" she asked.

"They're at home," he replied.

"If you want to work here, bring them with you when you come back tomorrow," she said, and summarily dismissed him.

The next day he repeated the process, and was hired. The work was stoop labor in the auto plant—the dumbest, dirtiest, most unpleasant jobs that no one else wanted to do. But, it was work—and, it was gas free—four hours a day, five days a week. It wasn't long though before it became full-time and Dad was happy. A month later I was born. Dad missed that day at work. It was one of two days he missed in twenty years at that plant. The other missed day was because of an industrial accident that cost him his right great toe.

He was never late. Not once. Although we were no more than twenty minutes by car from the plant, he would leave home an hour and a half before he was to start work, "Just in case something happened to the car, and I have to walk." Dad had a very strong work ethic and a tremendous sense of loyalty to Henry Ford.

But, in 1946, he had been in that horrendously loud, stinking, foundry for 14 years. The war was over, and Dad foresaw a great depression ahead, with all those millions of men coming home from the war to fill jobs that no longer existed (another great miscalculation). So, during the two weeks of the "grand reunion," Dad was busily looking at farms that might be just right for us—and he found one, he thought. It was 120 acres of mostly scrawny oak trees. There were about 20 acres of rocky ground that the salesman said were tillable.

The house had two stories and a full basement. It had two bedrooms and a sewing room on the second floor, a dining room, living room, bedroom, kitchen a full bath on the main floor, and a furnace, coal bin, and a deep-well room in the basement. Actually, it wasn't a bad house. In fact, compared to all of our relatives, and most folks in the general area, it was a great house. Except—it was haunted. But that's another story.

Chapter 16

THE FARM

IT was the middle of November, 1946, when we arrived in Fossil[1]. Mom and Dad thought they would be spending the rest of their lives there. Both of them were home, having been raised on neighboring farms during the early part of the century. It was near zero degrees and the wind was sweeping across the prairie in snowy, biting gusts. Our furniture had not arrived so we moved in with one of Mom's brothers, Dave, and his family, who had a house in town, about two miles from our farm.

Gladys, Dave's wife, did all of her cooking on a kerosene range. She was a great cook though, and I never heard anyone complain about quality or quantity. Dave and Gladys had four children, three boys and a girl.

On the third day the moving van arrived. All of Dave's family came out to the farm to help us unload. We had a household full of beautiful furniture that Mom and Dad had accumulated over their years of working in the factories of

Detroit. (Mom had worked several years spray-painting automobile dashboards in the Ternstead plant, one of the many factories that supplied the major auto plants with parts.) Dad had also packed every nut and bolt, every rusty, bent nail, and every tool he had ever come across. He was a saver—a pack rat. I suppose it had to do with the deprivation he had endured during the depression, but this was ridiculous. The moving company's bill was twice what the estimate had been. Dad had no choice but to pay it or they wouldn't have begun to unload the van. Those turned out to be very expensive rusty, bent nails.

One of the very first things Mom did was to get a telephone. I was one of those wall-hung jobs in an oak cabinet with a crank, a mouthpiece sticking out of its face, and a receiver on the end of a three-foot cord. We learned quickly that you should never be on the phone during a thunderstorm. Lightening would sometimes come screaming out of the mouthpiece and punch a hole in the opposite wall. Having that electrical flash pass through one's mouth would have been most unpleasant. We just never used the phone during storms.

Fossil was small. Our phone number was six. We had sixteen farm families on our party line, so whenever we answered our ring, we would always hear the "click - click - click," as receivers were picked up by the other parties on our line. This invasive practice was known as rubber-necking. There were damn few secrets in Fossil.

Arriving in November as we did, there was no way to generate any income so Dad busied himself fixing up the house. Although it was a fairly large, beautiful structure, it had been neglected by its previous owner. Actually, he had abandoned it, leaving the doors open to the wind, rain, sleet, and snow. One of the first things we discovered was that the house was settling. There was a huge support post in the middle of the basement that seemed to be sinking. Naturally, all of the walls in the house developed enormous cracks, and we didn't know where that would all end.

Dad broke out the concrete floor and began to dig down around that supporting post. What we found was that the post had been set on a huge, rounded rock, and it was beginning to slip off. The post had slid several inches, resulting in the damage we had seen upstairs. Dad rigged up several house jacks and managed to raise the main floor of the house to an even keel. Of course, that added several new, very severe cracks in every wall in the house. How he finally got that support post resituated so it would keep the main floor where he wanted it, I don't know. But he did. We filled in around the post with new concrete, and thought we were done. The rest of the winter was spent fixing up the damage, and collecting a small grouping of strange farm animals.

By strange animals, I mean creatures such as: a twenty year old swayback cow that I creatively named Elsie, one boar and three soon to be pregnant sow pigs, 150 scrawny leghorn chickens, two teams of horses, a dog, and two very tall, skinny, range cows. Those range cows really, really hated to have their tiny little teats pulled on at milking time.

The door to our barn had a threshold about six inches high that needed to be stepped over when entering or leaving the barn or any human would fall and break his or her face. Elsie was so old and arthritic that she couldn't lift her hind feet over the sill, or maybe she just forgot, but every time she traveled through that doorway she'd crash the front of her hind ankles into that threshold. She had the most horrible looking ankles of any cow I had ever seen, bloody all of the time.

We did manage to sell a few eggs and a little bit of cream, but that money amounted to the total income for our family during winter and spring of 1947. Such straights didn't faze any of our many relatives in the area though, who frequently

---

1. Fossil is a pseudonym for the town's name, but the characters and events are true.

arrived an hour or so before dinner. It was a crazy time—but there were many positives as well.

One night in February of '47, I walked home after an evening of playing spin the bottle with some kids in town. We didn't have any bottles, so we used a kerosene lamp chimney, and it worked just fine—until it shattered on someone's knee. I'd never heard of that game before and thought to myself that I could surely become addicted to it. It was about ten below that night, there was no wind, and the moon was full. I walked away from the two or three lights still on in Fossil and out onto the hardtop road that passed our farm. The crisp snow crunched under my boots as I headed for home. I was about half way there when I heard something. I stopped my crunching and listened. It was wolves, howling at the moon. Or maybe they were howling at me, or telling their friends what a neat meal was walking all alone. I picked up my speed dramatically and made it home safely just in time to prevent my heart from bursting.

In May, the boar pig managed to adequately service the three sows. All were pregnant. We were all pleased, but I'm sure not as pleased as our friendly boar. Actually, he was much more like a dog than a pig, but a Hell of a lot smarter. He had free run of the farm, and was always waiting for us in the yard when we returned from a trip to town. He would squeal and jump straight up and down and beg for us to scratch his back. He was a *great* pig. However, Dad figured that since his job was done, our friendly old boar could be sacrificed for our eating pleasure. Since uncastrated pigs have fairly foul tasting meat, the first order of business was to deprive him of his only claim to fame.

I went with Dad down to the little pig shed where we tied my friendly porker to the floor so he couldn't move. Then, with a single edge razor blade, Dad sliced my friend's scrotum, pulled out each testicle and severed it. Then he threw some flour on the gaping wounds to help congeal the freely flowing blood and untied him. I never heard such screaming before or since. I vowed that I would never let that happen to me. And it hasn't. At least not yet, and my hopes remain high.

Chapter 17

FOSSIL CONSOLIDATED SCHOOL

THE day after we arrived in Fossil, I started school. I was the sophisticated kid from the big, dangerous city of Detroit and a force to be reckoned with. I had just turned fourteen.

The school drew students from a very wide rural area. The school was quite small. Even so, given the nature of this wind-swept prairie land, it was a fairly imposing structure. Grades one through seven were housed on the first floor, grades eight through twelve on the second. It had been built in 1920 for $65,000. It had a 175-foot front and was 75 feet deep. It was brick, had two floors and a full basement. My class had seventeen students, including me.

It was on one of my very first days in school when I met my first challenge. I was sitting in a science classroom, waiting for the teacher, when some kid behind me (with a name like Adams, I was always in the front row) said something I thought was funny. I laughed out loud. A voice from behind me said crisply,

"What the Hell are *you* laughing at?"

I turned and was met by the snarling face of a blond Norwegian kid, Olaf. I had no idea who he was, except that he was significantly bigger that I was—but then, most everyone was. Straightening up in my seat, I brilliantly replied,

"I was just thinking how funny my fist would look in your face."

That was it. After school I met him and with my little body of coiled steel, beat the Hell out of him. He never challenged me again, and actually we became reasonably good friends. Years later, in prison for who knows what, another inmate murdered him.

My next challenge came from Earl, a muscular brute, short, but very strong. He didn't know how to fight though. I beat him fairly savagely, and, strangely enough, we too became good friends. Then, the physical challenges were over.

One day Petie, a sixth grader, heard me call someone a pimp. He had never heard that word before, nor had any of his buddies. So Petie and two of his comrades went to the little classroom on the second floor that doubled as a library to look it up in a dictionary. The principal of the school, Mr. Shraeder, walked by and saw them.

"What are you guys doing in there? You haven't been in the library in your entire lives. What's going on?" he asked them.

When Petie told him what they were looking up, it did my reputation with the school administration very little good.

Fossil was a small school, but I think I learned more in my two years there than in the next three years in four huge metropolitan Detroit high schools.

Because the school had so few students, everyone was expected to turn out for all sports. What a joke. I probably weighed eighty pounds. I was small, but wiry and strong. Even so, I knew enough not to turn out for football. Those huge farm kids would have killed me. I wasn't so fortunate when it came to baseball and basketball though.

I played one season of baseball for Fossil High School, and one for the American Legion team. Both were disastrous. My coordination in all sports was painfully terrible, but I generally had nine innings to demonstrate my incompetence in baseball. As I recall, I only earned first base one time in two seasons. And that was because a pitch hit me in my left hip. That monstrous farm kid who was pitching for the other team threw a fastball that I couldn't escape. It hit me on my left hipbone and I crumpled to the ground, out cold. They put a pinch runner, Duane, in for me. He immediately tried to steal second base. I regained consciousness just in time to see him slide into second base headfirst. Some observers said he was traveling at least thirty miles an hour when he hit the bag. He slid ten feet beyond the base and into short center field. The second baseman walked over and tagged him out. An inauspicious ending, I must say, to the one time I had painfully earned first base.

My fielding was on a par with my immeasurably incompetence at the plate. Our hapless coach tried me in every position except pitching and catching. I missed every ball that entered my domain. One time, while playing third base, I actually managed to stop a grounder. Delighted with my unexpected success, I picked up the ball and threw it as hard as I could, at least ten feet over the first baseman's head and into a grove of trees. The ball was never found.

Another time, I came running in from left field to catch a fly ball, only to watch it sail well over my head for a home run. I leaped awkwardly into the air in a futile and ridiculous attempt to save face. I managed an exceptionally rare corkscrewing maneuver in the air and plunged to the earth in a heap of humiliation. The coach was crying.

The basketball team was sorted into three levels of

competence by our coach: the "A" Team (the boys who were most gifted with motor skills), the "B" Team (the boys who were at best, mediocre), and the "C" Team (the largely incompetent). I was a substitute on the "C" team. I got to play in two games, briefly, during the one season I played.

One bitterly cold blustery night the team loaded itself into a frosty school bus and traveled across the snowy prairie to a small, competing school in Fertile. When the game appeared to be hopelessly lost, our coach put me in. Some fool threw the ball to me, which I immediately drop kicked into the steel rafters. The ball was retrieved and play began again. Within a minute, I was called for two fouls. I still don't know what I did wrong. In any event, I was summarily removed from my one and only basketball game.

Such was my athletic career at Fossil Consolidated School.

Chapter 18

FALL/WINTER, '46 - '47

THAT first winter in Minnesota was a jarring assault on all of my senses. I had never seen anything like it. Never before had I heard telephone or electrical wires howl and scream like creatures that belonged in Hell. Nor had I heard of storm windows for cars—but there they were—little plastic ovals with a strip of rubber around their perimeter. We would glue them to the inside of each car window, providing an air pocket of about a quarter of an inch between the glass and the interior of the car windshield or rear and side windows. It worked quite well. It became possible to see the snowbank or ditch just before plunging head long into it—a dubious benefit.

The icy winds that blew in from Canada and North Dakota were near paralyzing and frequently deadly. During blizzards, many farmers became disoriented and lost just trying to walk from their farmhouses to their barns to care for their livestock. They would eventually be found, frozen to death. The smarter farmers strung a rope between the house, barn and other outbuildings that would guide them even if they couldn't see.

Cross continental Highway 2 ran directly through the middle of town. It was twenty-five miles between Fossil and Crookston, the next town to the west. After one blizzard in the '30's, thirty-five people were found frozen to death in or near their cars along that twenty-five mile stretch of highway. It had been so cold their cars had frozen up and stalled even as they were being driven down the highway, leaving them stranded in this inescapable, penetrating, unforgiving cold.

It was preordained, I suppose, that some tinkerer would invent a supplementary heater for cars trying to operate in that dreadful climate. And so it was that a gasoline heater, tied into the car's fuel line, and placed in the front passenger seat's footwell was created. The most bizarre feature of this invention was that it actually worked. When ignited, it would blast intensely hot winds from its bowels—which was great unless you were sitting in the front passenger seat. There were a lot of heat-damaged and scorched boots, feet and ankles before the wrinkles were ironed out, but it eventually did serve a very useful purpose.

As cold as it was, Dad and I cut probably a hundred and fifty trees from our forested "farm" that winter. We bundled the trees together with a piece of chain and dragged them, six or eight at a time, with a team of horses up to the house. We would have used rope because it's normally easier than chain to work with, but all of our rope had frozen into stiff, coiled bundles of useless ice.

I learned a lot about cold in a very short time. One example: feet would stay a lot warmer, longer, if you didn't wear shoes. All that was needed were three pair of wool socks and several layers of paper in the bottom of your galoshes or boots. Shoes would constrict the blood flow and feet would freeze much more quickly.

We rigged up a miniature sawmill near the house so that we could cut the logs into furnace size pieces. It was a peculiar looking little mill but it worked. Dad had taken an electric motor from an old, discarded washing machine, attached various belts and pulleys, a twelve-inch rip blade which tore through our scrawny little trees like a hot knife through summer butter. The pieces were thrown through an open window into the basement where we would later split and stack them in the coal bin. Green wood is hard to get started burning, but once its going, it burns extremely hot. We always tried to bank the furnace fire with ashes at night, so we could get the next day's fire going with the coals. Sometimes it worked, sometimes it didn't.

Although the furnace worked, it had what appeared to be a distinct water line all around it about four feet up from the concrete floor. Another "Oh, Oh." Clearly the basement had been flooded, probably every spring since the house was built. So in a fit of rarely practiced preventative creativity, we decided to install a sump pump.

Dad broke out the concrete floor under a window that opened out of the side of the house near the septic tank. Then he dug a hole in the dirt big enough to hold a fifty-gallon oil drum. The sump pump was then installed in the oil drum, with the pump's screen-covered pipe resting near the bottom of the drum. Using large steel chisels and a five-pound mall, Dad and I took turns chipping channels in the floor leading to the sump. We figured the incoming water in the spring would drain neatly into the sump—and what do you know? It worked. And a good thing that it did, too. In the spring when the snow began to melt, and the frost in the ground began to thaw, the water began seeping in through the walls and the floor. The sump pump evacuated fifty gallons of water every three minutes for nearly two months.

There was a steel, decorative grate in the floor between the living and dining rooms, directly above the top of the furnace. The furnace top would get red hot when the fire was at its peak. The grate, while not red hot, was nevertheless hot enough to sear flesh. It was not something to step on with bare feet. Now that was an exercise in one-trial learning. There was no way to circulate the heat, so the only way it could get to the second floor bedrooms was through small vents, about 12" x 12," in the bedroom floors. The first winter I slept upstairs. If the wind blew at night, and it almost always did, I would have an inch or so of snow on my bed in the morning. It was great, if you were weirdly masochistic.

It wasn't all bad, though. Dad introduced me to what was to become one of my greatest pleasures—ice fishing. One brilliantly sunny day, when it had warmed up to about twenty below, Dad took me to Maple Lake, about a mile and a half from our house. The lake was long and narrow—about seven miles in length and no more than a mile and a half wide at its widest point. It was fairly shallow, too. Probably no more than forty feet in a few places. Just before the Great Depression, the lake dried up, and farmers living adjacent to it strung barbed wire fences across it and pastured their livestock in it. In the late 30's, the county government had a channel dug between a lake ten miles distant and filled the Maple Lake basin. It has never been dry since.

When we got to the lake, I saw several little shanties out on the ice. Dad knew who owned one of them and we trudged across the snow-covered lake to it. The owner, Mr. Gunderson, (Gundy) was expecting us and opened the door and invited us in. It was pitch black inside the fishing house and I couldn't see anything. I learned that the houses had to be light-tight. The exterior of each shack was covered with at least two layers of overlapping tarpaper to prevent any leakage of light. If there was any light in the house at all, the fish could see us hunkered over that hole and would hang back, out of spearing range.

We all sat on little apple crates in front of the hole. The

shanty itself had a framework of 2 x 2's covered first with cardboard, then with the tarpaper. Under the house were two 2 x 6's with their front ends beveled like sled runners, so the house could be towed, either by car or by hand to the most likely fishing spot.

It wasn't long before my eyes adjusted and I entered a world of excitement and awe, the image of which has stayed with me to this day. This little house, about 6x6x6 feet, had a hole in the floor about 2x5 at the far end of the house from the door. To our immediate right as we entered the little house was a small, pot bellied kerosene stove. It was drip fed by a coffee can full of fuel, which hung on the wall above the stove. The fuel line had a small valve that opened and closed the fuel line with a small turnkey. My Uncle Dave made them by the dozen in his backyard welding shop for just about all of the local fishermen. The stove was vented through the roof with a 4 inch galvanized stovepipe. It was a unique looking affair, but I never heard of anyone getting asphyxiated by fumes.

Gundy was sitting on a stool by the edge of the hole with the handle of a five-foot, five-tined, steel spear resting on his right shoulder. The top prong of the spear's barbed tip was nestled in a notch he had carved in the ice with it, about a foot below the water line. There was a rope tied into a loop in the opposite end of the spear. The other end of the rope was then securely fastened to the wall of the fish house. I learned that the purpose of this setup was to save the spear if a large northern were to wrench the spear out of the fisherman's hands after having been speared. Sometimes that did happen, especially if the fish was speared anywhere other than directly behind its head—right where the neck would be, if it had one.

As my eyes adjusted to the darkness, the hole in the ice became increasingly brilliant and clear. The ice we were sitting on was about four feet thick, below which the water was seven or eight feet deep. Gundy had sliced up a few potatoes and had dropped them into the water, so that the light penetrating the ice from outside would be reflected and give us a clearer view of any creature that might venture into our trap. Some folks, I learned, used crushed oyster shells (normally fed to chickens as a calcium source to harden the shells of their eggs). Later, in my own fishing adventures, I greatly preferred oyster shells as a reflecting backdrop.

Gundy had cleared the ice of snow in a three-foot wide swath around the outside perimeter of the house to facilitate the transmission of light for reflection. The water was extremely clear and you could see every pebble on the lake bottom. Gundy had a decoy, about six inches long, shaped like a fish, with a small screw with an eye in it screwed into its back, about midway between its head and tail. A swivel was attached to the screw eye. A fishing line was attached to the swivel, with its other end tied to a small stick he held in his hand. The decoy had a slight curve in its tail, so that when Gundy gently moved the end of the stick up and down, the decoy would "swim" in circles, tempting all sorts of creatures from the deep.

"There's one," he whispered softly.

Gundy moved slowly and surely to back the spear tine out of its resting place. Gradually he lowered the spear to within inches of the northern's back. The fish was barely moving. Its fins were undulating rhythmically as it held its position, carefully studying this strange, but appealing morsel.

Suddenly, there was a flurry of activity as the spear was thrust into the fish, just behind his head. The aim was perfect. The huge twelve-pound northern was paralyzed. He curled up, motionless, as the spear, with its captive, was pulled from the water. The door was opened and Mr. Northern was placed outside on the ice with three of his relatives. I was hooked. From then on I spent every spare minute I could sitting in a fish house, staring into a hole in the ice at lake bottoms, and an occasional fish.

The limit on northerns at that time was seven per day, and I rarely had a day where I came home with less than my limit. We would stack them like logs on our back porch (which served as our walk-in freezer). Whenever we had an appetite for fish, we would bring one in and shave off its scales with a paring knife or potato peeler, thaw it, scrape out what little viscera remained, cut it into steaks, drench the steaks with butter and flour and fry them up. Could life get any better than this, I wondered?

One day my cousin Leroy and I combined our fledgling intellects and gave birth to a brilliant idea. Why not go ice fishing in the dark? We figured we would lower a flashlight to the bottom of the fishing hole, and spear fish after fish as they came to see this attractive beacon.

One morning at 5:00 a.m. sharp he and I loaded our scrawny frames into our family's 1929 Chevrolet four door sedan and set off for the lake, armed with our spear and great expectations. It was bitterly cold but not windy when we arrived at our little fish house. We got the stove going and cleared the hole of four or so inches of ice that had formed since its last use. We tied a line onto the flashlight and lowered it to the water. It floated. Oh, boy. What to do? Well, the flashlight needed some weight if it was going to sink and do its deadly duty. So we put the flashlight in an old gallon pickle jar I had in the car, filled the jar with water for weight, put the lid on it and lowered it to the bottom of the lake. The batteries lasted just under two minutes in the water before they died. It was still pitch black outside, but our day of fishing was over.

Dejectedly, we walked back up to the car, and found that we had a couple of additional problems. One, we had a flat tire, and two, the radiator had sprung a leak and half of its alcohol contents had spilled into the snow. We had no tools to fix the tire, but we did have an old bucket.

We took the bucket and trudged back to the fishing shack where we filled it with water. We figured the leak in the radiator was probably a small one and filling it once would get us into town. We had to drive slowly though, because of the flat tire. It took us quite a while, and although we made it, we completely ruined the tire. Fortunately, we didn't have to drive on any pavement, so the wheel rim was spared. Unfortunately our pride was not.

Fishing the next spring, because it was somewhat warmer, required a fairly different technique. Dad would rent a little wooden rowboat from which we could cast our tantalizing lures. We never trolled. We would go out about seventy feet from shore and cast back toward the shore, reeling our lure back to the boat. I tried most lures and even some live bait like minnows and worms. Even orange wedges didn't work. Neither did anything else.

Finally, I discovered an almost magic lure. It was a Johnson's Silver Minnow. It was a bright silvery spoon with a single barbed hook protected by a weed guard. This turned out to be a northern killer of the highest order. Even at its best, removing barbed hooks from the snarling mouths of northerns is a dangerous activity and not one to be taken lightly. It has been estimated by people who should know, that each northern, regardless of size has close to three million teeth, each one razor sharp and longing to tear the flesh from its tormentor. I learned, though, that if I gripped them with my thumb and index finger by their eyes, they simply go limp, at least momentarily, giving you a small window of opportunity in which to dislodge the hook.

Then I would string them on a metal safety-pin-like stringer and drop them over the side before they ate my feet. The best day I ever had fishing with Dad I caught eleven fish in one hour. Dad caught none. I was elated, and he pretended to be.

Chapter 19

GO BACK TO DETROIT, MISTER

BY June of 1947, all cash reserves were gone and Dad had borrowed us into a couple of thousand dollars of debt. Mom's brother, George, loaned us the money, but of course, there was still no way to earn any money to pay him back. It was getting close to the time that Uncle George would show up with his directive to Dad that he was to return to Detroit so he could settle the debt he owed him, but I was oblivious to that.

Sure enough, one fine, sunny, Sunday afternoon in June, George, his wife, Ardith, and little boy, Jimmy arrived. As was their custom, they appeared in plenty of time for dinner. As we all sat about in the living room after the feast, George said,

"Lester, its time for you to go back to Detroit to work. You just can't stay here. You can't make any money here. And you owe me two thousand dollars. You've got to go back."

It about broke Dad's heart, but he had to admit he was in a jam. Here he was, sitting in the middle of his beloved prairie, with no money, and no way to make any. In June, he kissed Mom and me goodbye, and left for Detroit. Luckily, he had taken a year's leave of absence from Ford's, so he at least had a job to go back to.

One of Mom's brothers, Howard, was working at the Ford plant in Dearborn and living in the remodeled attic of a family acquaintance. That space consisted of one bedroom, a very small room under the eves with a toilet but no window, sink or tub, an eating area, and a small sitting area. The sitting room had a single bed in it, and a terrible, beat up couch where company could sit. Dad shared the $30 a month rent with Howard, and regularly sent money to Mom for our living expenses. This arrangement was to continue for a full year.

Fall came, school began and I started the ninth grade. It was 1947, I was the man of the house, and I thought I had everything under control. I was wrong.

During that year, from June of 1947 to July of 1948, my mother and I "batched it" on the farm. We managed to make a few pennies selling chickens and eggs, and a drop or two of cream once in a while. I tried to help out by selling Christmas cards to all of the town folk and farmers in the area. Many of the farmers couldn't write their names, so they were very proud of their beautiful cards with their names imprinted on them. I think my net profit was $10.12. But still, it was something and I felt like I was helping.

With my profits, I sent for a minnow seine from the Sears catalog so I could capture minnows at Maple Lake, about a mile from our farm. My plan was to sell them in the spring and summer months to hopeful fishermen as they headed for the lake. I figured I was about to parlay my puny funds into a great fortune. With the help of cousin Leroy and my new seine, I captured about a hundred huge sucker minnows, but no little shiners. My "minnows" were damn near big enough to eat themselves, ranging from four to six inches. I filled an old steel boiler with water and my enormous minnows, all of which died within 24 hours due to lack of oxygen. How was I to know that fish need air?

Two or three months after Dad left, Mom figured that our boar pig's meat had been "purified" enough and arranged for the butcher from the locker plant in the next town to come out and get him. I won't forget that either.

My friend was sitting on his haunches in the farmyard—sunning himself. He was probably wondering why the sows really didn't interest him anymore. He had what I remember as a faint smile on his face and I suspect he was reminiscing about much better days. A single shot rang out. He slumped to the ground with a .22 caliber bullet hole directly between his eyes. The butcher ran over to him and cut his throat to finish the job and bleed him so he wouldn't get his pickup truck so messy. Then he and his helper hoisted him into the truck and drove off. I can still see him there, bouncing around in the bed of the truck as it made its way back to the main road to town. I was heartsick.

Although many of our geographically close relatives shared great pork dinners of one kind or another for the next several months, I never took one mouthful of my old friend. Not one. I still get close to weepy when I think about him.

However, we did have three pregnant sows. One was a huge, black and white, 300 pound, friendly gal—another was a much smaller, near psychotic red freako—and the third was so nondescript I just can't picture her. My cousin, Leroy, came out to the farm one sunny afternoon to help me build a little "pig house." It was a low, teepee-like structure that we figured would be a great maternity ward when the time came.

The time came that afternoon while we were working on its roof. I spotted a newborn piglet wandering in out of the adjacent field, its eyes closed, its placental sac and umbilical cord dragging in the dust and dirt. When we went to rescue it we found nine more. We scooped them all up and put them in the little teepee. Then we went looking for "Mom," who turned out to be our little red psycho friend. When we found her, she was not in the best of moods. She wouldn't let us near her. If fact, she bared her nasty little teeth and threatened to attack. We backed off and left her to her own devices. Later that day, she did return, found her "children" and started acting like a mother. We had no more problems with her.

The next day our black and white friend decided it was her turn, and cheerfully spewed nine piglets into my waiting hands. One by one, I cleared the placenta from their faces and the mucus from their throats and made sure they were breathing. Mama pig seemed to be just fine, spinning her curly tail in a frenzied circle just before delivering the next one. We all went to bed happy, but –

The next morning when I went to check on her, she had a huge mass of tissue protruding from her vagina. I thought at first it was afterbirth, and tried to pull it out. It wouldn't budge. Mom had never seen anything like that before either, so we called Mr. Johnson, who owned the farm adjacent to ours, over to see if he knew what this was. As soon as he looked at her, he knew.

"She's thrown her womb," he said. "Just shoot her. She can't survive this."

It seemed that one of the piglets had scratched her before birth. That irritation was misinterpreted by the mother pig as being another piglet. She continued straining to eject this phantom baby until she expelled her womb.

We just couldn't accept Mr. Johnson's recommendation to kill her, so we called a vet in the next town. He said that he had been able to save horses and cows that had thrown their wombs, and would be willing to give it a try.

Mom said, "Let's try. Come on out."

When the vet arrived he examined her and decided to first try to reinsert the womb. He rigged up a block and tackle and hoisted her hindquarters up about three feet into the air. Leroy had come out from town to help if he could. He and I held her womb in a dishtowel stretched between us, to eliminate any weight or drag on the procedure. The vet smeared Vaseline all over her swollen parts and tried manually to stuff her womb back into her. It didn't work. It was too swollen. He decided to amputate. He tied her womb off with binder twine as close to the vaginal orifice as he could—waited a few minutes for the numbing process to take effect, and snipped off the entire womb with scissors. Then he pushed the bound stump back into her. We loosened the hoisting rigging, gently lowered her to the barn floor, and hoped for the best. The next morning she was dead. And we had nine brand new piglet orphans.

We went to town and bought several lamb nipples. These were fairly large, about three inches in length and a half-inch wide. Mr. Johnson devised a formula of milk and vitamin and mineral supplements that we blended and fed to those little creatures every two hours, around the clock. It wasn't long before their eyes were open, and they began to figure things out. If we weren't there on time with their bottles, they all lined up on our back porch, squealing at the top of their little pig lungs, until we showed up with their food. They apparently were imprinted and thought I was their mother. I played with them every day in a pile of hay down by the barn—and generally, it was a wonderfully warm, happy time—but not always.

One day in the fall, Leroy and I were playing catch with a football in our side yard. One time when he threw the ball to me it sailed over my head. It reached our back porch just as my mother came out of the house carrying a gallon jug of water. The ball struck her directly on the wrist and she let go of the bottle. It crashed into the top of her bony right foot. She screamed in agony, grabbed a nearby broom and came after me, cursing and flailing away with that miserable broom handle. Fortunately, I was young, lithe, very fast, and easily outran her. I did, however, think it might be a good idea to go to town for awhile, until things settled down around there. Leroy and I walked to town and shot pool in one of Fossil's many taverns until it closed.

When I got home, Mom was sleeping, and the next day was just another day.

Chapter 20

NEVER RIDE THE LEAD TOBOGGAN

THERE aren't many things for young folks to do in farm country, in the middle of winter on the prairies of Minnesota, so we tended to make our own entertainment. One such activity was to tie a toboggan or two to the rear bumper of a car, and see how fast we could get going, and how long we could stand it before we froze to death. Sometimes it was fun, sometimes it wasn't. Like the one time I tried it.

We hooked up two toboggans, one behind the other, to our pulling vehicle, a 1937 Chevrolet with more than a quarter of a million miles on it. There were four stupid kids out for a fun evening of riding that night plus our even more stupid driver. I climbed into the second position on the lead toboggan, and off we went. The country roads were compacted snow and ice. Nevertheless, the driver managed to get that old baby rolling about thirty miles an hour before my set of sliding boards hit a bump and I went flying off. I knew something was wrong when my back exploded in pain as the trailing toboggan hit me. When I regained consciousness, we all decided it was probably time to call it a night.

Chapter 21

THE STONE BOAT SAGA

A stone boat is a wooden sled, with a platform about six feet wide by ten feet long. It is used by farmers to haul the visible rocks and stones from their field in a generally vain effort to avoid breaking the points on their plows. I say visible rocks, because there was an unending supply of rocks and boulders under the surface. Each spring the repetitive actions of thawing and freezing would push up a new crop for harvesting. A single horse or tractor pulled the stone boat.

One fine sunny day in the winter of '47, cousin Leroy and I hitched up Queen, one of our horses, thinking we would have her take us for a sled ride over the snow to get the mail that had just been deposited in our mailbox on the main road. Getting to the mailbox was great fun. Getting back was not. As soon as we headed her for the barn, she accelerated to full speed. I was driving, or steering, or whatever you do with horses. I certainly wasn't controlling. Leroy huddled down behind me, using me as a convenient windbreak, and thought this was all great fun. We hit a bump and I went flying—right over Leroy and into the snow. I looked up just in time to see him careening wildly off the sled just a few yards down the path.

The horse didn't stop when it got to the barnyard. Instead, she tore around the barn at breakneck speed, stoneboat flying. Once around the barn, she ran directly into a heavy-duty, barbed-wire fence. That stopped her. But it also shattered the harness. We managed to peel the broken pieces off of her and get her reinstalled in the barn, while thanking God we were still both alive and able to move all of our limbs.

When Dad got home and took a look at the harness, he wasn't happy, but he took it in stride as he did most things. He wired it back together good enough so that it was usable as long as we needed it. Which, as it turned out, wasn't very long.

Grandpa Abbott, Mom's dad, had been staying with us for a couple of weeks when this event occurred. As luck would have it, he was standing in the living room watching our hapless adventure with the stoneboat. When Dad arrived home, Grandpa could hardly wait to tell him how stupid we had been.

"They had that cussed horse hitched up all wrong," he said. "I could have told them she would go crazy and do just what she did."

His vitriolic attempt to thrust us into a position where a sound beating would be unavoidable failed. Both Mom and Dad knew what he was trying to do and discounted his story. Mom, especially, had seen him in his sadistic mode far too often, but that's a story in itself.

Chapter 22

THE HAUNTING

AS I write this little story, it is September of the year 2000. I'm sixty-six years old and I have never had an encounter with a ghost—except once—when I was fifteen. Never before, never since.

It happened in the late fall of 1947. Dad had returned to Detroit to work, and Mom, my niece, Sonja, who was living with us at that time, and I were alone in the old farmhouse. The wooden stairway to my bedroom had a small landing on it halfway up, then it turned in the opposite direction and continued to the second floor. Straight ahead from the top of the stairs was a small room that Mom used as a sewing room. It had an eastern exposure, so it had a lot of natural light. She liked that little room and she spent many hours there. Standing at the top of the stairs, my bedroom was to the right—an identically configured guest bedroom to the left. Two things happened that effectively deterred me from ever sleeping up there again. The first was perhaps a bit bizarre, but not terribly frightening.

One evening I went to bed and directly to sleep around ten o'clock. At eleven thirty our dog, Blackie, began raising a horrible commotion outside. That was most unusual, since he only barked at strangers, and this was not a time of night one would want intruders lurking around. All of us were up quickly and gathered in the kitchen. We turned the lights on and very shortly, Blackie stopped his barking. We were certain that someone—or something—had been there, and we remained uneasy for several days—and we never forgot it. Our guard was up.

The next episode occurred just after Christmas in 1947. It was a very dark, still night. The ground was covered with a foot and a half of snow, and as I recall, it was about twenty below. Again, about ten o'clock, I climbed into my frozen bed, covered myself with a half dozen wool blankets, carved a little hole for my nose to protrude so I could breathe, and settled in for a short winter's nap.

I had only been in bed for ten minutes or so when I heard what I thought was someone slowly coming up the wooden stairs, each one of which had its own peculiar creak. When I first heard the stairs creaking, the sound was coming from about half way up the first set of stairs. One by one, the next step would emit its small, distinct whimper until the landing was reached. There was a pause. Perhaps twenty seconds. Then, as if proceeding up from the landing, the squeaking became increasingly loud and clear.

Finally, whatever or whomever it was reached the top of the stairs and stopped. Silence.

My heart was pounding. I tried to call out.

"Mom?"

But my voice caught in my throat, releasing only a scratchy whimper. No answer.

"Mom?" I called again, this time more distinctly and loudly. Again, no answer.

Then there was a tremendous crash, as if a large body had fallen against the wall right next to my bed. I screamed. My throat was dry. My eyes were wide open. I was terrified.

Mom raced up the stairs and burst into the room.

"What's wrong?"

I tried to tell her what had happened, my words tumbling out in no particular order. She recognized that I was badly shaken, and did her best to comfort and reassure me. She let me come downstairs, and sleep on the couch in the living room that night, and that's where I slept for as long as we lived in that house. We never told anyone about this frightening experience. Mom probably thought I had dreamt it anyway, and was just humoring me.

When we left Minnesota to return to Detroit, the farm had not yet been sold. We left the house full of the beautiful furniture Mom and Dad had worked so hard to accumulate. Several sets of relatives spent time in the house between the time we left and when it finally sold. They would take turns living there on weekends and showing the place to prospective buyers. When it finally did sell, we were told that there wasn't any furniture left in the house. No one knew what had happened to it.

It was only after several years had passed that one set of relatives mentioned to another that they had an unaccountable experience when they stayed at our farmhouse. They then related essentially the same story about the stairs and the falling body that had convinced me there was an entity in that house. They said they had never told anyone about it because it was too weird and scary. The couple listening to the story turned ashen. "That happened to us, too." Later, each of the couples that had stayed there overnight related that they, too, had that had precisely the same experience.

A few years later the house mysteriously burned down. No one knows how it started.

And, by the way, what was it, really, that so frightened our old dog, Blackie? Was it an intruder as we thought? Or was it something else?

That experience did not make me a great believer in ghosts. But it did make me a small one.

Chapter 23

WHITE BULL CALF

OUR first winter in Fossil was filled with unique happenings, but few were stranger than this one. It was sometime in February, 1947, when one of our very tall, red, range cows came into heat. Her bellowings were alternately loud, obnoxious, demanding—and plaintive. She needed her man. So Dad went looking for a stud bull. By what he thought was a grandly fortuitous event, he located a white stud bull at Benny Gudmundson's neighboring farm.

The snow was about three feet deep on the level, and when Mom and I saw Dad leading that stud bull across the open field between us and the road to town, we had to laugh. That "stud" bull was no more than a calf. He was not much taller than three feet and perhaps four and a half feet from nose to rump. He was pure white, except for the plentiful manure he had ground into his coat, had pink eyes, and a jaunty swagger, as if he knew what he was doing.

We turned the old cow loose in the barnyard with this

pathetic lothario. At least my mother and I had a great time watching this incredible exhibition. Dad had never seen anything quite like this either.

At first the cow would stand expectantly and patiently while "micro stud" attempted to mount and penetrate her. Alas, he fell quite short. He couldn't reach her—even standing on his tippy, tippy hooves. She would turn her head and look at him, probably hoping against hope that perhaps he could try a little harder or stand a little taller. Then she would walk away, bellowing in disgust, and he would fall to his knees, generally smashing his face into the ground. Then he would try again—with the same result. Over and over again they tried their coupling efforts. It never worked. Poor boy. He was probably beginning to ache somewhere back there and he had no idea why.

Finally Dad had what he thought was a stroke of unadulterated genius. Although the main floor of our barn was dirt, the animal stalls all had raised, wooden floors. So, just behind the stall floor, Dad dug a foot deep hole the width of the stall. Then he led the tall, red cow into her stall and tied her so that her back feet were in the hole. With the micro bull standing on a makeshift platform, and his girlfriend obligingly standing with her back legs in the hole, success was finally achieved. Or so we thought.

We sold that cow soon after as a pregnant animal for $75. Unfortunately, "Micro Bull" either didn't plant his seed deeply enough, or he was firing blanks. The fellow that bought what be believed to be a pregnant cow descended on us and demanded a $25 refund, which Dad had no choice but to pay.

My mother and I replayed that afternoon's scene in our minds a hundred times, but Dad never did see the humor in it.

Chapter 24

STUPID OLD COW

AKA

STUPID YOUNG BOY

THE only time I ever ran into a farm animal with a car, I figure was as much that stupid cow's fault as it was mine.

I was traveling west on a compacted gravel road out of Fossil one evening when I saw a cow up ahead, standing in the middle of the road. I slowed my car by downshifting, since the brakes were completely shot, and slowly approached the east end of the cow heading west. My goofy mechanical horn was blaring "ah ooo' ga, ah ooo' ga." The cow stopped dead in her tracks. I thought the cow would move, if not through intelligent thought about physical damage, perhaps by some primordial instinct for self-preservation. I was wrong on both counts. She didn't move. My car didn't stop. I was only going 3 or 4 miles an hour when I hit her.

She promptly sat down on my front bumper, bending up one of my headlights, which was mounted on the front of the fender, so that the beam pierced the evening sky at about seventy degrees from horizontal. Only then did she deign to saunter off. I swear she was grinning at me as she walked away. Although I did hurl a few well chosen epithets at the old cow, I rather liked the angle of the light beam (probably something related to primitive id urges), and so it remained in that position as long as we owned the car.

Chapter 25

SHIFTING GEARS AT 50 BELOW ZERO

WHEN it's forty or fifty below zero, not counting the wind chill which was an unknown concept at that time, most (but not all) things begin to stiffen up. And so it was with our '29 Chevy. Around the first of December, the little road from the highway to our farmhouse was drifted full of snow and impassable. Therefore, from about that time until spring we left her parked just off the highway. It was halfway decent shelter for me while I waited for the school bus that was frequently late, and sometimes didn't arrive at all, having slid into a ditch somewhere along the route.

Every once in a while I'd get that old baby started so we could run to town for supplies. One morning though, I tried to force the gear shift lever into reverse before the grease in the gear box had thawed enough, and broke off two little steel prongs that determined whether or not we had second and third gears. So, all we had left was first gear and reverse.

I drove the car in first gear, no more than ten miles an

hour, a mile and a half into town to Bud Benoy's service station. He tore out the floor boards, which were just that—boards, peered into the gear box, shook his head, squinted his famous squint, and said,

"I'll have to take this all apart to get at those chucks of steel. It'll cost you $30.00."

Well, I didn't have $30.00, so I crept over to Uncle Dave's house a couple of blocks away and related my pathetic story. Dave said,

"Well, let's take a look."

I pulled my car into the welding shop Dave had at the rear of his house where he moonlighted with welding jobs for the locals—generally for farmers who had broken plow points trying to till their near worthless rocky land. Dave took one look and said,

"Hell, I can take care of that in less than two seconds."

And he did. He simply took a welding rod, inserted it into the gearbox, and welded onto the broken pieces. First one, then the other. Actually, it probably took him five seconds. Then he welded the broken pieces back on the end of the gearshift where they belonged. My car was fixed, and so was I, at least for the time being.

Chapter 26

NEVER STORE FISH

IN YOUR UNCLE'S FLOODED BASEMENT

EVERY spring when the lake ice and snow began to melt, the level of the water in the lake would rise. The ice would thaw first at the shoreline, and then proceed toward the center of the lake until it had completely dissipated. A stream we called the outlet carried the surplus water straight through town, heading north for several miles. Many fish would follow the stream to spawn, after which most, if not all of them, died.

One morning before school, I noticed that there were a lot of perch in the stream, most of them just wandering around, seemingly going nowhere in particular. That evening, I asked my uncle Euclid (who was married to Mom's older sister, Bertha) if I could borrow his prized spear.

"Sure," he said, "Just be careful with it, and don't hit any rocks."

Euclid was a man you didn't mess with. He had a near crazy temper, and if he ever got mad at someone, it was usually for life. The only exception was his wife, Bertha. When he got mad at her, which was fairly frequently, he simply didn't talk to her, sometime for months. Since those two were the only residents of their town, Bertha's life was fairly barren of joy.

I gingerly took his spear, and with appropriate bowing and scraping, left for home. I could scarcely contain my excitement and anticipation of the next morning's adventure.

The morning broke clear, sunny and reasonably warm. About an hour before the start of school I arrived on the bank of the stream with my spear and a stringer, my emotions surging as I moved in for the kill. Stealthily, I moved along the shore of the stream peering into the turbulent water.

"There's one," I muttered to myself.

I saw what appeared to be the tail end of a perch right alongside of the bank. He seemed to be standing on his head. With the deftness of an old hand at such things, I thrust the spear into the water. The water exploded and I damn near lost my spear as my quarry fought to survive the attack. When I retrieved it, there was not one, but five perch on my deadly tines. Wow! They must have been spawning. Or perhaps they were just discussing how they might best avoid that guy up on the bank. Since there was no limit on perch, I speared another twelve before it was time to head for school. I strung all my fish on my stringer and tied the stringer securely to a small tree growing on the edge of the stream. The fish were in the water and secured. On the one hand, I was ecstatic. On the other, however, I was terrified. I had hit a rock with one of my final thrusts and bent two of the spear's tines badly. I careered off down the road to the schoolhouse where I spent the rest of that day fantasizing about my great adventure. I also began nearly nine months of tortured worrying about how I was going to tell Euclid about bending his wonderful spear after I had given him my word that I wouldn't do that.

After school, I retrieved my fish from the stream and took them to my uncle Dave's house. His basement had about a foot of water in it from the spring thaw, and I tied the stringer of fish there where they would be safe, cold and wet. Then I promptly forgot about them. Don't ask me why I forgot about such an important prize. I just did. I forgot a lot of things those days. Perhaps it had something to do with my great anxiety about Euclid and his cherished spear. About a month later, Leroy said,

"Hey, Glenn. Remember those perch you tied in our basement? Well, they got pretty ripe. Dad went looking for what might be causing such a stench and discovered them. I had no choice but to tell him that they were yours."

Uncle Dave had a relatively difficult time being civil with me from that point on.

Just as the winter spearing season was about to begin, and my date with Destiny and Uncle Euclid approached, the old Frenchman bought himself a new Skipley spear, the highest quality spear in the country. He told Leroy that he could have his old spear, and I was saved. My months of agonizing about my moment of truth with old Euclid were all for naught.

Chapter 27

FALL/WINTER, '47—'48

FALL in Northern Minnesota is crisp, sunny, and pleasant. It generally lasts fourteen to sixteen days. Then the cruel, cutting winds sweep down from the vast, barren plains of Manitoba.

Dad was back in Detroit, and we were struggling financially. I tried to earn a few bucks picking potatoes during the harvest in North Dakota. Since this was an agricultural community, the schools provided "excused absences" for any of us who wanted to help with the harvest. What a deal that was for the scrawny speckled kid from Detroit who didn't think much of school anyway. The downside was getting up at six in the morning, in the pitch black, and walking to town to catch the "potato truck." The truck was an open, two-and-a-half-ton staked brute that would haul all of us kids sixty miles or so to the North Dakota tundra. It was cold, back breaking work—but better than school, I thought.

Soon the winter was upon us in all its unrelenting fury.

Things that weren't supposed to freeze began freezing. Like the deep well in the basement. Our signal that something was wrong was clear and definitive. The water stopped running in our plumbing system.

Whoever had built this house had sunk a 95-foot well just off of the main area of the basement. It was a tiny room, probably not more than six by six by six. I don't know what I thought I was going to do, but I started to dismantle the top of the pump. When I finally managed to get the top off, it was clear that the pipe coming up out of the ground was frozen solid. It was 40 degrees below zero and falling that night.

I melted a washtub full of snow over the furnace grate and boiled the water on Mom's kitchen range. Then, teakettle by teakettle, I began to pour scalding water over the pump and down the one-inch in diameter well pipe. It didn't really take all that long, maybe thirty minutes, and I began to hear an ominous rumbling. Then, suddenly my whole world seemed to explode as the ice in the frozen pipe broke loose. Ice cold water discharged violently straight up into the low ceiling—and there I was—standing in a blinding shower of very cold ice water. Even I, at my young age, had done things that were a lot more fun than this.

It took probably an hour before I got the pump capped, but my trial and error techniques finally worked. I was soaking wet. I looked like a drowned possum, and couldn't remember ever being that cold. But, the pump was fixed. We had water in our system again, and I was a micro hero.

A few days later I flushed the toilet and sewage began seeping up out of the bathtub drain. Oh, oh. Now what. Back to the basement. I located the grease trap for the household drainage system. Its top was just about two inches from the ceiling. I didn't know at that time that it had been installed upside-down, and that its lid should have been facing down. I figured I would just unscrew the lid and remove whatever object it was that had gotten into the system.

I attached the wrench and began my efforts. Finally the top started to unscrew. Success! Just as I was about to remove the cap, my world erupted again. All of the drainage pipes in the house, which were full of sewage and other undesirable stuff, shot straight up into the ceiling, and there I was, standing in a shower of liquid muck. I thought to myself, "This isn't nearly as nice as the ice-water shower."

Well, the pipes drained and finally stopped spewing their awfulness on me. I recapped the grease trap, went upstairs and took a bath. Of course, the bath water, and all other wastewater simply drained into the pipes, waiting for me to do something stupid again. I decided to oblige.

In the side yard, perhaps fifteen feet from the house, was our septic tank. The previous owner had placed a large, ½ inch thick steel enclosure around the top of the tank. I think it was a piece of a smokestack from a steamboat. At any rate, its ragged top edge was about three feet from the ground. It had been filled with straw, supposedly to prevent the tank from freezing. That was a faulty assumption. Carefully, I crawled over the raw, sharp edges of the rusty smokestack and lowered myself into what was to become my next encounter with Hell.

I threw all of the straw out with a pitchfork, and with a great deal of effort, managed to remove the septic tank lid. Sure enough, the contents of the tank were frozen. I took an ice chisel (a six-foot long, inch-and-a-half thick, piece of steel, sharpened on one end) that was normally used for breaking holes in the lake ice for fishing, and broke through the septic ice. It was about eight inches thick. Now I needed help, so I called on cousin Leroy. Leroy arrived and we went to work.

I broke the ice loose and into manageable chucks with the ice chisel. Then I filled a galvanized bucket with frozen chucks of effluent. This was not a pleasant task. Cousin Leroy, on relatively safe ground up above, would haul the bucket up with a rope and dump its contents a few feet away. After an hour or so, enough ice and liquid had been removed to expose the opening of the sewage discharge pipe from the house. It too, was full of ice.

We connected a garden hose to the hot water tank in the basement, and I began shooting hot water into the pipe opening. Gradually, but surely, the ice melted and I fed the hose farther and farther into the discharge pipe. Without warning, the final bit of blockage broke loose, followed immediately by all the pent up liquid waste the pipes had been conveniently storing for us. The discharge blasted straight across the tank—hit its opposite wall, and there I was, in an exploding shower of putrid waste. I was trying hard to maintain my sanity. Leroy thought it was great fun and very funny.

We slid the tank top back onto the tank and covered it with straw to the very top of the smokestack. I decided it was probably a good time for another bath. After all, I didn't want to go to school smelling like this. Even barn smell was taboo in our little school, and that was noticeably less pungent that what I was exuding. But school is another story.

Along about the first of March, I saw an advertisement on a match book cover: *"Draw Me!"* the figure of a woman's head cooed seductively out at me. It was the first ad I had seen for the Art Instruction School Incorporated of Minneapolis, and it wanted me to enter their scholarship contest by drawing the figure on the match book cover and sending it in for their "judges" to evaluate. If it was good enough, the ad said, I would win a $220 course in cartooning. Wow! I went right to work copying that woman's head.

The next day I took my "sure to win" entry to Fossil's post office personally, and handed it to one of the two spinster sisters who were Fossil's joint postmistresses. They both smiled at me when I told them what I was doing, and wished me good luck.

A week later I got a letter from the Art Instruction

Company saying that although my drawing was superb and showed incredible potential, there were many other entries that were perfect. Unfortunately for me, all of the available scholarships had been given to them. However, they would really like to talk with me about their program since I was exhibiting so much talent. I agreed to allow one of their representatives call me for an appointment.

Two days later, a telephone call interrupted my evening's radio adventure with The Lone Ranger. It was the "talent scout" from the art school. Mom and I arranged to meet with him the following day during my lunch hour. It was bitterly cold but sunny that day, and Mom had walked to town to meet with us. Our meeting room was his car. The car was reasonably warm, since he had installed a new gasoline fueled car heater in the foot well of the front passenger compartment. Mom sat in the back seat and listened to the pitchman tells me how wonderfully talented I was. But I could be much better if I enrolled in their $220, twenty-two month correspondence course for cartoonists.

Mom said to me, "Is that really what you want to do, Glenn?"

Without hesitation, I nodded my head—and she signed the contract.

The first lesson arrived about a week later. I completed it immediately and fired it back to them. Their response was gratifying. They gently pointed out some of my mistakes, but were incredibly generous in their praises of my "talent."

The second lesson was a bit more difficult, but again, I was superb, according to my instructor. However, the third lesson began delving into the mysterious art of drawing with pen and ink. I was horrible. And they told me so. Oh, well, I was tired of this whole affair anyway, so I just quit. I figured if I wasn't sending in lessons, I wouldn't have to pay anything more. That is when I learned about contracts.

I battled with them for over a year before their dunning

letters became too frightening even for me. I cashed some of my precious bonds and paid them off. That whole experience was a costly nightmare.

In the summer of '48, I got a job in a tiny little butcher shop in downtown Fossil. The butcher and his wife lived in the back room of the store. He was an alcoholic and was drunk most of the time. His wife, a tall, emaciated, quite homely woman was very nice to me and to all of their customers. During the summer, many of the folks who lived at Maple Lake would telephone their orders in to us. Part of my overall responsibilities was to deliver these grocery orders. They had a turn of the century pick up truck they let me use for the deliveries. It had power nothing, and I had no driver's license, but all deliveries were made without mishap. One thing I learned, though, was that old animal bones smell bad, very bad.

Chapter 28

FOSSIL NOTABLES

LLOYD Remick and Roy Fitzgerald became two of Fossil's most famous residents. Both of them lived north of Fossil, but roomed in town and attended school there. They were ambitious young men, and when they heard of the mining boom on the Mesabe Iron Range near Cass Lake, just east of the Chippewa National Forest, they recruited two other young men, and set off to seek their fortunes. They left town with not much more than a mattress, a coffeepot, and other essentials for making camp.

Shortly after arriving in Cass Lake they started a taxi service. Transportation was poor and the ore mines were going strong. Their little business flourished. In a few months they were able to buy more cars and hire more drivers. Then buses were added. Their great insight, good fortune, and ambition grew that little business into what later became know as "Greyhound Bus Line."

Roy eventually split off from Lloyd, and with the profits

he had made on the Mesabe, started what would become known as American Airlines.

And then there was me. What more needs to be said?

Well, perhaps a little more. These three guys were obviously from the deep end of the gene pool. But who inhabited the shallow end? Probably seventy-five percent of the rest of the population of Fossil, if you ask me. Most, if not all, of the smart folks left town as soon as they realized that there weren't any gates, and by any means possible. The rest simply continued their boozing and brazen inbreeding as they probably had from the beginning of time. A few examples will give you just a bit of the flavor of what it was like trying to socialize in this tiny coagulation of humanity on the plains of northern Minnesota. Only the names have been changed to protect the guilty.

The first one that comes to mind is **Loren**. Loren was a dirt-poor farmer who volunteered to umpire Fossil's American Legion Baseball team in the summer of 1948. He was about 40 years old at that time and was a genuinely nice fellow. But his face! It was truly something to see. It looked like he had been smashed directly in the face by some brute force one can only imagine. His face, from the bridge of his nose to just above his chin was completely caved in. Most everyone had substantial difficulty understanding what he was saying, but in his umpiring role, only "safe!" and "out!" were critical anyway. And he also used hand signals. As best we could understand, he said that he had been kicked in the face by a horse when he was a young man. We believed Loren and forgave him for being outside in public when he was so ugly. But then we met his sister. She looked exactly like him. We all decided then that they were no doubt both products of either faulty eggs or spermatozoic dysfunction. Perhaps it was both. Then again, perhaps their anatomical similarity, in all its grotesqueness, was simply due to several generations of serious inbreeding.

Then there was the family **Lewinski**. There were six kids in the Lewinski family and every one of them looked exactly alike, whether male or female. Although the boys were all somewhat taller than the girls, all of the Lewinski kids had very large, sharp, beak-like noses, crossed eyes and pigeon toes. If you saw one, you saw them all. This outlandish grouping of humanity was one of the strangest sights I would ever see. One of the girls, Ora Lewinski, was in my grade. All of her dresses and skirts and blouses were home sewn from chicken feed sacks. Chicken feed was sold in fifty pound sacks made from about two yards of print material. Most farm wives used the material for dishtowels, but the Lewinski family was *so* poor that all of their daughters' clothes were made from feed sacks. Even in Fossil, children could be cruel, and Ora was frequently the object of their derision.

At the end of the eighth grade, my first school year in Fossil, all the kids exchanged little autograph books for the others to sign. When Ora gave me hers, I made a mistake that bedeviled me from that time until we moved back to Detroit. I made up the following verse for her:

> "There are tulips in the garden,
> There are tulips in the park,
> But the tulips I like best,
> Are *your* two lips in the dark."

She read the verse, and fell in love with me at that exact moment. She followed me around like a semi-comatose puppy for over a year. She was a nice girl and I could never be mean to her, so I tolerated her mooning as a true gentleman should have. That bit of compassion was my first lesson in learning how to handle future situations when young ladies would fall in love with me just because I was kind to them.

Dennis was a man about thirty-five, as best as I could tell. He was the only person I have ever known who had three nostrils. Two of the holes were more or less appropriately placed, but the third, somewhat smaller one (apparently not a functional nostril) was right in the center of the tip of his nose. He lived in a nasty little two-room house in town with his mother. The house had no plumbing, but then most houses didn't so that wasn't so unusual. What was unusual was that Dennis and his mother slept together on a horrible old mattress covered with rags in the middle of the floor. As far as I know, they never had any children.

Macon was the school bus driver on my route. He was also the sheriff. One night my mother and I were cruising along in our rickety old Chevy on a freshly graveled road, heading for Fossil. It was very dark. Both sides of the road had a rather deep ditch filled with icy water from the spring runoff.

Suddenly, we both spotted a man climbing out of the ditch to our left. He was soaking wet and had to have been freezing. I wanted to stop to see if we could help him, but my mother was scared out of her wits. She said, "Don't you dare stop. Drive into town and report it to the sheriff."

When we got to town, I quickly found Macon in one of the local taverns and reported our sighting of the UDM (Unidentified Ditch Man).

"I'll take a look," he said. He put on his red and black Mackinaw coat (the standard for men's men in northern Minnesota), blinked his bleary bloodshot eyes, and careened out the door.

Half an hour or so later, he returned with a fellow everyone called Buster. Buster was one of four boys in his family. His brothers were Otto, Robert, and Pete.

That fateful evening, Buster was drunk, as usual, and had fallen into the ditch full of icy water. He told Macon that he was walking to town from his house in Dugdale to get a much-needed drink. Apparently he had run out of moonshine and was going to have to settle for 3.2 beer that evening. He wasn't quite certain how he got into the ditch full of water, but he was sure glad that Sheriff Macon had rescued him.

Otto and Robert were the most famous of the four boys. Pete was more or less normal and became a car salesman in a nearby town. Both Otto and Robert were extremely adept at avoiding every known form of work. They lived with their mother in a two-story house in Dugdale, a little (emphasize little) town about seven miles west of Fossil. Otto slept in a bedroom upstairs. Robert slept with his mother on what appeared to be an oversized army cot in the living room. Robert was forty-two years old at that time.

Otto was about two years older than Robert. Being the more mature one, he decided it was time to leave home. He didn't have anywhere to go, of course, so he moved into an old, rusty, car body that had been abandoned in a field not very far from his house. He figured that such fine accommodations would do until he began to turn blue when winter approached.

Meanwhile, Robert began having difficulties with his mother, and she threw him out of the house. Homeless, broke, and stupid, he had nowhere to go either, just like his big brother. Then one day, seemingly out of nowhere, Robert had what was to him a brilliant idea. He walked out to the car body to see his brother. Sure enough, Otto was home. He listened with feigned interest to his little brother's tale of woe, then struck a deal with him that would benefit them both. Otto sub-let the back seat of his fine auto-body home to Robert for two bucks a month. It was great until the north winds started screeching around their sodden souls. At that point they both decided they'd had enough independence for awhile, and moved back in with their Mom, where they stayed until she died several years later.

Greg was a huge, semi-retarded man very reminiscent of Lennie in Steinbeck's *Of Mice and Men*. He lived with his parents on the family farm. It was a gorgeous place with 1,500 feet of frontage on Maple Lake. He earned a reasonably decent living as Fossil's drayman and iceman. As drayman, Greg would haul heavy freight from the railroad depot to folks in the greater metropolitan Fossil area who had ordered it, generally from their Sear's catalog. Things like ice boxes, or wood ranges, or perhaps a new chair or couch were typical of the items Greg delivered. He was always friendly and, of course, people were always happy to see him, since he generally had some great prize for them in his dray. His dray was a long, low, heavy, four-wheel wagon that he towed with a team of horses. The sides were removable to facilitate the loading and unloading of heavy merchandise. But that was only part of his livelihood.

In the wintertime, Greg would lumber out onto the frozen lake all alone, except for his horse, and cut huge blocks of ice with an eight-foot timber saw. The lake's water would regularly freeze four feet thick by December so the blocks were huge. Then he would latch onto the bottom of the block with a grappling hook. The hook had a chain attached to it which in turn was attached to the horse's harness. The horse would pull the ice block out of the hole where Greg would then cut it into manageable hunks of twenty-five pounds or so. He stored in his parent's enormous barn under burlap, straw, and canvas, where they remained until it was time to haul and deliver them to the surrounding farms and townsfolk.

Since almost no one had an electric refrigerator, a block of ice in the icebox served to preserve food, at least for a little while. As the ice melted, the water would drain into a large pan under the icebox, which hopefully would be emptied before it overflowed. The iceboxes were primitive, but better than a hole in the ground that some folks were still using to cool their perishables.

When Greg was about fifty, his folks died and the farm had to be sold. There was no place for him to store ice, so that business simply melted away. The dray business gradually evaporated as well as people stopped buying from the catalog and began buying their heavy goods in local stores.

One of Fossil's tavern owners, a man everyone called Candy because he was never without a piece of candy in his mouth, took pity on Greg and took him in. Greg's pay was only five dollars a day, but he had lots of fringe benefits. For example, Candy provided him with lunch and dinner and a place to sleep. His sleeping quarters were not enviable though. At least not for most folks. He would pull together three tables in that little tavern and make his bed on top of them. At least he was warm. And, Candy let Greg have all the beer foam he could handle. Greg was happy.

There is an almost limitless supply of Fossilites to thumbnail, but these few will serve as colorful examples of what happens when people stop attending to the gene pool and let its contents curdle.

Chapter 29

GRAY MILK

THE summer of 1948 was hot and humid. Flies and mosquitoes were devastating the peace of mind of most other living things, including all of our horses and cows—and we had almost no money. Being fourteen and broke isn't any fun at all. I couldn't even buy my girlfriend a Coke.

When I heard about an opening on a shirttail relative's farm for a hired hand, I jumped at the chance to earn some spending money, even if it was only $2.00 a day. Two bucks a day was better than nothing a day. Although the job only lasted two weeks, I got a jolt of a reality that was completely foreign to me.

This farm couple had three boys, about eight, ten, and twelve. The oldest one worked with me in the fields, shocking bundles of oats. As the old man cut the grain, the machinery would gather it and tie twine around it before disgorging it to the side. Our job was to collect four or five bundles and stack them, teepee like, so that any rain that might fall before the grain was thrashed would run off, rather than soak in. It was a primitive system, but it worked pretty well. Laboring in the fields in the scorching sun with the oat chaff sticking to my sweating, itchy skin was the most pleasant part of each day.

When dinner time came the first day, I entered into a twilight zone that I wish to this day I had never encountered. The house had no running water, so the entire family washed up for dinner in an enameled basin filled with very hard, very cold well water. Hard water, as opposed to soft water, contains multiple minerals that act in concert to prevent soap from emulsifying. The result, therefore, is that as soon as the first person begins to wash up, the water becomes riddled with a chunky scum containing soap, dirt, and small pieces of sluffed skin, which covers the water's surface. Each successive person needs to battle their way through this layer of unpleasantness in a vain attempt at getting either cleaner or better smelling than they were when they arrived at the wash basin. Essentially no one succeeded on either front.

There was one washcloth for the entire family and "guests," such as me. I have no idea how often they might have changed or washed that rag, but it was so sour, its stench would make your eyes spin and your toes curl. God, it was awful.

The food was terrible, and I did my best not to eat. Of course I couldn't not eat for two weeks, so I had to ingest some of their grotesque offerings. Peanut butter and jelly sandwiches for lunch in the field pretty much managed to sustain me as long as I was there.

The strangest food was gray milk. I had never seen gray milk before. I didn't drink any. My first evening there I went with the boys to their barn where they were to milk their four cows. It was then that I learned why it was gray. The barn had a dirt floor and was covered with bovine fecal and urinary waste, on which giant green flies were feasting.

The boys were barefoot and the animal's waste squished

up between their toes like a putrid jelly. The cows' udders were caked with the same toxic substance from sleeping in their own waste. Apparently, this was the usual state of affairs, and the boys went about preparing to milk.

They used a technique called wet-milking. They would squirt milk into their hands and rub it all over the cows' teats so their milking fingers could slide easily down these feces encrusted, milk filled appendages. That is how the milk got gray and why I elected to never drink any.

Bedtime was also a unique experience. I joined the three boys in a stiflingly hot upstairs bedroom where all four of us crammed into one full-size bed. I couldn't breathe. The stench from the mattress and its inhabitants was overwhelming. The mattress's fragrance was a putrid blend of stagnant urine, sweat, and body ash that I'm sure had no equal anywhere in this world. But there was still one other devastating odor invading my olfactory sensibilities. It was their feet. Never, ever, have I encountered any smell so terrible. I didn't sleep well for two weeks.

I decided not to extend my stay. I collected my hard earned $28, went home and took a very long, very hot bath. I vowed I would never entrap myself like that again as long as I lived, and I haven't—yet.

Chapter 30

CHICKENS

OUT behind our house, just a dozen or so steps from the rear door, we had a summer kitchen. It was a building about six feet wide and perhaps ten feet long. In it we had a hand crank operated separator for separating the cream from the whole milk, a four burner wood range with an oven, and a butcher's block. Its primary purpose, however, was to do heavy duty cooking and roasting during hot weather so that the main house could remain relatively cool.

Shortly after Dad returned to Detroit, we bought 150 Leghorn and 100 Plymouth Rock chickens. The Leghorns were small but great egg layers, each hen averaging between four and five a week. The Plymouth Rocks laid considerably fewer eggs, but we had the Rocks primarily for meat. They were huge, sometimes weighing more than ten pounds dressed and drawn. We ate chicken fairly often, and Mom canned many, using one of the very first Presto pressure cookers available for home use. Canned chicken is an Epicurean's delight! During the spring of 1948, we sold between fifteen and twenty Rocks every weekend to the "Lake Trade." Those were the folks who lived anywhere that required they pass our farm on their way home. I also invested my personal money in 100 newly hatched chicks that I bought through a mail order catalog.

    Before Dad left, he built wooden nests on the two walls of the barn that didn't have livestock stalls on them. These were great nests, lined with straw or hay. The idea was that these would be cozy, private little compartments in which the chickens could lay their eggs. Each row of nests had twenty compartments and there were four rows of nests. One of my jobs was to pick the eggs twice every day, once in the morning and again in the evening. It was a decent job except when a chicken was brooding. When a chicken is in a brooding mood, it means she has decided that she wants this particular egg to hatch. Of course, it never would because it hadn't been fertilized, and since she'd never had a sex education class, she didn't know any better. But, sitting there in her regal, protective, mother-to-be mode, she would tear the flesh from any hand that dared intrude. They are nasty, nasty birds that way. I came out of the barn after picking eggs with bloody hands more than just a few times. Although some chickens are more obnoxious than others, all chickens are abysmally stupid.

    In the fall of 1947, and the spring of 1948, we sold lots of chickens every weekend to the lake trade. Every Friday morning during the "kill" season, I would shoot twenty Plymouth Rocks before school. I was an excellent shot with my .22 caliber bolt action Marlin. The first step in the process was to go down to the barnyard and sprinkle seed corn kernels all over the ground. The chickens thought that was a great treat and would flock around for the feast. Then I would retreat to our back porch and call them: "Chick, Chick,

Chick . . . " in my squeaky, breaking voice. They would all stop eating, and stretch their necks up so they could get a better view of whatever it was that was issuing that irresistible call. They would stay in that "target" position for perhaps three or four seconds—which was ample time for me. "Pow," the rifle cracked, and a plump Rock fell, a bullet through its head. Then the process was repeated until I had my quota for the day. My last duty in this process was to behead and bleed them. Then it was Mom's turn.

While I was harvesting the week's chickens, Mom had gotten a substantial fire roaring in her summer kitchen range. On the range she had a huge galvanized tub full of boiling water. She would place four or five chickens in the boiler at a time and let them soak for just a few minutes. This process loosened the feathers so they could be more easily plucked. After plucking, the pin feathers (new, baby feather starts), were painstakingly removed. Then they were moved into the main house kitchen where the body hair was singed off over one of Mom's propane gas flame burner on her kitchen stove. Then they were gutted (a nasty process). The final step was washing the birds and storing them in the refrigerator until Saturday morning, when they would all be sold within a couple of hours. We sold a lot of chickens, but, as may be recalled, no minnows. No one seemed interested in my dead minnows.

My own attempt at becoming a chicken farmer was an unmitigated disaster. When my chicks arrived, I had no place to put them. You just don't put three-week old chicks out in the barnyard. They wouldn't last seven minutes. Besides dogs, pigs, and marauding wolves, we found that chickens, too, like to eat chickens. They really are nasty creatures.

Well, it so happened that Grandpa Abbott was living with us at that time, and had just finished building a large multi-room, two story doll house for my niece, Sonja. With appropriate permissions, I evicted the inhabitants of the house and moved my chicks in. I put a low wattage light bulb on the end of an extension cord in with them to keep them warm, and for two or three days, they looked really cute. All those tiny, fluffy things running around peeping. Then disaster struck. They contracted coccidiosis, a brutal, contagious, always fatal disease. Every morning and every evening I would cull those little things that had perished—until there just weren't any more.

Chapter 31

RABBITS

IN the late fall of 1947, I had two experiences with rabbits, neither of which was at all pleasant.

One sunny day, early in the morning before school, I spied a pair of brown bunnies scavenging some bits of food down by our barn. I got my trusty little .22 caliber bolt-action Marlin rifle and loaded it. Quietly, I opened our back door and slipped silently out onto our back porch. I took careful aim. "Pop. Pop," the rifle cracked, and I had two rabbits for that night's dinner. I ran quickly down to the barn and retrieved the spoils of the hunt. I scooped them up and ran excitedly back to the house to display my "kill" for my mother. She wasn't terribly impressed.

"You shot them. You clean them," she said.

I agreed, but it was time to get ready for school, so I promised I'd dress and clean them as soon as I got home.

Later that morning while sitting in study hall, I started to itch. Something was crawling on my skin. I scratched. Then I scratched some more. Finally, I discovered that it was fleas that were making me itch. Then they seemed to be all over me, crawling and nibbling, and sometimes drawing blood. I had one hell of a time for the rest of the day, until I could get home and take a bath and wash the fleas out of my hair and various body parts and crevices. That night, not wanting to infest myself again, I quietly buried the rabbits.

I still hadn't learned my lesson though. One bright, sunny afternoon as I was trudging through the snow on my way back to the house from the mailbox, I spied a little white bunny in the grove of trees to my left. We called the white rabbits snow bunnies, for obvious reasons, and I thought this little guy would make a great snack. I made it home through the snow as fast as I could and, passing on my .22, got my dad's twelve-gauge shotgun. I slipped a shell into the chamber, closed the weapon and crept as silently as I could back to where I had seen my prey. There he was, just crouched up against the snow and the bitter cold, trying to eat some tiny roots he had uncovered. I was no more than twenty feet from him.

I took careful aim, held my breath, and fired. "**BUH—LAM!**" the shotgun thundered, its sound reverberating loudly before being absorbed by the snow laden trees. The kick from the twelve-gauge just about knocked me down. It was the first time I had fired it. It was also the last time. I knew nothing about how to hold the weapon for firing, and it damn near tore my scrawny shoulder off. If muscles and bones have memories, I'm sure they're still mad at me for that stupidity.

The smoke cleared and I moved quickly to recover my prize. He wasn't there. All that remained was a bright red spot in the snow, and little bits of white, bloodstained fur. I was sick and thoroughly disgusted with myself. I had completely obliterated that little guy for what turned out to be no reason at all. I was repulsed by what I had done and felt terribly guilty. I trudged slowly back to the house and didn't relate that story to anyone for many, many years. If there is a bunny heaven, I sure hope he's there.

But it wasn't only rabbits that I stopped killing. Those two little episodes in my young life demonstrated to me with great clarity that I was not a "hunter." Unlike most of the other young boys in Fossil, I never hunted deer, or geese, or ducks, or platypuses, or anything else, ever again. Unpleasant as these two episodes were, they taught me a lesson about myself and about life that has stayed with me forever.

Chapter 32

UNCLE GEORGE'S BULL CALF

IN the late winter of 1948 Mom's brother George bought a bull calf for ten dollars from the county sheriff. The county had foreclosed on a small farmer for non-payment of taxes, and sold off all of his possessions for practically nothing. George, who never paid full price for anything in his life, saw this as a wonderful opportunity, since his sister, my mother, had a farm that could provide board and room. He told Mom that if she would let the bull calf stay with us and let him graze the pasture with our own livestock, when he butchered the calf in the late summer, he would share the meat fifty-fifty with her. Mom thought that was a reasonably good deal and agreed to it.

It wasn't long though, before she discovered that our two milk cows had no milk. They had been sucked dry by George's calf that obviously preferred sweet whole milk to grass. We told George about our concern and after several days he brought Grandpa out to our farm to see if he could remedy what to us was becoming an untenable and extremely irritating situation. Grampa rigged up a leather muzzle for the calf that had five four-inch sharp spikes protruding from it. He figured that when the calf approached a cow for his sweet repast, the spikes would jab her in the udder and she would move away, preventing him from sucking. He strapped the muzzle on the calf and turned him loose. We thought the problem was solved.

That evening, both cows were dry. He had managed to twist the muzzle enough that he could enjoy his meal without significant protest. No matter what modifications were made in the muzzle over the next three months, the calf figured a way around them. It was driving us crazy.

One day I captured the calf and attached about a twenty-foot chain on his muzzle so that I could lead him to a separate part of the pasture and stake him out, away from the cows. As I led him through some trees to his new grazing area, he decided he didn't like this idea very much and started to trot, with me flailing along at the other end of the chain. As we approached an oak tree about ten inches in diameter, the bull ran around one side of it and I decided I could stop him by running around the other side. Well, good grief. The calf probably weighed 400 pounds by then. I weighed eighty. What kind of a contest was that? The calf kept running at what I thought at the time was at least seventy-five miles an hour. I was whip-lashed back into the unyielding oak tree with significant force. Then, too late, I let go of the chain.

I was humiliated, bruised, furious, and bleeding from my encounter with the oak tree. When I regained my senses, I jumped up and started running home as fast as I could, to beg for sympathy. Unable to see clearly through my tears, I ran full speed into a two-strand barbed wire fence. That stopped me. I had torn a deep gash in my left shoulder and the blood was running freely. I figured then that this was probably not going to be one of my better days. I walked the rest of the way home, bloody, sweaty, dirty, and smelling like the bull calf. I had reckoned right—Mom did comfort me and cleaned and bandaged my wounds, at least my visible ones. But, the calf was free and continued his merry, sucking ways.

Mom cried a lot about our loss of milk and cream money. It wasn't much money, but it was some, and we had very little. Finally, I decided unilaterally to do something about this untenable situation. I called Mom's brother, Dave, to see if he would be willing to stake that horrible bull calf out in his yard until it was time to butcher him. He had plenty of room, and agreed to that arrangement. Then I called Uncle George, and explained that the calf was driving us crazy, drinking our entire milk supply day after day. I asked him if he would be willing to move the calf to Dave's house where he could stay for the next two or three weeks until he was butchered. George said," Sure, Glenn, no problem." He moved him the next day.

Two weeks later it was butchering time. But we weren't apprised of it. Uncle Euclid had agreed to kill, dress, and cut the animal into roasts, chops, ribs, etc. So, one fine evening, that is exactly what he did. Then they wrapped each piece in freezer paper in preparation for storage in the local locker plant. George had, without our knowledge, arranged to split the half that was to have gone to us evenly between Mom's sister, Bertha and her brother Dave. Mom never really got over this betrayal.

Part Three
DETROIT

Chapter 33

BACK TO DETROIT

IN the late summer of 1948, Dad drove from Detroit to Fossil to get Mom, niece Sonja, and me. The farm had been listed with a real estate company, but no prospects were in sight. We loaded ourselves, one suitcase each, and not much else into his 1936 Studebaker, said goodbye to nearby relatives, and left for Detroit. There were four families of relations that lived reasonably close and they promised they would keep an eye on our home and furnishings until it sold. We were naively comfortable with those assurances.

We got nearly to LaCrosse, Wisconsin, before the car threw a rod. It was one of the damnedest noises I'd ever heard. We got a wrecker from town to tow us to the nearest "reputable" mechanic's cavern that he called a garage. Parts were hard to come by, and the mechanic had to order a new rod and its necessary accessories out of Madison. It took a total of six days for the parts to arrive and for the installation to be completed. During the wait, we were spending what meager money we had on motels and greasy restaurant food.

Finally, the car was fixed. We loaded up again, and gingerly drove the rest of the way to Detroit without incident. About the only joy in that trip was the occasional appearance of a Burma Shave sign. These signs were one of the Burma Shave Company's favorite advertising methods, and everyone enjoyed them. They were a welcome break from the monotony of the highway. Some examples:

"The bearded lady
tried a jar.
She's now a famous
movie star."
BURMA SHAVE
Or
"She eyed his beard
And said, 'No dice'.
The wedding's off
I'll cook the rice."
BURMA SHAVE
Or
"Unless your face
is stinger free,
you'd better let
your honey be."
BURMA SHAVE

And so on and on, clear across the country.

It was sultry and very hot the evening we arrived at Dad's converted attic. No one was particularly pleased with our discouraging circumstances, but we were resolved to make the best of a very bad situation. However, I got myself into a jam with the Detroit police within the first week.

I went to my old neighborhood one day to visit my childhood friends. One of them, Hermie, had converted his rickety old bicycle into a motorbike by adding a goofy little motor on the bike's fork. It had a little wheel that pressed up against and spun on the sidewall of the front tire. That was the propulsion system, and it could pull that outlandish two-wheeled device at speeds up to thirty-five miles an hour—a more than ample speed. And it was for sale! I coughed up the twenty bucks Hermie was asking for it, and sped off. I had wheels!

The next Friday night after my big purchase, I again visited the old neighborhood. Four of us decided to take the streetcar to the Rex movie house, one of our favorite theaters. The Rex was located on Fort Street about five miles from the neighborhood. It was a small theater, with one aisle down the middle. Six-seat rows extended from the aisle on either side. The foul air was permeated with the stench of stale perspiration and garlic, no doubt from the epidural oozings of those who populated this seamy area of town. Every day three feature films were shown, accompanied by at least one cartoon and a serial, like Flash Gordon. Every so often while watching the films, we would hear a scream, as one of the resident rats ran across someone's feet. It added a little thrill to whatever film we were watching.

One evening soon after returning to Detroit, seven of us including me, decided that it would be great sport to dress up like hoods and attend the Gaiety Burlesque in downtown Detroit. We were all sixteen or seventeen and clearly didn't know any better. We dressed Billy up in a knee length fur coat and, pretending as if he were our leader, surrounded him as we purchased our tickets. Then, with two of us walking in front, two along side, and two behind, we escorted him down the aisle and found seven seats in a row. We thought it was a great scene and thought no more about it.

We enjoyed the show and left. We parted the curtains at the top of the aisle and started walking through the lobby. Even the slowest of us found it impossible to ignore eight huge, very mean-looking goons standing there in two lines, forming a very narrow passageway. Apparently, the burlesque's manager had taken our goofy ruse seriously and had brought in some hired guns. His attempt at intimidation worked exceedingly well. We minced our way through the narrow passage they provided and caught the streetcar home—and never, ever, pulled that stunt again. I thought to myself: "Whoa. This isn't Fossil."

Another Friday night, after our movie feast at the Rex, we took the streetcar back to the neighborhood. We walked a couple of blocks to Kelly's Drug Store, an old hangout where assorted lies and adventures were traded among the kids. It was about one o'clock in the morning when we arrived at Kelly's and began rehashing the wonderful movies we had just seen. A police car sidled around the corner and stopped. Two cops got out and ordered us to face the brick wall of Kelly's and spread eagle.

They frisked each one of us, and of course, found nothing. Then they started asking each one of us how old we were. When they got to me, I stuttered and stammered and finally spit out "seventeen." I wasn't. I was only sixteen, and I was out past the curfew that had been imposed after the riots. One cop didn't take kindly to my feeble attempt at lying. He opened the rear door of the prowl car and slammed me inside. He was not gentle. Inside the car was John, another acquaintance of mine from school. He had been picked up elsewhere. Both of us were in deep trouble.

The officers told the other kids to get the Hell out of there and go home. Both cops got back in the car and told us they were going to take us home and give our parents a lecture they wouldn't soon forget for allowing us to be out so late. They took John home first, and one of the cops went with John into the upstairs flat. While they were up there, the car's radio reported a family disturbance in a house about two miles away. The driver cop said that he and his partner would respond and let me out of the car. He told me that my punishment would be to walk home. Hell, to get back to my motorbike, I had to walk through a very large construction area, filled with the skeletons of new homes being built—and then through a solid black neighborhood. Given my fairly recent experience with race riots, I was scared to death, but I made it back to my bike about three in the morning. I revved that baby up and sped off into the night, heading for home.

When I arrived, I found Dad waiting for me. To say he wasn't pleased would be an immense understatement. Then, when I told him what had happened, his fury accelerated. He was ready to take me and go right down to the Fort and Green Precinct House and raise Hell. It took the full measure of my vast powers of persuasion to convince him not to do that. I knew that if such a complaint were registered with the precinct, I would be picked up and harassed by the cops every time I ventured out of the house. I didn't need any more trouble than I already had. He finally relented and acquiesced to my pleadings. We went to bed friends.

Dad was working the afternoon shift at Ford's because it paid a few cents an hour more than the day shift. He had been able to transfer out of the foundry and into a maintenance job, and the work was significantly lighter and easier on his aging, fifty-four year old body. His shift ended at 11:00 p.m. and he would arrive home at 11:30 every weeknight.

On Saturdays and sometimes on Sundays he had a moonlight job, working for another Ford employee who had bought himself a giant vacuum cleaner that sucked the soot from residential coal furnaces, related ductwork and chimneys. Dad was, in fact, a part-time chimney sweep. He certainly looked the part. When he arrived at home, he would be completely covered with fine, grimy, black coal soot. He could have screen tested for a role in *Chitty-Chitty Bang-Bang* and won it hands down. Since we had no bathtub or shower in our attic, he would have to use our landlord's bathroom to clean up. Using their bathroom for his bath was not pleasant, but we were only paying thirty dollars a month rent, and figured we could tolerate a few inconveniences. Thirty bucks a month was about half of what comparable housing would have cost, so we ground our teeth and plodded on.

Frank and Ann were our landlords. Both were from Germany and spoke broken English. Frank was severely crippled with arthritis, and his joints were nearly non-functional. He could walk, and he managed to keep his factory job, but he couldn't drive a car nor do much of anything else. Ann would rub him all over with Absorbine Junior every night when he got home. Then he would eat dinner and take up his place in an overstuffed chair he had positioned next to the radio. Ann would bring him a case of beer and set it down on the floor next to him, and he was set for the evening. He drank twelve 12-oz. bottles of beer every night before staggering into bed. The whole house was permeated with an unique blend of Absorbine Jr. and stale beer odors.

One morning in the spring of 1949, Mom got out of bed to start her day. Dad was still sleeping, but his right foot was sticking out from under the covers. It was not something easily ignored. His foot was wrapped in a huge bandage soaked with blood. Mom just about fainted. She awakened Dad and asked him what in the world had happened. He told her that a crate loaded with steel parts had fallen from a stack of crates and had crushed his right great toe. The workers at the Aid Station in the plant cut off his steel-toed work boots and immediately called in a physician who saw no alternative but to amputate the entire toe. That accomplished, and leaving him to his own devices about how he was going to drive his car, they sent him home. He did manage to get himself home and into bed without further incident, but he was in significant pain.

After relating his story to Mom, he went back to sleep for a couple of hours before deciding it was time to get ready for work. He sat up on the edge of the bed and promptly fainted. When he regained consciousness, Mom was able to convince him that it might be a good idea to take the day off. He did. That was the second of two workdays he missed during his entire work life at Ford's. The other day was the day I was born.

As bad as this living arrangement was, it was going to get worse—a lot worse. On the next street, a tiny house that I delivered papers to became vacant. The woman that owned the house lived next door to it and was also one of my customers. I inquired of her what the rent would be for the little house and she replied that it would be ten dollars a month—an unheard of price. When I reported this "find" to my parents, they rushed right over and closed the deal. The only furnishings we had were a bed, dresser, couch and a cheap dining room set, so moving was not a major problem.

The problem, as we very soon discovered, was that the place was infested with rats. They were everywhere. Their most disturbing presence, however, was when they would peer up at us from a hole in the bathroom floor and grin while you were sitting on the pot. We set traps and caught a few, but the others wised up and avoided the traps. Then we decided that poisoning them was the only answer, and we were very successful in killing many of them. They promptly died under our little shack and within a few days the place was permeated with the stench of rotting rats. God, it was awful.

From that point on, that home was referred to as "The Rat House." We lived there for just over a year, and I never brought any of my friends to our home. It was an appalling time for all of us. We were, however, able to save enough money by 1950 to make a down payment on a little four-room house in Lincoln Park, a suburb adjacent to the area in Southwest Detroit where the rat house was. It was a substantial step up from where we were, but a great distance from where we had started before moving to Fossil.

Chapter 34

THE PAPER BOY

ONE week after arriving in Detroit, I got myself a paper route for the Detroit Times, a Hearst Syndicate paper.

The Times was very good to all of its employees, including the young carriers for home delivery. My first route was noticeably less than satisfying. I had about eighty customers in a low-income housing project. The projects were comprised of obsolete, single story army barracks which had been moved from an army base that had been closed. It was four blocks long and two blocks deep. Each building housed either two or four families. The walls were so thin you could hear the people in the next unit set their table, converse, breathe, or otherwise engage in various bodily functions.

Collection day from each of my eighty or so customer was every Saturday morning. Far too frequently, when I attempted to collect my money for the week's papers, the man or woman would ask me to come back sometime next week (so they would have time to move). What kind of person stiffs a scrawny, fifteen-year-old paperboy? I could never collect enough money to pay my bill at the paper station. I was losing between one and two dollars every week. I said to myself, "Glenn, this is *not* a good job."

The realization struck me one fine afternoon that I couldn't get terribly rich if I continued to lose money every week. Even though I liked the other kids and the paper itself, I decided to seek my fortune elsewhere. I went to my station manager, Dick, and related my tale of woe. I told him,

"I am outta here. I can't stand losing money every week."

"So, you're a quitter, eh?" Dick queried.

"Well, no, I'm not a quitter. But I'm not stupid either. How do you suppose I'm ever going to get rich if I keep losing money to these jerks who skip and won't pay," I replied.

Dick came right back at me. "Go ahead and quit if you want to. I didn't think you were that kind of a kid, and I had you in mind for a very good route that's opening up in a couple of weeks."

He went on to explain that the route he was thinking of for me was six blocks of very nice settled homes right in the neighborhood where I lived. "But, if quitting is what you want to do, so long. I'll find someone else for this plum route."

I knew the area where he was suggesting my route would be. I only lived half a block from it and it was a nice, older, settled neighborhood. The prospect sounded good to me, so I decided to stick it out. Because of the tremendous amount of positive reinforcement that followed, that decision was one that changed my life, and I've been grateful to Dick ever since.

I learned very quickly that Dick liked to win contests. The manager for the branch that won the contest in each district got to accompany the boys as a sort of pseudo chaperone. Three contests a year were held, and each one was six weeks long. They were hard work. Every day after school, I would take the streetcar to the end of its line, where I had stashed my bicycle in a friend's yard. I'd ride my bike ten blocks to the paper station, fold my papers, stuff them in my white canvas paper bag with **"The Detroit Times"** emblazoned in orange and black ink on its front, try to stay out of fights (not always successfully), strap the bag onto my handlebars and take off to deliver my route. It took about thirty minutes to complete the route, after which I would head directly back to the paper station. By that time it was about four in the afternoon. There wasn't time to eat, so dinner on those nights generally consisted of potato chips and a bottle of orange soda pop. Sometimes it was pretzels and Coke—just to vary the cuisine.

There were typically six or eight kids ready to canvas each evening. We'd all load into Dick's brand new two-tone green Pontiac (sometimes two guys would need to cram themselves into the trunk), and speed off for a night of canvassing adventure. I only rode in the trunk one time—it was hot, stuffy, claustrophobic, and scary. Once was enough.

The interior of the car itself was not much better, but at least you could see out. It always had the unique scent of an unappetizing blend of adolescent boy body odors and Dick's ever-present cigar. That whole car trip was a terrific experience for anyone with masochistic tendencies. We never knew where we were headed—only Dick knew.

When we arrived at our destination, which could be anywhere from downtown Detroit, to the slums (black or white), to residential suburbs of every known ethnic derivation, Dick would drop us off in pairs. He would tell us how far to go, and what time he would meet us. He was always on time for the pickup and would then relocate us to a different set of blocks to be mined for subscriptions. This activity would repeat itself several times each evening before it was time to head for home. On a good night, I would gather six or eight new orders. Most guys would get two or three, but I was good. I was very, very good.

There were "BIG" trips, and "Little" trips. Big trips were won on a strictly competitive basis. The six boys who got the most orders in each district won the big trips. Big trips were always for four days, generally by chartered airplanes from Capitol Air, and all expenses were paid, including $5 every day for incidentals and souvenirs. They were wonderful. All of the trips I won were "big" trips, and I won every contest I worked. I won trips to Washington, D.C., Atlantic City, Boston, New York, and Miami. Little trips were always for two days with significantly less exotic destination cities—like Cleveland and Chicago. They were awarded to all boys who gathered fifty or more new subscribers but who didn't win one of the few highly competitive big trips.

I liked the kids I was working with. We ranged in age from fourteen to eighteen and all of us had far too much energy for the good of the paper station or the community at large. We were all good kids though—we just couldn't tolerate tranquility at any time or place for very long. One of the techniques that the Times had for utilizing this otherwise untethered energy was to conduct subscription contests for the boys in the metropolitan Detroit area. There were twelve delivery districts in Detroit, and each district usually had between fifteen and twenty substations, each with twenty to forty carriers, depending on the population density of the area. I was in the "R" district in southwest Detroit, Branch 13. We had thirty-two carriers, but only a few of us were "Big Guns." We were the elite of the carriers in our branch. All others were our "slaves" or "stooges," who did whatever we told them to do. It was great being a big gun.

I have some recollections about a few of those kids. Wayne, for example. Wayne was my age, but significantly bigger and stronger. One night, after an exhausting and relatively unproductive evening of canvassing during one of our seemingly endless contests, we were headed back to our paper station. Wayne was sitting in the front seat and I was sitting directly behind him in the rear seat. He mistakenly thought I insulted him in some way. He turned in his seat and without warning, hit me in the mouth as hard as he could, given the physical circumstances. He did have a quick temper. I don't remember if he ever apologized for that painful blunder, but luckily for me, we eventually became very good friends. He lived in "The Project" with his parents and two brothers, Bryant, and Bruce. When he got married at age seventeen, I was his best man.

Then there was Morgan. Morgan was a smart aleck who, like Wayne, became sexually active by the time he was sixteen. One evening Morgan was my canvassing partner when we were out mining for new subscriptions for the contest we were in at the time. We were in an unfamiliar but nice neighborhood and had just finished our assigned block. We were approaching the end of the street on our way to the drugstore on the corner to await our manager, Dick, who would then take us to a different area for more canvassing. We were just about at the corner when we met four guys a year or two older than we were (and, it seemed, much—much bigger), going in the other direction. Morgan and I were laughing and joking and thought nothing of it, until one of the guys yelled back at us,

"What did you call me?" addressing Morgan specifically.

"I didn't say anything," Morgan replied.

"Oh, yes, you did." the kid hissed, and without warning, brought his knee up sharply into Morgan's adolescent testicles. He was doubling up as the indescribable pain began coursing its way to his less than perfect brain, when his mouth was met with the upcoming knee of his assailant. Morgan reeled back against the brick wall of the drugstore, blood spurting from his mouth. He slumped to the sidewalk in bewilderment. He was in shock. The attacker and his laughing friends ran off into the darkness, and I was left to try to comfort him as best I could until Dick arrived. I couldn't have been more than five minutes before Dick showed up but it seemed a lot longer. He was appalled by what he found on that street corner, and furious. We loaded into the car and Dick drove up and down the side streets in a vain attempt to find those guys. We spotted a police prowl car and reported the incident, but as was usually the case that is where the episode ended. Morgan licked his wounds, literally, and we called it a night.

All of us guys in the paper station knew that Morgan had less than a sterling character. So, one summer night about six of us, including Morgan, descended upon the little cafe next to Kelly's Drug Store. It was hamburger and french fry time. As we approached the cafe, we noticed a guy, all alone, straddling his bike, waiting for who knows what. He was a pretty big kid, about eighteen. Good grief! It was one of Morgan's nemeses. They hated each other. We could understand why he might have hated Morgan. Morgan felt brave, though, and asked us if we would back him up if he picked a fight with this guy. "You bet," we all exclaimed in unison. We parked our bikes, and Morgan sauntered up to the (to us) stranger. The fool walked right up to him, called him a name even I can't repeat here, and spit in his face. Just as this happened, we all walked quickly into the cafe, leaving him stranded, alone, and extremely vulnerable. That kid beat Morgan about the head and shoulders with wonderful enthusiasm, until he finally squeaked, "I give." Those of us in the cafe thought this was great entertainment. Morgan didn't.

He eventually married Evie, my childhood girlfriend from the old neighborhood. Evie and I had been steadies at ages four and five. They had two children before this fine young man abandoned them.

Stevie was a tiny kid, very quiet, and a nice person. He,

like most of us, had a paper route in order to earn a few bucks to help out his family. He was another of Morgan's victims. One day Morgan had an idea that he thought would be great sport. While Stevie was folding his papers in the paper station, Morgan took a pair of wire clippers used for cutting the wires from the bundles of papers, and severed every other one of the spokes on the front wheel of Stevie's bicycle. When Stevie was ready to leave to deliver his route, Morgan asked all of us "Big Guns" outside to watch. When the weight of the bag full of papers hit Stevie's handlebars, the wheel collapsed into a totally non-functional oval. Stevie, without saying a word, put his bag of papers on the ground, straightened his wheel enough so that it would at least roll, slung the paper bag over his meager shoulder and walked off, pushing his bike, to deliver his route. Three days later little Stevie was hit by a car and killed. It was not a very pleasant time for any of us.

Jim was a very stocky red-headed kid who liked to bully anyone smaller than he was. One fine afternoon, I had my papers all folded and stuffed into my bag. I picked it up and started toward the door of the paper station to load it onto by bike's handlebars. When I got to the doorway, Jim stepped in front of it and blocked the exit. I put the loaded bag down, stared at Jim and said, "Get out of my way, Jim."

Jim moved back and continued folding his papers. I picked up my bag and started through the doorway. Again, Jim placed his mushy, outsized body directly in my path, grinning at me. Without thought of possible consequences, I dropped my bag and hit him squarely in the mouth with all the force I could muster. He could have killed me, but he didn't. He looked at me quizzically and stepped back. I never had a problem with him again.

Eddie was a kid two years younger than I was. He thought I was God and I never told him otherwise. One night Dick dropped Eddie and me off in a strange neighborhood to prospect for new subscribers. Eddie had a half-pint heavy glass milk bottle that he had just finished as part of his fine supper of milk and cookies. As we walked toward our designated street, he tossed the bottle to me. I caught it and tossed it back. Then we separated as he began to move to the other side of the street. Naturally, we had to throw the bottle harder and harder to compensate for the increasing distance. When we were about thirty feet apart, Eddie threw the bottle at me very hard. I caught it, but just barely. He knew the bottle would be coming back at him at nearly the speed of light, so, using the nearest shield he could quickly find, he ducked behind a telephone pole. I hesitated just long enough, I guess, for Eddie to become curious. He peeked around the pole to see what I was doing—just as the bottle reached his skull. The bottle ricocheted away, leaving a gaping, two-inch gash in Eddie's scalp. Blood shot everywhere. I thought I'd killed him. I ran over and tried to comfort him and tell him how sorry I was. Even though his scalp was wide open and blood was everywhere, he wasn't mad at me. We just sat and joked about this awful mess until Dick arrived. Dick wasn't happy. He took Eddie to the nearest medical facility, got him cleaned up and stitched, and brought him back to finish his canvassing with a giant bandage on his head. Eddie didn't get many orders that night.

One bitterly cold winter night Wayne and I were canvassing in a neighborhood far from home, in an area that had many two and three story apartment buildings. We were tired of canvassing, and looking for some reasonable excitement. We slipped silently through one of the buildings, removing the bulbs from the hall lighting fixtures. We would always leave one or two, so people could see that it really was a hallway, but we'd pocket the rest of them.

Then we went to the roof of the building, which was covered with ice, and of course had no barricade or banister to prevent people from walking right off the edge. We walked very carefully right up to the slippery precipice and looked down to the street below. It had two lanes of traffic moving in opposite directions, twenty to twenty-five miles an hour. We took careful aim and bombed a passing car with a light bulb. "**Pow!**" It sounded like a small bomb—perhaps a grenade. The driver never knew what hit him. He stepped on the gas and sped off into the night. "**Pow!—Pow!**" Wayne and I each hit our next moving target. This was great!

We were bombardiers!—and we had no fear of being shot out of the sky! We spent our ammunition, slipped carefully back from the edge, crept quietly down the stairs and out into the street to await Dick, who, none the wiser, would transport us to the next block he had targeted for us to canvass. Our adventure in the night sky was much better than canvassing. Wayne and I reminisced about that night for a long time.

The next spring, Wayne, Morgan and I decided to go to a baseball game at Brigg's Stadium, the home of the Detroit Tigers. We got our fifty cent tickets to the left field bleachers, settled in and started eating. There were multiple vendors hawking their tempting items up and down the aisles. By the way, there are no better hot dogs in the world, perhaps in the universe, than were sold at Brigg's Stadium. They were absolutely superb. We wolfed down two or three of those steaming delicacies slathered with mustard, along with a Coke, an Eskimo Pie and finally, a huge bag of peanuts, in the shell.

There were two older gentlemen sitting directly in front of us, and one was wearing a tan felt fedora, a brimmed dress hat that just about all adult men wore. The brim was just sitting there, empty and lonely. We decided that the brim would make an excellent home for our peanut shells. We must have heaped forty or fifty crushed and broken shells into that brim before the guy's buddy noticed. He thought it was a funny prank, too. Every time his friend turned his head, a few shells would fall out and land on him. The victim, however, remained clueless.

At that time, all of us were smoking cigarettes, as all great and grown up people did, and lighting them with matches, that were then dropped on the concrete floor. Everything was fine until a burning match that had not gone out ignited the scrap paper under the gentleman's seat in front of us. As the flames grew higher, so did our anxiety, and finally we had no choice but to let him know that he was about to burst into flame. He jumped up, peanut shells flying everywhere. He stamped out the growing inferno under his chair, spewed every horrible invective he could think of at us and sat down, fuming, so to speak. His buddy still thought it was funny—and so did we.

Then there was Angelo. Angelo was not a paperboy, but he worked for the Times as a swing branch manager in our district. He was only eighteen himself, so we all related well to him the two days a week he spent as manager of our branch. One summer day Angelo asked me if I would give him a ride to another branch to pick up some papers he needed. I had access to Dad's '36 Studebaker, so I said I would, even though I didn't have my driver's license or any accident insurance yet. What could go wrong? Plenty, as it turned out.

On the way back to our station, we unexpectedly came upon a traffic jam. I jammed on the brakes, which were next to useless mechanical brakes, and plowed into the stopped car directly in front of us. We didn't do any damage to Dad's car or the rear end of the car we hit, but the force of the collision drove the car I hit into the ends of a load of 2x4's protruding from the bed of a pick up truck in front of him, causing great damage to his grill, headlights and radiator.

Naturally the guy wanted to call the police. I didn't. I had no license, no insurance, and I didn't have permission to be driving. I was in deep trouble. It was only through very fast and very sincere pleading that we convinced our victim that we would get his car repaired by a body man we knew, and that it would be done quickly and professionally. Reluctantly he agreed.

We headed back to our own paper station and discovered that our day wasn't quite over. As we approached our destination, I made a 90-degree left turn to cross a boulevard. The latch on Angelo's door released itself and Angelo started falling out of the open door. Frantically, he reached for something, anything, to grab that would stop his plunge toward the concrete pavement. He managed to grab a corrugated asbestos heater hose from the foot well of the passenger compartment that wasn't attached to anything. He and the hose hit the pavement with a sickening thud and a nasty scream. I managed to stop the car and ran around to see if he was hurt. He was dazed, and felt rather silly, but he was okay.

Angelo did know a body man and within just a very few days, we fulfilled our promise to this understanding stranger. The bill came to just about two hundred dollars. Where was I going to get two hundred dollars? Then I remembered. I had more than that in War Bonds. Since our car had not been damaged, I figured I could cash in two hundred dollars worth of bonds, pay my bill, and Dad would never have to know of my stupid transgressions.

I went home, found enough bonds to cover my needs, and went to our local bank to cash them. I handed them to the teller. He looked at me, looked at the bonds, and said, "Just a minute, please," and disappeared into the mysterious catacombs that all banks have.

A few minutes later he returned and said, "Glenn, your father is on the phone. He wants to talk with you."

Oh, no. My anxiety level shot into the stratosphere.

"Hi, Dad."

"What in the world are you doing, Glenn?" he asked with a most unpleasant firmness.

I was undone. I had nowhere to go—nowhere to hide. I confessed the whole ugly story.

"Put the bank man back on the phone," he ordered.

I complied. The teller had been lurking in the background just within earshot. Dad told him it was all right to cash the bonds, and I walked out with enough cash to pay the body man. Ugly, ugly time.

But, back to the paper station.

One night Angelo took us canvassing. He dropped Wayne and me off in a new construction area where there were scores of homes in various stages of completion. The streets hadn't been paved yet and there were piles of construction materials everywhere. There were no streetlights either, so it was very dark. Wayne and I figured it would be great fun to build a roadblock across the street using concrete blocks that were stacked in front of every building lot, to be used for basement walls. We stacked the blocks two high completely across the dirt street. That didn't look like quite enough so we placed sacks of concrete mix on top of our barricade. Then we slipped back into the shadows to await our first victim.

Unfortunately, our victim turned out to be Angelo. He came zipping around the corner in pitch-black darkness, except for the pale yellow beams of his headlights. He didn't see the wall and slammed directly into it. Both of his headlights popped out of their moorings and hung dejectedly by their little wires, peering into the dirt and under the car. Fortunately, Angelo wasn't hurt, but he started to cry. The only little piece of mobile junk he owned was broken.

We felt awful. We rushed over to him and, while not admitting guilt for this mess, consoled him and told him we'd be happy to pay his repair bills because we were so appreciative of his willingness to take us canvassing.

When Dick was transferred to another branch, an overly neat little man named Wilson took over as our branch manager. Although we had no name for his behavior at that time, his neurotic symptoms were clearly those of a classic obsessive/compulsive personality. He had made cards for every customer on every carrier's route and had them all neatly filed in two cardboard boxes that he kept in his desk drawers. Every day he would go through his files to make sure that he was absolutely correct and up to date.

He would count out the papers for each boy's route one by one, and then verify the count by repeating it. It was weird, and he was getting on our nerves. Most of us big guns had a key to the paper station, so one Friday night we entered the place and threw his precious, neatly organized cards all over the place. We made sure that we were there the next day when he arrived so we could relish his anguish. It was a pitiful sight, watching Wilson cry—but it was a lot of fun, too.

Wilson smoked a pipe, and he had two or three of them. He always left one in the paper station in the unlikely event that he might leave home without one. Wayne and I thought that it would be a good idea to boobytrap that spare pipe. We carefully removed the tobacco from it and filled the bowl half full of wood and lead shavings from the pencil sharpener. Then we repacked some tobacco on top of the shavings so it looked like it had never been tampered with. We placed the pipe back in its resting place on Wilson's desk, and just waited. It wasn't long, maybe two or three days, before the trap was sprung. Wilson lit his spare pipe and inhaled a deep drag.

None of us knew how horrible this would taste or how dangerous inhaling smoke filtered through wood shavings and powdered lead was. I swear we thought old Wilson was going to croak. He hacked and spewed, coughed and spit, and finally lost his perfectly prepared and eaten lunch. Wilson was not a happy man. Wayne and I promised him that we would find out who did this to him—but, of course, we were never able to.

In what I thought was a laudatory effort to win us obviously hostile creatures over, Wilson told us that he owned a small plane that he kept at the Wayne County Airport, near downtown Detroit. At that point I was the biggest gun in the house so I was the first one he offered to take up. I thought that would be just great, so one fine sunny Sunday afternoon, I met Wilson at his house and he drove us to the airport. Sure enough, there was a little plane with two seats waiting just for us. We loaded in, strapped ourselves tightly, and Wilson turned the ignition key. The little engine sputtered and then roared to life, smoky exhaust spewing from its ports. We taxied down the runway and waited for permission to take off. Permission came. Wilson opened that little baby up and we screamed down the runway, both of us pressed into the back of our tiny seats. It couldn't have been twenty seconds and we were airborne. We climbed to 3,000 feet and leveled off, heading southwest. Before long we were over our own neighborhood, he said, but I couldn't recognize anything. It all looked the same to me.

Then he said, "Do you know what a chandelle is, Glenn?"

Having never heard of either a "chan" or a "delle," I replied, "No, I don't." Then he explained that it was a stunt, and he had his own modified version of it that he was going to show me.

"I'm going to pull the nose of the plane up," he said, "so that we'll be in a fairly steep climb. Then I'm going to level off and slowly throttle back the engine until it stalls. The plane will begin to fall, nose first toward the ground. It will be very silent with no engine noise. Only the soft whistling of the air as we fall through it. After thirty seconds or so, I'll restart the engine and we'll peel back, climb sharply and roll over at the top of the loop. Then we'll level off and head back to the airport."

"Oh, boy," I thought to myself. "What in the Hell have I gotten myself into here?"

Wilson pulled the nose of the plane up and began a

seventy-degree climb. He eased off on the throttle, slowly—slowly—slowly—the engine sputtered, coughed,—and quit. Dead silence. The prop was still. Then we began to fall. Down—down—damn near straight down toward the earth and certain death. My mind was racing, my heart crashing around in my bony chest. I thought,

"I really hope Wilson's not crazy and has decided to end his nasty little life with me as some sort of trophy. Perhaps he found out it was me that booby trapped his pipe—or shuffled his card files."

Just then he turned the ignition key, the prop spun twice and the engine roared to life. We were probably approaching a million miles an hour when he pulled the nose up and into a full power climb. At that point my stomach continued on its way toward the ground. When we were completely upside down in the loop, he turned the plane over, leveled off, and headed for the airport. Even though I didn't have many wits left, most of them having petrified somewhere up there, I managed a relatively weak, "Thanks a lot. I had a great time!" and immediately began planning my revenge for the unspeakable horror I had just gone through. It wasn't long in coming, but that's another story.

Chapter 35

SOUTHWESTERN HIGH SCHOOL

THE first of the four high schools I attended in the Detroit area was Southwestern High. Both my sister Dorothy, and my brother Harland, had graduated from Southwestern in the early '40's. That they graduated from high school was a fairly distinctive feat at that time since most of their peers had dropped out before graduation to enter the work force. In fact, most of my peers, like Wayne, Billy, and Jim dropped out too.

Southwestern was a serious study in contrasts, compared to Fossil Consolidated School. In place of the four classrooms that Fossil provided for all of its fifty or so high school students, Southwestern housed nearly 2,800 students. It was an entire city block long and three stories high. In addition, it had a full basement with classrooms and a fourth floor turret at both ends of the building. My homeroom was in the turret at the south end. A fifteen-minute homeroom session was placed between the second and third class session.

All classes were forty-five minutes in length, at least by the clock. To me, each class was at least four hours long. Classes for me were an interminable bore. I really didn't like school at all, but some experiences were deposited in my memory bank forever. Like skipping school, for example.

No less than once a week I would decide that it was not a good day for school, and would stay on the streetcar after it had disgorged most of its student passengers at the doorstep of the high school. Sometimes my comrades accompanied me. One fine day in the late fall of 1948, Wayne, Billy and I decided that we needed to see the toy display at the J. L. Hudson Company's department store. Hudson's was the largest store in Detroit, a full city block square and fourteen stories high. The twelfth floor was entirely dedicated to toys at Christmas time and their most attractive display was a very complex electric train setup. It was marvelous. It was hypnotic. We three waifs were standing at the display's edge, completely mesmerized, when two adult men sidled up to us, one on each side. One spoke:

"Why aren't you boys in school today?"

"Well, uh, what's it to you?" we responded.

"We're truant officers, and you look like you're still students. Why aren't you in school today?" they repeated.

Reaching boldly into my vast repertoire of excuses, I replied, "We're Catholic. We go to a Catholic school, and today is a religious holiday."

"Oh, izat so. What holiday is it?" one of them queried.

Since none of us was Catholic, we were stumped. We stood silent, staring at the floor, and wishing that we were somewhere, anywhere, else.

Then one of the truant officers spoke, "Look, you guys. We know you're skipping school. You each have your lunch sack. I'm going to write a note for you saying that you have been caught by us and that you're on your way back to school—

just in case another truant officer stops you between here and school."

Thanks a lot officer. We shuffled off and caught the first streetcar back to school.

The next morning we each had to report to Mr. Becker, the counselor for our class, to get a written "unexcused absence" slip in order to get back into the classes we had missed. Mr. Becker was a small man, perhaps five foot, six inches tall. He was about fifty years old, and balding. He had a face reminiscent of some sort of rodent, a mole, perhaps, and it was covered with flaking skin from a nasty case of psoriasis. But, he was a good guy.

"Hello, my stupid young students," he said as we stood before him. "What's the matter with you? Don't you know better than to be out in plain sight if you're skipping school? At least hide out in a dark theater or something. Stop being so dumb!"

He smiled as he gave us our entrance slips for class, and all of us remembered him fondly for many years. And, from then on, that is exactly what we did. We wound up exploring every majestic theater multiple times in downtown Detroit.

Then there was Mr. Breedlove, the teacher of the only biology class I ever took in high school. Biology class followed homeroom period in my turret, and Mr. Breedlove's classroom was in the basement at the far east-end of the building, as far from my homeroom as it could possibly be.

Every day, I would rush out of homeroom, race down the four flights of marble stairs, and fight my way through the throngs of students who were either just milling around or trying desperately to reach their own classroom destinations. I was late for biology just about every day.

Mr. Breedlove was a nice enough guy, but he had a physical impairment that was really distracting. He was cockeyed. Each of his eyes looked toward the outside periphery of his visual field - a lot like Marty Feldman. Since

I never knew which eye was looking at me, I figured it would be best to at least act like I was listening to what he was saying. Actually, it paid off with one of the few "B's" I got during my high school career. Useful information that I learned about amoebas, paramecium and cilia, remain with me to this very day.

During one of my frequent absences from my speech class, the instructor learned that my class was to choose one student to represent Southwestern High as a disc jockey for an FM radio station in downtown Detroit. Each high school in Detroit was sending a student representative who would conduct their own three-hour program that would be broadcast through loudspeakers throughout the school's cafeteria during lunch periods. Since I was absent and had no defense, the class unanimously elected me to be Southwestern's representative. A few days later I received a very long list of all the available music. I was to select which ones were to be played and write a script to introduce each piece. So I did. About a week before my virgin performance as a "DJ," I sent the station a list of the music I had selected, and the order in which each piece was to be played.

The appointed day arrived. It took two transfers and three streetcars (but only six cents in carfare) to finally get me to the station, but I figured that it was really a small price to pay to be able to legitimately miss school for a day. When I got to the appropriate offices of a very large building, I was given instructions on how to pull this off.

Directly in front of the desk provided to me was the broadcast booth with a large glass window, behind which was the fellow who would actually play the records. I was to give my eloquent and sometimes mildly witty introduction to each piece and then point to the guy in the control room who would then play the piece. When the piece was finished, he would point back at me and I would begin my introduction to the next piece. This sequence was repeated for three hours, pointing back and forth, back and forth, ad nauseum. Actually, I thought I had done really well. And I had.

When I left the booth at the end of my "performance," I was stopped by one of the station's executives. He told me that I had a very nice broadcast voice and that I should consider the possibility of a career in broadcasting. He told me that the station had a training program on Saturdays for future on-air personalities, and that the station would give me a scholarship to cover all costs if I were interested. What the Hell, I was sixteen, and thought that was a terrific idea so I signed up. It only took two trips to my lessons to determine that this was not what I wanted to spend the rest of my life doing. I relinquished my scholarship, and my broadcast career careened into oblivion.

I should probably mention that I played the violin in the school orchestra. Sometime during either the fifth or sixth grade, my parents experienced a revelation from somewhere on high, that I should and would become a great violinist. Their reasoning, I think, was that if I could play a musical instrument, I wouldn't be forced to live the life of a factory laborer like both of them had been compelled to do.

I started lessons with a group of other beginners in Boynton Elementary School, and with the help of weekly private lessons, soon was able to join the school orchestra. I took lessons for two years or so before moving to Fossil. Fossil was not as sophisticated in such things, so while we lived there, I took a welcome two-year hiatus from the squeak box. I didn't like to play much, and I certainly didn't like to practice, so I welcomed a break in at least this one aspect of my life struggles.

When we moved back to Detroit, the lessons began again, this time in earnest. I became a member of Southwestern's orchestra as well as the Detroit All-City Orchestra, which was comprised of the top music students from all of Detroit's high schools. It truly was quite impressive.

The practices were one evening a week at Central High School near downtown Detroit, and I could get to that school with only one streetcar transfer. Four times a year we would have a grand concert, when parents and others could gather to admire their offspring or musical friends and relatives.

Although it seemed like overkill to me, my parents also arranged for me to have private lessons one night a week. These lessons were taken in the Wurlitzer Building near downtown Detroit. My private instructor was Mr. Tierri, an Italian who claimed that he had played for the Queen of England. Whether he in fact played for her remains in doubt to this day. In my opinion, Mr. Tierri was a superb con man. He certainly had my parents convinced that I was progressing remarkably well. He charged two dollars for a thirty-minute lesson. I figured that added up to an enormous four bucks an hour. This guy was getting rich by telling parents how wonderful their kids were.

I figured I could use the money much more wisely than he could, and so every third week or so, I would simply skip the lesson. I would ride my bike to the old neighborhood gas station, where my friends hung out in the evenings, buy a Coke, and just hang out until it was time for me to be arriving back home. It was a welcome break from Mr. Terri, and I was two dollars richer. I did have a twinge of guilt every so often, but somehow I always managed to overcome it.

Another unpleasant bit of "life in high school" occurred nearly every day. On my way to Mr. Breedlove's class, I would meet Rameriz, a Syrian kid that I knew, going in the opposite direction. Rameriz was also a paperboy in the same district but in a different branch office than mine. He also won big trips whenever the Times held a contest. In fact, he won first place in every contest, with so many new orders that no one could possibly match or surpass him. Everyone else simply forfeited first place to him. It was a given.

Rameriz was a cheat though, and no one liked him or

respected him. The week before a contest was to begin, he would canvass his own route, asking his customers if he could change their name on the records to the wife's maiden name. Then he would put in a stop order on the married name of the customer, while simultaneously entering a new "start" order using the maiden name. The following contest, he would simply reverse the process. On opening day of every contest, Rameriz would have 150 or so "new" orders. It was ridiculous, but he was only rewarded, never disciplined for it.

Anyway, Rameriz knew I was also a paperboy, and every day when we met in the hallway, he would punch me in the shoulder or upper arm. It wasn't just a love tap either. Those punches really hurt. Rameriz was not terribly tall, but he was very strong and built like a small gorilla. Blasting someone in the arm was his way of demonstrating recognition and machoness. I hated it. I hated him. One day, as I pushed my way through the milling throng of students, he hit me—hard. I hadn't seen him or his painful punch coming and it infuriated me. I spun around and ran after him, careening from one to another of the oncoming students. When I caught up to him he had his back to me and didn't see me coming. I slammed my scrawny fist into the middle of his back with all the force I could muster. I don't think I was thinking about anything—just revenge—and perhaps that he would back off then, like Jim had done in the paper station. Alas, I was wrong.

Rameriz turned around and hit me as hard as he could, right in the stomach. I hit the cold marble floor with a sickening thud as the air rushed out of my lungs. Rameriz sauntered off, smirking, but he never spoke to me or hit me again. Later, I reconstructed my thinking so I could believe that such an embarrassment was a small price to pay for eliminating the source of continuous, severe arm pain. I laid there for two or three minutes, gasping, trying to catch my breath, thinking surely I was going to die. The other students just walked around me, having seen such sights many times before in those hallways. Finally, I could breathe in a reasonably normal fashion. I got up and found my way to Mr. Breedlove's classroom. I don't think I learned any biology that day, and, as usual, I don't know if Mr. Breedlove looked at me during that period.

Drafting class was my favorite class. I was relatively compulsive in this dimension of my life, and could create mechanical drawings that were superb. Each day, at the end of the class period, the students would store their drawings, taped onto a large drawing board, in their designated slot in a storage wall behind locked glass-paneled doors. At the beginning of class one day, I was about to retrieve my drawing board, when another of my nemeses, Zoltan, showed up. Zoltan was a pretty big guy and was generally quiet and reasonable, but that day he was in a surly mood. I don't even remember exactly what it was he did to me, but when I hit him, he went crashing through one of the glass-paneled doors, breaking out three panes. We stopped fighting, realizing that there existed the remote possibility that we might be in some pretty serious trouble. We were.

In a few minutes, the instructor arrived. He surveyed the mess in his compulsively organized little classroom and gently requested that the responsible parties confess. Zoltan and I gave ourselves up. Our punishment quickly followed. We were required to remove the entire door and, with our own money, pay to have the glass replaced—and we were to do it right then. He told us where a glass shop was located—just about three miles down the street toward the center of Detroit. He said he would call the store and let them know we were coming.

Zoltan and I removed the door, which was about six feet high by a foot and a half wide, and with one of us on each end, carried it through our laughing classmates and out the door. The streetcar stop was right in front of the school. The next streetcar clanged to a stop and we loaded ourselves and our door into it. A few minutes later we disembarked and walked with the door half a block back to the glass shop. It didn't take long to repair our mess, but when we tried to board a return streetcar, the operator wouldn't let us get on his streetcar with it. Instead of waiting for a more favorable opinion from the driver of the next trolley, we obediently started walking the three miles back to school. We arrived shortly before school was finished for the day, but we had time to reinstall the door, and complete our amends. The teacher was smirking victoriously as we walked out. Actually, Zoltan and I became fairly good friends.

World History was a class I detested. All those irrelevant names and dates. I just had a Hell of a time getting through two semesters of it. I barely passed World History One with a "D-minus," the lowest possible passing grade. I remember that the first semester was taught by Mr. Simon, a very tiny Italian guy. As usual, I had a front row seat, but it was also in the row nearest the door, so I thought I could hide from Mr. Simon—at least a little bit. As he droned on and on, I would slowly slip down in my seat, prop the huge history book up in front of me and rest my eyes. Every so often I would fall completely asleep. One day I was abruptly awakened by the crashing noise of Mr. Simon's own textbook slamming onto my desk's top. I awoke with a start. The whole class had been watching as Mr. Simon slowly crept over to me. They all thought it was very funny. I didn't. In fact, I thought it was pretty rude. I still do. I tried World History Two with a different teacher.

Mrs. Gray, my dusty old teacher for the second semester of World History, was completely unforgiving of my unwillingness to do any of the written work for the class. She failed me cold with three consecutive "E" grades. I didn't like Mrs. Gray very much. Besides, I was really getting tired of this.

As I began gathering failing grades, I knew that such stellar performance would not be adequately explainable at home, so I created my own little subterfuge for the benefit of my parents. With my silver tongue, I used my oratorical skills to convince a cute little girl who worked in the school office that I needed a blank report card. From then on I simply filled in the grades I thought I deserved. That forged card became my ticket to peace at home for the remainder of my tour of torture at Southwestern High School. It had grades on it that any parent would have been proud of, mighty proud indeed.

I knew everything there was to know about Hammurabi's Code, the Pharaohs of Egypt, the Tigris and Euphrates, and so on, and on, and on. But it was a good thing that I had my own report card.

In the second semester of my junior year an event occurred that sent my little mind reeling. I was taking a typing class because I thought typing would be easier than writing all of my reports in longhand. In my second semester a kid named Rudy sat next to me. Rudy had an older brother who created, printed, and sold those little eight-page comic books which depicted our favorite cartoon characters like Maggie and Jiggs, Blondie and Dagwood, Tillie the Toiler, etc., in various forms of sexual behavior, normal and abnormal. We thought they were great, but except for Rudy, very few kids, including me, would dare keep any of them on our person. Anyway, these little books clearly demonstrated that Rudy's mind was beginning to rot at a very early age.

One day in class he decided to make up and then type some really awful things about one of the girls who was sitting directly in front of us. He thought his filthy diatribe was funny, but I didn't, and I told him so. However, Rudy decided to carry his assault on the girl a bit further. He arrived in class early the next day and left his composition in the girl's typewriter. When she read it she immediately reported it to the instructor.

I guess I must have been wearing my near constant guilty look because that afternoon I was called to the principal's office. He accused me of having written the pornographic piece. I denied it of course. I asked him why he would think that I had written such filth. He then told me that Rudy had told him that I was the guilty party, and that he was just an "innocent bystander." Good grief. No matter how much I protested, I was in the soup with him. The principal told me to bring my mother to school with me the next day—that he wanted to tell her what I had done—and why he was, therefore, expelling me at the end of the semester. Rudy lived with his older brother and had no parents, so he was to bring his brother, the actual creator and marketer of the little books. What a joke.

That night, after due deliberation and in a state of high anxiety, I related to Mom the whole sordid story. Luckily, she believed me. The next morning she and I left our little house, walked to the end of the streetcar line, and rode that clanging steel carriage to school without speaking. Our meeting with the principal didn't last long. He just told her that because he couldn't discern just who the guilty party was in this nasty little scene, neither kid would be allowed to enroll for his senior year there. I was done—finished—with Southwestern High School. Overall, although there are a few fond memories, it was not a pleasant time.

Chapter 36

THE TELEVISION STAR

IN 1949, television was just beginning to be available to the general population, and very few homes had it. We certainly didn't, but an acquaintance of my parents who lived several blocks away did have one. That fact was most fortuitous when I learned that I had been nominated by my station manager to appear on a televised sports quiz show sponsored by the Times. Dad was working, as usual, the night I appeared on television, and Mom walked to her friend's house so she could watch her little boy. I arrived at the television station in downtown Detroit at the appointed time for an explanation by the host of the show of what was going to happen and what the rules of the show were.

There were two kids from the West Side of Detroit, of which I was one, and two kids from the East Side. The East and West sides were teams that were to compete against each other. All of us kids were either fifteen or sixteen. We were seated in metal folding chairs in a kind of semi circle, with the host to our left and a television monitor directly in front of us. The host gave each of us a newspaper bag and fifteen papers to put in them. A sports picture, which had to do with the preceding week's sports coverage by the Times, would appear on the monitor. The first kid who could recognize the picture and recall the reason it was in the paper would yell, "**Times**." He would then get the first chance to explain just what that picture represented. Every time a kid answered correctly, the host would "buy" a paper from him for fifty cents, which he then got to keep. At the end of the show, we could buy sports equipment prizes that were displayed on a huge portable room divider. Prices for these prizes were ridiculously cheap, like fifty cents for a really nice bat, or a dollar for a glove or football.

I watched as one or another of the other boys would yell the required "**Times**," respond with an accurate answer, and become instantly wealthier. I didn't recognize *anything*. Finally, when the show was nearly over, I saw a picture I thought I recognized. "**Times**," I yelled.

"Glenn," the moderator replied to me. My response was automatic—what General Semanticists call a "signal reaction."

Whenever I was called upon in school, my signal reaction was to stand up to say whatever it was that needed saying. When the moderator called on me, my signal reaction slipped into gear. I started to stand to give my answer. The paper bag with its fifteen papers still intact, had slipped down through the opening between the back of the chair and its seat. As I rose, the paper bag caught on the chair, lifting it off the floor. It banged noisily into the back of my legs.

"Whoa," the moderator cautioned, "Just sit down, please."

I sat, embarrassed and blushing through my sweaty freckles—and gave my answer. It was *wrong*.

Nevertheless, it was a great experience, and I'll never forget it. I had been on TV. Even if no one else in the city of Detroit had seen me, my Mom had.

Chapter 37

BLOCK-BUSTING

DURING the spring of 1949, when I was fifteen, I witnessed one of the strangest phenomena ever seen in Detroit's social history. It was known as block-busting.

We were still living in that miserably hot converted attic of Anne and Frank's home, in the house that smelled of Absorbine Junior and beer. The segregation in housing of Blacks and Whites was in full bloom, and everyday people, like us, never gave such things a second thought. On the street just across the alley behind us, a residential district for Blacks began and then continued for five miles or so to the Detroit River. The homes were very much middle class and, as far as I knew, there were no current racial problems in the neighborhood—certainly not for several square blocks. The tensions of the recent race riots had eased somewhat, but not entirely.

My paper route consisted of six blocks of White homes on the street directly in front of our house. Even though the racial situation in our immediate neighborhood was relatively stable, there remained a palpable uneasiness—and trust between races would be a very long time developing.

During the war, millions of poor, uneducated Blacks and Whites moved from the South to cities in the North, where work was much more available to them in the factories producing the machines and materials needed for the war effort. Many of the Blacks thought they were being liberated from the oppression they had endured in the South, since folks in the North verbalized a much more liberal and "tolerant" view of them. They were wrong. Segregation in housing, restaurants, and social activities of all types was in full bloom. In restaurants in our neighborhood, Blacks were served their food on paper plates with disposable utensils. Why? Who knows. I guess that the owners of the restaurants didn't want to "contaminate" their White patrons by serving them food on plates the Blacks had used. I had a deep-seated feeling of uneasiness about this practice. Even though they endured these nasty racist behaviors, the Blacks who went to work in the factories did enjoy a significantly higher level of income than they had been accustomed to in the South—and they wanted to buy their own homes.

Everything appeared reasonably normal in our neighborhood until the spring of '49, when a Black family moved into one of the houses on my route. Almost immediately, the house next to it went up for sale, then the house across the street, then two or three houses adjacent to them. Like wildfire, panic sales moved down the six blocks of my route. Within a month, my entire paper route was busted.

The dynamics of this process were triggered when the first family sold their home to a black family. Actually, they didn't sell to a family, they sold to a real estate agent who offered them whatever it took to induce them to sell—sometimes it was twice the fair market value of their home, sometimes more. Then he would immediately resell it to a

Black family. When the Black family moved in, the block was busted. White neighbors became nervous, expecting that the value of their homes would fall, and values did fall. But they fell not because the Black family moved in—they fell because the White families (subsequent to the first one) took whatever they were offered—sometimes half, or less, of the real value of their homes. Real estate salespeople from both races swept in and purchased as many of the homes as they could, at incredibly depressed prices. They could turn their home purchases into sales to Black families almost immediately at outrageously inflated prices, making enormous amounts of money for themselves. During the height of the panic, I counted eighty homes for sale in the six blocks of my paper route.

As my route became increasingly "Black," the real estate people conducting this extraordinary social symphony would break a block on the next street, in this case, Annabelle Street. Next came Liddesdale Avenue, Electric and Edsel. The same anti-Black sentiment infected the entire neighborhood. It took about three years to complete the transition from White to Black in a residential area encompassing twenty-four city blocks containing close to eight hundred homes. It was one of the most startling and depressing aspects of human behavior I have ever witnessed.

The "busting" stopped at Fort Street, a major, six-lane boulevard. It took about two years for the Black community to digest this major housing coup—before jumping across Fort Street to continue the practice in the neighborhood where I had been raised as a child.

I visited my childhood neighborhood with my brother, Harland, one summer afternoon in 1975. He still lived in a nearby suburb and was willing to take me back "home." But my home no longer existed—either literally or figuratively. It had been torn down to make room for a new expressway. And, the remainder of the neighborhood I had known as a child had been transformed. Most of the block was still there, but it was a slum. It was filthy, with debris everywhere. Rusting car hulks were parked in driveways and front yards, and on the street. The homes had not been maintained, and nearly every one of them looked as though it should have been demolished. That pleasant neighborhood where Ramie and I had our rubber gun battles had faded into history. The dark present was the reality now. It was heartbreaking.

It wasn't safe to be sitting in a parked car in that neighborhood anymore, so we didn't spend much time reminiscing. I went away from that experience saddened and depressed. My sadness continues.

Chapter 38

FORD BOULEVARD

THE summer of 1950 was morbidly hot and humid, as summers always are in Detroit. We were living in our repulsive little rat house and becoming increasingly sharp and hostile with one another. Although we had lived there a year, none of us had ever invited our friends to visit us. We were ashamed of this explicit symbol of the economic depths to which we had descended.

Dad, though, was willing to work the afternoon shift to earn a few cents an hour more. With the additional income from his part-time moonlighting job as a chimney sweep we had managed to save enough money for a down payment on a little, $7,000 house in Lincoln Park. It wasn't much of a house, but it sure beat where we were. It had two bedrooms, a kitchen, a very small living room, a full bath, and no rats—only mice.

It had a small, enclosed back porch that smelled of rancid urine. The fellow we had bought the house from had kept two large dogs in that small enclosure and, I'm sure, hadn't cleaned, or even rinsed the floor in all of the seven years he had lived there. It was awful. The thick, acrid fumes would cut our wind and curl the hair in our nostrils as we passed through it. We immediately learned to hold our breath when entering or leaving through the rear door of the house.

Dad and I set about to tear out the flooring, but quickly discovered that we had to tear out the lower portion of all of the walls of the porch as well. The urine had saturated the floors and was creeping up the walls. This "Yellow Menace of the Canines" was on its way, I knew, to engulfing the entire dwelling. It was not pleasant work, helping Dad to tear out the urine saturated materials, but it didn't approach my septic tank experience. After that unholy event, I knew I was able to deal with most anything.

Our little home was set back on the lot so that the rear of the house was bordering on an alley. Since we were at the very end of the block, we also had an alley running alongside of the house, next to the windows in both bedrooms. Across the alley behind our house, was a vacant lot. The story was that contractors had tried to build on it, and would excavate for a basement or a foundation, only to find that their neat hole had filled itself in by the next morning. It was like quicksand and very unstable. After several attempts by different builders, the city condemned the lot so that any future builders would be saved this expensive, but predictable, agony. Folklore had it that in the olden days before the city of Lincoln Park existed, a team of horses and a wagon had disappeared into this quagmire. The driver of the team escaped a similar fate—but just barely.

Evidence that foreboding things were happening subterraneously kept appearing. For example, every spring of the nine years we lived there, a mound would grow in the center of the alley that bordered our bedrooms. I don't know how tall that mound would have gotten because I kept chopping it off before it got big enough to defend itself. Whenever it got high enough that the undercarriage of our car would catch on it, I would level it off with a shovel so it was even with the surface of the alley. The interior of the mound was foul. It was black and oily, and smelled of sulfur. I suspected that it was a putrid zit on the Devil's backside, but I could never really be sure about that. I'd trim it down four or five times a year and pray that our house would still be on the surface in the morning. And it always was. Other people though, weren't so fortunate.

The City of Lincoln Park drew its water supply from the Detroit River, that brown, stinking current on its way to attack life in Lake Erie. Lincoln Park's city fathers decided to build the city's own water purification plant. It was to be located a mile or so to the East from our house and would be used to filter and sanitize our water, rather than forever having to pay the City of Detroit for that service. Since the river was about five miles directly West of our home, a tunnel to carry the water about six miles long would have to be built. Construction for the caisson began, and almost immediately serious problems developed. Industrial accidents killed three men in the tunnel within the first few days. The excavation continued.

Three or four miles of tunnel had been completed when nearly unbearable, putrid, black, oily junk began erupting through the basement floors and walls of the residences and businesses within a two mile radius of the tunnel. Large, open holes and eruptions occurred in streets and vacant lots as well. It was a disaster. Sulfur fumes were roiling out of the ground at scores of sites throughout the area. Homes were being destroyed. Tunnel construction was stopped and all efforts were focused on stabilizing the ground.

The first, and as it turned out, only, effort was to pour concrete into the open holes. A continuous stream of concrete mixer trucks poured load after load of concrete into the holes. Only after thousands of truckloads had disappeared into these boiling cauldrons did the eruptions slow down and, finally, stop. The city fathers reconsidered the project, and ultimately abandoned it. Perhaps buying water from Detroit wasn't so bad after all.

My bedroom was right next to the festering alley. Across the alley was a field about seventy five feet or so wide, next to which was Dix Highway, a four lane major road that was the main highway between Detroit and Toledo, Ohio. There were traffic lights on Dix two blocks in both directions from our house, so day and night we were treated to the sounds of accelerating, burping, and backfiring semi-trucks, spewing their lung-killing diesel fumes. It was especially obnoxious at night when we were trying to get to sleep.

One night, about ten o'clock, I was home alone when there was a knock on the back door. I opened the door to find a drunken guy about thirty-five or so. He had backed his car into the field between our house and Dix in an attempt to turn around, and had gotten it mired in the oozing muck. He wanted to know if I would use our car to pull him out. I said, "You bet!" and leapt into my rescue mode. I backed our car to within a couple of feet of the front of his car and got out. It was fairly cold that evening and the guy had on a leather jacket. He dropped to his knees in the slop to attach the chain, and as he did so his jacket fell open and a .38 caliber revolver fell out of his shoulder holster into the mud. He grabbed the gun and jammed it back into his jacket, mud and all. I didn't say anything, but the hair on the back of my neck was screaming.

He finally fumbled his way to a secure hookup and I pulled him out. He burped a "thank you," and spun off down the alley toward more solid footing. I later found out that he was a policeman who was off duty that night and lived just ten houses or so up Ford Boulevard from us. Nevertheless, the impression he left me with that night was a bit more than somewhat terrifying.

Another evening I didn't see anything—I only heard the sounds—but that was quite enough. It was about ten o'clock one dark evening and I was having a late snack in the kitchen. "**Stop!—Stop!—or I'll shoot!**" I heard a voice call out—followed quickly by three quick explosions, "**Blam!—Blam!—Blam!**" And then it was quiet. I didn't know what happened out there in the alley, and I didn't want to know.

One night, around two a.m., the police, with their squad car sirens screaming, had trapped three teen age boys on the roof of a small supermarket directly across Dix from our house. The kids had tried to break into the market through a skylight and had tripped a silent alarm.

The police were there almost instantly. The boys wouldn't come down, so the fire department, with its long ladders, was summoned. As soon as the ladders were positioned two of the boys surrendered and came peaceably down the ladder. The third one, who had to have been playing life's game with less than a full deck, jumped from the rooftop. It was thirty or more feet to the ground, and as you might expect, he broke both knees. The cops scooped him up and off they went to the local hoosegow and hospital.

As the police cars and fire trucks disappeared into the night, I thought to myself, "Man, life just doesn't get much better than this." But it did.

Chapter 39

LINCOLN PARK HIGH SCHOOL

WHEN we moved from the rat house to Lincoln Park and I started school again in the fall of 1950, I realized that my hatred of school for the past eleven years was not simply an extended fluke—I really *did* hate school. I immediately started haranguing my parents to let me quit. I was seventeen and wanted to go to work for the Detroit Times as a "Jumper." Lincoln Park High School was a large school, but not even close to the size of Southwestern. There were probably around twelve hundred students there.

I was never an easy person to get out of bed in the morning. Combining that innate predisposition to remain in bed with my intense dislike for school made getting up in the mornings next to impossible. Mom would call and call, but I always needed just five minutes more. I was late to school nearly every day, and just about drove Mom nuts. In utter disgust one day, and with a fury she could easily summon, she tore back the covers and emptied a full tray of ice cubes into my nest. It was not pleasant, and it did get me up. From then on all she needed to do was rattle an ice cube tray in the kitchen and I would hit the floor running. I thought it was a great example of one trial learning on my part.

City buses ran by our house on Dix Highway every twenty minutes, but I generally was able to catch a ride by hitchhiking. Whether I took the bus or hitchhiked, I could get to within about a half mile of the school, and would then walk the rest of the way. My first class was at 8:00, and wouldn't you know, it was World History II—and it was my second time around. My seat was directly in front of the teacher, and I was late three or four times a week. It was impossible to creep into class unnoticed, so I would frequently just go to a little hangout a block or so away and have a donut and a cup of coffee while waiting for second—or third, period to start. The first two of the three grading periods I managed to garner E's again. God, I hated that daily work! I just refused to do it. I did manage to find some ways to amuse myself though, so the Lincoln Park High experience wasn't a total zero.

Just inside one of the entrances to the school was a sort of anteroom where students could stomp or shake off excess snow before entering the main classroom area. The room had a soft drink vending machine. When the appropriate amount of money was inserted, it would dispense a single paper cup through a chute into the filling area. The pop would pour directly into the cup, which was standing on a drain that would carry off any spillage into a small holding tank. My job, as I saw it, was to screw up the mechanisms of this great machine.

The solution to my self-assigned project was simple. I would reach up into the cup dispenser chute and remove one cup. I would then puncture the cup's bottom with several holes and shove it back up the chute, always making sure that it was seated properly. The next unsuspecting student who felt the need for a soft drink would insert the appropriate amount of money. When the stream of drink stopped, the student would reach in and remove the empty cup that the pop had passed quickly through on its way down the drain. It never failed to piss my victims off. I thought it was great.

As the end of the semester approached, I figured it was time to have a talk with the teacher. I asked her if there was any way I could pass this course. I told her I knew everything there was to know about World History II, and I really needed to pass this awful course. She responded,

"Glenn, if you get an 'A' on the final exam, I'll pass you with a D-."

I did just that, passing with a score of 98%. She kept her word and I was finally finished with that bit of nonsense.

The school had two graduations a year, one in December and one in June. I volunteered to do some work with the graduation gowns following the December ceremony for some required student activity credit. I borrowed our brand new family car to drive to the school that evening, a 1950 Oldsmobile 88. I did my bit with the gowns with my usual high degree of excellence and started home about eleven p.m.

I was scooting down the road about fifty miles an hour, heading home on Dix Highway, listening to Dragnet on the radio, and congratulating myself on the fact that I might soon be free of school (except for night school), employed with the Times, and have pockets overflowing with cash.

Suddenly, with no warning or signaling, a car approaching from the opposite direction made a left turn directly in front of me. I slammed on the brakes, but it was too late. I clipped the rear quarter panel of the car and careened out of control. The steering wheel spun back and forth violently as the car ricocheted wildly from one lane to another. I couldn't stop it. The car then took a crazy spin and shot off across both lanes into oncoming traffic. I crashed head on into a pickup truck with four people in its cab—and stopped.

I crawled out of the wreck and after a cursory check, it appeared to me that the people in the truck were uninjured. I ran back across the highway to where the car I had clipped had stopped.

The driver, a young guy, was apologizing, and his young, very pregnant wife was in the car, screaming hysterically. It was a very nasty scene. It was miraculous that not a single one of the seven people involved in that accident was seriously injured. Traffic slowed. Some drivers stopped to see if they could be of any assistance. Very quickly the police arrived. They took statements from everyone involved and arranged for a wrecker to tow our beautiful new smashed-up Oldsmobile to a wrecking yard. They put me in the police car, took me to their station house and called my home.

Dad had just gotten home from his afternoon shift, and in fact, had passed the accident scene on his way home. He didn't know then that it was his car and his son that had been involved in it. He immediately came down to the police station to take me home. It was very strange. He asked if I was hurt, and when I said that all I had was a broken thumb from the spinning steering wheel, he was silent. He spoke not a single word all the rest of the way home. When we got in the house, he said,

"I'm glad you're not hurt, Glenn," and we went to bed.

I was heartsick, scared, and guilty. My great day had turned into a festering heap of fecal matter.

The next day our insurance company inspected the car and reported to us that it could be repaired. It had been damaged severely, very nearly a total loss, but not quite. We gave the go-ahead to have it repaired and within a couple of weeks, it was almost as good as new and ready to roll again. But it wouldn't be rolling for long.

By December, 1950, I had finally persuaded Mom and Dad to let me quit high school to become a jumper for the

Times if I promised I would complete that last semester by attending night school after work. O.K.!

I immediately went to the principal to let him know that I wanted to quit school at the end of fall semester. "Right," he responded lackadaisically, and signed me out. He didn't ask me about why I was quitting school, or what my motivations or needs were, or anything else. He just signed the appropriate document and handed it to me. I was free at last.

Chapter 40

THE JUMPER

THE Times had two types of delivery vehicles for getting its papers to its customers. One category of trucks was comprised of huge, two-and-a-half-ton staked trucks that delivered whole bundles of papers to home delivery substations, where paperboys would complete the delivery process to individual homes. The trucks in this fleet were known, oddly enough, as "big trucks."

The second type was a fleet of pickup trucks. In keeping with the sophisticated truck nomenclatures adopted by the Times, these vehicles were known as "small trucks." The small trucks all had specific routes throughout the city and suburbs. They delivered papers to street stands and retail outlets, such as small grocery stores, drug stores, or any other type of store whose owner could be convinced that selling papers in his store would be good business. All drivers purchased their own trucks and had them painted orange, with *The Detroit*

Times emblazoned on the side in black paint, the standard for Times trucks. All drivers had a jumper assigned to them.

The term jumper evolved out of the small truck operation, and was an apt term. Jumpers assigned to small trucks spent most of their workday standing on the truck's running boards, counting and organizing papers in the bed of the truck. The passenger window of the truck was open at all times when the jumper was clinging precariously to the side of the truck, getting prepared to "jump" off of the moving vehicle and run the papers in to the next sales site. Depending on the manicness of the driver, the trucks would slow down or stop to allow time for the jumper to jump off of the truck, deposit his papers appropriately, pick up unsold papers from the last edition, and jump back on the running board. In fact, most of the time the jumper would be back on the running board before the truck ever stopped. The jumper would tie returns in bundles of fifty for credit back at Times headquarters in downtown Detroit.

In the summer, the work for the jumper was stiflingly hot and humid—in the winter, unbearable cold. Actually, it was a horrible job—and dangerous. During the year that I worked as a jumper, three jumpers were killed—two by falling off of their trucks in traffic—one by being crushed against the loading dock by a truck driver who didn't see him. But, it paid exceptionally well. I started at $1.93 per hour, significantly more that my Dad was earning after what seemed like an eternity at Ford's. He was a little piqued at that.

Jumpers on "big" trucks worked hard, but were at least reasonably warm in the winter, and didn't have to worry about hitting the pavement at fifty miles an hour. They rode in the cab of the truck with the driver until it was time to off-load a substation's quota of bundles. Since all substation managers came from the ranks of the jumpers, I knew that being a jumper was where I would need to start my career climb with the Times. However, I couldn't go to work as a jumper if I was still in school. That's why I pestered my parents to let me quit.

Since jumpers had to be eighteen and I was still only seventeen, I had to lie to the Times about my age. The lying bothered me only until I knew for sure that the paper wasn't going to make me prove my age.

In January of 1951, I left school and started work as a jumper for the Times. I started as number twenty-five on the "extra list," which meant that twenty-five jumpers had to be absent for me to work. There were many weeks in the first two months in which I only worked a day or two. Sometimes none. Nevertheless, I had to be at the Times loading dock every morning at 8:00 a.m. to see if I was needed that day. By 8:30, I would know, and would usually have to hitchhike or take the streetcar back home.

Fairly quickly though, as jumpers quit, were killed or crippled or were promoted to managers of branch offices, I moved up on the extra list. It seemed like no time before the number of workdays had increased to full time employment—forty hours a week. My net paycheck for a full week was $64.44. The first two or three times I had a full week's work, I would go to a nearby bank to cash my check, and get it all in singles. What a wad! I was rich beyond belief! Was life great or what? Well, close to great, anyway.

One of the other jumpers, an Italian fellow named Zackaradelli (Zach), who was about twenty-three and very sophisticated from my perspective, suggested to me one payday that we might go shoot a few games of pool. Since I had honed my pool shooting skills to a keen edge in Fossil, I thought it was a terrific idea. He took me to a pool hall that must have been the Mother of all Pool Halls. It was the entire second floor of a block long building fairly close to the Times building. We climbed the wooden stairs, and as we entered the pool hall, I was overwhelmed by the vastness of it all. It was dimly lit, with most of the light coming from single pool table lamps illuminating each table. There must have been nearly a hundred tables, pool tables, snooker tables, and billiard tables. There were no women. This was a very serious man's domain.

After a few games of sloppy pool, Zack suggested that it might be fun to play for money. In my blithering naivete, I agreed. Zack let me win occasionally, but only when he wanted to. It took just about an hour for him to have my entire paycheck. Zack smiled and said,

"Now there's a lesson for you. Never play pool for money."

To drive the lesson home, he kept all of my money. From my point of view, the lesson had been overlearned.

Even so, I admired Zack greatly. After his day's work at the Times, he hired himself out as a bodyguard for whomever the winner was at a nightly floating poker game. He would escort the winner safely to his home, always clearly stating that there was no fee for the service. The big winners invariably tipped him generously though, sometimes a hundred dollars—sometimes more. I thought he was terrific.

Another memory that has stayed with me forever was the week that I substituted for the jumper who had the route containing one half of the Ford Rouge Plant. Every afternoon, between two and three o'clock in the afternoon, the day shift would end, disgorging thousands of production workers from the plant. We couldn't possibly deal with selling papers individually to the horde of sweating humanity that streamed around us, especially at two separate gates. So the driver and I set up a four by six-foot wooden folding table at each gate and stacked papers on them. Then we just sat back and watched the workers filing out of the plant. Some, about three hundred at each gate, would pick up a paper and drop a nickel on the table. Many needed change for larger coins or bills, and just took what they needed.

When the stampede was over, the driver and I picked up the money and any papers that might be left from both gates and retired to a neighborhood tavern to have a cool drink and count the money. It was unbelievable! With the thousands of papers sold that week, we were never short more than five cents on any day. Usually we were right on. I've never seen anything like that before or since. It certainly says something rather profound about the fundamental integrity and honesty of the working men and women in those days. I suspect things may have changed.

At the same time that I started jumping, I began night school. I elected to go to two different schools simultaneously because I was determined to keep my promise to Dad and finish high school. I also wanted to do it in the shortest possible length of time, and I couldn't get both of the classes I needed at just one of them. One of the schools, Cass Technical Institute, was very close to downtown Detroit and relatively easy to get to after a day of jumping and running through Detroit traffic, sucking exhaust. The other school, Northern High, was a considerable distance out on Woodward Avenue, the arterial that separated Detroit's East Side from its West Side, a very significant distinction for Detroiters.

I attended classes four nights a week, which was a cinch if I hadn't jumped that day. But when I had, it was quite a process. The driver would say "so long" at the end of his route, wherever that might be and I'd be on my own. I would check the addresses on the businesses and find a bus or streetcar heading in the direction in which the numbers were decreasing. That meant that I was heading, at least generally, toward downtown Detroit. Sometimes I would hitchhike. (As a footnote, I might add that in all the time I hitchhiked around Detroit, I never had a problem of any kind. It was a different time then.)

Classes began at 7:00 in the evening and lasted until 9:30. I would generally get to either Cass or Northern about six. I'd head for the latrine, strip off my sweaty shirt and try to wash the newsprint off my hands, arms and face in one of the sink basins. I still remember the smell of that awful green liquid soap and the brown paper towels I used to dry off with. Then it was time for class.

The class I took at Northern High School was a Literature class. All of my classmates were considerably older than I was—most of them were thirty or more years old. One lady was seventy. She had been working on her high school diploma just about her entire life after she immigrated here from Italy. It was in this class that I experienced something I had never enjoyed before. I was applauded for a poem I read in class one night. It was a poem that my Dad had recited to me from his memory, and I had found it in a dusty old book purely by accident. I thought it was wonderful. I pulled myself up as tall as I could in front of the class, and began my recitation:

FIFTY CENTS

I took my girl to a ball last night, 'twas such a fancy hop.
We stayed until the folks went home, the music it did stop.
Then to a restaurant we went, the finest on the street.
She said she wasn't hungry, but this is what she'd eat:

A dozen raw, a plate of slaw, some fancy Boston roast,
Some turtle stew, crackers, too, some soft-shelled crab on toast.
Next she tried some oysters fried; her appetite was immense!
She asked for pie! I thought I'd die, for I had but fifty cents!

After eating all of this she smiled so very sweet.
She said she wasn't hungry at all, and wished that she could eat;
But the very next order that she gave, my heart within me sank.
She said she wasn't thirsty, but this is what she drank:

A brandy, a gin, a big hot rum, a schooner of lager beer,
Some whiskey skins and two more gins did quickly disappear.
A bottle of ale, a soda cocktail, she astonished all the gents!
She called for more, I fell on the floor, for I had but fifty cents.

To finish up, this delicate girl cleaned out an ice cream can.
She says, "Now, Sam, I'll tell mama you're such a nice young man."
She said she'd bring her sister along next time she came, for fun.
I handed the man my fifty cents, and this is what he done:

He broke my nose, he tore my clothes, he knocked me out of breath.
I took the prize for two black eyes, he kicked me most to death.
At every chance he made me dance, he fired me over the fence.
Take my advice: don't try it twice, when you have but fifty cents.

The whole class stood, and while cheering, gave me my first standing ovation. What a feeling!

But back to my climb up the Times' corporate ladder.

I had to get to be number one on the extra list before the next step was possible. The next step would be a route of my own—and union membership. I never made it.

One fine afternoon in December, 1951, I was doing my thing with the papers in the bed of the truck. I was standing on its running board as it sped fifty miles an hour down the highway, heading for downtown Detroit. I finished my frigid tasks and began to move up the running board so I could put my head inside of the truck cab. I had just reached the window and had both hands on the sill when I slipped off of the icy running board. Instinctively, I held on to the sill and screamed. My feet and lower legs hit the pavement racing beneath me and bounced up. Again and again, my legs crashed into the concrete just ahead of the truck's rear tires. Luckily, the driver immediately saw what was happening and began to slow the truck gradually enough so that I wouldn't be catapulted from my precarious hold. When the truck finally stopped, my legs were both seriously injured, but not broken. The ligaments in both legs had been badly torn though, and I wasn't ever able to return to jumping.

Although I was close to the top of the extra list, I was not yet in the jumper's union. I had no representation and was forced to quit. I was devastated. I was eighteen, my legs were torn up, I had no job, and as far as I could see, I had no future. The only thing I had ever wanted to do was work for the Times—and now that wasn't possible. I went home to nurse my wounds, physical and psychic.

Chapter 41

BWANA DEVIL

IT was a brilliant sunny day in the late spring of 1952. I had begun to successfully sell "Kirby Sanitation Systems" and had money in my pocket, when I found myself developing a growing need for some potato chips. I entered the local Neisner ten-cent store where I knew I could buy a quarter's worth of chips from their bulk bin in the candy department. It was hot in the store—very hot. Air conditioning was extremely rare, and certainly didn't exist in any of the Neisner stores. The doors were open to allow the accumulating heat and vapors from the oiled wooden floor to escape into the street.

I recognized the pretty face of the smiling blond clerk. She had gorgeous, naturally wavy, blond, shoulder length hair and really was quite lovely. She had been in my English class at Lincoln Park High School, but we had never spoken.

"What can I get you?" she asked pleasantly.

"I'll have a quarter's worth of your finest potato chips," I responded with a twinkle in my eye.

When this major transaction was completed, I struck up a conversation with her, and between bites of chips, managed to wrangle a date to see the latest rage movie, "Bwana Devil," with her. Bwana Devil was the very first 3-D movie, and it was playing at one of downtown Detroit's majestic theaters.

The advertising budget for this new type of film must have been enormous. Ads were everywhere, in all media, newspapers, radio, and billboards. Robert Stack was the leading man and Alice Hayward was the leading lady. The story was written by Arch Oboler, one of radio's and Hollywood's most prolific and respected writers. Gordon Jenkins, one of the finest arrangers and musicians in the country, had written the musical score. With all of this, the movie was horrible. It had a very weak story line and Robert Stack gave an almost unbelievably blank, wall-eyed performance. It should never have been released, but we sat through it and we each finished our box of popcorn.

When we left the theater, we went to the parking garage where we had left Dad's sparkling, emerald green Olds '88. We found the car and got in. She said, "Did you notice those two guys standing back against the wall in the shadows?"

"No, I didn't see them," I replied. "But in Detroit there are always guys lurking in the shadows."

I thought no more about it, started the car, and wound my way down three stories of the garage and out into the night. I knew the city quite well and moved that great car almost silently through its bustling boulevards and avenues until I was back on Fort Street, the main drag back to Lincoln Park.

We had traveled perhaps two miles south on Fort Street, when she turned to me and said, "I think those two guys from the parking garage are following us."

I glanced in the rearview mirror. Sure enough, there was

a car directly behind us, but I didn't know whether or not it was following us, or just there. I sped up a bit. The driver of the car following us also sped up. I slowed down so he could pass. He slowed down. It was clear that this fool really was following us. I picked up speed again, and so did he. Fort Street had two lanes of traffic going in each direction, streetcar tracks between them, and a parking lane on each curbside. Traffic wasn't heavy that night, but it wasn't particularly light either. I started weaving in and out of traffic as I began to overcome and pass cars that were traveling the speed limit of thirty miles an hour. The car behind us remained right on our tail. Now I was getting worried.

Within three blocks I was hitting eighty miles an hour, running red traffic lights and slowing only a bit at major intersections. The car matched us, stupidity for stupidity. I was terrified. My date thought it was great fun. She suggested I turn off of Fort Street and onto one of the side streets, which were residential streets, and lose them.

"Are you nuts," I screamed at her. "It would be too easy for us to get trapped in a neighborhood we don't know."

We roared along, fast approaching Southwestern High School and approaching more familiar territory. I knew there was a police precinct station house at the corner of Fort & Green, just two blocks from the school and directly across the street from my favorite hamburger joint—Motts.

We finally reached Green Street—I slammed on the brakes and with tires screaming, spun around the corner and slid to a stop right in front of the police station's open garage doors. The driver of the car following us apparently didn't know this neighborhood—but he did recognize a police station—and continued on his way down Green Street and disappeared into the night.

The one time in my life that I wanted a policeman, there were none to be seen, not even at the Fort and Green precinct station. Good grief. Rear tires screaming and smoking, I backed out of their driveway and headed for home. I had seen a horrible movie, had the Hell scared out of me, and found out that this beautiful girl might be just a little bit strange. I guess the evening hadn't been a complete waste.

She was with me again on a very nice, sunny, summer afternoon when I was confronted with another piece of Detroit's violence. We were simply traveling south on Fort Street when we stopped for a traffic light. Another car stopped on our right. The driver got out, ran around the front of my car, reached through my open window, and grabbed the front of my shirt. He jerked me violently toward him, crashing my head into the steel lining along the upper portion of the window frame. He held me there and screamed in my face, "If you ever play games with me again, I'll break you apart!"

Then he let go of my trembling body, ran back to his car and sped off. I never knew what that was all about, but such events always tended to take the edge off of my day.

Chapter 42

DEATH RIDES THE NON-SKEDS

IT was the first of February, 1952. The ground was covered with a three day old layer of snow, which in turn, was covered with a fine coat of soot from the factories, stores, and residence's coal furnaces. I was eighteen, had bum legs, and out of work. I was beginning to know what depression feels like.

I had just completed an evening of feigned frivolity at Kelly's Drug Store, and was having a chat with one of my neighborhood friends, Jeno. It turned out that he, too, was not happy with the way his life was going, even though he had a job on the assembly line of Ford's Rouge Plant, and had a year old Chevy Bel-Aire. Nevertheless, he was depressed. I later found out that he was beginning what was to be a lifetime battle with clinical depression.

I don't remember how we got around to it, but we decided we should go to California to seek our fortunes. We had friends and relatives along the route, so we could sponge free room and board here and there. What the Hell. Let's do it.

It was very cold that February morning in Detroit. There was snow on the ground, but the sun was shining brilliantly. "A good omen," I though to myself as I finished up my last minute packing details. Jeno pulled his car up to our back door and honked. Mom and Dad were very sad. I kissed Mom goodbye—and then Dad. He was crying. I had never seen him cry before.

"I guess I haven't made a very good home for you, have I," he said through his tears.

"No,—no, Dad, its not that at all. Its just that its time for me to leave. I need to try my wings."

At that point, though, I very nearly changed my mind. Ambivalence swirled through me, and we hugged each other tightly. But I couldn't not go now, could I? I grabbed my scruffy suitcase and coat and stepped through the door they had opened for me. I threw my stuff in the trunk of Jeno's car, waved goodbye, and we were off.

Our first stop was in Cairo, Illinois, about 590 miles almost due south of Detroit. Jeno had an aunt living there and we could get something to eat. We arrived at their doorstep at 2:30 a.m. Not very good planning. He didn't want to awaken them, so we tried to get a little sleep in the car.

Jeno curled up on the back seat and was soon snoring loudly. I was left to my own devices in the front seat. I wound up with my body tortuously twisted. My lower body was crammed into the passenger seat footwell with my head resting on the seat. It was grotesquely uncomfortable and painful.

Finally, lights came on in the upper flat where they lived. Old Auntie was really surprised when she answered our knock and found us two things standing there. With true Southern hospitality, she invited us in. She was about to prepare breakfast, and true to Jeno's promise, graciously offered to share it with us. They were having fried eggs, bacon and grits with gravy.

We were starving. We sat down at the kitchen table with the rest of the family, seven in all, and prepared to placate our growling guts. I hadn't realized just how far south we were. What Auntie set before us just about made me vomit. The thickly sliced bacon had merely been warmed up. It was raw. The eggs had been very briefly dipped in hot pork grease and then served. They were raw, too, and covered with grease as well. I had never seen grits before, but I was able to eat a few of them. Jeno scoffed up this raw, greasy mess as if it was really good food. He loved it. I could see that our paths were beginning to diverge. We both took a short nap and hit the road again.

We were anxious to get to Hollywood, where Jeno's cousin, Bert, had a job and a room. We figured we could hang out with him until we both got jobs and could afford our own place. We barreled across Arkansas, Oklahoma, and the Texas panhandle, taking turns driving and sleeping. We drove that purring Chevy day and night, stopping only for gas and a sandwich here and there until we reached Phoenix, Arizona. That was our next stop for any real rest. The weather had been getting progressively warmer, and by the time we reached Phoenix, we were enjoying seventy degrees or more. It was wonderful.

We had arranged before we left Detroit to meet up in Phoenix with Jack, another guy about our age from our block in Detroit. We rendezvoused successfully and decided to take a slight detour and shoot up to Las Vegas, where another friend of ours, Gordy, was a staff sergeant stationed with the Air Force at Nellis Air Force Base. Gordy and his wife, Ilene, lived in off base quarters—a very nice little stucco house in a military housing development three miles or so from the base. They seemed happy to see us, so we moved in and stayed for three days and nights. It was great. They fed us wonderful meals, but we were all so socially inept that we never even thought about contributing to the cost of the groceries.

Every evening after dinner, we would all load up in Jeno's car and do the Strip. This was 1952, remember, and Las Vegas was very, very tiny compared to what it has become. Nevertheless, it did have several gigantic casino/hotels, like the Flamingo, the Sahara, and several others. Ilene had worked as a shill for several of the casinos so she knew her way around the strip. All of the hotels had big name Hollywood stars like Penny Singleton (who played Blondie in the Blondie and Dagwood movies), Carmen Miranda (a Latin singer with the trademark fruit basket hat), and many others. Each of them had a show that lasted about an hour and a half, so we could see three shows a night, just for drinks. We would each order a forty-cent beer and nurse it throughout the whole show. Then we'd move on to the next casino and repeat our little act. I was only eighteen, but I was only asked for proof of age one time during our entire tour. The waitress looked at my driver's license, handed it back to me, and served me my beer. She either couldn't add, couldn't read, or didn't really care. Perhaps all three.

On our first night there, I walked by a dime slot machine and decided to drop in the only coin I had. Voila! I hit the jackpot for seventeen dollars. I was rich! Luckily, Ilene said she'd hold my money for me and ration it out to me at five bucks a day, so it lasted for the entire time we were there. I don't know whether our sponge-like stay had anything to do with it, but soon after we left Gordy and Ilene broke up.

After the road we had traveled, we consumed the next bit of highway in what seemed like no time at all, and arrived at Bert's Hollywood rooming house around eight in the evening. Bert only had one bed, which he shared with Jeno, Jack took the couch, and I, being the lowest on this particular totem pole, slept on the floor. Although the days were warm and sunny, the nights were quite cool. I covered up with the only thing available, a filthy throw rug, and spent the night breathing whatever bacteria-laden horrendousness decided to leave the rug for the warm, moist haven of my nostrils.

The next morning, Jeno and I located our own room. It was very nice, located in an old residential district of Hollywood, surrounded by palm trees. We each had our own single bed to sleep on, and the bathroom was down the hall.

That afternoon, Jeno took me to the offices of the Los Angeles Examiner, the Time's sister Hearst paper, where I thought I might be able to find work, given the way I had excelled for the Times. I was wrong. They had nothing. However, they did offer me an opportunity to sell a life insurance policy available for five cents a week to all Examiner subscribers. They promised a commission of one dollar for every policy I sold. It wasn't much, but it was something. Jeno dropped me off on a street of apartment buildings and said he would come back for me in two hours, which he did. In the interim, I must have knocked on a hundred doors. I talked to many people. I sold nothing. I quit.

My next stop was at the Good Humor ice cream Company. I thought I might be able to sell a few ice cream bars in that glorious, warm city. I was wrong. Good Humor required its drivers to be at least twenty-one years old, and being eighteen, I didn't think I could wait that long. I soon found out that almost all employers required their workers to be twenty-one.

I was beginning to get seriously distressed about my career potential in Hollywood, when three days after arriving, I came down with the flu. It no doubt had been precipitated by that great stuff from Bert's rug. My distress accelerated. I was so sick I could barely see. My eyes ached when I moved them even just a little bit. My lungs were congested and I was spewing things never before seen in the medical world. My hair hurt. I was a mess.

It was nearly two weeks before I was well enough to begin thinking that it would be better to live than to die. I decided that my future did not lie in Hollywood and placed a collect phone call home. I asked Mom if she would cash in one of my insurance policies for whatever it was worth, and to send the check to me as soon as possible

A few days later, the check arrived and Jeno rushed me to the nearest bank to cash it. The teller said they would cash it, but it would take three days before they could be sure it had cleared and give me the money. I didn't need the money three days from then. I needed it *right now*. Well, that just wasn't possible.

Neither Jeno nor I had any money, except for a nickel that I had. We hadn't eaten all day so we stopped at a little neighborhood grocery store to see what we could get to eat for five cents. After due deliberation, we settled on a package of devils food Hostess Cup Cakes. We opened the package and each took one. We ate it slowly and deliberately so as to savor the flavor. Jeno immediately got sick and vomited all over the sidewalk. He was coming down with my flu. We crawled back into his car and crept slowly away from the curb. On the way back to our room, I said to Jeno, "When we get back to our rooming house, I'll call an airline and see if it will take this check toward the price of a ticket to Detroit."

Sure enough, Northwest Orient Airlines said they'd be happy to take the check and that their next flight would be at 4:00 p.m. We had just enough time to make it. I packed my bag, said farewell to my lovely sickroom and jumped back into the car.

We arrived at the Northwest counter thirty minutes or so before take-off time. I bought my ticket with my heretofore uncashable check and even got some change. I loaned Jeno twenty bucks and said goodbye.

The time for loading approached—and passed. Then there was an announcement over the loudspeaker that the departure would be delayed an hour. I bought a magazine and settled down to wait. At five o'clock there was another announcement. The flight was again delayed an hour. It happened again at six and seven o'clock. I went to the Northwest counter and asked what was wrong.

"Nothing is wrong," the agent replied. "This is a non-scheduled flight. We just wait until we have a profitable load and then we take off. You'll probably get out of here around eight."

What the Hell? I'd never heard of such a thing. No wonder the price was right. I picked up a newspaper to pass some time reading the national news. The headline screamed out at me: **Death Rides the Non-Skeds."** My heart was racing as I read the article. Apparently there had been a rash of airline crashes recently of non-scheduled flights, just like the one I was about to take. Oh, boy. What to do. Well, there really wasn't any alternative, and at eight o'clock, I boarded with the rest of my goofy compatriot travelers. We rumbled down the runway and took off, climbing steeply to a height just barely adequate to clear the mountains and headed east.

I was still hacking and spewing and blowing my nose, when, about a half-hour into the flight, a male steward brought us all a box lunch. I consumed my dry sandwich and apple and tried to settle down to sleep the rest of the flight. My sleep was fitful. I was coughing a lot. I was miserable.

Finally, the sun broke over the horizon, and its light began streaming into the cabin of the plane through the right front windows. Then the sun unexpectedly began moving. It seemed to be traveling to our right, toward the rear of the plane. Finally, its light was streaming in from the left rear windows. We had turned completely around! What the Hell? Then the announcement of the Captain:

"We ran into some unexpected turbulence and

headwinds last night. We used a lot more fuel that we had anticipated, so we're landing in Montana to refuel."

We landed at a tiny, unattended airport somewhere on the northern plains of Montana. The runway was covered with nearly two feet of fresh snow, which we hit at about 150 miles an hour. We stopped almost instantly. It was a serious jolt. The Captain spoke again, telling us that he had radioed for someone to come out and refuel us—clear the runway from snow—and that we would soon be off again. About an hour later we were in the air again, heading for Detroit.

We landed at the Detroit City Airport, and I dragged my coughing, spewing body out of the plane and into a taxi. It was still early in the morning when I arrived home. Mom was glad to see me, even if I was a mess, and made me a decent, fully cooked breakfast. Then I disrobed and fell into my own warm familiar nest, where I stayed for a week, recuperating from my adventure. When Dad arrived home from work that evening, we had a great reunion. He was happy that I was home again, but I'm sure had mixed emotions since I had tried my wings, and they had failed me. Now what?

Chapter 43

A SANITATION SYSTEM

(AND BEAT IT IF YOU CAN)

WHEN I had rested and recuperated from my trial trip into the "real world" with Jeno, I started looking for work again. I saw an ad for draftsmen in the Help Wanted section of the Times. Since I had some minimal level of talent in mechanical drawing, I swung myself into the next streetcar and headed for downtown Detroit. The organization I was applying to was a subcontractor for Chrysler Motors. They had the entire second floor of a building that was a city block long. There were more than a hundred drafting tables, with men hunched over them as far as I could see. I got the job and went directly to work. They supplied everything, pencils, T-squares, slide rules, and erasers for the occasional error I might decide to correct.

I was assigned to a senior draftsman who was creating a

drawing that would become the blueprint for the manufacture of an automobile engine block washing machine. The job paid two bucks an hour, and because they were in a rush mode, my workweek was ten hours a day, six days a week. Heavy. But, I was making $120 bucks a week—not bad for an eighteen-year-old beanpole.

However, sixty hours a week quickly became an exhausting pace especially for my bony hind end, perched on a wooden stool for ten hours at a crack. I started looking at the help wanted ads again. I found an ad that was extremely interesting. It talked about the enormous money that could be made selling some unnamed, mysterious product. It was what's known as a "blind ad." The address of the office that applicants were to report to was right down the street from my house, so I took a day off from my drafting job to answer the ad. I wanted to learn about this miracle product and the fortunes to be made peddling it.

I arrived at 9:00 a.m. on the morning designated in the ad, and although the place smelled strangely of mothballs, nothing about the premises gave me a clue about what the product might be. About fifteen other guys showed up as well. Then Al appeared. Al was twenty-four years old, with a chronic sinus condition. But he was a very friendly fellow and extremely articulate, even if his words sounded as though they were coming through his nose. He spoke softly and confidently and none of us could help but like him right off. He stepped behind a draped table, under which the "mystery product" was concealed, and began his pitch.

He brought out a glistening chrome plated aluminum Black & Decker motor and talked convincingly about its merits for at least twenty minutes. The next piece he revealed tipped us to the fact that it was a vacuum cleaner he was talking about. Al put on a wonderful "show" for two-and-a-half hours, without ever repeating himself. He seemed absolutely convinced that he had the greatest machine ever conceived, right there, before our very eyes. He convinced a lot of us, too. He built the value of that machine with a marvelous story about its every component. Its cord, for example, was twenty-two feet long, so it only needed to be plugged in one time to clean the entire first floor of the average home. The fine strands of copper wire were wrapped in silk fibers and then covered with a vulcanized rubber exterior coating that would last forever. And so the spiel went—on and on.

By the time he had finished, I knew I could clean carpets like they had never been cleaned before. I could also shampoo the carpet, wax the linoleum and hardwood floors with the floor polisher, sharpen knives and polish silverware with the "Handi Butler." I could also demoth closets with the "Crystalizer," a small, red plastic container that attached to the intake of the cleaner. The crystalizer was filled with "paradiclorobenzine" crystals (moth crystals) which would then be sucked into the whirling fan blades (6,000 rpm!), exploded, and blown out the vacuum's exhaust port. What a concept! To be moth-free and clean, too, and have sharp knives. What could be better? He certainly convinced me. I bought one on the spot for $188.80, including $5.50 for state sales tax. Everyone who showed up in answer to the ad wanted to be a Kirby salesman.

Al pulled out an "Aptitude Test," which we all took. Several of the least desirable applicants were weeded out because they "didn't pass the aptitude test." I later found out from Al that this was a ruse used to eliminate those applicants he didn't want to hire. He said he took a chance on me, even though he had never hired anyone so young before, because he knew I would be just great once I learned the techniques. And I was.

Mom thought I was crazy when I brought the shiny, very heavy vacuum cleaner home, but I knew I had made a deft financial move—and, more likely than not, she would learn to love it. Wrong again. She hated that machine from the moment she saw it until she died, decades later.

Because I was working sixty hours a week drafting, only the evenings were left to learn the machine's wondrous attributes and to put together a show of my own for Mrs. Housewife, USA. I watched Kenny, who was my district manager, put on a couple of shows, and I was ready. Our telephone solicitor made an evening appointment for me and I showed up at the house, showered, shaved and shined. I was full of stories about the multitudinous advantages awaiting this fine lady when she became the proud owner of a "Kirby Sanitation System."

It was a unit in the projects. Only poor people lived in the projects, and I suspected that this might be hopeless. I took a deep breath, thought "What the Hell, it'll be good practice, anyway," and knocked on the door. A frail lady about thirty-five years old in a very worn-thin cotton dress invited me in—and the show began.

The very first thing I did was explain why it was important for her to have that sturdy, stainless steel 3/4 horsepower power plant as the heart of her new cleaning system, even though there wasn't a carpet in sight—only linoleum with black paths worn in its veneer. Bit by microscopic bit I went through a mini-performance about every single thing I could think of about this beautiful machine's motor. During this time I was squatting and my knees began to ache. I stood up and my legs started to shake violently. Perhaps I was more scared than I thought. I quickly dropped again to my squat and continued.

I soon came to the "Crystalizer" part of my spiel. I filled the unit with moth crystals and asked her where there was a closet so that I could demonstrate how simple it would be to exterminate all undesirable life in her closets. She said she had no closets with doors on them, only cloth curtains. That wouldn't do, so I suggested we use her bathroom. I had two purposes in mind. One, I would ask her to get the machine after it had been running in there for a couple of minutes and she would see how light this little motor was; and two, she would get a first hand whiff of that horrible, noxious gas that had been created in her bathroom.

She agreed to the bathroom idea, and I set up the machine, turned it on and shut the door. I chatted aimlessly with her for two minutes, pulled the plug from the wall, and asked her to step into the bathroom and retrieve the Kirby, which she did. Then I asked her if I could open the bathroom window, so as to let those horrible fumes escape to the outside.

"My window doesn't open," she replied, squinting at me through watering eyes. "It's nailed shut."

Oh, boy. Why hadn't I checked that. On the other hand, who nails their bathroom, or, for that matter, any of their windows shut? Quickly, the house filled with paradiclorobenzine gas. It was awful. We did open the doors for some ventilation, but the gas had permeated everything. Not good–not good at all.

On with the show. Since she didn't have any rugs, I polished what was left of her kitchen floor, and with the rug nozzle, pulled some horrendous stuff from her couch and far too much body ash from her mattress.

"How much is that machine?" she asked. I told her. I also said that I would give her $10.00 trade in allowance for her broom, and—I would let her keep the broom. Wow. That was just too good. "Okay," she said, and peeled off $188.80 in cash for me.

I couldn't believe it. It was my first demo. It was in the "poor" projects. I had completely screwed it up and damn near gassed us. She had no carpets. But, I sold it, and made myself $45.00 for two hours work. I figured that was a lot better than the $2.00 an hour I was making as a draftsman, so I quit that job the next day and went to work full time as a Kirby salesman.

At 8:00 a.m. the next morning I showed up for work. There were about twenty salesmen in the meeting room, all sitting in folding chairs waiting for Al to call the sales meeting to order. Al took his place behind the table at the front of the room and pulled out one piece of the Kirby. He then explained, or demonstrated, every conceivable positive aspect of this piece. One day it would be the electrical cord, another day it would be the burnished aluminum housing of the motor or whatever. There must have been a million parts he could describe in infinite detail. When he had finished the demo, we would all stand, and with song book in hand, render three or four "Kirby Songs" in a weirdly cacophonous harmony. For example, to the tune of "*The Thing*":

As I was walking down the street,
One bright and sunny day,
I met a lady in her yard,
And to her I did say:

I am your Kirby salesman, Ma'am,
And if you'll let me in,
I'll show you something that is new,
And beat it if you can.

She opened the door and let me in,
And much to her surprise,
I showed her what was in the box
And opened up her eyes.

I cleaned her rugs and polished her floor
In nothing did I fail.
She said young man just leave it here
'Cause you have made a sale.

A LIKELY STORY

The moral of the story is
Don't ever be a dope.
'Cause you can make a Kirby sale
With work instead of hope.

So follow the road, to the end
No matter where it leads.
'Cause there are plenty of sales to be made
'Cause there are plenty of sales to be made
Fulfilling all your needs.

Then, at 9:00 o'clock, and with thousands of adrenaline molecules racing each other through our arteries, it was time for coffee at the nearest restaurant. There we would sit around for forty-five minutes getting wired on caffeine, munching donuts and telling lies to each other about our adventures in the unique world in which Kirby salesmen live. We would then return to the office where we would pick up the 10:00 o'clock appointments our telephone solicitor had made for us, and off we would go.

During my second or third show, I remembered how Al had demonstrated how he could stop the spinning of the buffing wheel on the Handi Butler, the power tool kit that came with the Kirby, by simply pressing his hand on it. The purpose of this demonstration was to show that even if one's hand might slip while polishing the silverware, the drive belt would slip on the spinning drive shaft and the wheel would stop. The problem with my demonstration that fateful day was that I had the grinding wheel on the Handi Butler, not a soft buffing pad.

I explained to my less than interested prospect sitting on the couch, just what I was going to do and why. I pressed my hand on the grinding wheel, spinning at 6,000 rpm, and it immediately tore through my flesh and to the bone. Wow! I pulled my hand back, spurting blood in every direction. I pulled a relatively clean handkerchief from my pocket and wrapped my hand with it, but of course the bleeding continued.

I suspected that it might be time to close this demonstration. I packed my machine up in a most haphazard and messy way and headed for home. It was not a pretty sight. That little lady probably recounted that ridiculous episode a hundred times. If she's alive today, she's no doubt still laughing.

I tried to put on four shows a day, at 10:00 a.m., and again at 1:00, 3:30, and 7:00 p.m. Sometimes I did, but more often it was two or perhaps three. Frequently, the lady of the house had no idea that she had agreed to a demonstration of a vacuum cleaner, and when she realized what was going on, refused to let me in. One day, though, I sold two machines and cleared over $100. Life was good. That first month in the business I sold ten machines and, counting my bonuses, cleared $720. That was major money. Was I flying high or what? However, although I was making very good money, I never did quite that well again. Before I knew it, it was July and time for our two week vacation to Fossil, and some great fishing.

Chapter 44

LAKE OF THE WOODS

THE day before we left for our two week vacation in Fossil, I washed and polished our car, and had it serviced at the dealership. I was proud of that beauty, and anxious to show it off to our Fossilite friends and relatives.

On the second Friday night in July, 1952, we loaded our sleek, deep green Olds '88 with the drinks and sandwiches we deemed necessary for the 1,000-mile trip and headed north on Highway 75. Dad always liked to start this familiar trip at night, so we could avoid heavy Detroit traffic. It was close to 300 miles to Mackinaw City, where we caught a ferry to cross the Straits of Mackinac into Michigan's Upper Peninsula. We picked up U.S. Highway 2 there and took it directly into Fossil, about 700 miles due west. I did most of the driving and loved it. We arrived in Fossil on Sunday afternoon, in plenty of time for a great meal laid out for us by my uncle Dave's wife, Gladys.

For a week we visited with old friends, schoolmates, and

assorted relatives. Some of the Abbott boys had arranged for Dad and me to accompany them on a fishing trip on the Lake of the Woods, an enormous lake in the northernmost reaches of Minnesota. In fact, most of the lake was in Canada.

So, one fine day Dad and I loaded our sparkling car up with relatives, Dave and his son Leroy, and Uncle Euclid, and headed north. Dave crawled into the back seat and immediately began sucking on his ever-present pint of Jack Daniels. We stopped in Greenbush and picked up Mom's brother Art, and we had a full house. Both Dave and Art were about two sheets to the wind by the time we got to Warroad.

We arrived in Warroad, a small village on the southern tip of the Lake of the Woods, around noon, hungry and ready to reel in giant fish of every known description. A very heavy, narrow, eighteen-foot boat came with the two-bedroom cabin we had reserved for us. There was a seat in the prow, one in the rear, and two additional bench seats in the midsection. I attached my bulky, very heavy Scott-Atwater 7.5 horsepower outboard motor to the transom. That thing seemed like it weighed seven hundred pounds. Wrestling that baby around was just about more than my slender, but wiry, body could manage, but I did.

We ate a sandwich or two, loaded our gear, along with the rest of our food and much booze, into the boat and headed out to sea. My heavy little outboard pushed us six fools along at about three miles an hour. We didn't know the lake. We didn't have the slightest idea about where to go to snag our quarry, so we headed for a small island we could see in the far distance. The wind was blowing gently, the sun was brilliant. We had two fishermen with fairly bleary eyes, three neophyte fishermen, and uncle Euclid in a long, low, overloaded, under-powered, very heavy water craft, heading out into unfamiliar waters. Sound stupid? It was.

Nevertheless, we did arrive safely at our island destination (a substantial length of time later). The wind was blowing at a speed we figured would push this goofy boat, with its even goofier cargo, at just about the right speed for trolling. Since it was my motor, I was in charge of operating that monster. I drove us about two hundred yards out, upwind from the shore, and cut the power. We all threw our lines, with various lures and baits attached, into the water and began trolling as the wind pushed us gently toward shore. When we got to within fifty feet or so from the shore, everyone would reel in. I'd fire my baby up and we'd head out for a repeat performance.

We had made probably fifteen such round trips, catching nothing but very small, inedible junk fish, when I let the boat get too close to shore before trying to start the motor. The two-foot waves began to break over the boat, and very quickly flooded both the boat and the ignition system of the motor. I pulled furiously and repeatedly on the starter cord. I couldn't get it started. We crashed into the shore, all of us soaking wet and swearing. Our lunch was totaled. Euclid was madder than ever. He didn't like my navigating. The only bit of food that survived was a quarter pound cube of butter, which Dave immediately ate, as if it might have been an Eskimo Pie. Dave always said that although he only had two teeth, they meshed, so he could eat just about anything. Then he took off all of his clothes, hung them on some bushes to dry, and fell into a deep slumber on the beach. Art also decided it was an appropriate time for a nap. The rest of us were sober, but decided that at least the drying out part of Art and Dave's routine might be appropriate. We all stripped and hung our laundry out to dry. We then lay back in the warm, sunbathed sand, and took a nap.

When we awoke, it was getting rather chilly. We dressed, and I went to work on the motor. The spark plugs had dried enough and it quickly started. We loaded ourselves into the boat and departed for our home base and the warmth and security of our cabin.

The resort had a fish house, a little shack where more

fortunate fishermen could store their catches until they were ready to pack up and leave for home. Art and Dave, who had both managed to keep a slight edge on, explored the fish house, and came back with several nice walleye pike, the best eating fish in the world (even if stolen). Although some of us were a bit hesitant to eat stolen property, we did, and they were wonderful—rolled in seasoned flour and fried in butter.

After a short nap to help get our digestive juices working on our feast, Dave and Art decided that they wanted to go fishing again, in the dark. That was ridiculous, but my rank on the totem pole was right at the bottom, so my opinion of their ludicrous plan meant nothing at all. I just refused to pilot them out there to what I knew would be certain disaster. Leroy volunteered to take them. He helped Art and Dave load their somewhat unsteady hulks into the boat and shoved off. Dave immediately laid down on one of the seats in the boat's midsection to take another nap and Art took up a position in the prow. He was to be the lookout for deadheads in the murky, black water sliding beneath the boat. He wasn't very good at his job. Leroy plowed directly into the end of a partially submerged log and sent his dad careening off his perch and into the bottom of the boat, and Art damned near out of it. That was enough. They all decided it was time to turn in, and headed back to the cabin.

When they arrived, they found that the sleeping arrangements had already been determined. Dave was to bunk with my Dad, Art with Euclid, and Leroy and I were to sleep on couches. We all turned in and settled down for a much-needed snooze.

About an hour later, a wild commotion in the cabin awakened all of us from our sleep. Art, who was in bed with Euclid, had decided he really needed to pee, and started to crawl over Euclid to get out of bed. However, on his way out of the sack, he had only gotten one leg over Euclid when he decided it was time to rest. Sitting there, straddling Euclid and facing the wall, Art decided he might just as well pee right there—and he did. His steaming stream hit the wall just above Euclid's head and splattered down into his face. Euclid woke up with a start, piss exploding off the wall and into his face, coating his one yellow tooth with a flavor he was unaccustomed to. He really didn't like that at all. He screamed a litany of the most God-awful cuss words at Art, threw him back against the wall, and got out of bed.

Within a minute he was back. He had Art's tackle box. Unceremoniously, he dumped the entire contents of razor sharp hooks and lures over Art's barely audible mumblings. Art spent the next hour or so picking hooks out of his bed, and gently dislodging embedded ones from his flesh. Then he went to sleep. Euclid sat up in a chair the rest of the night. I'm not sure that he ever spoke to Art again as long as he lived.

In the morning, we packed up the remaining wreckage of our belongings, ourselves, and headed for Greenbush where we dropped off Art—just Art, no fish. Our next stop was Fossil where we all regaled everyone else with lies about what a wonderful fishing trip we had just had.

Chapter 45

MIZPAW

AFTER a day or so of rest in Fossil, we loaded up again for another fishing and camping trip. This time we left the drunken uncles and Euclid at home. We took Dave's wife, Gladys and her three youngest children, Dale, age 16, Jerry, age 12, and Sharon, about 6 or 7. With Mom, Dad and me, we packed the car with seven people and set off for a lakeside cabin near the town of Ely. I have no idea why Ely was selected as a destination, since it was clear across the state, in the northeast corner, and a full day's drive.

The cabin was a very nice lakeside log house, with a great porch facing the lake. It was stunningly beautiful, and the weather held. We spent two nights there and had a wonderful, relaxing time. Dad and I fished from dawn to dusk both days and didn't have a single strike. Another unbelievably barren fishing adventure. Even so, it was fun, and Dad seemed relaxed and happy. It was good to see him so, after the financial disaster he had recently led us through.

We broke camp early in the morning and headed for International Falls, where one of Dad's younger brothers, Douglas, and his wife and family lived. Dad hadn't seen Douglas in many, many years, and I had never met him. International Falls is near the Canadian border and is very frequently the coldest spot in the lower forty-eight states. During the winters, it was mentioned on the radio weather reports as the "deep freeze" spot three or four times a week.

We arrived at Douglas's hovel just about noon. It was an appalling shack, set back perhaps twenty-five feet from the main highway leading out of town toward Fossil. It had four small rooms. The bathroom was outside, about thirty paces from the back door, and deserves special mention. I had never before, or since, seen anything like it. It was a three-holer. Why anyone would want, or need, to do their duty with two others in attendance escaped me, but there it was. And each hole had a horrible rag-wrapped wooden toilet seat attached to the boards around the hole, perhaps so the occupant would think he was defecating in style, I don't know. It was very full, too, and the smell was enough to melt a heavily reinforced armored truck. I spent almost no time at all in there.

I slipped quietly back into the house, where Mom and Dad were preparing to leave. It had been a very short visit. They had offered us nothing to eat, an absolutely forbidden breach of Minnesotan etiquette—everyone was offered a full meal, no matter what day or time of day. That's just the way it was, and is.

When we got out in the yard, and the adults were saying their awkward farewells, Mom took me aside and asked me to drive. Both she and Gladys were very nervous about Dad's ability to handle and control the car. Apparently, it was just too powerful for him, and he was making errors in judgment regarding passing other cars on the two-lane highway. I agreed and we loaded up.

I was driving, Dad was in the outside front passenger seat, and Dale was between us. Everyone else crammed into the rear seat. We pulled out onto the highway and headed south, toward Bemidji, where we would pick up U.S. 2 for the remainder of the trip to Fossil. Dad was very sad about the exchange, or non-exchange, he had just had with Douglas after so many years. He was silent as we sped along.

It was Sunday, July 27. It was a beautiful day. The sun was shining and the still air was about eighty-five degrees. Our vacation would soon be coming to an end. We were traveling at about seventy miles an hour when we came up over a slight rise in the highway. Then, there it was. Another car in our lane—coming directly at us. "*CRRAASSHH!*" We struck head on. It seemed as if our car had exploded. The noise was deafening. The front end of our car dropped when I slammed on the brakes. When the cars met, we became airborne. Our car flipped completely over and landed on its roof—skidded for a while and then rolled over into a ditch—upright, but facing backwards, toward the direction from which we had come. In an instant, several lives were devastated forever.

As we collided in that terrible moment, I was thrown up against the steering wheel, catching the lower section of the wheel with my abdomen. The force of the impact bent the steering column up through the windshield and the engine was driven back under my feet. My chin was cradled between my knees and I was spewing blood. I was bleeding from my penis and anus as well. Dale was unconscious and smashed down into the front seat passenger foot well. Dad was nowhere to be seen. I turned and looked into the back seat. The two children were screaming, but apparently unhurt. They crawled out of the car through the rear window, terrified and crying. Both my mother and Gladys were unconscious. Mom was spurting blood from a very nearly completely severed ear. Both of Gladys' arms were broken. It was unspeakably horrible.

The driver's door was unopenable. With great effort I

was able to move my body out from under the steering wheel and exit the car through the open passenger side door. As I did, I saw Dad's legs protruding from under the car. I stepped over them, and limped, bleeding and in shock up to the shoulder of the highway. Other motorists and people from the nearby town of Mizpaw who had heard the collision were beginning to gather. Someone called the nearest hospital, which was in Bemidji, about 120 miles away. Others did what they could to assist and comfort the injured.

The driver of the other car was a twenty-six year old woman. She was killed instantly when the steering column penetrated her chest, impaling her against the back of her seat. She had her two very young children with her but they were, miraculously, uninjured. Her mother-in-law, however, who was riding in the front passenger seat, was severely hurt. Both of her hips were broken, as well as both of her arms. The driver's husband was in Korea, where war was raging at the time. He was immediately notified and was in Bemidji within three days of the accident.

During the time we were awaiting the arrival of the ambulances from Bemidji, I never lost consciousness, so the horror of the scene was indelibly recorded in my mind. It was over two hours before the ambulances finally arrived from Bemidji. During that time, people from Mizpaw came rushing to the scene to offer whatever aid they could. There wasn't much they could do but hold blankets over our bodies to protect us from the blazing sun. Through my fog I heard someone say, "Never mind him. He's dead." Mom appeared to be the worst off of the survivors in our car. She was clinically dead. She had no blood pressure. The medics transfused her immediately, and with a great effort and a gentle assist from God, were able to get her back. There was blood all over her head. I was given an injection of morphine to ease my pain, and loaded into one of several ambulances that had arrived.

-ADAM

I don't remember much after that until I awakened on the operating table. I remember being given a spinal block so the only feeling I had was from the neck up. The surgeons opened my abdomen with an incision from my navel to as far as they could go. There was no apparent injury, so they began pulling my intestines out, eight or ten inches at a time. Then they would examine them in an attempt to find the tear. Every time they pulled, I would vomit. It was horrible. They finally located the source of the bleeding, and deftly sewed it up.

Then they went to work on my face, sewing up multiple lacerations, and removing glass splinters. Then I was sent to my room, which I shared with Dale, and fell asleep to the screams of the mother-in-law from the other car, who was just two rooms down the hall.

When I awoke the next morning, I could barely move, so I didn't, much. A catheter had been placed in my bladder. There were several people standing around the perimeter of the room, mostly relatives. However, the man sitting on a chair right next to me and holding my hand was someone I had never seen before. He said, "Hello, Glenn. I'm Reverend Norquist. Is there anything I can do for you?"

"How's my Dad? Is he o.k.?," I mumbled through my stitched face and the fog of morphine.

Reverend Norquist took my hand in both of his and said softly, "Your father is in Heaven, now."

"*No! No!*" I screamed. "**No! Oh, No!**" and then I burst into uncontrollable crying. After several minutes, I regained enough composure to ask how Mom was.

"She's badly hurt, Glenn, but she'll live. She's in a room just down the hall."

A doctor arrived with another shot for me, and I drifted off into the nether world of drug induced sleep.

I awoke the next morning to a smiling nurse. Her name was Julia, and she took very good care of me during the two weeks I was in the hospital. She gave me back rubs every day (but then so did three or four other nurses or aides). When I grew tired of hospital food, she would go out into the world and return with a hamburger and chocolate malt for me. She did every thing she could to ease the anguish I was going through. On the second day I was there, she came in to get me up, so I could begin to walk around. I took one step and my brain exploded with pain. I lost consciousness and slumped to the floor. When I awakened I was back in bed and a doctor was hovering over me.

"We need to get you to X-Ray, to see if we might have missed something. Sunday was a very busy day for us."

I was lifted onto a cart by two large nurses and then wheeled into Radiology, where they quickly determined that I had fractured my left hip. It was a hairline fracture, so it wasn't terribly serious, but the pain was severe for many weeks. I wasn't asked to walk anymore during my two-week stay.

I sat with Mom several hours every day. Her ear had been stitched back in place, and it began to appear that the reattachment was going to be successful. Her right wrist had been shattered and surgically repaired by a team of very busy doctors. Because the wrist joint is comprised of many very small bones, they made an incision on each side of her wrist, peeled back the skin, and simply wrapped the broken bones in stainless steel wire, hoping that the wrist might again become functional. They did a wonderful job given the technology of the day, and with considerable therapy, Mom eventually regained most of her wrist function.

Within three days, Harland and his wife Lorraine, and my sister, Dorothy had arrived. They were doing their best to comfort Mom and me. The hospital was full and there was no room for any of them to stay. Dorothy slept on a table in the blood-drawing room for the few nights she was there. I don't know where Harland and Lorraine stayed. I do know that they went to Fossil and helped to arrange a funeral service for Dad in Crookston. Then Lorraine accompanied Dad's body back to Detroit, where another service was held. He was buried in a beautiful cemetery in one of Detroit's nicest suburbs. I knew nothing of these events until quite some time after our release from the hospital.

Every day Julia would come into the room with a wheelchair and take me for a ride, sometimes even outside.

One day Julia said, "Would you like to take a ride, Glenn?"

"Yes, I would. I'd like to see the rest of the hospital." I responded.

She loaded me into the chair, and off we went, fast. She took me to the elevator, which took us to the basement. Then she said, "I'd like you to meet Mrs. Port. I've been talking a little about you to her and she said she'd like to meet you."

Mrs. Port had been a patient there for ten years. She had her own private room. I reluctantly agreed, not knowing what to expect. Julia tapped on her door, and when she heard the faint, "Come in," she pushed me through the door, and there she was—Mrs. Port.

She was a frail lady, about seventy-five years old. She had suffered a stroke several years previously, and was paralyzed on her left side. Her face was somewhat distorted, but her mind was sharp and her speech was reasonably clear. I had no difficulty understanding her. She offered her hand, and said, "Its really nice to meet you, Glenn. Julia has told me so much about you," and smiled a crooked, but beautiful smile.

I took her hand and replied, "Its nice to meet you, too, Mrs. Port. You have a lovely room."

And she did. She had the room painted in her favorite colors and had pictures of her family all over the walls. She had curtains on the ground floor windows, and carpeting on the floor. It was about as close to a home setting as one could get in a hospital. Julia excused herself, saying she'd be back for me later. Mrs. Port and I began a conversation and a friendship that lasted for many years. From that day on, I visited with her every afternoon for as long as I was there, and we wrote to each other for about four years, until she died.

One day I was sitting by her bedside and we were laughing and joking about one thing or another, and all of a sudden she exclaimed, "Get out of here, you old son-of-a-bitch!"

I was startled. I looked at her, but she was looking past me, toward the door. I turned and was even more startled. There, in the doorway, was a skinny man, over six feet tall—completely wrapped in several bed sheets, except for one eye, which seemed to be looking directly at us. He didn't say anything. He just turned slowly, and shuffled off, back to his own, considerably less luxurious room. I turned back to Mrs. Port.

"That old son-of-a-bitch always does that. He tries to come in here and get in bed with me. I hate him," she said, clearly quite distressed. I calmed her down and we resumed our conversation about friends, family, and food.

Every Sunday, her son would bring her a great home cooked meal that he and his wife had prepared for her. Mrs. Port invited me to share the coming Sunday's repast with her, and I accepted without hesitation. I appeared at the designated time the following Sunday and met her son and his wife. They placed a spread fit for royalty before each of us, and quietly left us two unlikely things to enjoy our meal in private. Besides the normal accompaniments like watermelon and salad, there was warm fresh-baked bread and, wouldn't you know it, all the pan-fried walleye pike we could ever eat in a week. It was a wonderful meal, with wonderful company. I think I loved Mrs. Port.

After two weeks, it was time to go. George and Ardith graciously said that we could stay with them while Mom recuperated and was well enough to travel. George arrived on Sunday to pick us up. We said our goodbyes to a small cadre of tearful nurses, loaded what little gear we had into his car and were soon on our way to Red Lake Falls, where George and Ardith lived with their ten year old son, Jimmy.

Mom and I were both depressed, but I was crushingly so. Since I had been driving, clearly this whole horrible ordeal was entirely my fault. The guilt was nearly overwhelming, and growing.

We stayed with George's family through the rest of August, September, and October. During that time, my cousins Leroy and Audrey (Uncle Art's daughter), were extremely kind and comforting to both Mom and me, and I'll never forget that kindness.

By late November, Mom was well enough to travel. We bought an old '37 Chevy for $150 from George, and with what few belongings we had, drove to my sister Dorothy's home in Royal Oak, a suburb of Detroit. Once Mom was safely ensconced at Dorothy's home, I left to visit Al, my boss with the Kirby Company, to see when I could go back to work. I discovered that he had moved to Battle Creek to open a new territory for Kirby sales. When I found out where he was, I hit the road, alone, for Battle Creek. Mom was safe, and I needed to earn some money and get our lives back on track.

Chapter 46

BATTLE CREEK

BATTLE Creek is a beautiful little city, just a bit over a hundred miles from Detroit, and I made it in a little over two hours. It was a road that I would travel many times in the weeks and months ahead.

When I arrived in Battle Creek, I quickly located Al at his new Kirby sales office. He had rented a tiny, narrow building on a small arterial that ran through an otherwise residential district. It had a basement where the sales meetings and songfests were held every morning and a ground floor, which housed his used machine rebuild and repair shop, and Sandy, the telephone solicitor. There was a laundry and dry cleaners nearby, and a drug store filled mostly with gift items from all over the world. But that's it. Otherwise it was residential.

Battle Creek, I soon learned, was the "Cereal Capital of the World." Several major cereal companies were located there, including Kellogg, Post, Ralston, and General Foods, among others. The whole city smelled of toasted grains. Probably half the population of Battle Creek was employed one way or another by the cereal giants. The cereal factories all utilized a four-shift, six-hour workday, so more individuals could be employed. It was a nice little city.

Al and his wife, Bonnie, were glad to see me. Al offered me a job as one of three District Managers, and a place to stay until I could get established and settled in a dwelling of my own. I accepted, and around mid-January, I moved a few belongings and myself into his home. My bed was their living room couch for a week, until I found a room of my own just down the street from the office. I was nineteen and the youngest District Manager in the history of the Kirby Company. As a District Manager, I thought, I'd be making big bucks and would be able to take care of Mom.

After my second week I returned to my sister Dorothy's house for a weekend visit. Dorothy's husband, Don, took me aside and told me that I would have to move Mom out of their house, and soon. I couldn't take her back to our home on Ford Boulevard because we had rented that to my friend Wayne's dad and his family, who were desperate to get out of the projects. Our deal was for a year, so I had to create another alternative. I agreed to move Mom as soon as I possibly could, and drove back to Battle Creek, head spinning.

It wasn't long, though, before I located and rented a twenty-six foot, singlewide house trailer. It was cheap, only $30 a month, and big enough for us two things, I thought. I closed the deal and the next weekend drove back to Detroit to get Mom and a few belongings like bedding, towels, dishes, clothing, and some food.

It was a raw, blustery, cold night in early February when we arrived at our little "home." The trailer house was heated by an oil stove just inside the entry door. It had no fuel. I found a five-gallon fuel can outside, near the back of the trailer, put it in the car, and drove to the nearest place I could find to buy some fuel oil. When I got back, Mom was really cold and not terribly happy. I nearly dropped my lower intestines hauling that can full of fuel oil out of the car and into the trailer. I then lifted the can and started to pour the kerosene into what I thought was the stove's fuel tank. It wasn't a fuel tank at all. It was a space between the outer shell of the stove, and the heating unit. The oil ran straight down between these two walls and out onto the asbestos tile floor. I had probably poured two or three gallons before I realized what was happening. Good Grief!

Mom and I both grabbed towels and bedding and began mopping up the oil. For more than an hour we worked furiously, soaking up oil with whatever material we could find, wringing it out outside, and mopping some more.

It was approaching midnight and the temperature was just barely above zero. We re-discovered the fact that hard physical work can sometimes keep a person from freezing. Finally, we thought we had it pretty well whipped.

I went outside and found the appropriate fuel tank, and poured the remaining fuel oil into it. I open the valve and went back into the house. I closed the door and finally got a fire going in the stove. As soon as the little trailer began to warm up, the air in the house turned to fuel oil smoke. We opened the door and whatever windows we could to ventilate.

The smoke kept coming. It was coming from the walls. It was coming from the floor. It was coming from everywhere, it seemed. The oil had reached the wood veneer covered walls, and was slowly creeping right up the wood. It had also penetrated below the tile floor and had dissolved the mastic holding the tiles to the sub flooring. Every time we took a step, black, sticky, oil soaked mastic would ooze up between the tiles. The heat was causing the oil to throw off horrendous, stinking, smoke and oil fumes.

Mom and I worked furiously, nearly the whole night through, but we finally got things under a modicum of control.

I deciphered the instructions on the minuscule hot water tank, took a tepid little shower, and raced off to try to sell a Kirby to some poor, unsuspecting housewife. Mom said goodbye and went to sleep, for three days and nights, as I recall.

I arrived at the office, sang a few songs, demonstrated to the other salesmen how the Handi-Butler grinding wheel should not be used, and headed off for coffee and donuts. During our absence, Sandy, our telephone solicitor, made our 10:00 o'clock appointments.

I put on three fruitless shows that day, but in the evening I sold a complete Kirby with every imaginable attachment to the owner of the largest carpet store in Battle Creek. Two of the storeowner's daughters, about my age, were there, watching my demonstration with unusual interest. They saw immediately that there was something there they wanted. Since the Kirby was the only thing available for purchase, they did their very best to convince their father that it was worth far more than my asking price. Dad peeled off the appropriate amount of cash, and I went home very happy. "Boy, if I can do this every day, I'll be a millionaire in no time," I thought to myself.

My luck didn't last, though. I had eight salesmen in my crew, and I was responsible for their training and their success. That meant putting on demonstrations for them in the homes of the prospects Sandy had found for them. If the sale was made, the trainee got the commission of $50 or so, and I made an override of $10. I was beginning to not like that arrangement. The eight salesmen did not comprise a static sales group either. In fact, my sales force was extremely fluid, with a turnover rate of just about 100% every ten weeks. The result was that I was training new men all of the time, and selling a machine or two for them, while going deeper and deeper into debt myself. I had to borrow money from Mom just to buy groceries and pay the rent.

Finally, sensing my growing desperation, Al decided to go with me on a show of my own, to see if he could be of any help. It was a single house in an average middle class neighborhood. The lady of the house was a black woman about sixty years old. She listened intently as I plowed through my spiel. I was pulling dirt and junk from everywhere into nine by nine-inch cotton test cloths. I had constructed an impressive array of filthy test cloths all around her when I finally got to the carpet. I only ran the machine for perhaps ten seconds when I could see that the test cloth was full and about to pop off the exhaust port of the machine. I stopped the Kirby, pulled off the test cloth and showed her a handful of black, greasy horrendousness. I said, "You must have coal heat."

"No, Suh," she replied. "I have hot heat."

I looked at Al, who was sitting in one of her coal soot infested overstuffed chairs, and blinked, in a silent symbol of disbelief. He just smiled. I went on with the task at hand. She said, "How much is this thing?"

"One hundred eighty-eight dollars and eighty cents, including tax," I replied. "Would you like to pay cash or, you can pay on time if you wish, with payments of $9.30 a month."

"I don't want no time payments." she replied. "I want to pay by the month."

At that point, I just sat down on my rump, from the squatting position I had been in, and looked plaintively at Al. I was about to lose it and he knew it. He stepped in at that point and closed the sale and I went home a little bit richer, money wise, that day.

By June, I was very discouraged. I called Wayne's folks to see if they would be willing to move out before the lease was up so we could come back home, and they agreed. I said my farewells to Al and his family, the two other district managers, packed our belongings in our car, and headed for Lincoln Park and Ford Boulevard.

It had been nearly a year since the horror of our accident, and no day had passed that I didn't relive it, sometimes several times a day, and frequently in my dreams. My depression was settling in.

Chapter 47

JUNK JOBS—1953/1954

IT felt good to be back in our little home again, but it was quiet and different without Dad there. In a day or two Mom and I were settled in and I started scanning the want ads for a possible job.

I immediately spotted an ad for route salesmen for the Fuller Brush Company. Hey, I could be a Fuller Brush Man. I applied for and got the job. I had to purchase a batch of samples to use as door openers, and I chose a giant box of sachet samples. From then on, our car smelled like a rolling house of ill repute, but I thought it was great. None of my buddies' cars smelled nearly as good.

It was winter and it was cold. One morning, on my very first stop, I was ushered into the living room by a very nice young housewife. I gave her a sachet sample and opened my case of goodies, which included a then new, unbreakable, plastic comb. Until then, most combs were made of hard rubber and would frequently break, but not this little beauty.

"This comb is absolutely unbreakable," I said as I began to double it in half, a heretofore most impressive demonstration. The coldness had, unbeknownst to me, made the comb extremely brittle, and of course, the comb snapped in two like a pretzel might. Good grief! I didn't sell any combs or anything else to that young lady. After three or four weeks of *very* marginal living, I went back to the help wanted ads.

In quick succession, I tried my hand at selling home incinerators, Catholic jewelry, and stainless steel pots and pans, all door to door. I earned almost nothing, but I did manage to sell one set of pots. I don't know what those folks did with them since they didn't look like they had enough money to buy food to put in those gleaming pots. But, they seemed happy with their glittering new possession. I thought of the old saying, "They were so poor they didn't have a pot to piss in." Well, now at least these folks did. Back to the ads.

The downtown Detroit headquarters office of the "**Best Known Sewing Machine Company**" was advertising for a sales/service representative. That sounded like good, clean, honest work so I applied for the job and was immediately hired.

I was sent to "school" for two weeks to learn how to sew, and how to diagnose minor problems, such as bobbin or thread tension adjustments. If the tension on either part was too tight, the thread would break; if it was too loose, the stitch would be loopy and loose. Both tensions have to be just right and in harmony with each other. It was a simple and very prevalent problem.

I was furnished a gray panel truck with "**The Best Known Sewing Machine Company**" emblazoned on the side in red. I was to carry two or three very nice new machines housed in walnut cabinets in the back of the truck at all times when making service calls in the event an opportunity arose to sell a new machine. I was paid $60 a week, and for that, I was expected to sell $300 worth of machines every week.

When I reported to work each day I would receive a

batch of names and addresses for people in my assigned territory (about a third of Detroit) who had called in a complaint or concern of some kind. These were work slips, indicating the nature of the problem I was to remedy. I made ten to fifteen calls every day, and was doing just great, I thought. I'd fix the lady's problem, collect a $5 service call fee, and be on my way to the next stop. But, I wasn't selling any new machines.

A month had passed before my supervisor called me into his office one morning. He said, "I'm going to ride with you today, Glenn, to see if I can figure out why you're not selling any new machines."

"O.K.," I said, and off we went.

When we returned to the truck after the first call, a simple tension adjustment, and a $5 fee, he said, "I know what your problem is, Glenn. That machine was twenty years old. You *never* fix a machine that old in the home. *Always* tell her that you need to take it back to the shop where our head technician will examine and diagnose the problem. Then you leave a brand new machine in a shiny new cabinet with her as a loaner. After two weeks or so, you call on her again with the bad news. Her machine needs major repairs and the estimate to fix it is never less than what the down payment would be on the new machine you had left with her. By that time she has been playing with her new 'toy' for quite a while and has been getting used to having this wonderful machine in her home. Closing the sale is relatively simple at that point. You should close three out of four."

I couldn't believe it. I thought that this company was a great company. I knew they made superior sewing machines. Mom had had one of their old treadle machine models in our own home for as long as I could remember. But these guys were dishonest scam artists, and I refused to play their game. I resigned that day and started scanning the help wanted ads again that night. Goodbye, Best Known Sewing Machine Company.

My next adventure into the work world was as a helper in the window display department for Montgomery Ward's Department Store. I was to assist the lady in charge of setting up displays of various kinds in all of the store's windows. Some displays were of clothing, some were of tools, some were of appliances or furniture, but all were beautiful and creatively constructed by Mary, my immediate boss.

Mary was about twenty-six and a great lady. She had a sparkling personality, loved her work, and had a great sense of humor. She was also very stooped over with a large hump on her back. It took only minutes for me to get beyond her physical impairment, and we shared many happy workdays together. The only problem was mine. I still hated to get up in the mornings, and so I was late for work nearly every day. Since I had to punch in on a time clock, the personnel officer quickly determined that punctuality was not my strongest asset. She warned me two or three times before I reached critical mass with her.

One morning I was sent to the third floor of the store, which served as a warehouse for all kinds of goods, to locate a refrigerator and bring it down to the display window that Mary was working in. I managed to find an appropriate candidate and strapped it to a large dolly. As I was moving this bulky machine into the freight elevator it started to tip over. I managed to keep it from crashing to the floor, but it did hit the side of the elevator, which scraped a long, very noticeable scratch in its side. Sheepishly, I took it to Mary. She sighed, and looked at me sadly. She had no choice but to report it.

Soon after, I received a call from the Personnel Office. The director wanted to see me right away. When I stepped into her office, she was smiling and very friendly. She said,

"Glenn, you don't like working here very much, do you? Why don't you just not come back? We'll find someone else."

Well, at least I didn't have to pay for the refrigerator. I was relieved. I retrieved my lunch sack from the locker room, had a cup of coffee at the lunch counter of the dime store across the street, and went home to scan the help wanted ads—one more time. This time I drew a blank. I rejected all commission sales "jobs," and I wasn't qualified for much of anything else.

About a year had passed since our accident, and all of the suits and counter suits had been settled. The total amount available for distribution to the injured parties was $20,000, $10,000 from each of the two insureds. The attorneys had agreed upon the amount each surviving person would receive, and my portion was $2,000. I immediately put the money in the bank to await an appropriate opportunity. Meanwhile, I sat down and dejectedly reviewed my dubious marketable assets. The list was very short. Then it struck me. What did I know most about? Carpets—from my Kirby days! Of course. That's what I could do. I could clean carpets.

I tore open the phone book to the yellow pages listings concerning carpet cleaning and found a business that sold carpet shampooing equipment. I rushed right out to the advertiser's address and met with Mr. Smith, the owner. He didn't shampoo carpets himself. He just sold equipment to optimists like me. He was a slick, smooth talking man of about sixty, with pure white hair and a neatly trimmed mustache.

When I left him an hour later, I had purchased a gigantic carpet shampooing machine and a wet-dry, five-gallon vacuum cleaner on wheels. Each machine was just barely within my lifting capacity, so even working by myself, I could manage to get them into my car. With my $1,250 investment neatly crammed into the back seat and trunk of our new '53 Ford two-door sedan, I drove to downtown Detroit and obtained a business license.

My next stop was the Detroit Bell Telephone Company where I arranged for Yellow Pages advertising. I used part of the money I had received in the accident settlement to equip and launch my new business. I named my company the "Esquire Rug and Carpet Cleaning Company," and was ready for business to roll in. It didn't, of course. I purchased some classified advertising in our local paper. Zero response. I had a small, 6 x 9 inch four page brochure made and passed them out all over the neighborhood. Zero response.

Finally, one of my sister's friends, Loretta, took pity on me and hired me to do three rooms in her home. She was a very pretty, thirty year old married woman with a couple of children. She liked to talk. I lugged my machinery into her very nice home and prepared it for its loss of virginity. The scrubbing machine had a cleaning solution tank on it that held three gallons of liquid. When I squeezed the appropriate lever, the solution would flow out of the tank and through the spinning scrubbing brush. It took me a little while to get on to the operation of this bizarre, heavy, spinning, water-spewing scrubbing brush. I found that if I gently lifted on the handle, the machine's spinning brush would move the machine to the right. Pressing down on the handle would move it to the left. Every so often I would squeeze my little lever and allow the cleaning fluid to saturate the brush.

The job would have turned out fine, except for Loretta's incessant interruptions. Every thirty minutes or so she would start talking to me and I would have to turn the machine off so that I could hear her. Although I didn't realize it at the time, the water-saturated brush was draining water into her carpet. I finished my scrubbing and proceeded to extract as much water from the carpet as I could with my great wet-dry vacuum. Then I brushed the nap on her carpet into an upright stance, got my fee from Loretta, and left, thinking I had done a fine piece of work. And I almost had.

Three days later, Loretta called and suggested politely that there might be a problem.

"Would it be possible for you to stop by and take a look at the carpet?," she asked.

"Sure." I said, and rolled over to her house as fast as I could. When I walked in and took a look at her carpet, I knew I was in deep, deep trouble. There were dark stains all over the heretofore light-colored carpet. What were those things? But it didn't take long to figure it out. Every time I had stopped the scrubber and allowed the water to drain, the water had saturated the jute padding under the carpet. The saturation had released the dark dye in the padding, which then bled up through the carpeting. Three rooms of wall-to wall carpeting were ruined. I offered to pay for replacing the carpet, but Loretta was a more than understanding and gracious victim and wouldn't hear of it. She just wanted to let me know what had happened so I wouldn't do it to someone else. I thanked her repeatedly, and with the appropriate degree of embarrassment and chagrin, backed out of her front door and life. I never saw Loretta again.

In a stroke of uncanny insight, I realized that I had no idea what I was doing, I put my machinery in my already overcrowded bedroom where it stayed, collecting dust, for the next six years.

Meanwhile, my social life had just about ceased to exist. Uncle Howard recognized my plight and invited me to attend his church one Sunday. He said there would be a multitude of good-looking, nice, Christian girls there, and I might spot one I liked. With nothing to lose, I spruced myself up as best I could and joined Uncle Howard and his wife, Alice, at the next Sunday's service. I wore my new corduroy slacks with slash rear pockets. Slash rear pockets were the fashion rage at the time. Instead of having a horizontal opening in the rear pockets, the opening was placed on an angle sloping downward to meet the opening of the front pockets. I was spectacular.

After the formal church service, everyone was invited to socialize in the basement and partake of coffee, punch, cake and cookies. I reached the head of the stairs and looked down. Good grief, there must have been a half a dozen beauties at the bottom of the stairs, chattering and looking up at me. Assuming my most sophisticated look, I started through the doorway. As I did so, the slash opening on my right rear pocket caught on the strike plate in the doorjamb. Jolted, I was spun around, crashed into the wall, and careened down the stairs. I landed flat on my back, staring up at my beauties, who were all laughing at my outrageous behavior. I was chagrined. I was humiliated. I was barely able to choke out: "Good morning, my lovelies, my name is Glenn." Even with my awkward, rude entry into this new world, I did find a girlfriend for the next several weeks.

It was now March of 1954, and I was twenty years old. A cease-fire had recently been negotiated with North Korea, and a tenuous peace existed. However, the military draft was breathing heavily on the back of my neck. It was impossible for me to find a decent job, such as a management trainee position, anywhere. No employer wanted to hire and train me just to see me leave for military service. So, I was left to choose from what I called junk jobs, paying little and leading nowhere.

I located my last junk job at Federal's Department Store, selling men's wear. It was not a bad job, it was clean and I was inside where it was warm. But that was about it. My pay was $1 an hour plus a three-percent commission of my day's total sales. I quickly determined that I would have to sell a hell of a lot of shirts at $2.95 to make enough to even pay for my gasoline.

My direct boss there was Mr. Heinie, a nasty, skinny man of about fifty or so. One leg was about six inches shorter that the other so he hobbled around our department, careening to and fro, eventually getting where he wanted to be. One day he silently approached me and without my knowledge began to observe my men's shirt sorting and displaying behavior. Suddenly, and without warning, he reached out and slapped my hand, saying, "That's not the right way to do it!"

Startled, I turned around, and staring into his blazing blue eyes, said, "Mr. Heinie, don't you ever touch me again, not *ever*!"

Taken aback by this direct challenge to his authority, he reeled backwards, glared at me, and slunk off to the slacks' area to attend his wounded psyche and regroup his composure. He finally came around though, and was overly solicitous of me for the next two months that I worked there.

I was realizing though, that I was never going to find a decent job as long as I was a prime candidate for the military draft. I went to my local draft board to see if they could tell me when I would be drafted. They explained that they had no idea when my name would come up and that it could be from a month to a year and a half or more. However, I was also told that I could always volunteer to be drafted. Since men who volunteered in this way would be the first called to fill the board's quota each month, I volunteered. Within three weeks I received my "Greetings" from Uncle Sam. I was to report to the induction station in Detroit on May 4, 1954.

Chapter 48

UNCLE SAM EVE

THE night before I was to report for active military duty with the Army, I cruised all of my usual haunts, looking for some last-chance excitement. After a couple of hours of fruitless searching, I wound up at a Big Boy drive-in restaurant, four blocks down Dix Highway from my home. A kid that I knew from school, Mickey, arrived about the same time, and joined me in my car for a hamburger and malt.

We were enjoying ourselves, minimally, and telling lies to one another about our worldly adventures, when the carhop came up to our window. We both knew her, and believed her when she said, "Hey, you guys. You see those two girls sitting at the counter in there?" gesturing toward great panes of glass that were the walls of the drive in. "They think you guys are cute and would like to meet you."

"Son of a gun. Maybe this night is going to be successful, after all," I thought to myself as I gave the go ahead for them to join us in my car.

The carhop returned to the restaurant, and after a brief wild jabbering with the two girls, the girls left their perches and came out to the car. They said that they had come to the drive-in with some guys, but they didn't like them, so they wanted us to take them home. We said something stupid, like, "Sure. No problem."

They climbed into the back seat of my car and we slithered out of the parking lot and onto a side street. We both thought that this evening might finally be "The Night," and were thrilled with our "catch." We hadn't counted on what should have been the obvious fact that their "boy friends," who were sitting in their car on the other side of the restaurant, could look right through the glass windows of the drive-in and see exactly what we were doing.

As soon as I pulled out onto the residential street I noticed that another car had done so as well. It was following us. The girls looked back and screamed, "It's them. They're following us. They're not nice. Try to lose them!"

I accelerated somewhat, but I could only go so fast in a residential area. I turned at the first side street I came to—and it ended—right there. In front of me was a huge expanse of undeveloped field, with grass and weeds a foot high. I had no choice. I roared straight into the field. My cohort and the girls were hanging on and screaming, "Don't let them catch us!"

I must have been going forty miles an hour through the dark, totally unfamiliar field when I hit an unseen, major, foot-deep hole. The car went airborne and then crashed to the ground. It bounced once and came to a brain-bruising halt. The engine died immediately. The car behind us was in hot pursuit. I didn't feel like talking to those guys right then so I grabbed the car keys, opened the door and ran toward the houses, forty or so feet away. Mickey fled through the passenger door and headed into the field. The girls were in the back seat, and neither Mickey nor I cared.

When I got to the houses, I began creeping along in the shadows, all the while maintaining a very low profile. I could hear some scuffling and shrieking in the distance and I said to myself, "That would not be a good place to be, right now."

I continued my hunched over, *very* low profile slither, first through one house's shadows, then the next. It was slow going, but I couldn't think of anything better to do at the moment, so I continued my tedious trek around the perimeter of a very wide circle. It took me perhaps two hours to reach the other side of the field. There was my car, sitting alone and apparently abandoned. No one was in sight. I dropped down and began crawling, very slowly, toward the car. All senses were on full alert. My antennae were fully extended for the vaguest cue that my enemies might still be lurking in the grasses, or worse, in my car, just waiting for me.

Dawn was breaking when I finally reached the car. I very slowly pulled myself up and peered into the window. *No one was there!* I breathed a deep sigh of relief, jumped into the car, slipped the key into the ignition and turned it. *Yes!* The engine spun over and started. I closed the car door quietly and crept away, thanking God that my crazy life had not ended in such a useless way.

I never saw Mickey again, but I did learn from mutual friends that they had indeed caught up with him. Using two by fours, they fractured his skull and both forearms. But he did survive.

You know, it really was getting to be time for me to leave town again. My brother, Harland, was to pick me up in just about two hours for my trip to the induction center.

Part Four
THE U. S ARMY

Chapter 49

HI, THERE, UNCLE SAM

MAY 4, 1954, was a beautiful, sunny morning. My pursuers had vanished, and I, too, was about to disappear into the waiting arms of my Uncle Sam.

Harland arrived shortly after 7:00 a.m. I kissed Mom goodbye and jumped into his car and we were off for Fort Wayne, a major processing center near the river, close to downtown Detroit. I was traveling light, carrying not much more than a change of underwear, my toilet case, and $35 in cash. The first day was consumed with indoctrinations, eating, showering, and trying to act cool. I didn't know anyone, and there were hundreds of us there that morning.

When I bunked down that evening, it was in a huge room with more than two hundred other guys. The steel bunks with their flimsy, well-worn mattresses, were stacked three high and fairly close together. The densely packed room was nearly claustrophobic. A few men seemed depressed and were quiet, but just about everyone else was filled with nervous energy, buzzing about how great or how horrible their lives in the Army were going to be.

And then I saw him. He was on the top bunk, two above me. He was the ugliest person I had ever seen. This guy was about twenty and he had several yellowish green snaggely teeth sticking out of his face. And he was grinning. It was Baccaduchi. He was hanging over the edge of his bed spewing friendly but grossly pornographic obscenities at his buddy who was sandwiched into the middle bunk between us. It was a simultaneously frightening and laughable scene. I didn't laugh. I didn't know if Baccaduchi was crazy or not and I didn't want my life to end my first night in the Army. Although I didn't have much to do with Baccaduchi during the remainder of my military life, he did play a significant role in my civilian life which was to come, somewhere down the road.

The next morning, after breakfast in the largest dining room I'd ever seen, we were loaded onto a train which had been reserved exclusively for our use. We began winding our way through and out of Detroit, on our way to Fort Smith, Arkansas and Camp Chaffee. It took me just under an hour to lose my thirty-five dollars in a poker game. But there was an up side, too. I met John-Bob, one of the finest people I have ever known, and we became friends for life. He wasn't one of those who profited from my lack of poker playing skill.

The first three days in Camp Chaffee were interesting and filled with activities of various kinds, most of which involved intelligence testing. Little pieces of my brain were being recorded somewhere in the Great Army Personnel Department. When asked what my job preferences would be in the Army, I responded with "Drafting" and "Radio Operator." That was the last I heard of those jobs.

We received multiple shots in our arms, rumps and thighs, but I missed the apocryphal one given in the testicles with a square needle with a rusty hook on the end of it. We had not yet been issued uniforms, so we were all in our civilian clothes, and some of us were getting ripe. Our heads were shaved to the bone as soon as we arrived. I had never seen so much ugliness gathered in one place. Not ever. Well, maybe in Fossil.

On the third day we were issued our uniforms and told that since we weren't going to be needing our civilian clothes for awhile, we should send them home to our mommies, who we wouldn't be seeing for awhile either. That accomplished, and dressed in our neat, new, ill-fitting fatigues, we were loaded into deuce and a halfs (two and a half ton trucks), and sent like unsuspecting virgins, "over the hill," where our infantry training was to begin.

Chapter 50

OVER THE HILL

THE trip "over the hill" was a short one physically, probably not more than three miles or so, but it was thousands of miles from the sanity and civility I had known. When the trucks stopped, we were in another world altogether. We discovered a world filled with hostility, noise, and degradation. *"WHAM! BAM! CRACK!!"* Red-helmeted cadre (our trainers) were slamming their billy clubs against the wooden side rails of the trucks.

"Get the Hell out of there, you miserable, ugly shitheads!!" they screamed.

Instinctively, we knew they weren't kidding. We grabbed our duffel bags with all of our belongings in them, threw them to the ground and jumped down after them. Several unsmiling cadres moved in then to help us get halfway organized into groups that vaguely resembled a platoon formation. There were three two-story barracks behind us. The lead cadre, Fedician, roared: *"When I call your name, pick up your bag and fall into barracks number one. O.K. Adams, Alexander W.——Adams, Glenn A.——" and so on until the first barracks was filled. Then barracks two and three were filled with unsmiling captives. When finished, two hundred and twenty men had been ensconced in their lovely new homes.

After assigning us to bunks, which were only two high this time, and with considerably more room laterally, we were pretty much left alone for the rest of the evening. After writing letters home, as ordered, most of us were able to get at least some sleep that night.

At five a.m. the next morning the front screen door of our barracks was nearly shattered by the force of Fediucian's blow. It crashed back against the wooden wall, as he blew his high pitched trainer's whistle, over and over, as he stomped through the barracks, slamming his club into the metal frames of our bunks.

"It's time to get up, you miserable pieces of dog shit!!" he screamed through a throat that must have been lined with a mixture of leather, moonshine, and gravel. *"It's almost daylight for Crissake!! Move your pansy asses—NOW!!"*

Once in a while he would pause to give special attention to a recruit who had not immediately leapt from his bed. He just grabbed the edge of the mattress and jerked upwards, sending the hapless fog-brained creature crashing to the wooden floor. The very first time I saw that happen, I suspected that such a ritual was not for me. So, for the very first time in my life, I decided that it would be a good idea to get up the first time I was called. This was a learned behavior, however, that endured only for as long as I was in the Army.

The company commander was a small man—in all respects. He was probably 5 feet, seven inches tall at most, twenty-two years old, and had earned his 2nd Lieutenant bars through ROTC in college. He did have shiny boots, and his uniform was always neatly pressed, but he was a jerk. His name was Desmond, but most of us referred to him as Lt. Despot. Every morning at 6:00 a.m., after breakfast, the recruits from our three barracks would form into four platoons in the company square, a hard packed dirt area in front of our barracks and alongside of our mess hall. Lt. Desmond, in his squeaky, barely post adolescent voice, would scream, *"Have you God-damned men defecated today?"*

We were greeted with that bellowed query every single day for eight weeks. And, I suppose, at least for the first week or two, for good reason. The multiple shocks our mental and physical systems were absorbing had slammed the anal aperture of most of the troops shut with a vengeance. That poor muscle was scared to death. Perhaps more accurately, it had been stunned into a state of stark paralysis. Lt. Desmond was a classic oral-anal military personality, and a fool to boot.

For reasons solely his own, he was very interested in receiving awards for having the highest percentage church attendance every Sunday of any company on the base. Therefore, we all were required to attend three consecutive services on each of eight very hot Sunday mornings.

Our general exhaustion, combined with the stifling heat of 100 degrees or more, and a relative humidity to match, caused many of us to drift off to sleep, even if we were actively trying to attend to the incredibly boring sermon. The ever-alert cadre, however, positioned themselves around the periphery of the room with ten-foot slender wooden poles. When they saw some hapless soul nod off into his own private dream world, they would reach over and whap him loudly on his barren skull. It was horrible. But, Lt. Desmond won his award each week for having 300% church attendance.

In the second week of training I had a molar extracted that had been giving me problems. That afternoon as we lined up for chow, a really big ugly guy jumped into line directly behind me. Our orders were to stand in line at parade rest (a semi-attention position with the feet spread about a foot apart and hands clasped behind the back). When the line began to move, we were to come to attention and take a pace or two forward and then resume the parade rest position until the line moved again. I had just come to parade rest when the "big ugly" moved in very close and positioned his genitals in my hands. I didn't like that. I couldn't turn around, though, and confront him. I tried to reposition myself so that I could free my hands of their unwanted contents. It didn't work. He simply moved with me.

Luckily, I guess, I was still bleeding from my recent extraction, so I saved up all the bloody saliva I could without choking, turned my head quietly, and let it go on his shiny boot. I suppose he could have killed me, but he didn't. He just moved back a bit, and I had no more trouble with him.

Around the fifth week of training, Lt. Desmond decided that it would also look good on his record if he had a very high percentage of his company donate blood. Even he, though, had a vague suspicion that he couldn't make the same demands of his troops at the blood drawing station as he did for church attendance. Nevertheless, he was bound to get what he could. He ordered the entire company to voluntarily donate blood. And, as it turned out, it was a good thing that he did. Not a single soldier's blood was acceptable, due to low iron counts. The medics alerted Lt. Desmond's superiors, who quickly determined that our poor showing was due to widespread fatigue, overwork and undernourishment in temperatures that regularly reached 115 degrees by noon. We noticed an immediate improvement in our rations (like fried chicken that wasn't bleeding), more free time on the weekends, and a training day that ended at two in the afternoon. Of course, to compensate for this kindness, we then began our day at three a.m., instead of our customary 5 o'clock reveille.

It was here that I first learned more than I ever needed to know about approach-avoidance conflicts. As mealtime was nearing, all the troops in each barracks became increasing tense, awaiting Fediucian's screaming whistle that signaled that we were to rush out of our building at full speed and into the chow line. No exceptions, no lagging. We were always starving, so when the whistle blew, we rushed out of the barracks and toward the mess hall. That was the approach part of the conflict.

The avoidance segment was simultaneous and came when, without exception, the first ten men in line would be hauled off to be servers in the chow line, and would eat last. No spinning in circles was allowed, and no crying either.

We all struggled on, through the firing range where we learned how to accurately fire our .30 caliber M-1 rifles and .50 caliber machine guns. Then through the week of bivouac, where we trained and slept in pup tents in the woods, and through the infiltration course where rattlesnakes and tarantulas lived and live ammunition was fired a few inches over our heads. We had other assorted humiliations as well, like gang showers in the forest under a single strand of cold water.

The infiltration course didn't provide us with a nice evening. The Army had staked out an area for itself on barren hardpan that was as hard as concrete and had sprinkled it liberally with some loose sand and gravel. Barbed wire was strung thirty inches from the ground. Our mission was to crawl under the barbed wire toward the machine gun nests that were firing .50 caliber bullets an inch or two over the barbed wire. Every fifth or sixth bullet was a tracer, so we could all enjoy the sights as well as the sounds of machine gun fire. We were to crawl the first half on our stomachs, with our weapons across our wrists; the second half on our backs, with our rifles on our stomachs, barrel aimed at our chin. When we reached the machine guns, we were to leap up, affix our bayonets and run screaming into a strategically placed hole in the ground where we plunged our bayonets into dummies, who were probably getting tired of playing the "enemy."

In the week prior to our turn through the course I noticed that many of the men in the company preceding us through basic training had significant wounds on both their elbows and knees. When asked, they responded that crawling through the infiltration course with the constant grinding and chafing on the rocks, sand and gravel, not only wore holes in their fatigues, but in their skin as well.

I didn't think that was acceptable, or necessary. The night before it was our turn for the course, I went to the base PX and bought a box of Kotex sanitary pads and a roll of adhesive tape. The next evening, before heading for the infiltration course, I taped a pad on the inside of each elbow and one on each knee. The course wore holes in my uniform and the pads, but not in me. I thought I was pretty clever, and I was. While everyone else was attending to their painful, bloody wounds that night, I was relaxing in my bunk and writing letters home.

Chapter 51

IT'S ALMOST OVER

THE end of basic training was drawing near. During the sixth week of training, I called a local air charter service to see if we could arrange for a plane to fly us Detroit guys home at the end of our training. I negotiated what I thought was a fair price, and spread the word among the troops. The day before graduation, I set up a table right next to the pay station where the troops would be receiving their month's pay. Around fifty guys signed up and paid their money to me, which I stored in the company safe that night.

Finally, it was graduation time, and a fine looking lot we were. We dressed like soldiers, marched in straight lines while doing precision movements as soldiers do, and were trained to kill with our bare hands if necessary. I liked to think of myself as a lean, mean, killing machine. My muscles were hard as pebbles and I had gained twelve pounds. I was 140 pounds of coiled steel, just waiting to be unleashed on the enemy.

It was a Saturday morning when we had our graduation parade. All of us had our duffel bags packed and ready to go the instant we were dismissed from our parade duty. We were dressed in our class A uniforms and were profoundly uncomfortable in the heat. Finally, it was over. We rushed into the barracks, grabbed our bags and ran for the buses that the airline had arranged for us. They took us to the airport and to what we all thought would be a giant silver bird that would fly us home and to freedom.

In twenty minutes we arrived at the airport. There, in the blazing sun, sat our plane. It was a rather small, rust colored, long obsolete, aircraft. Its tiny wheel at the rear of the plane where we entered her, managed to keep the plane's metal from resting on the tarmac. As we entered through the door at the extreme rear end of the plane, we began a very steep, perhaps thirty-degree, climb up the single aisle. Each of us found a seat and strapped ourselves in, expecting to take off as soon as the pilot boarded. And we did, but the pilots didn't get there until an hour and a half had passed. The temperature in the plane was at least 125 degrees. Our uniforms were soaking wet with sweat. Even our shoes were sounding squishy.

Finally, a couple of men about fifty years old and in civilian clothes arrived. They climbed the aisle with some difficulty, pausing now and then to quip with a soggy passenger. I thought to myself that the pauses were so they could catch their breath, rather than any attempt at human relations. They seemed decrepit, but then, so did the plane. It all fit.

They disappeared into their cabin, behind a scraggly cloth curtain, settled into their seats and fired up the two engines. We crept along the tarmac and out to the end of the runway to await our turn to take off. I looked around at the guys. They were not a happy bunch. They were hot, wet and scared. "Oh, well. Let's get this creature off the ground," I said to no one in particular. I was angry with myself for not having checked on the type of aircraft I had contracted for. What a dimwit!

The engines roared. The "Captain" let off on the brakes, and we began rolling gently down the runway. As we slowly picked up speed, our gentle rolling became a bouncing, lurching, straining extravaganza of sound and fury. Twenty feet or so before we would have crashed off the end of the runway into oblivion, the plane lifted up and we were airborne. The assembled troops gave out a spontaneous cheer as they realized they were still alive.

We climbed slowly up to about 10,000 feet, where, we immediately discovered, it was rather cool. The temperature in the plane dropped to near forty degrees. Our sodden uniforms became unwelcome blankets of near ice. We learned quickly what it was like to fly in a minimally pressurized plane. Our ears were alternately clogging and popping and we were all wildly chewing Chicklet gum in a vain attempt to equalize the pressures between our eustachian tubes and the plane's. We gave up on that fairly quickly and broke open our box lunches.

As I began to eat my stale bologna sandwich, I began to study with more than idle curiosity, the large piece of metal flopping and slapping against the fuselage of the plane. What the Hell?! Was the plane falling apart? I didn't want to start a panic, either in myself or among my frozen comrades, so I closed my eyes and tried to pretend that I was somewhere else, anywhere else.

We had been flying about four hours when one of the pilot's voices crackled over the intercom. Matter of factly, he said, "We are experiencing difficulty with our radio. We have lost contact with the ground, so we are landing in Indianapolis for repairs. We will probably be on the ground for two hours, so you can deplane and get yourselves a Coke or something."

We dropped out of the sky like a floating rock and taxied to a nearby hanger. The plane was heating up rapidly, so we didn't have much difficulty breaking our frozen uniforms away from the seats. We walked, fell, and tumbled down the ramp and out the door. Fresh air!

We had our Cokes, and a freshly made sandwich too, before reloading for a repeat performance of alternately sweltering and freezing. Our frozen forms landed in Detroit to a tumultuous cheer from the troops. We were survivors! We left the plane as quickly as we could and ran to the waiting arms of family and girl friends. No one thanked me for the arrangements I had made for the charter. Not even John-Bob.

When we entered the airport, we learned that the only information our families had received about us was that three hours or so before we arrived, the air traffic controller in Detroit had lost radio contact with our plane. No one knew whether we had crashed or simply disappeared. Apparently, the radio fix in Indianapolis just didn't work.

I only had ten days before I was to report to Ft. Lee, Virginia, for my second eight weeks of training, so I did my best to live very, very well for those ten days.

Chapter 52

FORT LEE, VIRGINIA

I began my second eight weeks of basic training at the Quartermaster School in Fort Lee, Virginia, twenty-three miles directly south of Richmond. The Military Occupational Specialty I was to learn was that of a Supply Records Clerk. That specialty had nothing to do with my recorded preferences, but that was okay. It sure beat an Infantry or Artillery assignment. I figured that these two months would be rather light and simple duty, since I already knew how to type. And it almost was.

My first encounter was with Derik, a tall, strong, lanky kid who had the seat next to me in typing class. It was important to me that I receive good grades since failure could mean reassignment to a much less desirable training program such as Baking School, or Fumigation and Bath Processing, or Laundry and Dry Cleaning Machine Operation, the Infantry or, worst of all, Graves Registration. All of the latter classes were being conducted simultaneously with mine, and were comprised of men in the shallowest end of the gene pool. And Korea was ever on my mind.

Every so often a speed and accuracy test was administered by the instructor to measure our progress. It was during these timed tests that Derik began his obnoxious campaign of harassment. He would simply reach over and slam the carriage of the typewriter back while I was typing. He would strike two or three times during every test and my anger was growing. As my grades slipped, my anger quickly evolved into fury. I asked him several times to stop his humorless stunts. He would just laugh, and continue his torment. I was becoming very tightly wound. And it was hot. *Very* hot.

After three weeks in the class I was ready to kill. I remember the day of climax clearly. The temperature had reached 105 degrees and we were given a ten-minute break, a common practice at the end of every hour during the workday. Behind our classroom, in the shade, there was a three-sided concrete bin for storing coal during the winter months. The walls of the bin were about ten inches wide and three feet high. I commandeered one of the bin walls for my private nest, stretched out on my back and fell asleep on the concrete wall's top edge.

I awoke with a start. I was falling! I tried to catch myself but only managed to scrape the heel of my hand on the concrete wall, all the way to the ground. There are more efficient and less painful ways to remove skin tissue, if someone wanted to see what their hand would look like skinless. Crash! Into the hard gravel I went. I picked myself up, bleeding and half dazed. And there was Derik, laughing like the fool that he was. For his own amusement he had tipped my sleeping form over the edge.

That did it. I jumped up and screamed at him, "You son-of-a-bitch! If you ever—if you *EVER* fuck with me again, I'll kill you!"

Derik sobered up instantly. He wasn't sure about this

situation. Was I serious? He had never had such vitriolic fury directed at him before. He elected to choose caution as his response and slowly backed away. His typing sabotage behavior ceased and he never spoke to me again. That made me very happy.

There were two Cubans in our company. One of them, Ricardo, was skinny, ugly, and sane. The other one, Emilio, was muscular, nice looking, blond, and insane. Ricardo did his very best to keep Emilio out of trouble, and every once in awhile he was successful. Emilio spent most of his free time in the evenings polishing his boots, swearing in Spanish, and sharpening his bayonet. He honed its blade with a whetstone for hours at a time until it was gleaming and razor sharp. No one bothered these two guys.

One day we were being marched from one classroom to another and I was two men behind Emilio. Our little platoon was called to a halt in front of our destination building and told to fall into the new classroom. As soon as the "Fall Out" order was given, Emilio spun around and without warning smashed his fist into the man's mouth who had been marching directly behind him. The guy went down, but remained conscious.

Spitting blood, the victim screamed at the Cuban, "What the Hell was that all about?"

One of his lower front teeth had cut through his lip and blood was flowing freely.

"You keep stepping on my heels, shit face. I don't like that. You shouldn't do that," Emilio replied in a low, very threatening voice.

The victim promised he wouldn't and slowly, cautiously, got to his feet. I'm sure his head was spinning as he walked with some uncertainty into the building.

Our classes ended around the first of October and it was time for permanent assignment. Everyone in the two classes preceding us had been assigned to the European Theater, and I expected that our company would be as well, since we were so close. We were all surprised, however, by an assignment to the Far East Command. I was ordered to report to Fort Lewis, Washington, for a more refined placement. Times were good, I was in great physical shape, I wasn't being shot at—and I was happy.

It was foggy and misting slightly when I deplaned in Seattle. I later learned that it's almost always misting slightly in Seattle, with or without fog and sometimes even when the sun is shining. I boosted my duffel onto my shoulder and had almost reached the front door of the terminal when I was stopped by a very large M.P.

"Where are you going, Soldier?" he asked.

I replied that I was to report to Fort Lewis. He asked to see my travel orders and when he was satisfied that I wasn't AWOL, directed me to an Army bus that was waiting for creatures such as me.

It wasn't long at all before my personal chauffeur dropped me off right in front of the unit headquarters of the company named on my orders. I was issued bedding and directed to a dark, empty, cold and damp barracks. I didn't care. I made my bed, then tore it up and crawled in. I was exhausted and gone for the night.

The next two days were spent just idling the time away and chatting with the new guys who were arriving almost by the hour. None of us had any duties. We were all just waiting to be told where we would be going next. That day came on the third day, and by that time there were several hundred of us.

Everyone was told to pack their belongings and report to the Assignment Building, a long, one story building with an adjacent chain link fenced holding pen. When I arrived at the assignment building I had to walk along the side of the fenced area, full of men who had already received orders for their next destination.

"Where are you going?" I asked one after another as I walked toward the building's entrance.

"Korea." "Korea." "Korea." one after another responded. "Everyone in here is going to Korea," one said. And it was true. I recognized some of them from Fort Lee.

The line I was in was moving slowly into the building. Finally, a clerk motioned for me to step up to his counter. "Name?"

"Adams, Glenn A." I responded, dreading his next move.

He pulled my card from his bin and scrawled a huge "J" on it. "What does that mean?" I asked.

"Japan. Our quota for Korea is filled today."

I breathed a deep sigh of relief and returned to the my barracks. The next morning Army personnel were kind enough to arrange for me to mop their infirmary's floors for four days while awaiting transportation to a troop ship in Seattle.

The fateful day arrived. About a thousand of us were loaded onto buses and transported to the Seattle waterfront, where the USS General William Mitchell awaited our arrival. Standing there, in our great looking fatigues and with our duffel bags at the ready, a deep, gravelly voice suddenly barked over a loudspeaker:

> **"WHEN YOUR LAST NAME IS CALLED, SOUND OFF WITH YOUR FIRST NAME AND MIDDLE INITIAL!! THEN PROCEED UP THE RAMP INTO THE SHIP!! LET'S GO!!"**

As usual, I was one of the first called. I boosted my duffel onto my shoulder and proceeded briskly up the gangplank, through the gangway and down several flights of very steep, steel stairs, into the bowels of the ship.

I was assigned to one of the main troop quarters, a room that housed about two hundred men. Down the length of the room were rows of several six-inch diameter steel poles. Four canvas bunks, each suspended by 3/8-inch link steel chain hung laterally from each side of the posts. Two feet from the outer edge of this column of bunks, another set of eight were stacked. Two inches were allowed between the foot of one bunk to the beginning of another. When the men were in their bunks, there was typically no more than six inches between their sagging butts and the fellow below them. I couldn't lie on my side without touching the guy hanging above me. Claustrophobic? Yes. Did it take very long for the air to foul? No.

I was on deck the morning we were gently nudged by powerful tugboats away from the pier and into the quiet waters of Puget Sound. A military band was playing and I was filled with a confusing mixture of emotions, sadness, excitement, guilt, anticipation, patriotism, fear, and relief. Soon, the tugs left us. We were under way.

Even in the smooth waters of Puget Sound, some men started getting seasick. Vomit began appearing everywhere. I had read somewhere that seasickness is largely in the mind, and that if I could just not think about it and try to keep food in my stomach, I'd be okay. And I was. I came close one night though, after wolfing down a whole box of Cheez-Its. Although I did manage to keep my stomach contents in place, I didn't eat Cheez-Its again for twenty-three years.

After breakfast every morning, since I had no specific duties, I would climb the near vertical steel stairs up to the main deck. It was late October and very chilly, but the air was fresh. I could breathe and enjoy an incredibly beautiful sunrise every day. At night, movies were shown on a rather makeshift screen set up on the fantail of the ship. There was only room enough for a hundred or so troops and the movies were invariably old and bad, but it was better than retreating to my stinking room, filled with my increasingly aromatic comrades.

The food was terrible. I don't know where they found those guys they called cooks. In any event, I managed to choke down enough to keep my gut in place for the fourteen days it took us to cross the Pacific. I kept physically fit by nimbly leaping from the trajectory paths of those troops practicing projectile vomiting. Next stop—Yokohama!

Chapter 53

JAPAN ORDNANCE COMMAND

THE morning we were to arrive in Yokohama, I took my place on deck early in the morning, before dawn. The waters were calm as we slipped slowly through a series of smaller outer islands. I could see the blinking lights of houses on the shores, and on several fishing boats plying the waters in search of their quarry.

The sun rose slowly from the sea, directly behind the fantail of the ship. It was a gorgeous sight with the sunrise behind us and the main Japanese island, Honshu, dead ahead. Several tugs came out to escort our giant ship into its berth. I retreated to my quarters to gather my aromatic belongings, and packed them tightly into my great looking duffel. I was ready.

The ship was secured to its moorings and orders were being barked in every direction by anyone having more than two stripes on his arm. Actually, disembarking from the ship was efficient and painless. About a thousand of us were herded into several railroad passenger cars that were lined up on narrow gauge tracks close to the pier.

The seats were four across, two on each side of a narrow aisle. It looked like a toy train. The seats were very small, much like seats for children. In each car, under a grate in the narrow aisle way, were two small hibachis, exuding heat and carbon monoxide from burning coals lying on a sand base. At the front end of our rail car was a small food service area, in which Army cooks and servers would prepare our meals. Actually, the food was fairly good, but I didn't see anyone ask for seconds. We filled our trays and returned to our seats where we sat and ate, hunched up and perched on our tiny seats. It was a ludicrous sight.

We were on our way to Camp Drake, a very large Army installation in Tokyo, which would serve as a Replacement Depot, a huge military personnel sorting facility. There we would be divided into several smaller groups and sent to Army posts throughout Japan which had requisitioned either additional or replacement personnel.

Tokyo is about a forty-five minute train ride from Yokohama, if you were on a normal train. We weren't. Our train had the lowest possible priority. It stopped to give the right of way to every moving thing, trains, buses, cars, rickshaws, pedestrians, and an occasional "honey wagon." At least it seemed that way to me. It took us all day to reach Camp Drake. I had mess in the dining hall and crashed into a bunk in my assigned barracks, wondering what tomorrow would bring. I was also wondering why I was so damned dizzy.

Morning came early the next day, and so did a nearly recognizable breakfast, and my dizziness. After eating, it was mail call time. Contact with home had been broken for at least two weeks—and for some of us, even longer. Through some miracle of Army efficiency, any mail that had been received at our previous posts or sent to the general Army

Post Office (APO) at Camp Drake, was waiting for us. The Army knew precisely where we were, even if we didn't.

Several hundred of us gathered in the "square," a large dirt and gravel area along side of the post office. As names of the recipients were called out by the sergeant dispensing the mail, a response could be heard from somewhere in the crowd, "**YO!**" and the letter would be sailed into the air in the general direction of the sound. Strangely, everyone got his or her mail, even me.

As I stood in this oppressive crowd, my dizziness increased and I had to find a place to sit down. I wasn't the only one experiencing this particular malady either. There were several of us. Then we figured it out. We were land sick. Our bodies and brains had become accustomed to automatically adjusting to the pitching and rolling of the ship for the last two weeks, and now that we were stopped on solid ground, our internal gyroscopes were continuously attempting to compensate for an undulation that no longer existed. I discovered that as long as I kept moving, the symptoms didn't exist. They only appeared when I was at rest. So, I kept moving as best I could until my physiology caught up with that reality. It took a little over a day.

After mail call it was lunchtime, followed by another assembly in the Company Square with our great looking luggage, stuffed with two weeks of dirty laundry.

As our names were called, we sounded off with the obligatory "**Yo**," grabbed our duffels and loaded ourselves into one or another of a waiting line of deuce-and-a-halfs. When our truck (one of three in our caravan) was full, we departed for the next destination in this great sorting process.

We bounced along the narrow highway, heading south, although I certainly didn't know we were traveling south at the time. After about three hours of careening around, sucking exhaust, and dodging oncoming kamikaze taxi drivers, (all of us driving on the wrong side of the road) we pulled into a compound of buildings, many of which had been bombed out or burned.

The trucks pulled to a stop in front of an intact two-story building. We were told that this would be our home for the next couple of days, while it was decided who would go where from there. We entered the building and found a large room filled with single army bunks. We each chose one, heaped our belongings on it, and headed for the mess hall, which was a separate building directly in front of the barracks. The food was good. In fact, it was the best Army meal any of us had eaten since entering the service. Could it be that this place was using real food? Then it was time for showers and our bunks.

Breakfast the next morning was a real surprise. I picked up a tray and utensils and approached the beginning of the serving line. The friendly cook behind the counter smiled and said, "Would you like eggs with bacon or ham, or pancakes?"

I had never heard such words in the six months I'd been in the Army. I was actually being asked what *I* wanted.

"Uh. I think I'll have bacon and eggs."

"And how would you like your eggs?" Good grief, I thought to myself. Was I in touch with a part of the real world again?

"Over easy, please."

And so began a year-long friendship with Van, once of the nicest, most competent people I came to know in the Army. One of his greatest pleasures was, I think, to have the troops compliment him on his cooking. He tried very hard to earn those compliments, too.

After breakfast in a large room filled with people I didn't know, I returned with the rest of the newcomers to our holding pen in the barracks. Every so often a clerk would enter the room, call off three or four names, and send them on their way to an assignment at another installation.

For two full days the process was repeated. On the morning of the third day, my name was called.

"Report to Lt. Tighe in the Headquarters Building across the street" the clerk told me.

I straightened out my wrinkled uniform as best I could, wiped the dust off my shoes, cleaned most of the tarnish from my brass, and walked over to the Headquarters Building. The first office I came to was "Personnel," a bustling room with about fifteen workers, both United States Military and Japanese civilians. I inquired about where I might find Lt. Tighe.

"He's out back, burning classified documents in the incinerator," one young trooper replied, and pointed me in the appropriate direction.

I found Lt. Tighe right where I was told he would be, stuffing one handful of papers after another into an incinerator. The smoke was heavy and the fire was hot. Lt. Tighe was a young First Lieutenant, busily feeding papers into his own private inferno. He was covered with smoky sweat and preoccupied with his task. He didn't notice me approach.

"Lt. Tighe?" I inquired.

He looked up at me, and squinting through the smoke replied, "Yes, I'm Lt. Tighe."

I snapped to attention, saluted and said, "Private Adams reporting, Sir. I understand you wanted to see me?"

"Yes, I do, and stand at ease. Your MOS is for a Supply Records Clerk, isn't it?"

"Yes, it is, Sir."

"Well, one of my men is going to be rotating back to the States in about two months, and I'll be needing a replacement for him. His name is Corporal Redding. Come with me. I'll introduce you to him and he can explain what the job is all about. Then you can decide whether you want this assignment or not," Lt. Tighe said, and together we walked around the corner and into the front of the building.

Just inside the front door, and directly across the marble hallway from Personnel, was a room, about twenty by thirty feet, with a chain link security fence around it, from floor to ceiling. It was a military library, containing great volumes of Army Regulations and books containing the nomenclatures of every piece of ordnance equipment known to man. There were also many shelves filled with expendable quartermaster supplies such as Army forms of a thousand types (some extremely sensitive), pencils, reams of paper, tablets, toilet paper, etc., anything that could and would be used up. Lt. Tighe introduced me to Corporal Joe Redding and his two assistants, both of whom would be leaving Japan within three weeks. Then he left us to get acquainted and to give me some time to decide whether I wanted the job or not.

For me, there was never a second's deliberation. I wanted the job. I wanted to stop traveling. I wanted a clean uniform. I *needed* clean shorts. The fact that Corporal Redding was a very bright, easy going, slow talking nice person was a bonus. After an hour or so of chatting, and a coffee break in the snack bar, I said goodbye to Joe and left to find Lt. Tighe before he changed his mind about me. I found him in his office, which was just down the hall a few steps from the library. He was sitting at his desk. I approached briskly, stopped and saluted. "Sir. Private Adams reporting."

Lt. Tighe returned the salute. "Well, what do you think? Would you like the job?"

"Yes, I would, Sir. I would like it very much."

"Well, then," he replied. "Report back to the barracks and tell them you'll be staying for awhile. They'll get you set up with sleeping quarters and answer any questions you might have about the Company. We are the 229th Japan Ordnance Command, and I think you'll like your duty here."

He smiled, we exchanged salutes, and I floated back to the barracks to start my settling in process.

I discovered very quickly that many items were rationed. The company clerk issued a ration book to me with coupons in it for many items in short supply. Things such as typewriters (one a year), whiskey (one fifth a week), and what I discovered was to be my fiscal salvation, cigarettes (one carton a week). But more about that later.

On the second floor of the barracks building, there was one very large room that housed about eighty men. There were both single and two decker bunks, and I was lucky enough to be assigned a single one, and by a window, too. I was accustomed to sleeping with windows open, so I could breathe fresh air through the night, rather than my own exhaust fumes (and in this case, the exhalations and other gaseous expulsions from eighty other men). Although it was a battle, and took awhile, I finally got the guys closest to me to accept fresh rather than stale air at night.

Directly across the hall was a huge latrine and shower room, from which the obnoxious sounds of vomiting and dry heaving were frequently heard from those who had partaken of too much Kirin beer or saki that night.

The remainder of the second floor was comprised of smaller, six man rooms, generally occupied by those of sergeant rank. There were no officers in our building. They had their own quarters, either on or off base.

One morning, soon after I arrived at the JOC, I was awakened when my bunk began to dance around just a bit. I looked up and saw that the lights hanging from the ceiling were swaying back and forth. It was my first earthquake. It only lasted a few seconds but the uneasy, queasy feeling the earth's movement generated was one I would remember forever. I found though, that earthquakes were very common, and it was rare if a week passed without experiencing one. I learned to simply "roll" with them, and the shifting footing soon became an expected part of the Japanese Experience. They were never pleasant, but tolerable.

I learned my job duties quickly, and began to relax for the first time in a very long while. I was beginning to get to know several of the other guys, and they were great. In the fifteen months I was there I never witnessed or heard about a single fight among our troops. Most of them were college graduates, but if not, had extremely high scores on the tests that were administered when they entered the service. It was an extraordinary group of men. I later learned that because this was a replacement depot that assigned personnel to military posts in a very broad geographic area, the guys in personnel tried to keep the very best and brightest right there at the JOC. It certainly worked out well for me.

I settled in and was relaxed for the first time in a very long while.

Chapter 54

AL

THREE weeks after beginning my job, two of the men who were there when I arrived were rotated back to the States, leaving just Joe and me. Then Al arrived, fresh from the basic training, to join us in our little cage. Al was about my height, but very skinny and very hairy. He had a very thick beard and hairy arms and hands (except for his palms, of course). He, too, was a draftee and from Detroit. He fit right in to our little group. Joe would soon be leaving for the States, discharge and reentry into the real world. It was to be just us two Detroit things left alone to manage our domain. And it worked. It worked very well.

Al didn't get off to a very good start in Japan though. Al was quite bright and had completed one year at Wayne State University in Detroit before flunking out. It wasn't that he couldn't do the work. He had simply been directionless, waiting for his call from Uncle Sam, as I had been. He had a brother, his only sibling, serving in the Navy on a ship anchored off the coast of Turkey. Al would have volunteered for the draft earlier than he did, but his dad had died at age forty-five from a heart attack and he didn't want to leave his mother alone for very long. When he knew that his brother would be discharged in less than seven months, he said to himself, "Let's go. Let's get it over with," and volunteered for the first available draft.

Six months later he joined me at the JOC. Al hadn't been with me for two weeks when he got word that his brother had been drowned while returning to his ship from shore leave. His water taxi had capsized in rough seas, and the entire complement of men aboard had been lost. Al was crushed.

The Navy inquired of Al whether he would like to fly to Turkey and escort his brother's body home to Detroit. The Navy said they would pay all transportation and other costs incidental to the trip. Al said he would like to do that. He knew that his mother would be devastated and would need his support. She had lost her husband just three years previously, and now this. Al was all she had left of her family. He put in his request to the Army.

He was denied. *Denied!* What the Hell? For what possible reason? His presence in Oppama, Japan, wasn't critical to the success of the Army's Far East Operations! He appealed and was immediately denied again. The refusal was worded something like: "He's already dead. There's nothing you can do about that." Unbelievable.

From that point on, Al declared his own private war against the Army. His response to any request made of him by the Army was always a minimal one. He failed every inspection while he remained in Japan. Of course, he was consequently awarded several punishments for these failed inspections, but in Al's twisted, hostile thinking, he was winning that stupid war. I felt sorry for him, but nothing I said made any difference at all. And, as history duly recorded, the United

States Army in Japan did not collapse because of Al's actions. As things cooled down a bit we became fast friends and remained so for many years after our Army "experience."

Al and I together quickly determined that many of the tasks we were responsible for had been done the hard way by our three predecessors. As smart as they were, they worked dumb. We began streamlining the operation. Joe and his buddies had canvassed every office in the Headquarters building each month for their supply needs, which they would then collate, order and distribute. That was damn near a continuous undertaking, since our operation had about 2,000 personnel, including both military and Japanese civilian workers. I appointed one individual in each area to bring me a list of their needs once a month. Simple? Yes. It cut our work time by more than ninety percent. Within three months, as the new system was implemented and minor bugs worked out, Al and I found that we could very effectively and competently fulfill our responsibilities in the equivalent of three full work days a month. We were on vacation!! With full pay!! At least Al was on full pay. I had an allotment deducted from my pay and sent home to my mother.

Once a month I would purposefully leave out an important item when ordering supplies or forms from the Forms Distribution Center in Tokyo. I would then write up a request to Lt. Tighe for a car and chauffeur to drive me or Al to Tokyo to obtain these critical items, which were "inadvertently omitted" from our order. Al and I took turns taking these mini-vacations in mid-week and enjoyed them immensely. Although he never let on, I strongly suspect that Lt. Tighe knew exactly what we were doing. It was a kind of silent game. We did a great job for him in our cage, and then there was a reward. It was a wonderful system.

Al and I discovered very early on that we were living in two very different worlds within the Army. One was our job, where Lt. Tighe was our immediate supervisor and our coworkers were intelligent, decent people. The other world was that of the soldier, with frequent inspections, war games in the cold, muddy woods, qualifying with weapons and gas masks and all the rest. We both loved our jobs, and appreciated Lt. Tighe. We both disliked the Army, with its regimentation, and frequent absurdities.

Lt. Mar was in charge of our lives once the workday ended. He was also our paymaster. At the end of November, 1954, I reported to him to receive my first pay in Japan. He peeled off $30 in script, a funny looking greenback substitute used for money overseas. "Thank you, Sir!" I responded and retreated from his office into the hallway of the barracks.

Thirty dollars? That's all that remained for me after the allotment to my Mom had been deducted. How was I going to live on a dollar a day? Everyone else had eighty or more dollars heaped upon him or her at the end of each month. On the other hand, I wasn't going to starve. I had a nice warm Army bed and a terrific wardrobe. Things could have been worse—a Hell of a lot worse. Like Korea, for instance. I guess I didn't have it so bad.

The fact is, I had it great. The things that happened to me and around me during my fifteen months there were indelibly etched into my memory. Many little stories have been told and retold, others have not. I'll relate just a few to enhance the picture of the Zeitgeist.

The head janitor for our building was Yamamoto-san. He was a man around fifty or so, weather worn and about five feet high. His office was an enclosed space under the stairway next to Lt. Tighe's office. In his cramped quarters he had installed a cot, a stool, and a small table on which he did his necessary calculations, and ate his lunch. He lived in Tokyo and commuted daily by extremely crowded trains. It took him just about an hour and a half each way. Mr. Yamamoto and I became fast friends. Although he couldn't speak any

English, we were able to communicate fairly well with the Japanese I quickly picked up.

One day, Mr. Yamamoto came to me, and was fairly distressed. He needed some lumber to complete a project he was working on and there wasn't any available in our immediate area. He had found what he needed at another location on our sprawling base and wanted to know if I would talk to Lt. Tighe about letting him go over there to pick it up. We walked across the hall to Lt. Tighe's office and I explained the situation. During this exchange, I had to ask for clarification, several times, in Japanese, from Mr. Yamamoto. When it was concluded, Mr. Yamamoto had his permission, and I had duly impressed my boss with my uncanny linguistic ability. We requisitioned a Jeep, drove over to the lumber site, and picked up a few sticks of lumber. Mr. Yamamoto smiled. So did I.

There were rare occasions when the previous evening's activities rendered me nearly useless the following day. Mr. Yamamoto took pity on me and my greenish gills and offered to let me rest on his cot under the stairs until I felt well enough to face the world again. He would pour me a cup of tea, close the door and lock it. Then he would busy himself in the immediate area for an hour or so, all the while keeping a close eye on the situation. If it happened that I was needed for something only I could respond to, he would surreptitiously enter his office and awaken me. He was a fine fellow, he was.

The second, and the last Christmas I spent at the JOC, Mr. Yamamoto showed up one morning with a Christmas tree as a present for me. I was astounded! He had transported that tree by himself on an extremely crowded train all the way from Tokyo. He was so proud and happy when he presented the tree to me. I thanked him repeatedly, and later that day, returned the favor as best I could with a fifth of Seagrams. That made him even happier.

Al and I set the tree up in a makeshift stand, and decorated it with lights and ornaments we bought at the Post Exchange. It was wonderful. It was festive. It was a reminder of home. It was ordered taken down. I don't remember just from whom the order came, but it was loud and clear. The order said that the tree was a fire hazard. We were devastated. I immediately appealed to Lt. Tighe to see if he could engineer a reversal of that order. Within the hour, the order was amended.

"If the electric lights are removed from the tree, it can stay."

Hallelujah!! The world was right again. My respect for Lt. Tighe was growing each day.

Chapter 55

RETRAINING SGT. WYRENS

SGT. Wyrens was a tall, fully-figured, master sergeant from Central Command in Tokyo. His boss had sent him down to our operation to see if he could determine how we were doing things so efficiently, so he could implement necessary changes in their own situation. Sgt. Wyrens wore quarter-inch thick glasses, which made his eyes look like tiny, nasty little bb's. And he was stupid, really stupid.

The first day he was in my office, he started ordering me around as if he were in charge.

"Do this! Get me that! Take your coffee break now! You can take a leak tomorrow!" he was fond of saying.

I didn't like that. I asked Lt. Tighe if I had to obey Wyrens' ludicrous commands, and gave him some examples of what I meant. Lt. Tighe said, "No, you don't. Tell him I want to see him, *now*."

When Wyrens returned from his meeting with Lt. Tighe, he was a changed man. A metamorphosis had taken place in the rank order of things, and he was now *my* slave. He became the student, as was appropriate. He also asked my permission to take *his* coffee, lunch and pee breaks and was generally a docile pet for the remainder of his month's stay with me. It was almost as if I had grown stars on my lapels.

An evening came during Wyrens' stay when we all had to qualify with our gas masks. The entire company was transported to the "gas tent," a 400 square foot tent filled with tear gas. Everyone was to don their masks, enter the tent, remove their masks and respond to a series of questions.

The entire time in the tent was probably no more than three or four minutes. I was exempt because I was experiencing a series of boils at the time from eating indigenous contaminated strawberries. I had two active boils at the time (of a series of seventeen that eventually erupted from my poisoned blood); one was located under my belt, which was quite uncomfortable. It was a picnic, though, compared to the excruciating pain of the boil coming to a head inside of my left nostril.

The whole left side of my face was distorted from the swelling. Whoever was responsible for making such decisions agreed with my contention that tear gas would be intolerably painful on the raw meat of boils. I was along for the ride, though, and for me, (except for the boils) it was a lovely evening.

Goofy Sgt. Wyrens, standing in a small group of guys outside the tent, and with watery eyes that were tinier than ever because of the tear gas, told what he thought was a funny story. It took him probably four minutes to tell the whole, very detailed, unfunny tale, and then he laughed hysterically at his story in what was something like a high-pitched squeal rather than a legitimate laugh. A few of the guys listening chuckled politely. Just then two more guys joined the group.

"What's so funny?" they asked.

Because Sgt. Wyrens had been so incredibly ludicrous, I

said, "Sgt. Wyrens just told a funny story. Why don't you tell these guys, Sergeant?"

And the blithering dolt launched into an exact, word for word, replication of his stupid story. This time we all laughed wildly. Someone in the group said, "What's going on? What's so funny?" just to get him to repeat the story.

This pitiful scene repeated itself at least a dozen times. We finally grew tired of toying with this poor creature and left him alone so he could have some time to ruminate on the finer details of his great story. In two weeks he took his huge frame, tiny eyes and dull intellect, and quietly disappeared into the mists of Tokyo. Life in our cage returned to its normal pace.

Chapter 56

THE BLACK MARKET

I had only been with the JOC about a week when I met Ralph. Ralph was the same rank as me, a Private First Class. He stopped me one day in the hall and introduced himself. He had been in Japan about six months so he was fairly well acclimated to all this newness that was raining down on me. He suggested that we go to Yokohama together on the weekend and he could show me the sights and some of the do's and don'ts of life in Japan. We had a great time and were the best of friends for as long as I was in Japan.

Ralph knew how short of cash I was and suggested that I might want to sell a carton or two of cigarettes on the Black Market. He explained that with all consumer goods being so scarce, I could sell just about anything and double my money. At that time I was smoking up my one carton a week allocation myself so I didn't have any to sell on the Black Market. Ralph explained that many of the troops that didn't smoke would just give me their ration book coupons for cigarettes. They weren't going to use them, and they really didn't care who did. I said to Ralph, "Well, where is the Black Market?"

"It's everywhere," he replied. "Just walk down the street in Oppama, or Yokohama with a carton of cigarettes in a paper sack under your arm. Someone will ask you if you want to sell it. Never take less than 600 Yen."

So, I decided to try it. An eighty-cent carton of cigarettes was the equivalent of about 300 yen. If I could double my investment every few days I could probably repair, or at least periodically patch, my ludicrous fiscal circumstances. I invested eighty cents in a carton, stuck it in a plain brown paper sack as instructed, and left on a weekend pass for Yokohama, all alone.

Twenty minutes later I arrived at the main rail station in Yokohama. It wasn't ten minutes after I detrained and began walking toward the main street of the city when a young man approached me.

"Cigarettes?" he asked.

"Yes," I replied nervously.

"Ekura deska?" (how much).

"Six hundred Yen."

"Dijobu," (O.K.), he said, and promptly peeled off six 100 yen notes from a wad of bills that was unseemly huge for such an ill-dressed young man to have. But there it was. My deal was completed. I stuffed my ill-gotten gains into my pocket, thinking, "Boy, that was easy. Perhaps my money worries are over." Perhaps not.

When I returned to camp later that evening, I checked in with the trooper who was in charge of quarters. He said solemnly, "The Marine M.P.'s (Military Police) were here looking for you. You're to report to their office as soon as possible. Go."

"Oh, no! My first microscopic excursion into the Black Market has been discovered. "What am I going to do?," I thought to myself as I hustled over to the Marine compound on our base. (Our base was a tri-service base with complements of Army, Navy and Marines.)

When I arrived, I was told that the men who wanted to see me were out, but that I was to wait for them. I sat down in a pool of heavy sweating and nervousness to contemplate and await my fate.

About an hour passed before two Marine M.P.s arrived. They were large men, all spit and shine, and ominously impressive. They called me into an interrogation room and sat me in a single wooden chair facing them.

"First of all," one of them said, "you need to know that you don't have to answer any of our questions. You can leave anytime you want to. You should also know that if you attempt to leave, we have the right to stop you and to shoot you if necessary."

That statement added a whole new dimension to this ridiculous scene, and I replied, "Ask me anything you like. I haven't done anything," I said, trying to straighten up even more in my chair.

"You know why you're here, don't you?" he continued.

"No, Sir, I don't," I responded.

"We think you do." And after a moment's pause, the questioner said, "We want to talk with you about your Black Market activities."

"What do you mean?" I replied. "This isn't happening," I thought to myself, as visions of Leavenworth and a huge roommate named "Mary" flooded my mind.

"You've been selling Army blankets on the Market, haven't you. We have the evidence. We found a laundry bag with your ID number stamped on it in an alley in Yokohama. It was packed full of Army blankets, waiting to be picked up by your contact," he said.

There was no humor or any other kind of leeway in his accusation. He was deadly serious. But when I heard what it was that they thought I had done, I was so relieved that I cracked a small smile. That was the wrong thing to do. They immediately perceived my smile of relief as my acknowledgment of guilt, and further, that I was laughing at them. That wasn't good.

"That couldn't have been my laundry bag, Sir. I don't know anything about black marketing blankets. My laundry bag is tied onto my bunk," I said.

I was gaining a little confidence that I might get out of this situation unscathed yet.

"Really?" he responded. "Well, why don't we go take a look. By the way, what color is your laundry bag?"

I didn't know what color my laundry bag was. Until that very moment I didn't care. Who would? All of the bags were a very faded shade of brown, blue, or green.

"I think it's blue," I said, "But I'm not sure."

"Well, let's go take a look," he said, and we all walked outside, loaded into their Jeep, and drove to my barracks.

We went upstairs to my bunk, and sure enough, there was my bag, tied to my bunk, as I said it would be. But it wasn't blue. It was a nasty, faded, shade of green. Now what?

"O.K. You're not under arrest, but we'll be keeping an eye on you."

They left me to wallow in my guilt, paranoia, and chagrin. I never heard from them again, but I was looking over my shoulder for months.

Chapter 57

SOLDIER OF THE MONTH?

FIVE months into my tenure at the JOC, the officers decided it would be a good idea to create and implement a "Soldier of the Month" program for the enlisted personnel. In its second month Lt. Tighe nominated me, as did Ralph's direct superior. Several others were nominated as well by their superiors, but the contest was really only between Ralph and me.

Part of the criteria for determining who would be the next Soldier of the Month was an interrogation by a six man examining board comprised of both officers and high-ranking enlisted men.

I reported at the designated time, snapped off a salute, and took my seat in a metal folding chair directly in front of the examining panel. I was asked a lengthy series of questions about military concepts of one type or another, such as General Orders, Military Courtesy, and put through a short exercise of drill executions. After about an hour, I was dismissed. Then it was Ralph's turn. He went through the same process and felt he had done quite well. And he had done very well. His overall score was 99%. Unfortunately for Ralph, I had scored 100%.

So, I was Soldier of the Month the next month, and Ralph was Soldier of the Month the following month. I was excused from all extra duties for the month following my selection, like mopping floors or latrine duty. My picture, an 8 x 10 glossy, was posted on the company bulletin board for all to see, and either applaud or ridicule. The award also carried with it a three-day pass. Actually, the pass was superfluous since I was the one responsible for ordering blank passes from our supply source in Tokyo, I already had my own personal pass, good for anytime.

It was during my tenure as Soldier of the Month that a General from Central Command in Tokyo decided to visit our operation. Part of his mission was to inspect the troops. The morning of the inspection was a bright, sunny Saturday. Our entire company was formed in front of our barracks, in Class A uniforms, with shiny shoes and our weapons.

I had completely forgotten about the inspection until five minutes before we were to fall out for it. I had donned a pair of shocking pink socks when I went to breakfast that morning, thinking it was really funny. When the order came to fall out for inspection, I completely forgot about the socks as I hurriedly prepared my weapon and myself. So there I was, standing there as if I were a real soldier, straight as an arrow, in fairly shiny shoes, reasonably clean brass, and pink socks.

I probably would have gotten away with it too, except for the General. He thought my hair was too long. It wasn't, but he didn't ask me for my opinion. That was called a "gig." A soldier could get gigged for all manner of real or imagined offenses, such as a dirty rifle, scuffed shoes, moldy brass, not being able to recall your own name, and sometimes, even pink socks.

Chapter 58

COMMAND INSPECTION

LT. Mar's office assistant was Sgt. Boudrou, who had been in an airborne division at some time in his career and wore his parachutist's pin with great pride. His boots were shined to the brilliance of glass, and you could cut teak with the crease in his pants. He was all soldier. He hated me. Every day he found an excuse to come into my little cage and harass me with statements like, "Shine your brass with a Hershey Bar this morning, Corporal Adams?" or "Who pressed your shirt, a blind, armless, crazy person?" Obviously, he didn't accept me in my "Soldier of the Month" role.

It got old very fast, but he was relentless. Not a day passed without at least one disparaging, unnecessary verbal barb. After a few months I got my chance to even the score. Our company was due for a command inspection by a General and his staff officers from Central Command in Tokyo. We had about four months warning.

The barracks building in which we lived also housed Lt. Mar's office and an adjacent office for Sgt. Boudrou. In Sgt. Boudrou's office there was a small library of Army Regulations, which were to be kept current at all times. It would be a primary target of the inspection team, which would be looking for currency and relevance of the library materials. Sgt. Boudrou, with his shiny boots and immaculate brass, was responsible for the library.

He came into my office one day and didn't slam me in the face with one of his obnoxious remarks. In fact, he was quite contrite. I'd never seen him like this before. He said, "Corporal Adams, my library is going to be inspected by Central Command. Would you be willing to help me get it current? It's a mess, and I don't even know where to begin. I'd really appreciate your help."

I said that I was really busy, but that I'd think about it and let him know. He left, boots gleaming, but I clearly perceived a hint of anxiety as well. I walked across the hall to Lt. Tighe's office and related Sgt. Boudrou's request for my organizational talents.

"Am I obligated to do that for him?" I asked.

"No. You're not obligated. You can do it if you wish, but you certainly don't have to," he replied. I caught just the hint of a smile on his face as he responded.

"Thank you very much, Sir," I said, and retreated to my wire cage. I related what Lt. Tighe had told me to Al. We looked at each other and laughed out loud. We had that bastard now.

Every three or four days Sgt. Boudrou would slither into my office and ask if I had decided when I could do his books. My reply was always the same: "No, I haven't. I'm very busy. I'll let you know."

As the weeks passed, Sgt. Boudrou became increasing anxious. He was almost fawning now. It was sad in a way, to see this great paratrooper nearly begging, but I was enjoying it immensely. Finally, the time came. Just a week before the inspection team was due, the company was ordered by Lt. Mar to don its war gear and move to the woods for war games. It was cold and raining that night and playing in the mud was not appealing to me. I walked over to Sgt. Boudrou's office and said, "I can do your books tonight, Sergeant."

"What?!" he replied incredulously. "We're playing war games tonight. You have to be in the woods."

"I don't know what to tell you, Sergeant," I said sadly. "Tonight is the only night I could possibly fix the mess in your library before Central Command gets here. But,—it's up to you. I can do it tonight, or———." I never finished the sentence.

"O.K., O.K.," he said. "I'll arrange it. Get what you need and report back here after chow tonight."

I smiled, and assured him that his library would be unassailable by the inspectors. I congratulated him on his foresight, thanked him, and left.

That night, while the entire company was rolling in mud and shooting blanks, I was comfortably ensconced in Sgt. Boudrou's warm, dry office, listening to the radio, drinking hot coffee from the mess hall, and reveling in my victory over stupidity. It took me less than forty-five minutes to bring his library up to currency. He passed the inspection with flying colors. Not a single gig, and I was his hero, even though he knew he had been had. That episode was one of the sweetest, perhaps *the* sweetest, of my brief Army career.

Chapter 59

SAY WHAT?

I was about ten months into my tour when Lt. Tighe stopped into my office one day.

"Do you have a couple of minutes?" he asked me.

Was I going to say no? "Yes, Sir, what can I do for you?"

"Have you ever thought about making a career of the service?" he said with a straight face. He was serious.

"No, Sir. I sure haven't."

"Well, I'd like for you to consider it. The Army needs really good people like you in its officer ranks, and if you give me permission, I'd like to nominate you to West Point."

I was stunned. No one, other than Al, had ever suggested that I might go to college. But West Point? No, I didn't think so. A military career was several places below the last item on my personal list of career alternatives.

"Well, thank you very much, Sir?" I replied. "It's wonderful of you to say that, but I'm really looking forward to my release date. I don't think I would like to make a career of the Army."

Lt. Tighe appeared disappointed, but he understood. We talked for probably two hours that day. I was beginning to think that he was an even finer, more astute gentleman that I had previously thought.

The fact was, I had already written to Wayne State University in Detroit. I knew that if I could be accepted there, I could get out of the Army up to 90 days early. The university's response indicated that they would send an entrance examination to the Education Officer at the JOC, who would then proctor it for me. The university would then let me know about my application after it had received the results of the examination. I made the necessary arrangements, and in just about a month, my tests arrived. I received a phone call from the Education Officer and a time was scheduled for the six-hour test. I took a series of major tests, involving English, Mathematics, and Literature, and a number of sub-tests that purported to measure my understanding of logic, the depth and breadth of my vocabulary, and my reasoning ability. I thought most of them were relatively simple, and waited to hear from Wayne State.

I didn't need to wait long. The Admissions Officer of the university responded within two weeks. I was accepted! I could start as early as Winter Quarter, which was to begin on February 6, 1956. I rushed through all of the necessary paperwork for an early release, hand carrying what I could. My early release was approved, and in mid-January, I reported for the last time to Lt. Tighe.

I went into his office that last morning and stood before his desk. He looked up. "It's time for me to go now, Sir," I said.

"Goodbye, then, Glenn. The very best of luck to you. You've been a fine soldier and you're a wonderful asset to your country." He looked up at me, and I swear, his eyes were teary.

I choked out a raspy goodbye and saluted. He returned

my salute. I turned and silently left his office. I returned to my barracks where an olive-drab Army car was waiting to take me to Camp Drake. It was a long, lonely, ride through the falling mist that morning. I was leaving everyone I had known and lived with for fifteen months. It was a much different feeling than saying goodbye to one or two fellows as they rotated home each month. This time the separation was complete. It was from everyone. I was filled with ambivalence. I hated the Army, but I liked and respected the guys I had been living with for over a year. Three mornings later I was on the ship, the USNS General E. D. Patrick, plying its way through the outer islands and into the open sea.

Chapter 60

THE OTHER JAPAN

CONCURRENT with my Army life at the Japan Ordnance Command, was a semi-real life, off base. Unfortunately, my financial resources were essentially non-existent, so, unlike many of my counterparts, I didn't get to see much of the country other than those areas located within a very short radius of Oppama. Even so, life off base was not dull.

I had arrived in Oppama in late November and my acclimation began immediately. One of the first things any occidental would notice was the unique smell of the Orient. Inside of most buildings, the heavy fragrance of incense was ubiquitous. Walking down the main street in Yokohama, individual sidewalk vendors in tent-like structures, sold everything imaginable, from cameras and silks to teriyaki chicken kabobs and Saki, an excellent rice wine. The chicken pieces were cooked over a charcoal-laden hibachi, and smoke billowed up from the juices dripping onto the hot coals. It was wonderful!

Not so wonderful were the smells from the toilets in most public buildings and homes, and from the multitude of canals that interlaced the city. The canals were largely open sewers. Most people had a small room in their house or business that served as a toilet. It was like an outhouse inside. Smells inside of the buildings were generally controlled with powdered lime, but when the "Honey Man" arrived to empty the pit into wooden buckets on his ox-drawn "honey cart," all bets were off. It was terrible. Usually, the honey man would clean out three or four residences' toilets in one trip, so the neighborhoods would be olfactorily decimated for days at a time as he slowly made his rounds. When his wagon's buckets were full, his ox would pull the wagon to the nearest available farmer and dump his precious cargo into the farmer's concrete holding tank. When the time was appropriate the farmer would fertilize his crops with honey. The honey helped strawberries grow to the size of small peaches. It is also the probable cause of my series of boils. Perhaps the boils were God's punishment for my having eaten of the forbidden fruit, locally grown strawberries.

Frequently, while strolling the streets of Tokyo or Yokohama, a virgin would be offered up, almost always by her pimp "brother," a skinny little guy with a belt eighteen inches too long. These guys all had at least a hundred virginal "sisters" (virginity guaranteed!). The fawning pimps would sometimes follow me for two blocks or more, trying to sell (or rather rent), their human wares before giving up.

Ralph saw what was happening one evening and said, "Look, Glenn, every Japanese in Yokohama knows just by looking at you that you're new here. You look so wide-eyed and naive you make me cringe. If you want those guys to leave you alone, you need to assume an air of sophistication. You need to look like you've been here forever and know exactly what you're doing and where you're going. It's simple. Just lower your eyelids to half-mast and walk briskly, as if you had a purpose, or a destination, even if you don't. Be suave!" I did. It worked.

A few public buildings and private businesses that had survived the terrible bombings of the air forces still had intact plumbing, but very few. One of the latter was the Matsuya Department Store, housed in a six-story, quarter-block-long building in Yokohama.

As Christmas approached in 1954, I thought it would be nice if I sent oriental Christmas presents to my many nieces and nephews in Detroit—things such as lacquered jewelry boxes, or glass encased geisha dolls, or Japanese toys. I walked the mile or so from the base to the town of Oppama the following Saturday. On my way I took a shortcut through the hills and discovered that they were riddled with caves. I later learned that the entire country of Japan was permeated with such recesses, grottoes and tunnels. We were fortunate that Japan surrendered when it did. A land invasion of the country would have killed and maimed hundreds of thousands on both sides.

When I reached the town, I caught one of the frequent, fast trains to Yokohama. I donned my sophisticated look as I detrained, and walked briskly to the Matsuya Department Store. No one ever looked more sophisticated, except perhaps, Ronald Coleman. Ralph had been right. No pimps, prostitutes, or beggars stopped me even once.

I entered the store and approached the nearest counter. A young Japanese girl asked in Japanese if she could help me.

I didn't know much Japanese yet but I was able to say, in a mixture of English and Japanese, "Toy department, **do**'ko **des**'ka?" (Where is the toy department?)

I had no idea what she then replied, nor did she of my response in English to her. It was immediately apparent that we were in a linguistic deadlock. She was embarrassed, and held up her index finger, "Cho'te a ma'te," (Just a minute) she said, and disappeared into the cavernous store.

"Just a minute" was one of the few phrases I knew at that time, so I quietly bided my time just looking at items in her showcase while she was gone. She returned shortly with her supervisor, an attractive Japanese lady in her early twenties.

"May I help you?" she asked in slow but impeccable English.

"Yes, you can," I replied. "Where is your toy department?"

She looked at me quizzically for a moment, and then in a flash of understanding and insight, she smiled and motioned for me to follow her. We wound our way through the crowded store and up a flight of stairs. She led me graciously across the store to a distant corner of the second floor. She stopped, and pointed with great satisfaction, to the store's restroom. She had misunderstood my request for "toys" as one for a "toilet." I smiled at her, bowed, thanked her profusely, and dutifully entered the restroom. I fulfilled her expectations of me in the restroom and eventually found the toy department on my own. My nieces and nephews told me later that what I had found for them was wonderful and that they were thrilled to get them. My odd little experience in the "toy" department had been worthwhile after all.

Chapter 61

HEAVY-DUTY CROWDS

I learned early on to never try to take a train anywhere at rush hour. But it was *always* rush hour, except in the dead of night and I just didn't travel very much in the dead of night.

Japan's population in the mid-fifties was around ninety million, plus the occupation forces. That was more than half of the entire population of the United States, packed into a land area about the size of California. I'm certain that all of them conspired to be on my train, no matter what train I was on, or where I was going.

Railroad personnel, standing on the loading platform for the trains, would run as fast as they could in the ten feet or so they had for acceleration, and slam their bodies into the train's patrons bulging through the train's open doors. They kept battering until everyone was wedged inside and the train's doors could close. I never worried about falling down on my frequent railway excursions, or even holding on to anything. No one *could* fall down.

Every once in a while I would miss the last train from Yokohama to Oppama and have to negotiate the lowest possible fare with one of several taxi drivers waiting for such an opportunity. Midnight was our curfew time and we needed to be back on base by then or have our passes revoked for a week. One evening Al and I struck a deal with one of them and then, much to our regret, said, "Hi-ah'-ku," which means hurry up or go fast in Japanese. The driver aimed to please. He roared out of the alley we were in, through the city, and onto the two-lane highway leading to Oppama. Al and I looked at each other as we careened along, each having the simultaneous insight that we had said the wrong thing.

"Good grief! This guy's going to kill us," I said to Al as one oncoming speeding vehicle after another thundered past us heading into Yokohama.

"Kee-o-skeh'-tay!" (take it easy, or slow down) we both pleaded. The driver would laugh, slow down for an instant, and then be right back up to ninety kilometers an hour. We were really getting scared.

"Perhaps we can bribe him," I said to Al and pulled out two cigarettes from my pack and offered them to the grinning driver while again requesting that he slow down. Again, a smile and momentary slowing. As we approached Mach 2, we gave him all the cigarettes we both had. It made no difference at all. We just closed our eyes and hoped for the best as our rolling death trap plunged ahead through the darkness.

When we did arrive at the gates of the JOC, both Al and I were absolutely sober. We had made it back before curfew, and although we hadn't been killed, the ride came at a high cost emotionally. Our driver was grinning.

We weren't. That was the last time either of us ever said "Hi-ah'-ku" to a cab driver, or anyone else for that matter.

Just off the base, about a hundred yards down the road to

town, there was a tiny little bar. It had two small tables, three stools at the bar, and a slot machine. It was convenient and a lot quicker than walking across base to the Navy Enlisted Men's Club if all you wanted was one quick beer before turning in. One night I walked down to the little bar with Ralph. When we walked in, there was a huge American sitting on a stool at the bar. He was wearing a letter sweater that I thought might be from Southwestern High School in Detroit. I struck up a conversation with him, and sure enough, he had graduated from Southwestern before joining the Marines.

He didn't look familiar so I asked his name, which I *did* recognize. Then it came back to me. Six years previously he had been a little squirt that Wayne and I used to like to tease. In fact, one day when our juices were running particularly strong, we stuffed his little frame into a hall locker and locked him in it. We thought it was great. He didn't. As he threw back one whiskey after another, I considered the situation and elected not to remind him of who I really was.

There was a grotesquely ugly, heavy set bar girl in there that night. She was floating around trying to make a score. She reminded me of a ghost, the way she slithered from one patron to another. And, lucky me, I knew the Japanese word for ghost: o-bak'a-san.

When it came to be my turn for her pitch, after having been summarily rejected by everyone else in the bar, I cleverly addressed her as "O-bak'a-san," thinking I was being cute because of her resemblance to what I thought a Japanese ghost might look like. Clearly, that was the wrong thing to say. She hit me with her gnarled fist squarely in the mouth. I fell off my stool onto the floor, moaning and spitting blood as she turned and ran out the door, screaming Japanese obscenities at me. Apparently, o-bak'a-san did not mean ghost. It *did* mean, "Go to your death," or some such epithet. She had been terribly insulted. As far as I know, she never returned to that little bar. She's probably still running through the streets screaming at me.

It was beginning to dawn on me that this was not going to be one of my better evenings. The bartender gave me an ice cube, which I wrapped in my handkerchief and held on my lip. The bleeding stopped eventually, and I walked back to the barracks, fell into my bunk and into unconsciousness. Another great evening in the Land of the Rising Sun.

There were wonderful times too, and I learned more that I thought possible in just fifteen months. I visited the Imperial Palace on New Year's Day, 1955. I saw the Emperor as he stood on his balcony with his family. He smiled and waved to the slowly passing throng. There were hundreds of thousands of people, perhaps more than a million, in that crushing human mass passing ever so slowly before the Emperor. It was frightening.

Being crushed in that crowd was more than educational. It was a pathologically claustrophobic situation. I couldn't move in any direction, except little by little with the flow of the people. I was immensely relieved when the review was over and the crowd began to disperse. I found I could actually breathe all by myself, without the help of the human bellows pulsating on all sides of me.

About midway through my tour, I decided to have my portrait done by a Japanese photographer in Yokohama. I dressed in my finest civilian clothes, shined my shoes, and leapt onto the next train headed into the big city. I located a photographer on one of the main streets and struck a bargain. He was good—*very* good. He created a portrait, in profile, that was handsome indeed. It was so good in fact, that he chose to place it in his shop window as an example of his artistry. It also provided me with an unusual opportunity to impress my friends whenever I was anywhere near the photo shop with one of them.

Overall, my time in the Orient was a series of unique

events—experiences I'll never forget. With its bumps and bruises also came unique events that just couldn't have happened anywhere else in the world. Most importantly, I met people that changed my life. But, it was time to begin thinking about reintegrating into American society. It was time for me and the USNS General E. D. Patrick to become intimately familiar with each other.

Chapter 62

THE USNS E. D. PATRICK

I managed, somehow, to be assigned most unpleasant duties on the way home. I was assigned to latrine duty in an area located as far forward as one could get in the ship. Overall, the duty was relatively easy, cleaning up the sinks, floors, and toilets after each morning's toileting ritual. The worst part of the duty was cleaning the urinals, which were fifteen-foot long metal troughs. The troughs had seawater running through them in a continuous flush. The toilets were situated over a six-inch waste pipe, also outfitted with a continuous flush system. In rough weather it was not at all unusual to have the flush line back up as the ship nose-dived into the valley between two mountainous waves. When that did happen, the ice-cold seawater would come spurting up through the toilets and the drains in the urinals—carrying with it whatever it had managed to collect on its merry trip through those lovely tunnels. If one of the troops were on the pot at such a time he would be treated to an ice cold douching. If he were standing in front of a urinal drain, he would get the eruption in his face. When my morning chores were done, I was free for the rest of the day to do whatever I chose to do.

We were about halfway across the Pacific when ominous thunderclouds appeared on the starboard horizon. The storm was clearly visible. Rain was pouring from the black clouds, and lightening was flashing between the clouds and increasingly rolling seas. By the time the main storm reached us, we were in forty-five-foot waves. The bow of the ship would climb the watery mountain, pause for an instant, and then crash loudly into the trench between each wave. The ship was rolling in a figure eight pattern, its huge twin screws flailing in the air as we careened, side to side, and up and down, over and over and over. Everything not fastened down was flying everywhere. Most of the men's stomachs were not fastened down.

At mealtime, when we had to climb the near vertical steel ladders to the mess deck, we pulled about two, two-and-a-half G's when the ship was surging upward. We would simply stop our climb, and wait for the rapid plunge downward, at which time we were essentially weightless. We just loosened our grip a bit on the handrails and floated up a few steps.

The mess hall itself was a mess, literally. Trays were flying off the tables and crashing onto the floor or into the bulkhead. Most of the troops were sick and vomit was everywhere. Even the servers in the food line were in terrible shape. They would just turn their heads, vomit on the floor, and then continue serving. I learned to hold down the tray with both elbows, while scooping food, which wasn't bad at all, into my face. It wasn't a good idea though, to look out of the window. One minute I could see nothing but sky, and the next, nothing but boiling waters. There really wasn't any place to go, so I wisely decided to make the best of it. After all, I was going home and I only had one boil left on my body. Those were two good omens, I thought, of better things to come.

By the third day in very heavy waters, the storm was beginning to subside as we punched through seemingly endless now twenty to thirty foot waves that crashed over the bow of the ship. No one was on deck. But, we told ourselves, we were heading for San Francisco, and freedom for all of us draftees. By the evening of the third day, the storm had calmed substantially. I went out on the fantail of the ship where I could get some fresh air, but in a protected area where the screaming January winds couldn't reach me. I looked out at our wake, which had been absolutely straight since the beginning of this wonderful cruise. It was turning. No, *we* were turning. We turned completely around and started retracing our watery path. Oh, no! Had Formosa blown up? Had North Korea or China invaded South Korea again? Had we forgotten something?

Finally, the announcement came. A deep voice blared over the PA system that a Coast Guard weather ship, stationed out in the middle of the storm we had just passed through, had a sailor on board that was deathly ill. The best guess the Coast Guard personnel could make was that the young fellow had appendicitis. Since we were the nearest ship with a hospital on board, we were elected to rendezvous with the weather ship as soon as possible and to bring the stricken sailor on board for an examination and probable surgery.

Well, o.k. We all breathed a sigh of relief that the problem was a relatively simple one and we were not going to war. War was a very real concern for all of us. Sometime in 1955, General Chiang Kai-Shek had moved his defeated army from the mainland of China to Formosa. Ships from our Seventh Fleet had formed a barricade between the mainland and the General's evacuation armada. The Communist Chinese had installed major artillery batteries along their coastline and were watching our every move with intense interest. If they chose to, they could have blasted Chiang Kai Shek's flotilla or us, at any time. The big Communist guns remained silent. The evacuation was a success.

We rendezvoused with the weather ship in the middle of the night, and circled each other until daybreak. We were right back in the middle of the storm again. Forty-foot waves were crashing over us again. The feeling in my gut as the ship did its figure eight plunge from the peak of each wave to its valley, was not pleasant. But we were going to be heroes so this mild discomfort was a small price to pay, I told myself.

The seething waters were just too rough to use a breeches buoy to transfer the patient, so volunteers from the weather ship brought this very sick young man over in a small motorized craft they had on board for emergencies. There were many attempts to connect with this bobbing, weaving, matchbox of a craft as it raced up and down eighty feet or more near our huge ship. Finally, ropes between the two were secured and the little boat was brought safely alongside. The young patient was transferred and a wild cheer went up into the raging winds from a thousand onlookers. All of us were at least a little proud of what had been accomplished.

Two hours later an announcement came over the PA system: "You will be happy to know that our young patient is doing fine. It turned out that he did not have appendicitis as suspected. He was constipated."

Constipated?! Constipated?! What a jerk! We had lost over two days trying to rescue a constipated fool in high seas. Oh, well. C'est la vie. Besides, it was nearly time for lunch.

Four days later we arrived in San Francisco. We were loaded onto buses for transfer to the Army facility where we would receive our orders for our individual separation destinations. As we pulled around a corner, on our way to the freeway, a small group of black teenagers standing on the sidewalk, looked up, smiled and gave us the finger. Nice. Real nice. Welcome home!

I flew across the country to Ft. Sheridan, near Chicago, Illinois, and was quickly processed out of the United States Army on February 4, 1956. I then caught a plane to Detroit, just across the lake and about a fifty-minute trip. It was snowing hard when my plane left Chicago, and in fact was the last plane that was allowed out that night. Detroit, however, was completely socked in and the nearest place the plane could land was in Buffalo, New York. The airline offered us a choice: it would either put us up in a hotel that night, or until the weather cleared, whichever came first. Or, they would pay for a train ticket from Buffalo back to Detroit. Since a connection could still be made that night, I elected the latter option. I arrived in Detroit at 8:00 a.m., twelve hours after beginning my fifty-minute flight. I took a cab home from the train depot, hugged my mother, ate breakfast and slept for two hours. I had the next day to rest and recuperate a bit. Then it was time to drive in to downtown Detroit and register for classes at Wayne State University. A new world was dawning.

Part Five

ACADEMIA

Chapter 63

WAYNE STATE UNIVERSITY

FEBRUARY 6, 1956, was a bitterly cold, overcast, typical winter day in Detroit. Soot from the factories had covered the new snow with a disgusting film of black. I never learned to like black snow. I had no civilian clothes suitable for immediate use, so I donned my sleek Class A Army uniform, buffed my boots and drove into the city.

The sprawling campus of Wayne State University was situated about three miles west of the heart of the city, in the midst of some of Detroit's worst slums. Racial segregation in housing in that area was sharp and distinct. The dividing arterial between the East and West Sides of Detroit is Woodward Avenue. On the East Side it was a solidly Black slum for several miles. On the West Side were the White slums, matching the Blacks mess for mess, brawl for brawl, killing for killing. Policemen walked their beats in that area four abreast, arm in arm. It was not a place for casual wandering off campus. At the heart of these despairing clusters of humanity was the cultural oasis of Wayne State University with a student body of over 30,000, 13,000 of whom were in various graduate schools.

I walked into Old Main, the most senior building on campus. Old Main began its life as Detroit Medical College in 1868. It now housed most of Wayne University's administrative offices, including the advising and registration functions. I found an advisor and sat down in a chair next to his impressively old, oak desk.

"What would you like to major in?" he said.

Tough question. I didn't know where to begin. Business Administration was the only major course of studies I had ever heard of, so my response repertoire was fairly constricted. All I knew was that by starting college I was able to get out of the Army 90 days early. I had never given any thought to what my major might be.

"Perhaps Business Administration," I offered. "What classes would be appropriate for me to start with if I were to major in Business Administration?"

Luckily, I had been assigned an advisor who recognized that I didn't know what I was doing.

"Why don't you start with some general university requirements," he said. "These courses can be used in just about any major, and it will give you some time to decide what it is you want to do."

That sounded like a very good idea to me. He signed me up for classes in English Composition, Astronomy, Modern Day Problems, Public Administration, and History, which comprised a full load of 16 semester credits. I thanked him and slipped across the street to join a very long line waiting in the bitter wind to enter the bookstore.

After purchasing my books, which ranged in price from $3.95 to $5.95, my next stop was in the Student Union Building. This was a classic, imposing edifice. It was a very old 14 story hotel that had been converted by the University into student housing, student services such as counseling and advising, a huge cafeteria, and many faculty offices. It even had a swimming pool in the basement. I talked with a Veteran's Advisor and signed up for the Veteran's Benefits that were available to me under the provisions of the GI Bill. At that time the amount was about $130 a month, which was enough for tuition, books, supplies, and gasoline.

The first semester was a struggle for me. I was twenty-two years old and I had been out of an academic setting for nearly six years. I hadn't done terribly well in the ones I had been in either. Nevertheless, I wound up my first semester in June with 2 C's, 2 B's, and a D, for a GPA of 2.25.

After the first semester, when the school officials thought I might be serious about attending college, my scores on the entrance examination that I had taken in Japan were evaluated. I had scored quite well, and was awarded a total of 22 semester credits. I must have been brilliant! In any event, I figured I had earned the summer off from studies.

I began to relax a bit, and even enjoyed my status as a sophisticated, world traveled, veteran of the military. But I really missed my old Army buddies. Sometimes, in periods of acute depression, I would think about re-enlisting. But that was insane. I hated the military life. So, with the help of a bottle of cheap wine, I was able to throw off those crazy little thoughts without too much difficulty.

I had joined the active Army Reserves as soon as I had been discharged, so I had a little contact with the military life. This time, however, I was a Company Clerk, and enjoyed my one-year commitment immensely. I had a two-hour meeting one evening a week, and two weeks of active reserves at Camp Murray in Wisconsin during the summer of 1956. My total obligation to the military was eight years, two years active duty, one-year active reserves, and 5 years inactive reserves. I managed to get through my reserve years without being called up to participate in a military action in some exotic land far away. I was extremely pleased when I received my final release from Uncle Sam in 1960.

Chapter 64

THE CARPENTER

THE first summer home, I decided to fix up the little house Mom and I were sharing in Lincoln Park. The stimulus was a mouse I saw staring at me from a hole he had chewed in a corner junction where two walls met the ceiling. I swear he was grinning at me, and I took up the challenge.

I decided to replace the decrepit lath and plaster ceiling with white, interlocking asbestos tile squares. "Should take about a week," I told Mom.

I covered the living room rug and what furniture we had with newspapers and brought in a ladder. With crowbar in hand, I nimbly ascended the ladder and punched my first hole in the ceiling. I began pulling the lath and plaster down and soon I was in a storm of powdery plaster dust, millions of bits of loose asbestos insulation, and accumulated debris that had been lurking up there, untouched, since the beginning of time. What I found was an architectural disaster that took me the entire summer to repair.

Whoever had built the original little house had installed a brick chimney in the living room which served to vent a small oil burning stove, the only source of heat, other than our bodies, which didn't amount to nearly enough in Michigan winters. The problem was that he had cut the hole in the roof for the chimney before he began building it. As he proceeded to mortar one brick upon another on his way to the heavens, he discovered about halfway up that he wasn't going to meet the hole he had prepared in the roof. He then began angling his brickwork back toward the center of the house and eventually made it through the hole. The resulting chimney was severely and dangerously bowed. To compensate for this nasty situation, he placed a 4 x 4 brace between the chimney and the outer wall of the house. Over the years, the constant pressure had skewed and distorted the living room walls and ceiling into geometric chaos. Nothing was square. No standard piece of anything would fit anywhere.

In addition, when I reached the walls with my ceiling-removing activity, I discovered that the walls, too, were badly skewed and that the wall studs were constructed with severely scorched 2 x 4's, apparently salvaged from a building that had burned down. I wound up carefully replacing every stud, one by one. As I installed a new stud, I would remove the burned out original. I slowly worked my way around the room until at least the walls were safe and structurally sound. I did the same with the ceiling joists, carefully calculating the potential domino effects of removing any piece of lumber. It took a long time, several weeks in fact, but finally the room was ready for new wall and ceiling materials.

For the remainder of the summer, I kept busy installing pieces of a beautifully grained wood paneling. I custom cut each piece to fit the skewed walls so that everything at least looked straight. I installed horizontal two by three-inch furring strips across the ceiling joists, which would serve as a base for stapling the decorative, interlocking acoustic tiles in place. It was looking good.

    I arranged to have natural gas brought in from the street and installed an attractive gas space heater. Finally, I ordered wall to wall carpeting installed and I was done, just in time for the crispness of fall. It was beautiful. A veritable doll house. Mom was happy and warm.

Chapter 65

BACK TO SCHOOL

MY second semester at Wayne was interesting and a lot more fun. Both Al and John-Bob had been discharged from the Army by then and had joined me as students there. Al suggested that I might try Psychology as a major. Being rather suggestible at the time, I enrolled in the introductory course. Unfortunately, it was held at 8:00 a.m., and I was late for class almost every day.

The instructor was an unconventional little man, short of stature and about sixty years old. He had three identically cut suits—one brown, one gray, and one blue, each worn for a week at a time. The cut of the suits was vintage 1900, with little decorative belts on the waist. He was owned by a very compulsive personality that required him to fill three walls of the classroom's blackboards with tiny, very neat writing, outlining the contents of the day's lecture. Without fail, his outline was completed before his lecture began at 8:00 a.m. sharp.

He didn't like my being late, and dropped me from his class three consecutive times. Although he never took roll, he knew precisely who was there and whether or not they had been on time. Every third time I was either late or absent he would drop me from his class. I had to report to him each time and humbly request reinstatement. After the third conference with him, he declared me incorrigible, gave me a "C," and with great relief, passed me out of his life.

I also enrolled in the introductory class in Sociology. That too, was an experience not easily forgotten. In fact, it was nearly beyond belief. The class was offered in an offensively hot portable building in which Detroit's humid, stale air frequently soared to over 100 degrees. The instructor was a slight man of about thirty-five. He was about 5 foot, seven inches, and 120 pounds. He wore an ill-fitting Army belt, cinched up tightly around his 28-inch waist. Sixteen inches of excess belt hung loosely from its grossly tarnished brass buckle. But it did hold up his very baggy pants. He stood in front of the class, droning on and on about nonsensical sociological concepts while staring at the ceiling. If he wasn't staring at the ceiling, he had his eyes closed. Not once did he make eye contact with anyone in the stiflingly hot classroom. At least once per session he would actually fall asleep while lecturing. Unbelievable! I finally stopped going to his class altogether, except for exam days. Most of the course content was common sense anyway, and I passed with no difficulty.

Funds were always in short supply, so I got myself a job driving a Yellow Cab from 6:00 p.m. until midnight, six nights a week. The job was exhausting, literally. The cab had a severe leak in its exhaust system that kept the worn out hulk filled with deadly carbon monoxide. I cruised the streets of Detroit seeking paying fares, and usually found some. I never had a repeat customer, however, and I only got ripped off once.

I had been sitting at a cab stand one night, trying to read

some boring text book, and get some fresh air circulating through the old wreck's interior, when a drunken black man of about forty opened the back door of the car and lurched into the back seat. He gave me an address and off we went. The destination was squarely in the midst of a very bad neighborhood. I stopped the car and told him what the fare was. His slurred response was, "I got twenty-eight shents. That'sh all I got. You want (burrrp) to do shumting about it?"

He threw the change into the front seat, opened the door and tumbled out. Since it was neither the time nor place to argue, I sped off and headed for safer ground. Then I radioed my dispatcher with my story. He said, "Don't worry about it. It happens all the time. The company will take the hit, not you."

I hustled back to the cab terminal in downtown Detroit and turned in my rolling death trap and my resignation. Surely, there had to be other ways to pick up a couple of bucks.

It was about midnight when I got home that evening. We were entering what would be an extended period of extremely cold weather, and I quickly discovered that our water pipes under the house were frozen. I dug out an old blowtorch of my father's, put on my warmest long-johns and outerwear, grabbed a flashlight and slipped under the house.

The crawl space was nearly nonexistent, being perhaps eighteen inches from frozen ground to frozen pipes overhead. I inched my way in on my back and examined the situation. I fired up the blowtorch and slowly turned it down to a fierce, blue searing flame, and began the slow process of thawing the pipes from where they emerged from the ground, to where they entered the house from the crawl space. It was agonizing work. I was lying flat on my back, holding the blue-flamed inferno overhead and trying to thaw the pipes without setting fire either to the house or myself, while ten degree, forty-mile-an-hour winds blasted through the crawl space opening. It wasn't long before even my shorts were near frozen. That is generally very unpleasant for me. It took about half an hour to thaw the pipes and reinstate the water flow. No pipes had been broken by the freeze, but this scene was to be repeated half a dozen times before the cold snap released its hold on us.

I finished my second semester at Wayne with good grades and moved through the next three, completing general university requirements, with no difficulty. It was in my fifth semester that I got my first taste of Graduate School course work, and I liked it. It was a night class in Family Relations, and Al and I took it together. One of the students in the class was a stunningly beautiful blond woman of about twenty. I struck up a conversation with her one evening during a break in the two and a half-hour class. Here I was, the sophisticated veteran, telling wonderful stories and making great progress with this beauty who stared at me with rapt attention. She just couldn't take her eyes off of me as I spun one yarn after another. Al stood by, simply smiling at me. Then it was time to return to class.

When we sat down, Al turned to me and said, "You don't know that you're bleeding, do you?"

"What?!" I exclaimed.

"You've got blood all over your face from a razor cut," Al said. He could barely contain himself. He thought it was extremely funny to see his old Army buddy putting on airs while bleeding.

I slipped quietly out of the classroom and into the nearest latrine. Was he pulling my leg? I looked into the mirror. No. He wasn't. I had nicked myself high up on my left cheek and had a stream of dried blood about six inches long trailing down from it. I was chagrined. So that's what she was staring at. It wasn't me with my wonderful stories—it was my blood-encrusted face. That was the last time I talked with that lovely blond lady.

During the next three semesters, I took an additional five graduate courses, four of them at the doctoral level. It was great and I was beginning to feel relatively good about myself and my place in the world.

At the end of my sophomore year I needed summer work, but summer work was simply not available. I answered an ad for a route salesman for the Jewel Tea Company and applied for a full time position. I had never heard of the Jewel Tea Company before, but I was to learn that it was one of the largest retail organizations in the country with gigantic supermarkets throughout the East, Midwest and South. The man who interviewed me was a fine gentleman of about forty. He explained that the job involved servicing customers on ten separate routes. I was to service one route per day during the week, taking orders and delivering the products the customers had ordered during the previous stop. Most of the products were food products—staples that needed no refrigeration—but Jewel also had a retail catalog for each customer that contained everything from panties to power mowers. The man who had the route previously had completely screwed it up, provided extremely poor service, ignored customers, and had generally been an obnoxious jerk. My job was to straighten that terrible mess out, provide service excellence, and return the route to profitability. "No problem," I said, and prepared to demonstrate my finely honed people skills.

In less than a month I not only had the route cleaned up and straightened out, I had generated several new customers. I had my work day so efficiently organized that I was generally through for the day around two o'clock, leaving much more time to work on projects around the house. At the end of the summer my boss was sad to see me go, but understood and we parted friends. He had no difficulty finding someone to take over the rejuvenated route. I often wondered what exotic paths my life would have followed had I stayed with the Jewel Tea Company.

Violence was still prevalent in Detroit, and I was privy to some of it. One example that stuck in my memory occurred late one night as I was returning home from a date. It was about 2:30 a.m., and stiflingly hot and humid. I was traveling east on Livernois Avenue, singing a Kirby tune to myself, when I saw a scuffling between two people just ahead. They were standing in the street alongside the open door of a parked car. As I approached, I recognized that one of them was a woman. The man with her slammed her in the face with his fist, knocking her backward onto the car seat. Her legs sprawled crazily as she slumped, unconscious, to the pavement. I stopped my car by the curbside, and as I did so, he saw me. He jumped into his car and sped off, leaving his victim in the street. I ran over to her. She was regaining consciousness as I approached, and was bleeding from a severe cut above her swollen eyes. I helped her to her feet and managed to get her into my car. I asked if I could take her to the Fort and Green police station which was just a mile or so away.

"No," she said. "Just take me to a gas station where I can make a phone call. I don't want to report this. He'll kill me if I do. I can call a friend to come and pick me up and take me home."

I took her to a service station several blocks away and waited while she made her call. In just a few minutes, someone arrived in a car and took her away. She waved and smiled at me as she slipped off into the darkness of Detroit, battered but apparently, not yet broken.

One afternoon when I arrived home, Mom was visibly shaken. She said that two plainclothes policemen from Detroit had been at our house for about an hour that day. She said that they had asked whether or not we had any guns in the house. Mom told them that we had a .22 caliber rifle, but that was all. They then searched the house and garage looking for guns. Of course they only found the rifle she had told them about. They then said that they had picked up a couple of delinquents in Detroit, each of whom had zip guns. Zip guns are single shot, home made pistols, typically used by small time thieves and adolescents short on testosterone who felt they needed to boost their masculinity up a notch or two. When asked where they got the guns, those jerks, whoever they were, told them that I had made them for them. They gave them my name and told them I lived in Lincoln Park.

Since I was the only Glenn Adams living in Lincoln Park, they were obliged to pay me a visit. I never found out who had reported this ludicrous lie to the police. It remains a mystery. It was also a mystery just why it was I had survived for so long with my cat deficit.

As I left the campus of Wayne State the next day, I decided to see what was available at the Detroit Animal Shelter. Wouldn't you know it, they had just under a thousand cats available for adoption. Big cats, little cats, micro cats, of all colors and descriptions where screaming at me, vying for my attention. All but one, and he was a runt. He was a small yellow kitten, about six weeks old, and he looked just miserable. He didn't say anything. He just looked at me, his eyes saying, "Please?" He was irresistible. I paid my two bucks, picked up the little guy and headed for home.

"What shall I name him?" I said to myself. "Well, Self," I responded, "he doesn't look very ferocious. Let's give him a ferocious name. Cat, henceforth, your name will be 'Igor'!"

Three nights later, Igor was sleeping peacefully with me when suddenly he began to do flip-flops in the bed and acting quite ill. I comforted him the best I could. Early the next morning I took him back to the pound where I had gotten him. The diagnosis was immediate. DISTEMPER! Oh, no! I had never seen an animal survive distemper. The veterinarian examining Igor said perhaps there was a slight chance he could be saved, and gave him an injection of something. Igor was miserable. He crawled over to me for protection from his invasive tormentor and hid his face in my arms. I think it was at that point that Igor identified with me so completely that he began to think he was in fact, me.

He survived the distemper and became the best pet I ever had. He would wait patiently on our front porch for me to come home from Wayne every afternoon. As soon as he would see me he would run as fast as he could to meet me. He would leave the ground about twelve feet from me, and fly through the air into my arms. What a wonderful animal Igor was. When I would walk to the neighborhood grocery store, Igor would follow and wait just outside of the door of the store for me, just like a faithful dog might. I had never seen anything like it.

I was the only human Igor tolerated, though. He would tear anyone else to shreds. Anytime we had company, I would have to lock Igor in my bedroom, where he would sulk until the house was clear of all intruders. I never worried about being assaulted while driving, if I had Igor in the car. I figured if such an event were to begin unfolding, I would simply hand Igor to them who would then proceed to rip out their arteries. He was a great cat.

Igor and I had been near constant companions for about a year and a half when he disappeared. I had very strong suspicious that our neighbor's teenage boy had done Igor in with his bow and arrow. I'll never forget Igor.

Just a block from Wayne's campus, the great radio station, WXYZ was housed in the Macabee's Building. WXYZ originated and was the only home ever known by both the Lone Ranger and the Green Hornet radio dramas.

On a Saturday afternoon in the fall of 1956, I learned that Mioshi Umeki was going to be a featured singer on our local version of the nationally broadcast *Dick Clark's Dance Show*. Ms. Umeki was very petite and pretty and a very famous pop singer in Japan. I had heard of her while I was in Japan but had never seen her perform.

I thought it would be both fun and interesting to watch her act, so I showed up in my very best sartorial regalia. I was standing in the back of the room waiting for her to begin when Pat Boone entered and passed directly in front of me. I had no idea who he was at the time, but his face was already made up with pancake makeup and he was stunningly handsome. He didn't even look real. It was only after several weeks that I learned who he was. Then Ms. Umeki finished her songs and disappeared backstage.

"What the Hell," I said to myself. "Let's see if she'll talk to me."

I sent a note to her by a station messenger asking if I could have her autograph. I received an immediate positive response, along with a request that I come to her dressing room.

I quickly discovered that she spoke essentially no English. So, with my childlike Japanese, I managed to invite her for a cup of coffee in the building's cafeteria. Unbelievably, she accepted and I escorted her through the crowd and into the restaurant. She sat quietly while I approached the counter and ordered two cups of coffee. My hands were shaking so badly that the cups were nearly empty by the time I got back to our table.

I sat down with her and for the next twenty minutes carried on a conversation of sorts in Japanese. It was great until I noticed that a rather large American man was staring at us. It wasn't long before he approached and introduced himself as Mioshi's manager. He said it was time for her to go, and swept her away.

I never saw her again in person, but we did exchange one set of letters. She went on to a role in television as the maid in the series, *Eddie's Father.*

Chapter 66

A WAY OUT

AS graduation time began to loom on the horizon, I began to feel a little anxious about what my next step was going to be. I went to the Career Counseling Office to talk with a counselor about what might be available to me. He administered an aptitude test of some sort to me and made an appointment for the following week for an interpretive session. When I arrived I had high expectations that he would be able to help me straighten out my career path. I sat down in a chair alongside his desk. He looked at me and said, with no humor at all, "Guys like you disgust me. Your scores are extremely high. You can do anything you want to do."

That was it!! That obnoxious, hostile statement was my entire career counseling at Wayne State University. I left his office overwhelmed with confusion and disgust, and headed for Dr. Browne's office on the next floor. Dr. Browne was a psychologist who specialized in General Semantics, a study of language and the meaning of words. He was Al's advisor, and I had met him about a year previously. He was a good head, and Al and I used to tease him about his specialty by asking if he had designed any new ashtrays or coffee mugs in his class in General Ceramics. I wanted to talk with him about my future, but I never got to his office that day.

On my way down the hallway, I passed a bulletin board outside of the office of the Chairman of the Psychology Department. There, in blazing green and white, was a brochure from the University of Oregon. Its bold headline screamed at me:

"Come to the University of Oregon in Eugene. Our two-year master's degree program in Rehabilitation Counseling is looking for bright young people. Our graduates will be trained to work with physically or psychologically impaired people to help them enter or re-enter the world of work."

What *really* caught my attention was the fact that this was a program sponsored by the U.S. Department of Health, Education and Welfare and offered successful applicants a $200 a month stipend the first year of training, and $220 a month the second year. My letter of inquiry was in the mail that evening.

A few days later I received an informational packet, an application, and a request that I take the Miller's Analogy Test as soon as possible, and to have the results forwarded to the U. of O.'s Psychology Department. I found out when the next Miller's was to be given, sent in the test fee and steeled myself for what I presumed would be a relatively tough test.

The day of the test was very bright and sunny for February in Detroit. I revved up my '53 Ford and roared off, over the dormant volcano in the alley, and headed north on Dix Highway toward the "Big D" and Wayne State. I was no more than two miles from home when my radiator blew a hole in itself and I lost all of my coolant. There wasn't time to take public transportation, so I had no choice but to call and cancel my testing appointment. I was informed that for a fee of $25 I could arrange to have the test administered individually. The following Monday I reported to the Testing Center and made the appropriate arrangements.

When my make-up test day arrived, I showed up, on time, at the designated office. I was met by a wrinkled old crone who led me into an extremely small room barely big enough to hold my chair and small desk. The crone turned out to be my test proctor and she took her job very seriously. She pulled her chair up right next to mine, whipped out her stopwatch, read the instructions to me, and I was off. I looked at the first question. My brain spun around and I damn near panicked. "This is to that as blank is to whatever."

I was to fill in the blank by choosing one of four alternative words or concepts, most of which I had never seen before. Perhaps I was in deep trouble. I had never been involved with mind bogglers like that before. I responded to two or three questions—and then the old crone said, "You have fifty-five minutes left."

She began the countdown. Every five minutes she would let me know that I was that much closer to a terminal state.

"You have fifty minutes remaining. You have forty-five minutes remaining," and so on and on.

I wanted to bust her in her tobacco-stained little teeth, but that wasn't a particularly sensible course of action, so I just ground my own and plodded on. When I finally finished the test, I was completely drained. My brain had nothing more to give. I arranged to have the results sent to the U. of O. and limped out of the office in my sweat-drenched clothes, found my car and drove home in a daze.

"That did it. I'll never get into the University of Oregon now. I may have to go to work somewhere. Oh, no!" I murmured to myself as I steered my little Ford to the nearest Mott's hamburger joint for some serious nourishment and self-pity.

I finished my course work and prepared for graduation.

I was going to be the first college graduate in the entire Abbott/Adams family conglomerate, and I must say, I was pretty proud of that.

Of the hundreds of students who graduated that evening, I was the only one who managed to trip while ascending the stairs on the way to the stage by stepping on the front of my robe. Nevertheless, it was a great evening. Al graduated the same night. We were both college graduates! What do you know! "Not bad for a high school dropout," I thought to myself.

When Mom and I got back home, we found that I had received a letter from the University of Oregon that day. I had been accepted into the Rehab Program!! Wow! What a day that was.

Chapter 67

THE REPO MAN

SINCE I didn't have to report to Oregon until late September, I still had the summer for work. However, jobs were really scarce. Detroit was on the brink of what became the longest steel strike ever, 96-days. All plants that depended on steel in the manufacture of their products, like refrigerators and stoves, tires, and wiring companies were preparing to shut down. When the strike did come, Detroit essentially shut down. Every day additional tens of thousands were laid off from their jobs. It became an economic disaster for the people of Detroit and its suburbs.

Soon after graduation I explored the summer job listings in the student placement office. That took less than a minute. There simply were no summer jobs. I wandered out of the building and over to the Macabee's Building for a cup of coffee and serious thought about what was to become of me now. Who walked in at the same time? It was Baccaduchi!! Even though he was neatly dressed in a business suit, I recognized him immediately. His yellowish/green incisors were unmistakable. I hailed him and he joined me at my table with coffee and a huge fat-heavy sweet roll. We reminisced briefly about our great Army careers, and then I explained my "lack of summer job" dilemma. Baccaduchi wiped the strawberry jam from his cheek and said, "My company is hiring. Their main office is right across the street. Why don't you apply?"

"What does your company do?" I asked.

"We're in the financial business," he explained. "We have seven different companies. Some of them loan money to individuals, others deal with large corporations. We also have a very large insurance company, underwriting individuals, cars, and companies. I work in small loans. Come on. I'll introduce you to my boss. Just don't tell him you're looking for temporary work or you won't be hired."

We finished our coffee and walked briskly across the street to the offices of Amalgamated Loan Company. After Baccaduchi introduced me to his boss, he disappeared and I never saw him again in my entire life. Boss Man gave me a really stupid Wonderlik Aptitude Test, from which I promptly blew the lid. He was surprised and said that he had never seen anyone get all of the questions correct before. Then came the tough question.

"You have a college degree. Why do you want to work with a small loan company?" he asked with some interest.

Good question. Revving up all available brain cells, I responded, "I've always been interested in the world of finance. From what Baccaduchi told me, Amalgamated is deeply involved in a wide range of financial activity. You're a large, international company, and I'd like to be a part of your growth."

Good answer. Boss Man smiled. "What a find," he must have thought and hired me on the spot. I was assigned to a branch office just two blocks from my home in Lincoln Park and started work the following day. For the first two weeks I was in training with a muscular brute who had been with the company for three years.

Amalgamated had three of their companies housed in this relatively small office of eight workers, including secretarial support. One was a small loan company that made loans of up to $500 to people momentarily down on their luck. This company generally took whatever furniture and appliances the person had as collateral. Interest rates were just barely legal and a hair this side of usury.

The second company in the office was an automobile loan company, financing cars up to a $5,000 value. Again, interest rates were at the legal limits.

The third company underwrote automobile insurance policies for the cars the auto loan division was financing. Since they would not insure a car they hadn't financed, or finance a car that wasn't insured by them, it was a kind of dark, symbiotic relationship, and an extraordinarily profitable one.

My job involved telephoning delinquent payers with a strong request that they make their payment right then, that afternoon. Almost all calls had to do with late or missed payments on automobiles. Sometimes people came in with the cash. Frequently they did not. Then I would make a second call. This time there were no pleasantries. *"Be in our office by 5:00 p.m."*

If they failed to show, their name, address, and a description of the car in question went into the "REPO" box. I spent about half of my time for the remainder of the summer working repos. That was exciting, dangerous work, but it was not fun. If we had to remove a car from the man's real property, like the driveway or garage, he had every legal right to shoot us both quite dead. Mom was not particularly pleased with my line of work that summer.

The repo guys always went out in teams of two. We would

meet at 3:00 a.m. at the office and drive to where we knew the car would be. We'd park about a block from the house and quietly creep up to the car. If it was unlocked, we were in luck. But that was a rare occurrence. My mentor had a cigar box full of ignition keys, one of which would almost always fit the car we were after. Amazing. However, if he couldn't find a key that would work, he had tools that he could slip into the door alongside of the window, and trip the locking mechanism. In any event we were generally in the car within seconds. He would get behind the steering wheel and I would push it by hand into the darkened street. Then I would run back to the company car, start it, and roll up behind the target car as silently as I could. I would slowly push the car about two or three blocks away from our victim's home, park it and lock it. Then we would go to the nearest open service station and call the police to report the repossession. That was followed by a call to the nearest towing company to have the car towed to an impound lot.

The morning following a repossession was fairly predictable. The person who'd had their car taken would call the police to report his car as stolen. The police would reassure him that it had not been stolen, it had merely been repossessed. They would tell the person to call their finance company to get it straightened out. And they always would.

When they called they were told that for us to release their car from the impound lot, they would need to come to the office, bring their account up to date, pay the wrecker and impound fees, and give us two month's payments in advance, in cash. Most of them couldn't come up with that much cash, but we had a solution for them.

We'd walk them across the room and have them apply for a $500 small loan, thereby sinking our hooks even more deeply into those hapless souls. It was a disgusting job. It was dangerous, and I hated it. But, it did provide sustenance throughout the summer, and I didn't get shot.

Then, it was fall and I was nearly twenty-six. It was time to leave black snow and crime and head for the lush green fields of Oregon. There I would meet a stunning woman who would change my life forever, but that's another story....

I backed my '53 Ford into the ramshackle shed we referred to as our garage, removed the tires and placed blocks under the wheels. The rocker panels were completely rusted out from the salt Detroit spread on its streets to melt the ice and snow. It also melted the metal from the cars that traversed those streets. I often wondered whether there was collusion between the International Salt Mine and the automobile companies. No car body lasted more than three years.

Chapter 68

THE UNIVERSITY OF OREGON

MY red-eye flight from Detroit to Eugene via Portland was, for me, unusually uneventful. I took a cab from the airport to downtown Eugene and the Eugene Hotel. I knew that a second cousin of mine, Violet, worked there as a waitress in the hotel's restaurant. I had met Violet and her two children in 1945 when Dad took me with him on his fruitless quest for a suitable farm. Her son was a year or two older that I was—her daughter a year younger. I was twelve at that time and I hadn't seen any of them for more than thirteen years.

Violet seemed delighted to see me and bought me breakfast. We chatted a bit, as she was able between customers, and we got reacquainted. She loaned me her car and pointed me in the direction of the U. of O. campus. It was misting lightly as I approached the campus some ten blocks or so away (I was to learn that it is *frequently* misting lightly in western Oregon). I was struck by the lushness of the lawns and trees, all meticulously and beautifully manicured. And clean, fresh air, tinged with the mixed fragrances of sweet evergreens, sawmills and freshly cut lumber. What a wonderful change from Detroit. The mist and occasional real rain were small prices to pay for the beauty in which I found myself. I was worlds away from the dust, grime, soot, crime, and black snow of Detroit, and I was truly happy.

As I approached the campus, I decided to drive through some of the surrounding residential area. Two blocks from campus I pulled off of 13th Avenue onto Ferry Street, and as I did so, I spotted a lady putting a "Room for Rent" sign in her living room window. I sidled over to the curb and walked up to the front door. The lady who answered was about 50 or so and very pleasant. She had a face that reminded me of some sort of bird. A canary, or parakeet perhaps. As we trotted up the carpeted stairs to inspect the vacant room, I wondered how her spindly little legs were able to support her. The room was huge, clean, and had its own window. It was gorgeous. And it had a full bath just outside my door. There was an identical bedroom and a landing at the top of the stairs that she also rented out.

"How much are you asking?" I queried.

"Twenty-five dollars a month. The other bedroom is rented to Dan, an Army Captain, and the landing is rented to John, a young graduate student from Dartmouth. The landing rents for only $15 a month. I vacuum the rooms every day, and wash and change the sheets once a week," she said.

Without hesitation I said, "I'll take it," and moved in that afternoon. We exchanged dollars, receipts, and names. I smiled when she said I could call her "Birdie." Of course, what else could her name have been?

I moved my belongings into the room and walked the two blocks to the campus. God, it was beautiful. Most of the brick buildings were quite old, but new ones were being built and there were a few surplus Army buildings being used as temporary offices for some functions like Admissions, Registration, and Counseling.

My first stop, however, was Condon Hall, just inside the boundary of the campus. Condon Hall was a very old two story brick building and the home of the Psychology Department. Condon was later nicknamed either "Condom Hall" or "The Pain Building" by my fellow graduate students and me. Which name was used by the students was determined daily by whether the Psychology faculty had really screwed us that day, or had merely inflicted psychological terror on us. I located my contact person and advisor, Dr. Scobbaggin and sat down in a hard wooden chair next to his desk. Dr. Scobbaggin was a slight man, probably close to forty and about 5', 8" tall. His hair was cut in an obsolete and unfashionable crew. Perhaps, somehow, he perceived that I thought he looked ridiculous. His first words to me were, "Where the Hell have *you* been? Classes start next week!"

Somewhat startled, I replied, "I know they begin next week. That's why I'm here a week ahead of time!"

A bit more of decreasingly hostile verbal sparring ensued, and we finally settled down into a relatively reasonable conversation. He outlined the courses I should register for and I headed for the registration office.

"That guy's really weird, and power drunk as well," I thought to myself as I meandered across campus. Just how weird he was I would only learn much later. But it was a beautiful day and, in spite of Scobbaggin, I was on top of the world.

I made the necessary arrangements to initiate my $200 a month Rehabilitation Counseling stipend, and enrolled in fourteen graduate credits, which included the first quarter of a year-long seminar with the head of the Psychology Department, Dr. Leeper.

The first quarter in his seminar seriously rattled my sensibilities. In fact, the first day was enough to energize my fledgling anxiety neurosis. The twenty new graduate students were sitting around a quadrangle of tables with Dr. Leeper. No one in the room knew anyone else. Since none of us had any notion about the intelligence or skill levels of the competition sitting there, the anxiety in the room was palpable. Everyone could see and hear everyone else. There was no place to hide.

Dr. Leeper, in his soft monotone, and through a five pound white mustache, which nearly covered his deep purple lips, droned his introductory question: "Can anyone tell me what Psychology is?"

A hand shot up, and Dr. Leeper acknowledged it.

"Psychology is the study of people," the curly-haired student said with great pride and satisfaction.

"That's understood." Dr. Leeper replied somewhat condescendingly. "Can you take it a little deeper?"

The young man was devastated. He had just shot his entire load and it had turned out to be a blank. He declined to continue and slumped down in his rock hard chair on his increasingly numb gluteus.

No one else decided to volunteer a guess as to what Dr. Leeper wanted for a response, so he began his lecture. It was as if someone had pulled down the shades and switched off the lights. I don't think I understood anything he said for the next two hours.

"Oh, man," I thought to myself. "Am I in the wrong world, or what?"

When the first session was over, I hooked up with the student who had embarrassed himself. We introduced ourselves to each other and headed for the nearest coffee shop to ruminate and exchange anxieties. His name was Don and he had a wife, Betty, two very young children and a degree in Physical Therapy. Don had moved his family from their home in New York State to enter this program, so he had an enormous investment in being successful. He and his family lived in married student housing in the Amazon Projects, a very large cluster of obsolete one and two story Army barracks that had been moved to a site just off campus.

Two days later, after classes, Don asked me if I was ready for the Qualifying Examinations.

"Qualifying Exams!!?? What are they?"

"They're comprehensive exams on several different areas of Psychology," Don replied. "All of us in the program in Psychology must take and pass the quals before we can be legitimately admitted to the Rehab Program. Didn't you know that?"

No, I didn't know that. It was news to me. How could I have overlooked such a crucial, required event? I crammed down a ham sandwich and a cup of pea soup at the cafeteria, and decided it was definitely time for a nap. I walked slowly back to Birdie's, crawled into bed and fell into a deep slumber.

When I awoke, it was ten minutes to six. THE EXAM STARTED AT SIX!! I leapt out of bed, head swirling. I ran down the stairs and out into the mist. When I got to the Pain Building, it was precisely six o'clock. I sat down in a chair, received my copy of the exam, and nearly panicked. The test was 450 questions long, 50 on each of nine areas of Psychology: History, Abnormal, Social, Physiological, Experimental, Educational, Counseling, Learning, and Statistics. The entire test had been written by Psychology Department faculty who were experts in their respective areas. There were damn few places to hide in that room.

There were several students in the room who had failed the first time they had taken the test a year previously, and were retaking it. If they failed it again, they could pack their bags and head for home and the consolation that only Mommies can give. Fortunately, I passed the Quals on the first trip through, and avoided a year-long anxiety state. Don wasn't so lucky.

Chapter 69

ARLENE

THE next afternoon I thought it might be a good idea to visit the Counseling Center and familiarize myself with it a bit since I would be spending considerable time there. The first floor of the old Army building housed the offices of Registration and Financial Aid, with the entire second floor dedicated to counseling rooms, faculty offices, and testing.

I climbed the stairs and began wandering down the hallway, casually inspecting each room. I came upon a small, closet-like room, filled with filing cabinets, a dim light and no windows. There was a young lady in the room, facing away from me. She was bending over one of the lower file drawers, pulling out one file after another for reasons only she understood. She appeared to be working very hard and was quite preoccupied with her task and didn't notice me for two or three minutes. I leaned casually against the door casing and enjoyed the view. It was a nice view.

Finally, she must have sensed that someone was there and turned to face me. She stood up and I was transfixed by her loveliness. Even though she was flushed from the heat and perspiring, she was the most beautiful woman I had ever seen. She was about five feet two inches tall, blond, and with stunning blue eyes. She was absolutely lovely.

"May I help you?" she asked politely. She seemed a bit flustered as she tried to brush out the damp wrinkles from her skirt.

"You certainly may," I said, and proceeded to provide her with some vaguely legitimate reasons for my presence. I learned that she was also a beginning graduate student, majoring in Educational Psychology and that she had a scholarship that provided her with twenty hours of work a week as a psychometrist in the Counseling Center.

Then I asked, "When is your next break? I'd like to buy you a cup of coffee."

She smiled and replied, "Right now."

It was the middle of the afternoon as we strolled slowly over to the Student Union Building (The SUB), and it was hot and sultry. We settled down at a table with our coffee and for the next hour of her ten-minute break we exchanged information about ourselves and began "The Dance." Her name was Arlene, she was twenty-two years old and from Seattle. Her only sibling was a brother, Nick, seven years her junior. She had attended Whitman College, a private undergraduate school in Walla Walla, Washington. Her outstanding academic achievements as a Psychology major had earned her a work scholarship as a psychometrist at the U. of O., which allowed her to pursue graduate work. And there we were.

It was way past time for her to be back at work, so we walked outside and on the sidewalk, said our farewells. I said, "Thanks for sharing your day with me, Arlene."

She smiled and said, "Thanks for keeping me awake this afternoon."

I chuckled, waved goodbye, and walked slowly back to my room on Ferry Street.

"She is unbelievably perfect," I muttered to myself. "I think I'm going to marry that girl."

The following day I was back in the Counseling Center. I found Arlene and asked her if she would like to have a cup of coffee with me at Tino's, a little pizza joint just off the campus.

"Sure," she said, and gave me directions to her little upstairs apartment that she shared with Carol, another Whitman graduate.

That evening I borrowed Captain Dan's car, picked up Arlene and cruised down to Tino's. Neither of us had enough money for food, so we just ordered a cup of coffee and took up the dance where we had left off the day before.

After an hour or so the waitress became tired of bringing us refills and finally just left a large pot on our table. I guess she had observed this scene before. We were there for nearly five hours. Everything we shared with each other seemed to mesh. Even the ideas and concepts that we differed on were complementary, balancing counterpoints. But it was one o'clock in the morning. It was time to go back to our respective homes and call it a night. Tomorrow would be another day.

"How perfect can a woman get?" I asked myself as I slipped between my sheets.

The Canadian geese were honking in the distance as they made their way south on their annual migration. How much more pleasant that was than the cacophony of police sirens and gun shots of Detroit. "I must be in Heaven," I muttered as I fell softly into a deep, deep sleep.

The next morning Dan could tell that my previous evening's excursion had been successful and again offered his car to me. Dan was stationed in Portland, where he lived with his wife and children on weekends. But during the week, he had no real use for his car and he let me use it for the entire quarter.

Because of the relatively high humidity during the late fall, winter, and early spring in Eugene, students especially but townsfolk as well, adopted the nickname "Webfoot" as a reference to themselves. Captain Dan really *was* a webfoot. I had never before, or since, seen a web-footed person. His toes had no separation at all. They only had very fine, faint indentions between them. His feet were somewhat like solid blocks of wood. But, he had gotten along just fine for over thirty years. I don't know how he managed all of the marching and concomitant wear and tear of Army life, but he had. I thanked him for his generous offer of wheels. Delighted, I ran off through the fog and mist to class.

As soon as classes were done for the day I was back in the Counseling Center. There she was—my beautiful Arlene. She smiled approvingly as I approached. I said, "Dan has let me borrow his car tonight. I'd like to show you the beauty of the lights of Eugene from the hills tonight. Would you like to do that?"

She said that she had never seen the city at night from the hills and would very much like to do that. My heart was crashing around in my chest and I thought to myself, "I think I'm falling in love." We agreed on a time for me to pick her up and I was there. It was not a time to be less than punctual.

That evening as we exalted in the panoramic beauty of Eugene, we learned much more about one another. As that wonderful evening drew to a close, I drove her back to her apartment, taking the most circuitous route I could legitimately create. As we were saying good night, she told me that I should know she was pinned.

"Pinned? What's that?" I said. "Does it hurt?"

"No, it doesn't hurt, Goofy. See this little pin on my coat? This is a fraternity pin. Tom, the fellow I was going with at Whitman gave it to me before he left for graduate school at

Brown University. It's just short of an engagement ring," she replied. "I think he's planning to give me a ring during Christmas break."

"So?" I said. "I don't care if you're pinned. You're not engaged now, are you? He's three thousand miles from here. I'm not. Clearly, you and I have a lot in common. Let's just keep things as they are. We'll get to know each other better and we'll see what happens, o.k.?"

"O.K." she said in a tone that was a blend of excitement, enthusiasm, and trepidation.

We spent every available minute in each other's company until the Christmas break. One evening though, shortly after we began serious dating, I just about did myself in. My two roommates, John, Captain Dan, and I were having dinner at Foo's, a very nice Chinese restaurant on Eugene's main street, when Arlene entered with an older couple and took a booth across the room from us. My adrenaline surged. "There's my girl"! I exclaimed to my friends.

Summoning my worldly sophistication in such matters, I ordered an exotic drink, complete with a ridiculous tiny umbrella, to be delivered to her at her table.

She couldn't see me across the darkened room, so after a minute or two, I sauntered over to her table. When she saw me, she about lost her sensibilities. Stuttering, she awkwardly introduced me to Mr. and Mrs. Harris, (who happened to be her fiancée's parents). I didn't have a clue as to who they really were until later that night, when she was able to explain to me how embarrassed she was. I thought it was funny, but I didn't laugh. Rather, I apologized profusely. She laughed her little laugh and we picked up where we had left off.

At Christmas break, she went home to Seattle and Tom, and I flew home to Detroit to get my car. I needed my own wheels if I was going to be really serious about this situation.

By the end of the first two quarters, all but two of us had switched from the Psychology Department's program to the

School of Education's program. The only students left in the Psychology Department were Don and me.

Another one of my classes was Clinical Psychology, taught by Professor Beuler. Beuler hated psychiatrists and never let a session be completed without a vitriolic diatribe, ranting against "those know-it-alls who know nothing at all."

Directly in front of me sat a young student, just a few years older than me. He had a very questioning, inquisitive mind and would frequently ask Beuler penetrating, cogent questions. He had a very loud, booming voice and was most impressive. In a very short time I learned that he too, had a work-study arrangement in the Counseling Center, and further, that he had known Arlene longer than I had. His name was Gil and was married to a young lady named Phyllis. They were from North Dakota and so we regaled each other with exotic tales of cold and lutefisk. Arlene and I became lifelong friends with Phil and Gil and have delighted in each other's company and accomplishments ever since.

Chapter 70

CROSS COUNTRY—ONE MORE TIME

THE airline took good care of me on my flight back to Detroit, but my head was aswirl with the sounds and sensations of Eugene and the University of Oregon. I knew now that I could be competitive at the graduate level and had made two very good friends, Don and Bill. Bill was a very easy going, tall young man who eventually became the director of the Portland Juvenile Center where he spent his entire career. The three of us spent many evenings, and some afternoons, drinking beer, exchanging anxieties, and wondering what was the matter with our advisor who was acting increasingly loony.

And then there was Arlene. She was in my thoughts almost constantly. My mind was filled with her delicate fragrance, her lilting laughter, and her challenging intellect. By Jove, I think I was in love. What was I going to do about that?

Detroit was cold but clear when I arrived. The black, salty

slush from a recent snowfall was everywhere. The city's snowplows had nearly buried cars that were parked along curbsides on the main streets, while the side streets in residential areas remained sheets of solid ice. Mom was glad to see me of course, and within the next few days we visited both Harland and Dorothy and their families.

A few days before I had to leave, I ran an advertisement in our local Lincoln Park paper, The Mellus, for a companion who might be heading west and willing to share expenses and driving. The day the paper hit the streets, I got a call from a young guy who was returning to his Army base in Amarillo, Texas. We talked on the phone and agreed on the arrangements. The morning we were to depart he arrived at my home on time and we loaded his duffel bag into my sleek, rusty car.

I had decided to take Route 66 across the southern part of the country, hoping to miss the wind and snow that scream across the plains states. What I didn't calculate was that the highway was also more than a mile high in some places like New Mexico and Arizona. I discovered that wind and snow screamed there, too.

My hopes for a reasonably intelligent, conversational, driving companion were dashed almost immediately. The man was stupid, refused to talk, and damn near ran us off the road the first and only time I let him drive.

We arrived in Amarillo just before I thought I might kill him. I ejected him at the gates of the Army base there and sped off. Even though his monetary contribution helped somewhat, I would much rather have paid all of the expenses and been alone with myself than alone with that mute idiot.

I was a bit west of Amarillo, maybe fifty miles or so, when I decided to call it a day, and stopped at a motel on the high plains, precisely in the middle of nowhere. There was a general store across the highway from the motel, but no other life in sight for fifty miles. Television didn't exist in motels then, so I set my alarm for 4 a.m., and immediately crashed into a dank, musty mattress.

The next morning I was up at four, well before daybreak, and eager for a fresh day of travel with my only companion, my car radio. I must have heard "El Paso" by Marty Robbins 5,000 times since leaving Detroit. It was a great song, but even great songs, if repeated often enough, will destroy one's mind. I slipped outside and into my frozen car. I pushed the starter. Nothing. Nothing!!?? My battery was dead.

I knocked on the door of the manager's office to see if there was anyone there who could help me with a jump-start. A frazzled, sleepy-eyed, very obnoxious, overweight woman answered my knock and told me she couldn't help me. She did say that the store across the highway would open about eight o'clock and that they might be able to do something for me.

"I'm going back to bed now. I suggest you do the same," she said, and slammed the door in my freezing face.

Thoroughly castigated, I made my way back to my unit and took a three-hour nap. When I awoke there were stirrings in the store across the highway and it appeared that it might be open. I ran across the barren, wind-swept highway to the store, and sure enough, they let me in.

I explained my dilemma to the old craggy-faced bewhiskered storeowner who was reasonably sympathetic and responsive. He said that a young Indian boy would soon be arriving and that for five bucks he would help me get my car started. I bought an apple and sat down on a rickety wooden crate to consume my breakfast. Soon after eating it, my blood sugar was up to approximately normal, my feeling of light-headedness disappeared and the Indian boy appeared.

He said he figured he could get my car started by pulling it, so he fired up a very old, dilapidated truck sitting behind the store. It was a stake truck such as one might see hauling corn to a processing plant. He let the truck idle for a few minutes to make sure the engine was warm enough to pull me without stalling. He then drove it across the highway and attached a twenty-foot heavy-duty chain to the front of my car frame. He gently towed me back across the highway and stopped behind the store. He got out of the truck and said, "I'm going to pull you around the store. When we get up to ten or fifteen miles an hour, pop the clutch. It should compression start."

"O.K.," I said, and girded myself for the ride. And what a ride it was. He took off at fifteen miles and hour and never slowed down. He roared around the store five or six times, never missing an opportunity to hit a foot deep, frozen chuck hole. I was ricocheting crazily around behind the wheel, popping the clutch with regularity until the engine finally caught and roared to life. "Whoa!" I screamed to no one but me, and signaled the kid to stop.

Eventually, he noticed my signals and slowed to a stop. I thanked him profusely as he disconnected his chain from my car. He grinned a yellow-toothed grin, took my five bucks and wished me luck. I slipped out onto the highway, headed west, and was on my way again.

I slowly climbed in altitude until at about 5,000 feet, I spotted a billboard advertising an auto mechanic and gasoline just a few miles further west. Relieved to see the station open, I pulled in, shut off the ignition, ordered a tank full of gas and went inside to get out of the bitterly cold wind.

In just a few minutes, my tank was full and I went out to try to regain some of the time lost in my dead battery fiasco. I turned the key. Nothing. "Oh, shit! Dead again," I muttered. Here I was, in the middle of the high plains, a dead battery, and a dwindling cash supply. I was rapidly becoming really sick of this adventure.

I re-entered the gas station and explained my plight. The guy in charge, a young fellow of about thirty, said he'd take a look at it and see what he could do. The room I was in was about fifteen by twenty feet. There was a pot-bellied stove with no glass in its door and a serious fire roaring in its guts. Around the stove sat three older gentlemen, probably in their sixties or seventies, telling lies to one another and spitting snoose juice with great regularity and accuracy on the nearly red hot sides of the stove. The spittle would pop and squirm and quickly evaporate, just as another juicy gob would hit it.

Trying to be as uninterested as I could be in their spitting and lying contest, I looked out the rear window. There I saw an Indian man of about forty or forty-five approaching. He was walking slowly against the wind, and stooped with an apparently very heavy gunnysack slung over his shoulder. Behind him in single file were his wife and five stair-step children.

When he finally arrived, he came into the station, but the rest of his family remained outside in the bitter cold. He wiped the frost from his near frozen face, and with lips that could barely function, said that he had a car battery in his gunnysack. He wanted to sell it to the service station owner so he could buy some food for his family. He wanted two dollars for it. The station manager said, "I'll give you fifty cents for it."

The Indian said, "No," slung the sack over his shoulder and trudged off. He walked across the highway, battery bouncing on his low back and kidneys, his family in single file tow. He and his ragged entourage slowly disappeared over the wind swept horizon.

An alarm bell went off in my head. "This guy is one tough cookie," I thought to myself. Sure as Hell I was going to have to buy a new battery from him at some inflated figure. I had no choice. The mechanic had worked on my car for about an hour when he came back into the station. "Well," he said. "One of your battery posts is shot. It's really loose, but I managed to shore it up a bit with some wire. It's makeshift, but it'll get you down the road a piece further."

I breathed a sigh of relief that I wasn't going to have to buy a battery, and steeled myself for his answer to my next question. "How much do I owe you for your time?" I asked, waiting for the axe to fall on the few bucks I had stashed in my right shoe.

He screwed up his face as if in deep thought, scratched his greasy head and spit on the stove. Then he said, "Oh, seventy-five cents should cover it."

Good grief! I paid him his seventy-five cents and, very happy with his response, prepared to leave. One of the old gentlemen made another sloppy contribution to that poor stove's belly and said, "Looks like snow out there."

Chapter 71

SNOW?——WHAT SNOW?

I walked out into blazing sunshine and got in my car. There wasn't a cloud in the sky. Except for the wind, it was a gorgeous day. I spun that old eight cylinder over, eased out onto the highway, and, with muffler now shot, roared off, heading due west, blue-black exhaust spewing out of my hind-end.

After breakfast at the first quasi restaurant I came to, I hit the highway again, pressing on, ever forward. Then I saw it. It was a very large highway sign heralding the approach of Las Vegas. I had promised myself a short stay in Las Vegas, and perhaps more than a few hands of blackjack. After calculating my needs, I thought I might have about twenty bucks I could risk at the tables. I figured with my winnings I could get a huge, flame-broiled steak dinner, a baked potato with all the trimmings and perhaps a piece of apple pie alamode for three or four bucks and maybe even a decent room for the night.

The old Ford followed my gentle commands to leave the main highway and headed north by northwest. I climbed steeply up the mountain's side, higher and higher. The road was getting narrower and less well maintained. Then it turned from hardtop to gravel and I was getting increasingly concerned. I'd been to Las Vegas before, and this didn't look at all familiar.

I finally arrived at my destination, Las Vegas, and my bewilderment cleared. I was in Las Vegas, New Mexico! Here I was, on a mountaintop, in late December, in a micro town with frozen, rutted dirt streets, looking for non-existent casinos. I checked my map again. Good grief! I was two states off. I spun the Ford around and gingerly retraced my path back down the mountain to Route 66. The whole misadventure cost me more than half a tank of gas, three hours of time, and a substantial amount of pride in my navigational abilities.

I wasn't back on the right track for more than twenty minutes when the gathering storm clouds began to release their wintry contents. The snow was falling heavily, and the wind was screaming horizontally across the highway. It was heavy. It was fierce. It was a blizzard like I had seen only once before, and that was in Minnesota. But here I was in the South, where folks sip mint juleps and tea. What's wrong? I was nearly a mile high. That was what was wrong. I hadn't counted on that.

The blizzard was blinding. I could only see three or four feet in front of the car. The bug screen that I had in front of the radiator to keep mosquitoes and other insects from clogging it in summertime Detroit immediately filled with snow and my temperature gauge rose steadily higher. I moved very slowly to my right, hoping to feel my front tire slip off the roadway onto the shoulder, where I could stop and have a chance to reconsider my perilous situation. I was in luck. Just as my wheels slipped off the highway and onto the shoulder,

I could see three other vehicles. It was a small rest area. Several cars and light trucks had pulled off to wait out the storm. Large tractor trailers were speeding past at forty or fifty miles an hour, clearly oblivious to the possibility that they were not immune to being killed.

I jockeyed my car around so that I was facing the highway and shut her down. I was on the brink of boiling over and was praying that my mechanic friend's battery post wiring job was still intact. I got out and removed the ridiculous bug screen from the front of my radiator and settled down to wait it out. Those old, spitting buzzards around my mechanic's stove were right. They knew more than all of our modern weather forecasters put together. The storm lasted about three hours and then trailed off into light flurries.

The snow on the highway was packed fairly solidly by the truck traffic which enabled me and my traveling compatriots to make our way slowly into Flagstaff. I stopped at the first motel with a vacancy sign and got my five-dollar room. When I tried to open the car door, I had to push snow that had piled up to about two feet on the level. I crawled into my room, turned on the heat and lights, and sat down on the bed. It was New Year's Eve, 1959. Heavy snow. No traffic. No sound. It was the quietest New Year's Eve I had ever heard. It was also the loneliest.

In the morning, after breakfast, I stopped at the first service station I found and had tire chains put on the rear wheels. I puttered off, clunking along on the plowed, but still very icy highway, heading this time for Las Vegas, *Nevada*.

I wasn't on the road ten minutes before my car radio died, leaving me completely alone with my miserable thoughts. My mind was turning to gruel, and it was hard to concentrate on anything, so I mused about Arlene and the great dinner she would have for me when I got back to Eugene.

When I arrived in Las Vegas, I couldn't wait to turn my

twenty bucks into a small fortune. The vision of my great, wonderful steak dinner was still fresh in my mind. I'd have my dinner, maybe catch a show, and even find a decent bed to sleep in. Anxious to strike it rich, I stopped at the first casino I came to on the way into town. I found a seat at a blackjack table, and within three minutes had lost my entire twenty-dollar stake.

Discouraged and road weary, I piled back into my rusty Ford and drove to the nearest service station where I had the chains removed from the rear tires. I had a hamburger instead of steak—and pressed on—through Barstow and then Bakersfield, where I picked up old Highway 99 and headed north. My mind was soon nearly completely gone and I decided it would be good to rest for awhile. I picked out a cheap looking motel and slept for five or six hours. Then I was back on the road again.

As I began to climb toward the summit of Mt. Shasta, the roads again turned to slick, glare ice. I had the chains reinstalled and crept back onto the highway. I didn't dare go more than thirty or thirty-five miles an hour in such treacherous conditions, and soon it was pitch black as well. It wasn't long before I was joined in this nightmare by hundreds of Washington State residents returning home from the 1959 Rose Bowl. I have no idea who Washington played that year, or any other year for that matter. I have never been particularly interested in watching giant hairy simians crashing into one another.

These fans, however, were some of the most aggressive, obnoxious drivers I have ever encountered. They would roar up behind me blasting their horns and flashing their headlights into my weary, bloodshot eyes, demanding that I get out of their way. Of all my adventures on this perilous trip cross-country, this was distinctly the most harrowing, frightening, and maddening. I steadfastly refused to speed up, but whenever the opportunity arose, I would pull off on the shoulder and let a batch of screaming meemies by. It wouldn't be but a few minutes, however, before another caravan of obnoxious, Washington football fans would replace them. God, it was awful.

I rolled into Medford, Oregon completely exhausted. My brain was gone, and I was on automatic pilot. I stopped and had my chains removed and that helped somewhat. The constant rumbling and clanking of the chains was finally over. It wasn't far now to Eugene, and I was determined to complete my trip that day. The fact is I had no more money for motels, so off I went, again.

I arrived in Eugene about eight in the evening, absolutely exhausted, an empty gas tank, an empty stomach, and two dimes in my pocket. I dropped one of the dimes into the first phone booth I came to in Eugene and called Arlene.

She was thrilled to hear that I had made it safely, and said, "Come over right now. I'll fix you something to eat."

What comforting words. In ten minutes, I was in the arms of my sweetheart. She prepared a wonderful dinner, poured us each a glass of Thunderbird wine, and I fell asleep. I was finally home.

Chapter 72

TIME TO GET SERIOUS

THE next morning I met Arlene at The Side, a wonderful, old time eatery just a few steps off the campus. It had booths all along three walls, and tables in the center. A short staircase led to a mezzanine, where small booths were arranged around the entire perimeter. Arlene was wearing her brown tweed mid-calf length winter coat, and was truly a vision of loveliness. I could hardly stand it. We climbed the stairs and commandeered a booth and ordered breakfast. Only then did I notice "IT." She was wearing a stunning diamond engagement ring. Oh, oh.

I slumped in my seat, not knowing really where to go with this.

"I see you accepted Tom's ring," I said.

"Yes, I did," she replied. It has been planned for a very long time—and I don't know where you and I are." Her tone was plaintiff and questioning.

Was I some sort of idiot? Yes.

Summoning what small mental reserves I had to the forefront, I said, "Well, what are we going to do? You and I love each other. How can we continue going together if you're wearing Tom's ring? This situation is ridiculous."

Then it struck both of us simultaneously. The solution? We could simply pretend that I had given her the ring. That would solve everything at least temporarily, on one of the coasts anyway. Happy with our ingenuity, we dove into our breakfasts. We'd figure the rest out later.

It wasn't long, though, before Arlene began getting significant pressure from her mother to get back to Seattle and choose her wedding dress. There were many plans to be made: a guest list, invitations, church, wedding dinner and reception, and on and on——.

I had put Arlene in a truly untenable position. Well, actually, we had both managed to put everyone concerned in untenable places and we shared that responsibility. Finally, I made up my mind to resolve this, one way or the other. On Valentine's Day, 1960, I proposed. Her acceptance was immediate. Now, what about Tom?

"I'll write to him tomorrow and cancel our engagement," Arlene said.

"Great," I replied, and thought the problem was solved.

But Tom didn't think so. He wrote back, neglecting to even mention her letter. She called him on the telephone. He refused to discuss it. All he would say was that things would work out and he would be home soon. Arlene wrote several more letters, each one a bit more aggressive and determined than its predecessor. Tom ignored all references to a breakup. He *appeared* to be in complete denial. However, Arlene and I were in Heaven. She gave her love to me, and I have been thankful every day since for that gift.

Meanwhile, Tom was not in denial at all. He was marshalling whatever resources he could to help him understand what was happening. He talked with Arlene's parents, Sam and Rosemary, and with all of his and Arlene's mutual friends, trying to find out who I was and what in the world I was doing with his fiancée.

What he did find out displeased him greatly. He discovered that I was from Detroit, the Murder Capital of the World, and I was four years older than Arlene. Without question, he must have thought, I was nothing but a Detroit hood, preying on Arlene and her innocence.

During spring break, Tom arrived in Eugene unannounced and ensconced himself in Arlene's apartment to wait for her. That evening after a pizza dinner at Tino's, Arlene and I pulled up to the curb alongside her apartment. The engine had barely stopped when her roommate, Carol, who was painfully aware of Arlene's dilemma, came rushing out of the shadows to the car.

"Tom's upstairs!" she exclaimed in a near panic state.

Arlene turned to me and said, "You'd better go. I'll take care of this. I'll call you later," and went upstairs to her apartment and a weeping Tom. I almost felt sorry for him. Almost, but not quite.

About two hours later, Arlene called me and said that she had given Tom his ring back and thought that things were finally settled. Tom was on his way to Seattle. We agreed to meet in the morning for breakfast at the Side. All was well, once again.

Chapter 73

DON'T STICK YOUR FINGER IN MY EYE

WINTER and spring quarters at the U. of O. were relatively uneventful. I did quite well academically. I even impressed Dr. Leeper, the Chairman of the Psychology Department, so deeply with a lengthy (but brilliant) paper I did on the relationship between psychology and religion, that he asked me if he could have a copy of it for his personal files. Of course I agreed.

Near the end of Spring Quarter, I was just about to complete a seminar on Counseling Procedures, when one of the louder, more obnoxious students made what I considered to be a spectacularly stupid statement. Up to that point I had generally been a fairly quiet person and the other students were shocked, but pleased, at the depth, length, and incisiveness of my attack. No one in the room liked the other student and all were happy to see someone finally challenge him and his incessant, generally irrelevant, pseudo-intellectual babblings. I was near completion of my

Psychology/Religion paper for Dr. Leeper and had scores of philosopher's, cleric's, and psychologist's thoughts and theories right in the front of my brain.

I let him have it, directly between his stunned eyes. I started quoting the theories of William James, Max Wertheimer, John Watson, Abraham Maslow and a dozen others.

I even drew from the writings and teachings of Leona Tyler who was nationally renowned and on the U. of O. psychology faculty. When I finished, the other students applauded. I was very pleased. My heart must have been pounding away at 150 beats per minute, pumping pure adrenaline through my arteries. The loudmouth cringed in his seat and was silent for the remainder of the quarter.

Two weeks later, I received a letter from Robert Thorndike, a world famous psychologist at Columbia University. He said that I had been strongly recommended to him by Professor Warnath (the instructor who had witnessed my devastating attack), inviting me to apply to their doctoral program and study under his tutelage. I wrote back, thanked him for his invitation, but declined his flattering invitation. I needed no more experience in the East. I had also had enough of the world of Academia for awhile. I was happy where I was. I felt that I was home free in this program. I wasn't—but we'll get to that down the road a bit.

Chapter 74

THE BIG HORN MOUNTAINS

WHEN spring quarter ended in June, Arlene returned to her home in Seattle for a brief stay and then attended summer school in Eugene. I flew home to try to sell Mom's house in Lincoln Park and move her to Eugene. Cousin Violet had offered to have Mom live with her until more permanent arrangements could be made, and I thought that idea would solve a lot of problems. Sister Dorothy and her family had moved from Detroit to California sometime during the previous year, and Harland and Lorraine had their hands full raising a burgeoning family.

We had very little luck in our attempts to sell the house and finally decided to accept the only offer we had. It was from a schoolteacher and her husband, a long-haul truck driver. The terms of the sale were no money down and $75.00 a month. It seemed like our best alternative at the time. Arlene arrived in late July, just in time to help pack and get ready to drive back across country.

Because so much was happening on so many fronts, Arlene and I decided to get married quietly, and did so at the first Justice of the Peace we found. We decided not to tell anyone and to play it cool for awhile. Things would sort themselves out soon, we thought.

The old Ford I had in Eugene was near death. Her body was completely shot. The rocker panels had totally disappeared, the grillwork had rusted and fallen out, and I was getting just under 150 miles per quart of oil.

It was time to contact Uncle Howard again. With no hesitation at all, he loaned me $2,000 to buy a new Nash Rambler. It was black, and had a bench seat in the front. We packed every square inch of that car's rear seat area and trunk with "stuff," collected our first month's house payment, and left for our first stop, Aunt Emerald's apartment in Hammond, Indiana, just outside of Chicago.

We hadn't gone more than 100 miles or so before we realized that a group of fools as mechanically incompetent as I was had put that car together while the inspectors on the final assembly line took their two-hour cigarette break. Nothing fit. The entire dashboard was off about a thirty-second of an inch. It was just enough so that none of the knobs would pull out or work correctly. I could barely get the hood open because the latch was improperly aligned. It got 200 miles to a quart of oil. Instead of having an old lemon with 80,000 miles on her, I now had a new lemon with practically no miles. And it did get a bit better oil mileage. A giant leap ahead in my mystical world of technology.

We had traveled almost 300 miles exactly when we arrived in front of Em's apartment, stiff, stupid, frustrated, and very uncomfortable. The three of us had been sitting, jammed together, straight up, with very little legroom, for over eight and a half hours. We pried ourselves out of the car, stretched, tried to shake the cobwebs from our collective brains, and rang the bell.

Em answered the door and invited us in. We exchanged pleasantries, and had a bite to eat with her and her husband and their daughter, Joanne. We called it a day and crashed, but we knew that something had to be done about the traveling situation. It was just too crazy to continue as it was.

The next morning I went out and purchased three packing barrels from the Mayflower Moving Company, and we began culling stuff from the car. By the time we had filled the three barrels, we had created a nice, comfortable niche for Mom in the back seat. All three of us could breathe again! I made arrangements for the three cartons to be shipped to Violet's address in Eugene, and we were off again.

Just west of Chicago we picked up I-94 and headed to Minneapolis for a short visit with my Aunt Dorothy, before aiming for Fossil and the 1960 version of *THE FAMILY REUNION*. The reunion was held at Uncle George's lakeside cabin on Maple Lake. Poor Arlene. Imagine meeting the entire Abbott Clan at once? What a shocker.

We arrived a bit late and had to park a little way from the cabin, on a one-lane dirt road leading to it. As soon as the car rolled to a stop, we were surrounded by several of the Abbott men, most noticeably Dave, who was a bit more than three sheets to the wind. He had his bottle tucked under his arm, bleary eyes, a four-day growth of beard, and no teeth. When I introduced him to Arlene, he said, "Well, aren't you the chesty little one!" and gave her a very wet welcoming kiss.

Then he said, "You know, someone once said that when your hind end gets heavier than your ideas—its time to sit down." And he did—on the front bumper of our car. He was only there for a minute or so before he rolled gently off into the roadside weeds for a snooze.

Arlene was then introduced to the rest of the clan. George had his boat in the water and was willing to take anyone water skiing who dared to do so. His only takers were his son, Jimmy, Arlene, and me. Jimmy and Arlene were quite good. I wasn't. I crashed very early on and, through very moist lungs and with my suit around my ankles, said: "I don't want to do this anymore." I never have.

We stayed for a few days, visiting with friends and relatives. One of the highlights of this time was a Walleye fish fry put on by Aunt Bertha in their converted chicken coop in the one-family "town" of Benoit. Bertha did all of her cooking on a wood range, had no running water or bathroom, but was the best cook within a thousand-mile radius. She fried up some Walleyes for us one afternoon that remain in Arlene's and my memories as the best fish that we ever ate, before or since. And then, it was time to leave.

We pushed on relatively uneventfully until we began our climb into the Black Hills National Forest in South Dakota. As we picked up altitude, our brand new Rambler began to sputter and lose power. On some relatively shallow inclines, I couldn't get it above twenty miles an hour. It was frustrating and exceedingly dangerous.

I stopped at a Rambler dealer in Rapid City, South Dakota to see if they could determine what the problem was. The mechanic diagnosed it immediately. He said the carburetor had been adjusted at the factory for sea level, and was simply not functioning properly at higher altitudes. He made the appropriate corrections for us, and we surged out of Rapid City in a cloud of blue smoke, heading up and into the Big Horn Mountains and an unforgettable experience.

It was a beautiful, warm, sunshiny day as we began our descent from the summit of the Big Horn Range. The road was narrow, drop-offs sometimes half a mile deep, and very few guardrails. It was spooky driving. Then, as we rounded a bend, I spied a lake down in a shallow valley to our left. I turned off the highway and eased us down a winding, dirt road to the lakeshore. There was a single, small trailer house on the edge of the water where a man of about forty was living with his teenage daughter.

They came out to greet us and were very friendly. I supposed that they didn't have very many drop-in visitors out there in that stark wilderness. I asked if it would be all right if we did a little fishing in the stream.

"Why, no. We wouldn't mind at all," the man replied. "But you don't need your fishing pole. My daughter will show you how to catch fish with your hands."

"Are you kidding?" I thought as we walked to the edge of the stream. The water was perhaps two feet deep, running gently out of the lake on its way to somewhere. We could see several two to three pound trout swimming lazily downstream, presumably on their way to their spawning grounds. The young lady stepped gently into the water and waded out to midstream about ten feet from shore. She stood there for a minute or two, staring down into the water. Then she slowly, quietly, lowered one hand into the water, palm open toward the oncoming flow. Suddenly, she thrust her other hand into the water, grabbed a beautiful trout and threw it up onto the bank, right at our feet. I was still reeling in disbelief when another fish joined the first one on the bank.

"It's easy," she said. "Come on in. I'll show you how to do it."

I took off my shoes and socks, rolled up my pants as far as I could, and slipped quietly into the water. I joined the young lady and began an experience that I will never, ever forget.

"Here comes one now," she whispered quietly. "Just put your left hand down into the water in front of its face. When it tries to turn and go around your hand, move your hand, keeping it directly in front of its face. It will soon quit trying to move around you and stop, presumably wondering what to do. That's when you thrust your right hand down and grab it tightly just behind its head and throw it up on the bank. That's all there is to it!"

I tried to do exactly as she had described, but I missed the first two. Then I got the hang of it, and threw four consecutive, beautiful rainbows up on the bank. The water was extremely cold, and my bony legs and feet were turning blue and getting numb. I crawled up onto the bank and dried off. Then I noticed that there were a few fish loitering just under an overhang of the bank. Quickly, I was down on my stomach peering into the slow moving water. Arlene sat on my legs so I wouldn't slide completely into the stream. I slowly slid my hand down into the water. I felt a fish or two, and was getting ready to try my luck at grabbing one, when the young lady said, "I wouldn't do that if I were you. There are a lot of poisonous water snakes that live under those overhangs, and they're not very nice at all. You wouldn't want one of their bites!"

I was up and out of the water as quickly as I could be, and that was very fast indeed. We thanked the man and his daughter for their hospitality and kindness, packed our fish and ourselves into the car and headed back up the dirt trail to the highway. About ten miles down the road we came to a rest area with picnic tables and fire pits. We stopped, cleaned our fish, and had one of the most wonderful, magical meals any of us had ever had. The whole experience was unbelievable, and I loved telling this story as often as I could for the rest of my life.

In another day and a half we arrived in Eugene, bleary eyed and exhausted. I drove straight to Violet's house where we unpacked Mom. Violet prepared a great dinner for us and after dinner, Arlene and I left to take care of our own business.

It took less than a week before all of us realized that there were too many cooks in Violet's kitchen. Mom decided she wanted to visit her daughter Dorothy and her family in California, and flew off. She stayed several weeks.

Chapter 75

THE LITTLE HOUSE

ARLENE and I immediately began searching for a suitable house for Mom in Eugene. It wasn't long before we found a little house on Agate Street, just three blocks from the University of Oregon's campus. An eighty-something widow lady named Mae had lived there alone for several years. Her children now wanted her to move to Roseburg and into a senior retirement complex where she could have excellent care, good food, and a safe haven.

Mae fell in love with both Arlene and me right off (at least she pretended to) and wanted us to have her house. She said she knew we would care for it. It was a nice little house but it needed work—lots of work. Mae wanted $5,500 for it, and she wanted cash. So we set about trying to put $5,500 together. I had clear title to the Rambler, even though I was paying Uncle Howard $50 a month on it. He trusted me enough that the title was never even mentioned in our loan agreement. I took the title to the local bank and borrowed

$1,500 against it. The bank loaned me $3,500 on the property itself, and the real estate sales person took her $500 commission in monthly installments.

We put together enough to pay Mae her price, and even moved her to Roseburg, a town about two hours south of Eugene. Then, it was time to go to work. The little house had potential, but at that point it was quite dirty and smelled very much like an old lady, older socks and the sickeningly sweet odor of body ash.

The first project we undertook was the living room. Mae had painted the fireplace bricks with a dark brown enamel and blocked the opening with plywood so it was unusable. The hearth tiles were mostly broken, and the whole fireplace wall was a dreary mess. Arlene and I worked every moment we had. We re-faced the brown enamel fireplace with new, twelve by two-inch decorative bricks of tan and muted pink and tore out the entire hearth. The evening that we reset new ceramic tiles for a new hearth was extremely stormy and windy. We lost power and heat, so Arlene and I finished the job by candlelight, in the cold. It could have been romantic, except that our freezing fingers were about to fall off from the cold. We painted the living room and replaced the rotten carpet with a new one. The smell was beginning to disappear.

There was a back room in the little house where Mae spent most of her time. She had a free standing pot bellied stove installed in the middle of the room. It was vented straight up through the ceiling and roof. She also had an old, turn of the century washing machine in there, which I suspect she rarely used. The rest of the house was heated by a very tall, narrow, gas heater in the living room. That heater had no fan on it, so while the living room would boast a temperature of 95 degrees, the rest of the house was much cooler, dependent entirely on heat movement by convection. When we realized that the icy draft across the floor frequently reached a speed of ten to twelve miles an hour, we knew that something had to be done.

We tore out the stove in the back room and disposed of it. We patched the resulting hole in the roof, and installed an acoustical tile ceiling and new linoleum. We installed baseboard electric heaters to eliminate the oil smell and even out the heating. By Jove, it was beginning to look like a livable little place. We put new wallpaper on the walls in the single bedroom, and cleaned and painted the tiny bathroom. It was ready.

I called Mom at sister Dorothy's house in California, and told her that it was time for her to come back to Eugene, but didn't mention her new abode. She agreed to come right away, and I'm sure she did so with great trepidation and anxiety about what the future held for her.

Arlene and I met her at the train station three days later, and told her we wanted her to meet someone before we took her back to Violet's house. We pulled up to the curb in front of her new little home, and we all got out.

She must have thought it somewhat weird though, that I had a key to the front door and no one was home. It was warm and cozy when we walked into the living room, and the smell of freshness was everywhere. "Here you are, Mom. This is your new home," I said.

She was astounded.

"For me? This is mine?" she asked as tears welled in her eyes.

"Yes, it is, Mom. It's all yours."

Arlene and I were smiling broadly and she knew it was true. We went out for dinner at Tino's and then we took her back to her new home.

We told her that the next day we would come by and take her grocery shopping so she could really get settled in. She was ecstatic. Arlene and I left, feeling very proud and content with both our project and ourselves. It was time to start the new academic year.

Chapter 76

THE LAST LAP

MIDWAY through fall quarter Arlene and I decided that our living arrangements were ridiculous, and decided to "come clean" so we could get our own apartment and begin acting more or less like sane people. We told my mother first and she was very accepting and happy for us. Then we drove to Seattle to tell Arlene's folks. They were stunned, but they didn't attack. We left them alone for awhile so they could digest the news. When we came back about two hours later, they had incorporated the news reasonably well, and gave us $150 which we eventually used to buy a new stove. We then returned to Eugene and made arrangements to move into married students' housing in the Amazon Project where Don and Betty Angell lived.

The next week we moved in, elated with our new living quarters. It was completely furnished, so we stashed our $150 stove money for use later on down the road. It had a kitchen, small dining room and living room, two bedrooms, a bathroom with shower, and a centrally located, four-foot high, oil-burning heater. The walls were so thin we could hear the people in the adjacent apartment breathing, so we were generally very quiet as we went about our business. But, we were finally legitimate.

I began the winter quarter with a flourish, and enrolled in some great academic adventures. I was formally introduced to General Semantics in my Public Opinion and Propaganda class, and it changed forever the way I would view the world and think about things. I learned about Alfred Korzybski, Wendell Johnson, and Sam Hayakawa and many other contributors to this (to me) new and exciting system of thought. Although Korzybski wrote at a level that was nearly incomprehensible, there were a few people in the world who understood what he was saying and subsequently wrote books and articles in a simpler language that most of us could understand and appreciate. He began a movement that would seriously challenge the then current Aristotelian system of thought and logic.

Hayakawa ("Language in Thought and Action") interpreted Korzybski at a fairly juvenile, but accurate level. Johnson, however, writing in books like "People in Quandaries" was just right for most graduate students. I loved it. It helped make sense out of so much nonsense in our world.

In the winter quarter, I had my first experience with counseling while being observed through a one-way glass by my peers and instructors. It was a little spooky, but helpful as well. My first "client" was a seventeen-year old female high school student who had been referred by her high school counselor. He had tried to help her, but wound up going in circles, so he referred her to the "experts" at the university. Although I didn't realize it at the time, the young lady was exhibiting classic symptoms of schizophrenia. She went on and on, almost making sense, but not quite. I didn't know how to turn her off and terminate the interview. It went on for over two hours when it should have ended after fifty minutes. The students who were watching finally grew weary and went home. Finally, my instructor knocked on the door and interrupted the session so I could escape. She was then referred to the hospital in town for psychiatric treatment.

The next day my "counseling" was staffed by my peers and by faculty. They asked questions of me such as, "Do you know that every time she mentioned sex, you looked out the window rather than at her? Why do you suppose that was?" or, "It seemed to us that you were completely taken in by her nonsensical babblings," and on and on for an hour.

It wasn't at all comfortable examining those questions, but I did learn a lot.

The next individual I drew as a client was also a seventeen year old schizophrenic, but this one was male. Although he was still in school, he claimed to have a part-time job in one of the local mortuaries. He said that one of his greatest pleasures was watching corpses being cremated in the incinerator. He said that when the bodies became very hot, they would start to sputter, pop and jump around on the table as various muscles and ligaments were affected by the intense heat. I had seen frog legs do a similar dance in a frying pan, so I didn't know whether to believe him or not about humans. I still don't. He, too, was immediately referred for psychiatric treatment.

A day or so later, Arlene and I decided to take Mom to a movie. The film playing at the only theater in Eugene was "Psycho," with Anthony Perkins and Janet Leigh. We thought it would be a psychological thriller of some kind, but what we saw about did us all in. It was horrific and we didn't sleep well for several weeks.

Three days after having seen the movie, I received a small package in the mail. It was wrapped in plain brown paper, with no return address. I opened the package and found a paperback mystery novel by Agatha Christie. Inside of the book was a typewritten note. While I can't remember the exact wording of the message, the meaning seemed abundantly clear.

It offered advice about shaving with a straight razor, saying that drawing it back and forth across the heel of the hand could sharpen the blade. I was cautioned to be very careful not to cut myself, but if by chance I should slice a hunk of meat from the heel of my hand, I was to eat it so it wouldn't go to waste. The note also made reference to a dentist in the novel that had drilled into the nerve center of one of his patient's teeth. The note said, "He should have had more practice before being turned loose on the public."

I took this to mean that I should not be counseling people with serious mental problems when I had so little experience in such things. It rambled on for two or three paragraphs of similar craziness, and was signed "Anne Ghaard," which I interpreted to be "On Guard." Both Arlene and I were freaking badly.

I immediately took the book and its wrapper to the post office and reported it, hoping that they could in some way trace its origin. They couldn't, but referred me to the F.B.I. offices in their building. The agents we talked with were of little help either, but they did call in a psychiatrist to read and interpret the note, to see if there was indeed a serious threat. The psychiatrist studied the note carefully and said that a woman had written the note, but that there was "little chance of her acting on the implied threat." Great.

Arlene and I returned to our apartment in Amazon to consider our dilemma. Then it struck me. Perhaps this note came from the crazy young man who said he liked to watch cremations. I knew that he had been released from psychiatric confinement, but I had no idea where he was - or what sex he was - or wanted to be. We were spooked enough that we moved in with Don and Betty a few buildings away, and slept on their couch for several nights. We were terrified. After a week or so, our anxiety had dissipated enough so that we were able to move back into our own place, but we didn't sleep well for a very, very long time. We never found out who had slipped us that nearly intolerable bit of misery.

Sometime near the middle of November, Arlene and I were having dinner in our small abode. She looked up at me and said, "Glenn, I think I'm pregnant."

We were delighted. We were scared. We hadn't exactly planned on having a child so soon, but we reassured each other and ourselves that everything would work out. The baby was due in late June or early July, so we'd both be able to complete our academic programs. I could then get a great job as a Rehabilitation Counselor and God would provide.

In Winter and Spring quarters I enrolled for practical experience in Eugene's local Vocational Rehabilitation office. I met several really wonderful people in that office, including the supervisor, Jim Booth.

Jim was a World War II veteran who had been seriously wounded in a South Pacific battle. As soon as he could be moved, he had been sent to New Zealand to recover and begin his rehabilitation. Jim's nurse, Beth, was a very pretty, caring American serving her country in this way. They fell in love and were married. Jim, among other serious wounds, had lost an eye and wore a patch over it for the rest of his life. Jim was a great man, very bright and full of humor. He took a liking to me and offered me a job as a counselor in his Medford office after I graduated. Oh, Boy. Now we were all set: a new baby, a new job, and a new life—come June.

Only one step remained before my hire was confirmed. I was sent to Salem for an interview with Mr. James, the Director of Oregon's Vocational Rehabilitation Office. I drove the seventy miles to Salem on the appointed morning and began my interview with Mr. James at 10:30. It was a simpatico meeting and our personalities meshed nicely. It was about noon when the interview and tour of the facilities ended, and he invited me to have lunch with him and his wife, Silvia, at their home.

When we arrived at their home, Silvia had lunch prepared and on the table. She was a lovely and gracious lady with very long, flowing, neatly arranged black hair. We all continued our conversation about the needs of the rehabilitation movement, and everything was progressing smoothly until I bit into the second half of my sandwich. The strangeness I felt in my mouth, I discovered, was one of Silvia's long black hairs. What was I supposed to do? I couldn't remove it without embarrassing everyone, so I simply swallowed it. No one, except me, was any the wiser. I was able to control my gag reflex and continued with the rest of my sandwich without further incident. I got the job.

The quarter ended in mid-June and I was supposed to start my new job on July first. Arlene was still very pregnant, so Jim let me work in the Eugene office until Kim was born. In the middle of the night on the 1st of July, Arlene appeared to be in labor, so I rushed her to Sacred Heart Hospital, adjacent to the U. of O. campus. She was in labor for nearly thirty hours.

Finally, early in the morning on of July 3rd , Kim appeared in all her glory. Arlene and I both thought she was absolutely beautiful, even though she was covered with bloody debris and very bruised. This tiny little thing blinked at us with silver-nitrated eyes and said something, but I didn't understand what it was. Her head was shaped like a torpedo from being squished through the birth canal and squeezed with head clamps–but she was stunning.

In three days, Arlene was ready to leave the hospital. I took her and Kim to Mom's little house and immediately left for Medford and my new job. My plan was to locate a place for us to live, and then move Arlene and Kim into our new home.

Chapter 77

MEDFORD

THINGS were working out on the financial front, kind of. I sold the rotten lemon of a Rambler and reverted to our hunk of barely mobile rust. I packed that baby as full as I could with our meager belongings and headed due south, bound for Medford and another adventure.

Just south of Roseburg, the car began to fill with smoke. I pulled off on the shoulder of the road to see if I could determine what the problem was. I did. The muffler had a hole it its top, allowing fiercely hot exhaust gasses to blast directly up against the rear floorboards. The rear foot-well carpeting had caught fire and was smoldering, dangerously close to flame.

I immediately unloaded everything from the affected area onto the gravely shoulder of the highway. Then I dashed across the road to the nearest house and breathlessly explained to the woman who answered my frantic knock what was happening. I asked if I could borrow a pail of water to douse the fire. She immediately complied and I ran back across the road as fast as I could without losing much of my precious water.

When I got to the car, I found the carpeting glowing red hot and very close to combusting into a raging inferno. I poured the entire contents of the bucket onto the bright, reddish-orange carpet and reeled back. Steam and ashes burst from the car. I choked and sat down in the gravel to clear my throat and lungs from the acrid carpet smoke. I sat there for a while, contemplating my situation and wondering if I could make it to Medford without another fire. Finally, I stood up, repacked the car, returned the bucket to the kind lady, and slipped back out onto the highway. In just about an hour I was safely in Medford. I employed the first muffler man I could find to replace the mass of rusty holes that were then very inefficiently serving as a pseudo muffler.

I located Richard, the man who was to be my supervisor in the Rehab office. Although I had met him previously in Eugene, I really didn't know him well at all. He was married to a schoolteacher and had one son. I don't remember much about Richard's wife, except that she had the dirtiest fingernails I had ever seen on any one, let alone a professional woman. I couldn't imagine when she had last washed her hands. After appropriate introductions, she fried some thin bologna slices in a greasy pan and warmed up some potatoes left over from their dinner, and I settled down at their table for a great repast. After dinner, they set up a very old, very musty Army cot for me in their living room and I tried to sleep.

The next morning Richard and I left for our office near the center of town. It was really quite nice. It had two counseling offices and a very nice reception area where our secretary worked. She made our appointments for us and typed our reports. She was a good and steady hand.

Richard, on the other hand was covering his well-justified feelings of inferiority with a facade of intellectual sophistication and authority as "Senior Counselor." He rapidly became nearly intolerable to be around. Nothing I did was quite right. Every report needed a minor change or two. It was exasperating, and I was silently furious most of my working day. Fortunately, much of my caseload was located in Klamath Falls, with a few folks living even a bit further east in Lakeview, a small dot in the desert of Eastern Oregon. At least I could escape from Richard's supercilious, overbearing presence for three days at a time every other week. The down side was that I also had to leave Arlene and Kim alone.

Within a week I had located and purchased a two-bedroom home just a few blocks from the office. I was able to get it for almost nothing down with payments of $75 a month. It came completely furnished, had two bedrooms, a living room and kitchen, and a screened sleeping porch. We stashed Kim in the smaller bedroom and commandeered the other one for ourselves. It was full of very valuable antiques, and a bed with a horse hair mattress. When we got into bed it sounded like the mattress was full of cellophane. We eventually got used to the crunching, but it took awhile.

The back yard was small, but did contain a very large, productive black walnut tree, and a Bing cherry tree. At Christmas time, since we had no money for presents for other people, we packaged up cute little mesh bags of walnuts and gave them away. All of the recipients seemed to appreciate that gift very much.

The lady that lived next door should have lived in Fossil. She was that ugly. She used to trap Arlene whenever Arlene was outside, and regale her with stories about how she used to service whole lumber camps all by herself when she was a young woman. She seemed very proud of that, but I suspect it was all in her head. Her face would have stopped an oncoming locomotive dead on its tracks.

In the middle of the winter, I called Arlene one night from Klamath Falls to see how things were going. She was in tears. She had stepped on a board on the dirt floor of our garage and severely punctured her foot with a rusty nail protruding from it. I said I'd be right home. I cancelled my appointments for the next two days, packed my bag and headed for the Green Springs Highway, a narrow, violently twisting two-lane suicide run through the Siskiyou Mountain Range.

It was snowing. That highway was as treacherous a road as I had ever seen in clear, dry, broad daylight. At night, in a blinding snowstorm it was terrifying. I crept over the mountains and through the pass to Ashland where the road became a relatively straight shot on Highway 99 to Medford. I arrived home about midnight. Arlene and Kim were asleep. I woke Arlene to inquire about her foot. She was really happy to see me and explained that after talking with me on the phone, she had gone to the local medical clinic for a tetanus shot, so all was well.

I wasn't so far away the next time a much more serious disaster struck. I was working on reports in my Medford rehab office when a call came in from Arlene. She was near hysteria. She said she had inadvertently thrown an aerosol can into the fireplace with some other trash. She lit the paper in the trash and when the flames heated the aerosol can to the critical-mass temperature, it exploded. It blew itself straight through the fireplace screen, leaving fiery debris everywhere in the living room. She said she had ten fires going simultaneously. She took Kim out of her little bathtub, stashed her in her crib and threw the water on the fires. She made several trips with that tub, until all of the fires were quenched. Then she had called me. I rushed home to comfort her, and help her clean up a seriously distressed living room.

I think it was March or April when Arlene informed me that she was pregnant again. We were delighted. From the looks of Kim, we figured we really knew how to make brilliant, handsome children, and began to look forward to our next arrival with great anticipation.

Chapter 78

DISILLUSIONMENT

WE had a cold snap in the spring of 1962 that threatened to freeze the blossoms in the peach, pear, and apple orchards which surrounded Medford. I knew that the smudge pots had been lit the previous evening, but I wasn't prepared for what greeted me in the morning. I got up about six and went into Kim's room to check on her. As usual, she was babbling contentedly, waiting for us to start stirring. I looked down at her smiling face and was stunned. Her face, especially about the nostrils and mouth, was absolutely black. I picked her up and went back into the other room to show her to Arlene, hoping for some explanation from my groggy friend. Oh, No! Arlene's face looked just like Kim's. She looked at me and laughed. "What's the matter with your face?" she asked.

All three of us were covered with soot from the smudge pots. A heavy fog had settled in the valley during the night and the oily smoke from the pots had nowhere to go. It couldn't rise and drift off like it should have, so it sought out every damp aperture it could find to settle on, or in. It was an eerie spectacle, but it *was* funny.

My client load was fairly typical. All of the people I worked with were adults (at least seventeen) with some type of physical or psychological impairment that prevented them from being competitive in the labor market without some special assistance. The work was fairly routine, but two cases were clearly fixed in my memory forever. One was Joe, a man of about thirty-five, who suffered from cerebral palsy.

Joe had been unable to find work of any kind throughout his life and was receiving financial assistance from the Klamath Falls Welfare Department. He had a small room with a hot plate for what little cooking he could do and was simply wasting away. I determined fairly early that he was quite bright and eager to find some way to become self-supporting.

I also discovered that he was very mechanically adept, and further, that he loved working on vacuum cleaners. Doing the fine bench work allowed him in some way to largely control his muscular spasms. Over the next few weeks, with wonderful cooperation from Julia, the administrator of the welfare office in Klamath Falls, a plan was developed to set Joe up in a vacuum cleaner sales and repair shop in Lakeview. There would be no competition for him in such a business, and Julia agreed to a unique, formerly unheard of cooperative plan wherein Joe would continue to receive his welfare subsidy while getting his business established. The plan also provided for the Oregon Rehabilitation Division to purchase his initial inventory of used vacuum cleaners and repair parts. We located a suitable location for Joe in a vacant building with living quarters in its rear half. It was right on the main highway through Lakeview, a perfect location. One weekend in the late fall of 1961, we packed him up and moved him into a new life.

When the Lakeview Chamber of Commerce heard about Joe, the Chamber arranged for a luncheon where he would be the guest of honor. That was a wonderful day. All of the business people chipped in with enough money to buy him some very nice used furniture and appliances for his new home. Joe was deeply moved, and was unable to control a torrent of tears. No one had ever been this kind to him and he was overwhelmed. His business flourished and Joe became one of the most active members of the Chamber. This experience certainly gave me enormous satisfaction, and some degree of pride.

The other case that stands in sharp relief in my memory is that of Tommy. Tommy was a senior in high school, and an all-state athlete in baseball, football and basketball. In addition, he was a very handsome young man, and had athletic scholarship offers from a dozen major universities.

Early one very foggy morning, he was awakened by a phone call. The voice on the other end was an orchardist who wanted Tommy to help light the smudge pots in his apple orchard. Tommy agreed, and within a few minutes a pickup truck with its bed full of other young men arrived.

Tommy jumped into the truck bed with the others, all of whom he knew, and sped off into the foggy darkness. They were nearing the orchard when the driver lost control of the truck, ran off the road and slammed into the bank of a very steep ditch. The kids in the bed of the truck were catapulted out, flying over the cab and landing in every possible contorted position.

Two of the kids had severe spinal cord injuries. Tommy was one of them. Richard and I flipped a coin to see which of the boys we would work with. Richard drew the less serious case who, although badly injured, was only paralyzed from the waist down. I drew Tommy, whose fracture was in the cervical area. Tommy was a quadriplegic. The world as he had known it ended forever that cold, dark, foggy morning.

A profound depression had submerged Tommy in a quagmire of hopelessness. His parents had converted their dining room into a bedroom for him and that is where I tried to counsel him. His plight overwhelmed me. I couldn't think of much else. I discussed the case with our consulting physician, a psychiatrist, and Arlene. Everything I tried with Tommy failed. I was getting nowhere with him and becoming fairly depressed myself.

Combined with this wretched situation was the fact that we simply were not making it financially. After two pay raises, I was still bringing home only $371 a month. Every other month or so I would have to borrow money on one or another of my life insurance policies until there was nothing left to draw on. We were going in the hole every month, even using up the few pennies we had stashed away for Kim, for food. Add Richard into the mix, and the circumstances were simply intolerable and out of control.

I got a part-time job selling Kirbys, and did sell one, but only one. Clearly, something had to be done.

Chapter 79

A FRESH START

I went to the library and dug out a book that listed all of the community colleges in the country. I identified several in California, Washington and Oregon, and wrote each of them a letter of inquiry about possible employment with them. Among those few that responded was Everett Junior College in Everett, Washington. Everett's college was where I knew that our old friend, Gil Carbone, was employed, so if by chance I was hired, Arlene and I would at least know one couple and their family.

A series of letters was exchanged between the Dean of Students, Jeanette Poore, and me, which resulted in an appointment for an interview on the University of Oregon's campus with Everett's Dean of Instruction, Bill Stewart. Bill and I very nearly missed each other due to a misunderstanding about where we were to meet. We accidentally found each other in the parking lot as we were both preparing to leave. We retreated to the Student Union

Building, had a cup of coffee, and a very nice mutual interview. Bill said he was impressed with my qualifications and would recommend to Jeanette that a job offer be made to me. Then he returned to Everett, and I returned to Medford to wait.

Ten days later, I received a call from Jeanette. She wanted me to come to Everett for an interview with her and the college president. We set a time and date, I borrowed money for the flight to Seattle, and with love and good luck wishes from Arlene, was in the air in three days.

The plane assigned to the milk run from Medford to Seattle was a very small, light aircraft that bobbed, rolled, rose and fell abruptly with each gust of wind or passing bird. Just before landing in Seattle the plane hit an air pocket and I dumped an entire cup of coffee down my front, badly staining my shirt, tie and composure. "Oh, well. Maybe they'll understand," I half-optimistically thought to myself.

Arlene's parents met me at the Seattle/Tacoma airport and drove me to their home in West Seattle. They loaned me their car to drive to Everett, which they said was easy enough to find. "Just head north on Highway 99 and you'll run right into it" they said.

Sure enough, they were right. I found the college with no difficulty, parked my car in a visitor's spot, walked into the Administration Building, and directly into the men's latrine. I cleaned myself up as best I could, combed my hair, hitched up my pants, checked my fly, and headed up the marble stairway to Jeanette's office.

Jeanette was a very nice lady and put me at ease right off. We chatted for about an hour. About what, I haven't the slightest recollection. Then she took me into the president's office and introduced me to Dr. Berg, a tall, impressive, articulate ex-army officer. We exchanged pleasantries for five minutes or so, and he turned me back to Jeanette. Obviously, this was going to be her decision.

Our next stop was in the office of Howard Larsen, a young

man of about thirty-two, who was in charge of Student Activities. If I were hired, Howard would be my immediate supervisor. If hired, my job was to be the Coordinator of Student Activities for Men. It wasn't exactly what I would have chosen, but I had to get out of Medford. Howard and I got along just fine.

I returned to Jeanette's office and learned that my starting salary, for nine months, would be 50% higher than I was then earning in a full year as a rehabilitation counselor. That pleased me. I bid appropriate farewells, floated down the stairs, and into Sam and Rosemary's car. I had three hours before my scheduled flight back to Medford and I thought I had plenty of time.

I would have had enough time, too, if I hadn't gotten lost and hopelessly entangled in shift-change traffic from the Boeing plant. I couldn't turn off at my designated street because I was locked into a middle lane of traffic. I had to travel two or three miles beyond my turnoff before I could get turned around and headed back, and the traffic was bumper to bumper, stop and go, nearly all the way to Sam and Rosemary's house. The time was relentlessly ticking away as my flight time approached with increasing speed. And there was nothing I could do about it except sweat and try to control my mounting anxiety.

I finally found their house. They jumped into the car and drove me to the airport as fast as they dared. I did make my flight, barely, and was off, into the clouds and a thorough buffeting before reaching the airport in Medford. Arlene was there with Kim, anxiously waiting for me and whatever news I might have about an escape from Medford. She was pleased with my report. We drove home, had a great talk and laugh over my misadventures, and crashed into our cacophonous horsehair mattress.

Ten days later I was in the Employment Security Office in Klamath Falls, awaiting my next client, when a telephone call came in for me. It was Jeanette. She made me a concrete contract offer. I accepted immediately. She was pleased and said she would send the contract to me for my signature. My starting date would be August 2, 1962.

I called Arlene immediately to let her know the terrific news. She was excited and happy and said, "You better get home as soon as you can. We've got a house to sell!"

Oh, yeah. A small detail. But, I was confident we could pull it off.

Chapter 80

HIGH ANXIETY

AS soon as I got home, we stuck a "For Sale by Owner" sign in the front yard, made the house and yard as presentable as possible, and waited for the hordes of prospects out there straining to flood through our doors. We waited, and waited, and waited some more. No one came. Arlene and I would sit in the living room looking out the window at passing cars, some of which slowed down, or even stopped at the curb, and looked. But no one ever came in. Days went by, then weeks, and more weeks. We were beginning to feel a sense of panic. We had to sell that house, and no one was interested. What were we going to do?

Two weeks before we were going to have to leave Medford, the Oregon State Commission for the Blind opened a new office in town. Richard and I paid a friendly welcoming visit to the office where we met its administrator, Clyde. He was a very pleasant man of about forty-five, and, wouldn't you know, he and his wife were looking for a house to buy. I told him we had one for sale that he might be interested in, and arranged for him to come and "look" at it. Clyde was blind, as was his wife, Rita. Both of them had enough vision to tell daylight from dark, but that was about it.

I picked Clyde up the next afternoon and drove him to our home. He went through each room, inspecting everything with his hands and other senses. He liked the house and made me an offer right then for our full asking price. We were thrilled. All of us went to a real estate attorney's office the following day and finalized the transaction.

It was in mid-July when we began packing our U-Haul trailer. It was 115 degrees that day, and even hotter in the trailer. Clyde came over to help us pack the trailer, and in spite of his lack of vision, did an extremely efficient job. The next morning we pulled out, heading for Everett and a whole new life.

By the time we got to Seattle, the heat, the pregnancy, and the stress had gotten to Arlene. She was very sick. We altered our plans and stopped at Arlene's folk's house where she immediately took to bed. I knew that she and Kim were in good hands, and left the next morning for Everett to locate housing for us.

With the help of the President's secretary, I found a very nice, clean, two-bedroom house just south of town that would suit us perfectly. The landlady, a librarian in the Everett Public Library, believed me when I told her that we would take very good care of her property, and even knocked off $5 from the $75 a month rent if I would mow the lawn at her current residence. I agreed, and the deal was sealed.

I roared back to Seattle where I waited for Arlene to become well enough to travel again. It wasn't long before we arrived in Everett, unpacked, settled in, and I reported for work. It was August 2, 1962. The world was good.

Chapter 81

EVERETT JUNIOR COLLEGE

I entered Jeanette's office full of anticipatory neural firings and reported for duty. Her first order of business was to inform me that my assignment had been changed. Instead of being the Men's Activities Advisor, I was going to instruct two classes of a Career Planning course for half of my load, and do individual counseling for the other half. This new assignment was much more in line with my abilities and proclivities and suited me just fine. Then she showed me my new office. We didn't have to go very far.

My "office" was a small storage closet in her office that she had asked the janitor to clean out for me. It was about four by six feet with a sloping ceiling that I managed to crash my head into with monotonous regularity for the next nine months. There was no window, so if I needed to shut the door for a counseling session, I would soon be suffering the consequences of oxygen deprivation. Fortunately, I didn't have Seasonal Affective Disorder (SAD) as well or I would have gone completely mad. I did my best to spend as little time in that closet as possible, and frequently moved my counselees to the Student Center coffee shop for counseling sessions. My second year was much better, and I received an office full of windows overlooking the lush, green campus.

Over twenty additional faculty members were hired that year and for the first time ever, faculty numbered over one hundred. The campus was first occupied in 1958 so it was new and fresh. The student body was growing rapidly each year and Everett had become the largest community college west of the Mississippi.

In early October Jeanette ask me to accompany her to a professional meeting for all northwest student personnel in Gerhart, Oregon. I thought it would be good for me to meet my colleagues from around the Northwest so I readily agreed.

When we arrived we checked in at the "hotel," which was a very old, very rickety, two story wooden building. The wind was fierce that chilly night on the coast, and at times I was sure that the whole crazy structure would collapse and disappear, scattering itself and my remains over the sand dunes.

There were hundreds of people there for the conference. We had dinner with some other faculty from Everett and some acquaintances from the U. of O. rehab program. After dinner the Chancellor for Higher Education for the State of Oregon gave a brilliant, articulate speech. I thought to myself, "This is where I belong. I'm finally home."

I silently congratulated myself on my astute career move, thanked Jeanette, and retreated to my room. I listened to the howling wind and prayed that I didn't disappear in the middle of the night.

Chapter 82

YOUTH OPPORTUNITY CENTERS

ON the 30th of October, Arlene began feeling very strange. It appeared to me that she might just be about ready to deliver our second bambino, so we loaded up and headed out. We dropped Kim off at Carbone's home for safekeeping and reported to General Hospital in Everett. Within just an hour or two, Beth was delivered. Beth was beautiful, with quite a bit of blond hair that soon disappeared and didn't reappear for two and a half years. During that time she looked remarkably like Nikita Khrushchev, the leader of the Soviet Union. Beth, however, was a lot more pleasant and easier to get along with.

I visited Arlene in her room right after inspecting Beth to make sure she had the appropriate number of fingers, toes, arms, legs and heads. After passing inspection, Beth was taken to the nursery and I went in to visit Arlene.

Arlene, smiling happily through her morphinous fog said, "That was so easy! Let's have another one!"

I smiled back at her and suggested, "Perhaps we should wait until your anesthetic wears off before we start working on another one. Then we can talk about it."

Three days later, Arlene came home with Beth warmly swaddled in blankets. Kim, after working the wrinkles out of her nose, very shortly became the second "Mom" and was of enormous help to Arlene. Beth was upside down with regard to night and day. She decided to be up and alert all night, and would sleep all day. It took just about a month of screaming nights to get her squared away. Then all was well on the home front.

I learned my job responsibilities quickly and was greatly impressed and stimulated by the numbers and intelligence of the faculty and administration. It was wonderfully satisfying, both for Arlene and me. However, something that really disturbed me was that nearly all students were declaring a bachelor's degree as their minimal academic goal. Most of them had done poorly in high school and had neither the knowledge or intellectual capacity to compete successfully in even the least academically demanding program we offered, let alone in the university programs they aspired to.

I did some in-depth research of the student population and determined that by the end of two years after their entry, more than 92 percent of them had dropped out. Most left the college either for academic incompetence or because they were vocationally directionless. A faculty member I know quite well once said, "Our students may be stupid, but at least they're unmotivated."

But, there were no other community colleges within seventy-five miles, so there was always a fresh line of students at the door. No one had paid any attention to what was happening to those poor souls that entered our academic meat grinder. The administration simply didn't want to know the information I was discovering. If the students didn't cut it, that was their problem, not ours.

Early in the spring of 1964, Arlene informed me that we were going to be the happy parents of another child, due probably, sometime in early August. We were very pleased and looked forward to another beautiful, brilliant addition to our growing family.

As the spring quarter was coming to a close, Jeanette informed me that there would be no summer work for me that year. My anxiety level ratcheted up several notches. I thought I would have full employment during the summers, but Jeanette had decided to give the work to someone else that year.

Just prior to reaching a full-blown anxiety state, I received a call from a professor in the Education Department at the University of Washington. I had been recommended to him by a mutual friend as someone who might like to help him out with a project of his during the months of July and August. He explained that his department had funds from the Federal Office of Employment Security to work with sixty unemployed college graduates in an attempt to prepare them to work as job counselors in their newly invented, and soon to be implemented, Youth Opportunity Centers. He was looking for three instructors, each of whom would bear responsibility for twenty students. I was enormously relieved and asked him what the salary would be. He responded, "Nine hundred dollars for each month."

That was nearly 50% higher than my salary was at the community college, so I accepted his offer immediately. I reported for work as an instructor in the School of Education at the University of Washington on the first of July.

On August 5, 1964, our only son, Kevin, was born. What a terrific kid. He, too, was a handsome child. The day after he was born, I reported for work at the university, and was greeted by my class of twenty students who had prepared a basket full of presents for Kevin. One of the gifts was a small football which all of them had signed. I was deeply touched.

I worked the two contracted months and met many faculty members who seemed impressed with my range of knowledge and competence. It was a good and valuable experience and I never forgot it. When I returned to work in the fall, I was named Director of Counseling and Testing. I was twenty-eight years old. It was a role I fulfilled for the next twenty-plus years.

Chapter 83

PLUSES AND MINUSES

It was sometime in April of 1966, and the world was coming to life again. The birds were welcoming the warmth with their constant chattering and songs, and our lives were moving along as we had dreamed they would. I came home from work late one afternoon, and Arlene as usual, was preparing dinner. She looked at me and said, "Glenn, I need to tell you something."

I looked at her quizzically and she responded, "I think I'm pregnant again."

She wasn't sure what kind of reception that news would stimulate, since we had pretty much decided that our family was complete.

"Well, I think that's just fine," I replied.

We hugged each other and reassured ourselves that everything was going to be o.k. We would welcome our newcomer with great rejoicing. She breathed a sigh of relief and was very happy. I helped her set the dinner table, we had a wonderful meal, and all was right with our world. Dawn, our last child, was born in November and we couldn't have been more pleased. She was reminiscent of a porcelain doll, almost a miniature person, and very bright. Dawn was destined to bring much additional joy into our lives.

My visibility in the professional academic world was increasing and I was invited to speak at a convention of the Mathematics Association of America. That year the meeting was held at the University of Victoria in Canada in June, 1966. Arlene accompanied me and we made a rare mini-vacation of it.

Early in 1969 I received a phone call from Dr. Larsen, the gentleman who was one of the first individuals to interview me for the Everett job. He had since received his doctorate from Stanford and had moved on to a professorship at the University of Washington. He urged me to apply to their doctoral program in Higher Education, indicating that there would be no question about my acceptance into the program. Further, he would be happy to be my advisor. He offered two scholarships to me. One was funded by the Kellogg Foundation and the other by the Federal Department of Education. I was flattered, of course, and immediately applied for a sabbatical leave from Everett so that I could begin my studies in the fall. The leave request was granted and I made the necessary preparations to enter the university in the fall.

During the summer of 1969, however, I ran directly into a serious problem. It occurred one afternoon when I was carrying a box full of books up a flight of stairs, on my way to load them into my car. Crushing chest pain gripped me and I had to stop and rest until the pain subsided. I knew from my days as a rehab counselor that I was having an attack of angina. I drove directly to my physician's office, near Providence Hospital in Everett and checked in. He saw me immediately and wired me for an electrocardiogram.

The results were not good. He referred me to Dr. Nathan,

an Everett cardiologist for further evaluation. Dr. Nathan attached electrodes to me and administered the Master's Two-Step, a relatively minor exercise stress test. He didn't like what he saw on the electrocardiogram and referred me for an immediate heart catheterization at Swedish Hospital in Seattle. I was thirty-five years old.

The day of the examination was frightening. I was flat on my back on a small operating table, surrounded by nurses in training, the physician who would be doing the heart catheterization, and Dr. Nathan. Dr. Nathan was there to support me and to learn as much as he could about the procedure.

A small puncture was made in my left femoral artery and a catheter was carefully inserted and threaded up the artery and into my heart. I could watch the procedure on a television monitor positioned just to my left. Then the dye, an iodine solution, was injected. It felt warm, almost hot. Then my heart ejected it into my arterial system and I thought my head would explode. It was an extremely hot sensation throughout my body, but especially in my brain. Pictures were taken, and I received another blast of iodine dye, and then another and another. I began to get nauseated and couldn't watch the procedure any longer. I closed my eyes and pretended I was somewhere else—anywhere else.

Finally, it was over. A pressure bandage was applied to the wound in my groin and I was transported to a hospital room for recovery. I was released the next day. A very worried Arlene picked me up and drove me through the rain to our home. Three days later we both visited Dr. Nathan for an interpretation of the test results.

He looked very concerned as he began his explanation. "Your left coronary artery is nearly eighty percent closed, Glenn, and your right coronary artery is fifty percent closed. We'll try the most conservative treatment possible at this time and have you enroll in a cardiac exercise program. Perhaps we can develop some collateral circulation to take some of the burden off of your compromised arteries."

The next day I enrolled in the cardiac exercise program offered at Everett Community College's gymnasium. I worked very hard for several weeks—sit ups, walking, stretching, and various other exercises. It began to pay off. I could do increasing amounts of physical work before angina pains began, and I felt I was really accomplishing something. And I was, for awhile. In fact, I got through nearly five years before becoming completely incapacitated.

I did extremely well at the university and was highly regarded by all of my professors and colleagues for my comprehensive knowledge of community colleges and the work world. At the end of the first year I returned to full time work as the Director of Counseling and Testing at Everett, but continued as a full time doctoral candidate at the university as well. My dissertation, completed during the 1971-72 academic year, was unique, exquisitely complex, but presented in such a way that it was simple to understand. It was laboriously typed, word by word, on a manual typewriter.

During the oral defense of my dissertation, one of the professors asked me a particularly stupid question. My answer was, "I think that's bull shit." Everyone else in the room agreed with my assessment and laughed out loud. Although taken aback at first, so did the questioner. The whole experience was a very good and positive one. The committee members were asking me questions that they really didn't know the answers to. I had discovered an enormously powerful statistical analysis for my data, called a randomized block design. That analysis was able to evaluate multiple variables simultaneously with very little room for error. The study was tight. It was unique. It was important.

Following the orals, I was asked to step outside and wait in the hallway while the dissertation committee members evaluated my responses. Within five minutes, I was welcomed back into the examining room and introduced to the committee members by Dr. Larsen, my advisor, as "Dr." Glenn Adams. Everyone stood and applauded. I was very happy indeed.

The university decided to submit my dissertation for consideration for the first annual award by the College Placement Council. The competition was international in scope, and included doctoral dissertations and masters' theses in the areas of counseling, placement or career planning from colleges and universities throughout the United States and Canada.

All of the submissions were evaluated and judged by a panel comprised of experts from Purdue University, UCLA, General Electric and the Ford Motor Company, under the direction of the College Placement Council Foundation's Research Committee.

Ten weeks after submission, I received a phone call from the Council, indicating that my dissertation was the unanimous choice of the judges. I was presented with their First Annual Award for Excellence in Counseling, Career Planning and Placement. I was ecstatic. When the $1,000 award check arrived, I immediately gave $100 to each of our children. It was a very small token of my appreciation for their patience and cooperation while I was immersed in my writing.

My days and nights had been full. From the perspective of a husband, father, and professional person, I was very happy. However. . . .

Part Six
MY REAL WORLD

Chapter 84

PREPARING TO DIE

BY the winter of 1973-74, chest pain was ever present. In addition to long acting nitrates, I was consuming more than forty nitroglycerine tablets daily. My disease had progressed to the point where the slightest emotion or physical activity would precipitate crushing, agonizing, chest and arm pain. Even walking across our living room was something to be considered twice before undertaking it. At night the pain of angina would awaken me. Clearly, something had to be done, and soon.

Dr. Nathan recommended an immediate cardiac catheterization and arranged for the procedure to be done by Dr. Robin Johnston, the catheterization specialist at Virginia Mason Clinic in Seattle. But first, I had to be withdrawn from all cardiac medications. The withdrawal took three days, and by the end of that time I was engulfed in continuous, intractable chest pain.

It was a cold, blustery day in mid-April when Arlene drove

me to my catheterization appointment. She dropped me off at the appropriate door and left to find a parking place. I wandered into the clinic and found my way to the "cath lab," where the operation was to be done. I didn't see Arlene again until after it had been completed.

All clothing was removed and I donned a light blue hospital gown with the standard open back. Although it was stunning, I wasn't in much of a mood to dwell on my sartorial splendor. Dr. Johnston's professional but friendly manner eased my anxiety somewhat. He injected a small amount of numbing medication into my left groin. He then made a small incision in my left femoral artery and inserted a catheter, snaking it carefully up into the left ventricle of my heart. I was watching the procedure on a television monitor placed on the wall to my left, and could see the tip of the catheter enter my heart. The iodine-based dye was injected, and once again, I could feel its warmth as it surged out of my heart into my arterial system. My angina was raging. I thought I was going to die right there on the cath table. Dr. Johnston injected liquid nitroglycerin into my hand, and the pain gradually subsided. Several more attempts were made to visualize and photograph my heart's arterial system, interspersed with overwhelming anginal pain followed by large doses of nitro. Finally, bathed in sweat, I heard him say, "It's over Glenn. You can relax now. I'm going to apply a pressure bandage to your wound, and you'll be on your way to your room in just a few minutes."

I breathed a sigh of relief and closed my eyes. Soon an orderly arrived and transported me through the chilly halls, up several floors on an elevator, and into my room where Arlene was anxiously awaiting my arrival. A ward nurse and the orderly slid me gently onto my bed, checked my wound, and disappeared. Arlene and I talked a bit about the procedure, but I was just about ready for a nap. She was happy to see that even through this mess, my sense of humor remained relatively intact, and agreed to leave me alone for awhile. She slipped through the doorway and into the catacombs where she eventually found the cafeteria and coffee shop.

Late in the afternoon my cardiologist at Virginia Mason, Dr. Hughes, stopped in to give Arlene and me the findings of the catheterization. He said that they had found a ninety-five percent blockage of the left anterior descending coronary artery but that it was probably graftable about one third of the way down. He also indicated that there was a fifty-percent closure of the circumflex artery, a relatively small artery near the top of the heart. He said that my case had been discussed at their Cardiology Conference and the consensus was that open-heart bypass surgery should be undertaken at the earliest possible time.

The news was not entirely unexpected. Nevertheless, it was devastating. That evening was one of the worst of my entire life. It was time to tell the children. After dinner, as we all were sitting around the table, I said, "Listen guys. I have something to tell you."

The chatter stopped instantly and all eyes were upon me. I took a deep breath, and began: "The results of my latest tests at Virginia Mason indicate that I need to have open heart surgery, and I need to have it as soon as possible."

As I tried to continue with a reasonable explanation of what the problem was and how they were proposing to fix it, my voice caught in my throat and I began to sob. Kim was twelve, Beth was eleven, Kevin was nine, and Dawn was seven. I don't think Kevin and Dawn fully realized the import of what I was saying, but Kim and Beth did. Soon they were crying too. Arlene came around the end of the table and stood behind me, holding my shoulders, saying, "Everything is going to be all right."

We all tried very hard to believe her. After all, we had

four beautiful children to raise—and I was only forty years old.

Later that evening, after I had composed myself a bit, I telephoned both my brother Harland, and my sister Dorothy, to let them know what was happening. They were shocked, of course, but fully supportive. They both wished me good luck and God speed in the adventure before me.

Three days later Arlene and I had an appointment with Dr. Jackobie, the cardiac surgeon who would be operating on me. Because the cardiac team had recommended immediate surgery, we were prepared to have the surgeon explain what exactly the surgery would be, what we should expect, and be assigned a room for surgery the following day.

Dr. Jackobie came sweeping into his little office where we had been directed to wait for him, still in his blood-stained operating clothes from a surgery he had just completed. He was a big man physically, probably six feet three or four, and about fifty-five years old. He greeted us rather gruffly, and sat down at his desk to review my file. Arlene and I sat there, nervously fidgeting in our chairs, wanting to get on with it. After three or four minutes he said, "It looks like something I can do. I'll have them schedule you for May 14."

"May 14th!" I exclaimed. "That's nearly four weeks away. The other doctors said that the surgery needed to be done immediately. We thought that immediate meant right away."

"Well, now," Dr. Jackobie shot back. "Just *who* in the Hell do you think *you* are? There are several people ahead of you waiting for this surgery. You'll get your bypass when your turn comes. I'll see you then," and we were summarily dismissed.

I slipped two nitro tablets under my tongue, and Arlene and I made our way out of the hospital and to our car. We were both baffled and scared. She drove me home, where we waited, day by day, for the 13th of May to arrive, the day I would be admitted to the hospital. Those days were excruciatingly long and both physically and psychologically painful. My medications were helping me to tolerate my situation, but all of us were anxious to get this behind us.

And the anxiety *was* great. After all, the surgeons had only recently moved from experimental heart surgery on dogs to experimental heart surgery on humans. I was to be one of the very first—humans, that is. I was very frightened, but also fairly philosophical. I told myself that there were no guarantees in life, and whatever was meant to be, would be. I believed I had been a good person, for the most part, and I had made my peace with God. I knew that the children were in good hands.

The thirteenth of May finally arrived. I packed a small bag of necessary toiletries, my new robe and slippers, and loaded myself into our car. We left home early in the morning and all of the children were waving to us as we pulled out of the driveway and headed for Seattle.

Arlene carefully weaved through the heavy morning traffic and we arrived at the hospital at just about nine o'clock. Arlene stayed with me for most of the day as the nurses and technicians pricked and probed and ran numerous tests on my blood, blood pressure, and a few other vitals.

Arlene stayed as long as she could, and then left for home to attend to the children and respond to the dozens of phone messages that had accumulated during the day. We hugged, and kissed each other goodbye. Both of us were a little teary at that point. Both of our minds were full of anxiety, concern, hope and wonder. We told each other that everything would be just fine, and agreed to meet again soon.

Following dinner, my entire body was shaved, except for my head. Apparently they didn't want any wild hairs getting into their work site, and that was probably a good thing. Just before lights out, an orderly arrived and attempted to insert a catheter into my bladder. He was uncommonly inept. After several unsuccessful attempts, he gleefully declared victory.

He asked that I attempt to urinate to see if his makeshift

plumbing system worked. My plumbing worked. His didn't. My gown and sheets were distressingly wet. I said, "That's enough. You will leave now."

Chagrined, he packed his miserable equipment and disappeared into the cool marble hallway.

I called for Mary, my main nurse. Mary was a vibrant young nurse who exuded confidence and demonstrated competence. In less than a minute she had the leaks repaired and the system working flawlessly. Then she changed my sheets, gave me something to help me sleep, and wished me good fortune for my adventure the following morning.

I awoke late in the afternoon the next day. I had a bandage on my chest, and tubes and wires protruding from everywhere it seemed. There was what seemed like a four-inch diameter corrugated tube in my throat. I was cold. It was hard to swallow. I retreated to the relative warmth and pleasure of sleep. Arlene had been there, but I don't remember that.

The next morning, May 15th, I awakened with wires and machinery everywhere, but my breathing tube was gone. I was cold, very cold. I was shivering constantly. There was good reason. In order to control the fever after the surgery, Dr. Jackobie had prescribed an ice bed for me. I was lying on a rubber sheet that had ice water circulating through a network of tunnels within the sheet. I was on that bed for three days, during which my shivering progressed to constant spasms.

After three interminably long, painful days and nights, I was taken off of the ice sheets and allowed to warm up. Two or three days later I was moved from intensive care to my own room, and I began my program of reintroducing my muscles to the world of work. The exercises were slowly paced, beginning with gentle, slow walking in the hallways, and progressing to stationary bike riding and light weight lifting. Arlene was there every day to cheer me on. All of the kids came down, too. A new life was beginning. The phrase "Being Reborn" took on a whole new meaning for all of us.

My pain was gone! My old enemy (or maybe friend, I don't know), angina, was not there. I was chest-pain free. I was a new man. I learned, though, that it took six hours for Dr. Jackobie to do the graft on the main left artery, and he didn't think it would be wise to keep me open any longer to complete a planned graft for the circumflex artery.

On the tenth day following my surgery, Arlene arrived to take me home. My body felt as though it had been hit by a freight train. Every muscle, every cell, was writhing in pain from my convulsions on the ice bed. I accepted that as a small price to pay, but it did take several weeks before the muscle pain dissipated.

Arlene and I reviewed all of the cards and letters I had received during my hospital stay, and they were impressive, both in numbers and in the messages of support they contained. I also learned that thirteen of my colleagues from the college had donated blood for me. It was a wonderful expression of love and concern. I was deeply moved. I only used eight pints, so the blood bank's storehouse increased at least a little bit.

After about six weeks I felt strong enough to return to work at the college. I started with half days, but soon progressed to a full work schedule. I was walking regularly, increasing my distance and speed every day. It was about November as I recall, that I borrowed Arlene's bicycle to take a tour around the neighborhood. I hadn't gone much more than a block when I was gripped by chest pain. I stopped immediately to rest, and the pain subsided. Was this my old nemesis, angina, back for a curtain call? I was concerned. I got back on the bike and slowly pedaled home. By the time I got to the house there was no longer any doubt. It was angina. No one was home when I got there, so I just sat in my chair at the kitchen table, wondering what was ahead for us.

When Arlene came home, I told her I thought I might be developing angina again. She was very concerned, but supportive. We made arrangements for me to see Dr. Nathan the following day.

Dr. Nathan scheduled me for a number of tests, including another angiographic study. The pictures showed a complete failure of the graft Dr. Jackobie had performed. The grafted saphenous vein from my left calf had collapsed and had been reabsorbed by my body. It had simply disappeared. The operation had not worked. Further, an 80% blockage of the right coronary artery was discovered and the 50% occlusion of the circumflex was still there. The problem in the right artery was a new blockage that had generated just since the surgery in May. Why was I disintegrating so fast? There were no answers.

Again, I was placed on heavy doses of nitrates and other cardiac medications and told to exercise as much as possible. That worked for about eleven months, before the pain became unbearable and intractable. I wasn't at all looking forward to another session with my obnoxious surgeon, Dr. Jackobie, and was greatly relieved when we discovered that he was no longer at Virginia Mason. Dr. Anders, a young, bright, very confident heart surgeon, had replaced him.

When Arlene and I met with him, and heard what he had to say, we were deeply impressed. He explained in full detail just what needed to be done and how he proposed to do it. He also said that my recovery in the hospital would be much more comfortable this time, since he would be using drugs, not a primitive ice bed, to control post operative fever. He said that he would be using the saphenous vein from the calf of my right leg for the graft. His information was complete, his confidence reassuring. I was scheduled for surgery on December 11, 1975. I was forty-two years old.

On the 10th of December, 1975, I was admitted to Virginia Mason Hospital. The routine was much the same as before. Tests and more tests were done. Arterial blood was drawn for a determination of blood gases. My body was shaved from stem to stern and beyond. Arlene stayed with me as much as she could, and was there all day. We said goodbye to one another again at the elevator. We hugged and kissed, and she disappeared through the waiting elevator doors.

I returned to my room and stood by the window. I knew where she had parked our car and that I would be able to see her once more as she pulled out of her space and headed toward the freeway entrance. It was snowing heavily but the streets were warm enough to melt it as soon as it landed. There she was! I smiled, waved, and choked out a nearly inaudible goodbye. I took a deep breath and returned to my bed.

By evening, I was ready to go. Mary, my nurse from the first surgery, was on hand to lend support and encouragement one more time. I asked her if it might be possible for the catheter to be inserted after the anesthesiologist had done his thing. She replied softly, "Of course it can, Glenn. I'll see to it." Relieved, I took my sleeping potion, talked one more time with God, and prepared myself not to wake up again.

But I did wake up. The next afternoon, after six hours of surgery, I awakened in the Intensive Care Unit. There was Bertha, my main ICU nurse, smiling and offering comforting words. She had been my ICU nurse following the first surgery as well, and was distressed to see me back so soon. Bertha was a small woman, probably thirty years old, and extremely competent. She helped me hold myself together for the frequent mandatory coughing exercises to clear my lungs, and was a wonderful translator of my condition to Arlene. I think I fell a little bit in love with Bertha.

I spent three days in the ICU, and then six more in a private room on the ward floor. Cards and letters again flooded in from friends, coworkers and relatives. I learned that this time sixteen of my colleagues had donated blood. I was overwhelmed with feelings of gratitude. Dr. Anders stopped in to see me every day, sometimes twice. He was a wonderful man, and I'll never forget him.

On the morning of December 20th, I was discharged with a new, operational plumbing system in my heart. My angina was gone and my body and soul were not wracked with pain from unnecessary ice-induced spasms. I really felt quite good, and I was home for Christmas. It was a very good Christmas. I hadn't died after all.

Now it was time to learn to live again. That's not always easy. I learned that depression was a frequent companion of such life threatening surgeries. I made contact with Dr. Murray, my psychiatrist friend and met with him several times during the next few months, slowly working through my mental miseries.

Within six months I thought that I was strong enough, both physically and psychologically, to return to work at the college full time.

Chapter 85

SURPRISE!

FOUR years passed swiftly by and in the fall of 1979, Kim went off to the University of Puget Sound in Tacoma. Beth was a senior in high school and would soon follow Kim to UPS. Kevin was a sophomore and Dawn was about ready to begin high school.

On September 13th, 1985, my sister Dorothy telephoned to let us know that Mom had died. She said that Mom had passed away in her little home the previous evening, from an apparent heart attack. Mom had lived in that cozy little nest that Arlene and I had made for her longer than she had lived anywhere else in her life, and had been extremely happy there. Arlene and I arranged to drive to Eugene immediately to help with whatever needed to be done. All of our children arrived a couple of days later. Brother Harland and his wife, Lorraine, were also able to attend the funeral. It was a sad time for all of us.

In the spring of 1986, my blood pressure began to soar.

Dr. Nathan was trying everything he could think of to control it, but it kept climbing. The highest reading that I know of was something like 220/115. That is stroke territory. I was reporting in to the Everett Clinic, where Dr. Nathan had his practice, every day to have my blood pressure taken, but nothing was helping. Dr. Nathan would manipulate my drugs every so often, but day by day my condition was worsening. I should have been hospitalized until my raging blood pressure was under control. But I wasn't. It was June and I was hoping to make it to the end of the academic year when I could rest. I didn't make it.

My last day of work was Friday, June 13, 1986. Spring quarter ended that day for me and for Kim, Kevin and Dawn who were all students at Western Washington University in Bellingham. Arlene and I were planning to drive up there to help them pack and move home for the summer, so I stopped on my way home from school and rented a large U-Haul trailer. I got the thing home and backed it carefully into our driveway. It was hot. I wiped the sweat from my forehead and got out of the car.

As soon as I stood up next to the car, my vision went crazy. I couldn't see anything. My visual field was a chaotic swarm of kaleidoscopic colors. That's all. I felt weak. Slowly, I let myself down on the driveway. I was on my hands and knees, blind, scared, and bewildered, when Kevin arrived home. He found me and helped me to lie down on the concrete. Then he ran to get Arlene, who was gardening in our back yard. Someone called 911. Arlene was there immediately to comfort me while we waited for the ambulance.

I don't remember the trip to the hospital, or much of anything else for a day or two. I had no idea what had happened. I was undergoing CT scans and skull x-rays, but no damage was showing up. An electroencephalogram showed chaotic activity in some parts of my brain, but Dr. Nathan assured us that I had not had a stroke. He was wrong.

The blockage had occurred in the left occipital artery, causing a near complete loss of sight in the right hemisphere in both eyes. Apparently, there had also been a slight stroke in the temporal lobe as well.

I was very confused, and very dizzy. I couldn't stand without holding on to someone or something. I remember standing in front of the mirror one morning two or three days into my hospitalization, knowing that I was supposed to shave, brush my teeth and comb my hair. But I didn't know how. I was terrified. I made my way back to my bed, weeping.

Arlene and all of the children were with me every day, encouraging and supporting. My emotions were extremely labile. I could move from wild, inappropriate laughter to tears instantly with no apparent stimulus. It was a very crazy and deeply foreboding time.

Finally, I was released from the hospital. Arlene helped me into the car and we rode home in near silence. I was half blind, with serious field cuts in the vision of both eyes. Trying to make sense out of this new world I had entered was exhausting and debilitating mentally. I plodded through each dark day, a prisoner of my deep depression. A stroke was not what I had expected at all. I suspected that some day I would probably have a fatal heart attack, but a stroke? It had never entered my mind. Now here I was, half blind and with a short-term memory that had been obliterated.

I entered the rehabilitation program for stroke victims offered through Providence Hospital in Everett. It was extremely frustrating. My visual field was constantly moving, undulating. I just couldn't get a sharp or clear focus on anything. However, slowly, over several months, my mind became more clear, and I was able to read, albeit with great difficulty, and word for word.

Finally, after a year and a half or so, I was functioning reasonably well and I was beginning to pull out of my doldrums. Then one night in December of 1987, around two in the morning, I awakened with that old, familiar crushing chest pain of angina. "Oh, shit," I said to myself. I got out of bed, took a nitroglycerin tablet, and fixed myself a cup of cocoa. The pain subsided and I returned to bed. The same thing happened the next night, and the next. Then it began happening during the day. There was no question in my mind. It was angina. And the progress I had been making with my depression ceased.

I was having dinner with Arlene one evening at one of our favorite restaurants, when she looked directly at me and said, "Glenn, how much longer am I going to have to live with your depression? When is this going to be over?"

I diverted my eyes from hers for a moment, and then said, "I think angina has returned."

I explained to her what had been happening over the past several days and nights. She was shocked, but somewhere, deep down, I suspect she was expecting such a revelation.

"Have you seen Dr. Nathan?"

"Not yet, but I'm scheduled to see him next week," I replied.

We finished our meal, paid our bill, slipped off into the night, and headed for home. She must have been thinking, "Oh, God. What next?"

I saw Dr. Nathan early in January. He scheduled and performed a heart catheterization to see just what was going on. What he found was a major blockage in the bypass graft. That graft was the only piece of my cardiac circulatory system that was keeping me alive, and it was over 90% clogged with something. He couldn't determine whether the blockage was a clot, or a large plaque buildup. We decided on the most conservative course of action and began a series of heparin shots. I gave myself the shots in my abdomen three times a day for a month.

I was again scheduled for another catheterization in February. No change. Another month of heparin shots. Thirty days later, the third cath was done. Three caths in sixty days. No change. If it had been a clot, it would have begun to dissolve somewhat. Now what? If I had been a bit more sophisticated, I would have asked to be hospitalized and put on a heparin drip, along with whatever other clot dissolvents were available. I also would have known about the toxic effects on my kidneys of so much dye. But I wasn't that smart, and Dr. Nathan elected not to tell me.

By then there were several heart surgeons practicing in Everett, but none of them wanted anything to do with such a high-risk procedure as another operation would have been. I said to Dr. Nathan that I would be willing to go to Texas, or California, or anywhere a surgeon could be found that would take the risk. Dr. Nathan replied:

"Well, Glenn, if you're that determined, I want you to make an appointment to see Dr. Steward at the University of Washington's Medical Center. Take this film with you so he can see what we found."

I scheduled an appointment with Dr. Steward as soon as I could and Arlene took me to the university to meet with him. He was a nice young man and very sympathetic. He reviewed the films and said, "We've got to get in there right away. We have five heart surgeons on staff here and I know one that can do this job." He scheduled me for an appointment with his colleague, Dr. Ivey, and we met with him about a week later.

Dr. Ivey, a kind and gentle man, had reviewed the films and was well prepared for us when we met with him in his little office in the concrete catacombs of the University of Washington Medical Center.

"This will be a relatively high risk procedure," he said. "But I'm confident I can do this job. However, we need to do it now, so let's get you scheduled."

Within a week my chest was torn asunder for the third time.

But, I woke up again. Damn. Must be my stubborn English blood. The drugs they gave me were terrific. I don't remember much of anything. I do know that they had a hard time getting me to breathe again and I was on a ventilator for a day or two longer than they anticipated. During that time I couldn't talk of course, but I was able to scribble a few notes to Arlene.

One asked for some morphine. I thought that was great stuff. Ten days after the surgery I was released to home, more or less sane.

The college granted me an extension of my leave without pay until September of 1988, at which time I was expected to be back on the job. When that time arrived, many of the sequela from the stroke were still present and debilitating. I asked for an extension of another year's leave without pay but was denied. Apparently, the college administration was simply tired of dealing with me and my problems, even though I was just fifteen months short of qualifying for retirement and had served with distinction for eight presidents.

Damn, I hated little people in big jobs. Still do. Always will. After careful consideration of my alternatives, which were two in number: I could fight to stay on board or I could resign. I elected to resign.

A few weeks later a very nice letter from the President arrived:

> *Dear Glenn:*
>
> *I want to take this opportunity to express my personal appreciation to you for the many years you have served the students, staff, and administration of Everett Community College. Your performance has consistently demonstrated the highest levels of dignity, competence and professionalism.*
>
> *During the nearly quarter century of outstanding service, both to us and to the community college system*

in Washington State, your ideas, your initiatives, and your programs have served as models of excellence.

Throughout the late 1960's and early 1970's, our state's community colleges experienced an explosive period of growth. The excellence of your innovative models in Student Services Programs captured the imagination of developing colleges across the state as standards toward which they all would strive. We are extremely proud of you, your accomplishments, and the legacies you have left us.

Some of your accomplishments over the years include: your development of a unique instrument for measuring the effectiveness of our administrative staff; grant proposal reader/evaluator for the U.S. Department of Education in Washington, D.C.; textbook reader/critic for several collegiate book publishers; and many major oral and/or written presentations to highly influential agencies and industrial organizations. You are also known as the Father of the Community College Placement Association of Washington—a high honor, indeed.

Letters in your personnel file indicate that you were extraordinarily well thought of by your professors at the University of Washington. It might also be noted that you were the recipient of the College Placement Council's First Annual Award for Research for your doctoral dissertation—an international prize.

You represented the College exceptionally well in all of the committees you chaired or served upon, both in the College and in the larger community. The classes and seminars you established and taught have been emulated statewide.

You are greatly admired by your colleagues who hold you in the highest esteem, both as an individual and as a professional. All of us are saddened that your incredibly productive career was cut short by ill health.

I could list several pages of individual accomplishments that will stand in the history of the College forever. However, let me simply express again my appreciation, respect, and admiration that all of us who were fortunate enough to have known you, have for you. Your extra efforts will always be remembered, for very few, if any, individuals have had a more pervasive, lasting, or positive influence on the College than you have had.

My very best wishes and warmest regards to you and your family.

Sincerely,
Bob
President, Everett Community College

And so ended my days at Everett Community College and in the world of work. It was a somewhat bittersweet ending, but not altogether unwelcome.

Now I was free. I was free to enjoy my remaining time with my family. I was free to immerse myself in long-neglected projects around the home and to exercise my dormant carpentry skills. I was free to write, and to remember, and to write some more. My leaving the college was one of the best, most constructive events of my life—as was my first contract, engineered by Ms. Jeanette Poore. I am happy now and I am content. It truly is a wonderful life.

I have at times considered returning to Detroit to view the wreckage of what was once a beautiful and dynamic city. But then I am reminded of Thomas Wolfe's warning explicit in the title of his last novel *You Can't Go Home Again*. It's quite true, and so I'll be content to remember my home town as I wish to remember it.

End

Epilogue

WHAT started as a gleeful romp through the craggier recesses of my mind, developed into a simultaneously happy and sad excursion through time.

As I moved from episode to episode through my memory, I came to realize more clearly than ever before what an incredibly exciting and wonderful life I have had.

I am today who and what I have been becoming all of my life. I thank all of you who have touched me, for good or otherwise. You have sharpened my perceptions and my understanding of life.

Some might say that my body has betrayed me. I don't feel that way. After all, how many people get to live their lives twice: the first time in "real time," the second through the recording of these exquisite memories. I have lived what I believe has been, on balance, a good life. No one could, or should, ask for more.

In the Rockefeller Report on Education in 1958, one statement, above all others, caught my attention:

"What most people want, young or old, is not merely

security, or comfort, or luxury, although they are glad enough to have these. Most of all, they want meaning in their lives."

It was profoundly true then. It is still true and so it shall always be.

Arlene and I have tried, and succeeded we believe, in the task of imbuing all of our children with the three essentials for living a reasonably joyful, effective, and productive life: a sense of honor; a sense of values; and a healthy sense of humor. With these three values in place, they'll be able to survive just about anything.

Finally — if anyone should ever ask you when you should stop telling your children bedtime stories — the answer is never. And if you should ever run out of bedtime stories, get out these reminiscences and read about the old days when I was a kid, when movies cost a dime, and gasoline was 20 cents a gallon, and all the wonderful, preposterous, tragic, comic and improbable tales of my life.

Hopefully, this brief essay will help you, Arlene, and all of the children and grandchildren to remember me and to keep me with you always. You have been, are, and will be, my reasons for being and the meaning in my life. You have my love — without conditions — forever.

This has been an experience none of us will ever forget.

Edwards Brothers Malloy
Thorofare, NJ USA
September 27, 2013